UNLAWFULLY AT LARGE
A DCI Jack Tyler thriller

Mark Romain

Copyright © 2020 Mark Romain.
All rights reserved.
ISBN-13: 979-8-6154-5573-5

The right of Mark Romain to be identified as author of this work has been asserted by him in accordance with sections 77 and 78 of the copyright, designs and patents act 1988.

This book is a work of fiction and any resemblance to actual persons, living or dead, is purely coincidental.

This book is dedicated to my mother, Sheila Rose Romain, who sadly passed away on 7th January 2020, shortly before it was finished.

Rest in peace, mum. We love and miss you very much.

ACKNOWLEDGMENTS

Edited by Yvonne Goldsworthy
Cover design by Woot Han

And I'd like to say a special thank you to my brilliant little team of test readers, Clare, David, and Darren, for all the great feedback you provided while I was writing this story.

ALSO BY MARK ROMAIN

TURF WAR

JACK'S BACK

THE HUNT FOR CHEN

THE CANDY KILLER

CHAPTER ONE

Tuesday 4th January 2000

Detective Chief Inspector Jack Tyler of the Area Major Investigation Pool sat at his desk at Arbour Square in East London and stared blankly at the computer screen in front of him.

It was a cold, wet Tuesday morning in early January, and the sky outside his window was a depressing battleship grey, which pretty much matched his mood.

Heavy sleet was falling and a fierce wind was making the old building's windows rattle. Despite the arctic temperatures that prevailed outside, the cast iron radiator inside his office was belting out so much heat that he was beginning to feel drowsy.

The little portable radio on his window sill was playing quietly in the background, and he had just listened to Bill Withers singing *Lovely Day*, which was somewhat ironic because it was anything but.

The hourly news bulletin came on, and the lead story was a regurgitated piece about the TV soap star who had strangled his supermodel girlfriend at their Chelsea flat during the early hours of New Year's

Day after a cocaine-fuelled night out on the town. Having killed her, he had promptly gone on the run.

"*Craig Masters, who plays loveable rogue Steve Michaels on the popular soap, Docklands, was last seen driving his Bentley over Lambeth Bridge during the early hours of New Year's Day,*" the announcer was saying in his clipped monotone. "*His current whereabouts remain unknown but police are following a number of leads. A spokesperson for the award-winning programme said...*"

Tyler leaned over and switched the radio off. An AMIP Team from West London had taken the job, and it was their problem, not his. He leaned back in his chair and stretched expansively. This was his first day back at work since Christmas Eve when he'd broken up for the yuletide festivities, and he was finding it really hard to motivate himself and get back into the swing of things.

It had been such a wonderful break, and so desperately needed after the gruelling caseload he'd been carrying these past few months. Since wrapping up the high-profile Whitechapel murders case in early November, the team had taken three other jobs in quick succession, a householder who had been killed and then set on fire following a dispute with his builder, a domestic, and a gangland shooting.

In dire need of some time off, Jack had driven up to the Norfolk coastline to join his parents at their country retreat in Wells-Next-The-Sea straight after work on Christmas Eve.

Over the next three days, he had eaten and drunk far too much, enjoyed a couple of wonderfully lazy afternoons curled up on the couch watching festive films on TV, and played charades and board games with the assembled family during the evenings. His elder brother, Henry, had also been there, along with his gorgeous Italian wife, Sophia, who Jack secretly thought bore an uncanny resemblance to the '60s actress Claudia Cardinale. She certainly had the same come-to-bed-eyes.

To the surprise of everyone in the Tyler clan, Jack had – in a moment of spontaneity the day before – invited Kelly Flowers to accompany him on the trip. With their relationship still in its infancy, Kelly had been more than a little apprehensive about meeting his family, but she needn't have worried. Everyone had taken to her immediately, so much so that when the visit came to an end on the twenty-seventh, his parents had gushed over Kelly in a way that they never had with his ex-wife, Jenny.

"Mark my words," Jack's father had whispered in his ear as they'd embraced prior to Jack setting off on the long drive back to Essex, "this one's a keeper."

The words had resonated strongly with Jack, who suspected that his wise old dad might well be right.

Instead of partying in the New Year, as had become the annual custom since his messy divorce five years ago, Jack had arranged a romantic getaway for the pair of them in a cosy four-star hotel in the heart of the New Forest. It was a picturesque, ivy fronted Edwardian building, surrounded on all sides by pretty meadows and sprawling forests. Their luxury room had contained a working fireplace and a fancy jacuzzi, and for the next three days they had only ventured out to take invigorating afternoon walks and to enjoy their evening meals in the hotel's Michelin rated restaurant. But, as the saying went, all good things must come to an end, and now it was time for him to get back to the grind.

As much as Jack genuinely loved his job, he was finding today's humdrum return to normality so incredibly boring that he was seriously considering popping into a local travel agent at lunchtime. He had tonnes of leave left, and a week's skiing in the Alps later this month or early next would certainly hit the spot. He wondered if Kelly skied; he would have to ask her later.

Jack took a sip of tepid coffee and grimaced.

Pushing the mug aside, he stifled a yawn and tried to force himself to concentrate on the task at hand. He was halfway through reading a lengthy forensic report that was so incredibly dull it was literally sapping his will to live.

With a laboured sigh, he started reading a new paragraph that was just as full of technical gobbledygook as the preceding one. Only half understanding some of the scientific phraseology, he found himself struggling to pronounce a particularly tongue-twisting word that seemed to contain almost every letter of the alphabet.

What possible justification could there be for having a word that long? he asked himself huffily.

Conscious that he had a telephone conference booked with the scientist who had written it straight after lunch, Tyler decided to skim over that section and return to it later if necessary.

The telephone suddenly rang, startling him. He scooped it up halfway through the second ring, grateful for the distraction. "DCI Tyler," he said, massaging his eyes.

It was DCI Andy Quinlan.

"*Morning, Jack,*" Andy said, sounding as though he bore the weight of the world on his slender shoulders. "*This is just a courtesy call, really, but I thought you'd want to know. I've just discovered that the drug squad's producing our old friend, Claude Winston, from The Ville today. Apparently, they've got him for a three-day-laydown.*"

The Ville, or HMP Pentonville to give it its full name, was the North London prison in which Claude Winston, a Bethnal Green-based pimp and drug smuggler with a nasty habit of shooting police officers, was being held on remand while awaiting trial for two counts of attempted murder, possession of a firearm with intent to endanger life and possession of two kilos of cocaine with intent to supply. He was there because Jack and his partner, DI Tony Dillon, had arrested him while investigating the Whitechapel murders late last year.

At the time, Jack had been so snowed under hunting down the serial killer the media had tackily dubbed The New Ripper that his boss, DCS George Holland, had insisted he hand Winston's case over to Andy Quinlan's team.

Tyler sat bolt upright in his chair, unsettled by the news. "Now why would they do that?" he asked in a voice thick with suspicion. "And how the fuck have the jammy buggers managed to get him for three whole days?"

When Her Majesties Prison Service granted the police permission to produce a prisoner for interview purposes, it was under the strict proviso that the inmate was returned later that same day. When investigations were protracted, and the interviews were likely to span several days, the prisoner had to be collected each morning and returned every evening without fail. It was a complete ball ache, but that was the way that the archaic system worked.

A nasty thought occurred to Tyler.

"You don't think they're looking to do a deal with him behind our backs, do you?" he asked. The words tasted even worse than his cold coffee had.

At the time of his arrest, Tyler knew that the drug squad had only considered Winston to be a fringe player. However, since his incarceration, intelligence reports generated by both NCIS – the National Crime Intelligence Service – and the guys at MIB – the Met Intelligence Bureau –suggested that Winston had forged links to the Turkish and Albanian organised crime cartels that dominated London's prosperous opium trade.

Knowing how these things worked, Tyler wouldn't be surprised if it transpired that some conniving bastard at the drug squad was trying to persuade Winston to trade information about the cartels in exchange for a more lenient sentence.

"*I've been asking myself that same question since I found out,*" Quinlan said gloomily. "*But Winston would have to have some pretty spectacular information to sell if he wanted a text worth the paper it's written on, bearing in mind what he's been charged with.*"

When a prisoner became a Confidential Human Intelligence Source – a CHIS – and provided information that assisted the police in preventing or solving serious offences, they were automatically entitled to receive a letter – commonly referred to in the trade as a text – from the Crown. This was traditionally served on the presiding judge in the privacy of their chambers by a CHIS handler at the start of the trial.

Apart from the judge, the handler, the ACPO – Association of Chief Police Officers – level officer approving the deal, and a high-ranking lawyer from the Crown Prosecution Service, no one else would ever know it had happened.

Jack sighed miserably. "Well, you've just brightened up my day no end," he said, running a hand through his short brown hair. "Do you know where they're taking him?"

"*He's going to KF, or so I'm told.*" KF was the phonetic code for Forest Gate police station in Romford Road, East London.

"Have you spoken to George Holland yet?"

"*Not yet,*" Quinlan said. "*I thought you'd want to be the first to know.*"

"Bloody marvellous. Dillon's not going to be a happy bunny when I tell him."

Claude Winston sat in the back of the grubby people carrier, quietly watching the world pass by through tinted windows that were streaked with rain. He was being driven along Romford Road towards the Stratford one-way system, and they were moving at what felt like a snail's pace. Traffic had been so bad this morning that the eight-mile journey from Islington had already taken them well over an hour. Still, he wasn't complaining; it was better than sitting in a cell and staring at four walls.

The people carrier slowed to a stop as it tagged onto the end of a long line of vehicles being held at a red traffic signal. The driver cursed the traffic, and then the weather. He complained that his throat felt like he'd swallowed sandpaper and announced that he could murder a cuppa, which triggered an argument over whose turn it was to get the drinks in.

Ignoring the banter from the three detectives who were escorting him, Winston glanced out of the side window at the sodden pedestrians who were scurrying hither and thither along the crowded pavement like a bunch of drowning rats. Some were huddled over with their collars pulled up high; others were hiding underneath umbrellas that did little to shield them from the sideways driven rain. All of them were getting in each other's way and most of them looked as miserable as sin.

He watched dispassionately as a limping vagrant of Eastern European appearance hobbled from doorway to doorway on a pair of crutches that were too short for him. The dishevelled man was soaked through, and as he came to a wobbly halt underneath a large canopy suspended above the entrance to an Ironmonger's, the proprietor came rushing out and shooed him away.

Winston grinned mirthlessly. *Another example of the milk of human kindness*, he thought bitterly. *And they have the nerve to call me ruthless!*

As the lights started to change, an elderly Indian woman with a bright red Bindi on her forehead dashed across the road directly in front of their vehicle. He'd once asked an Indian punter what the dot signified, only to be told that it was a reset button for the husband to press if his wife ever displeased him. The drunken Indian had then teetered off, still chortling to himself over his joke, without giving Winston his answer.

The woman wore a thick green coat over her sari, but all she had on her feet was a pair of wafer-thin sandals. He shook his head in amazement – *someone ought to tell the silly cow to put on some Wellingtons next time she goes out in the rain.*

Holding her umbrella high, so as not to decapitate anyone coming the other way, the woman shimmied through a succession of puddles, trying to avoid the deepest ones with varying levels of success. As she reached the safety of the pavement, a fierce gust of wind caused her umbrella to collapse in on itself, and while she was trying to straighten it out, a lumbering HGV drove through a puddle the size of a small lake and drenched her from the waist down.

Winston chuckled to himself. *Classic,* he thought. *Maybe she needs her reset button pressing.*

It was a huge relief to be away from the claustrophobic confines of the prison, with its endless concrete corridors, all separated by locked metal doors or steel bars. Spending Christmas and New Year inside had been one of the most depressing experiences of his entire life, and he had no intention of repeating it.

Shifting in his seat to ease the numbness in his buttocks, Winston let out a restless sigh and stretched his one free arm above his head.

"Keeping you awake, are we?" the sombre looking detective he was handcuffed to asked in his deep baritone voice. It was the only time the man had bothered to address Winston all journey.

Winston responded with a surly grunt.

Winston's escorts, all big lumps with broken noses and barrel chests, had obviously been handpicked for the job because of their formidable size as opposed to their social skills, but with his reputation for violence, that was only to be expected.

Detective Sergeant Declan Bale, the man in charge of relocating Winston from HMP Pentonville to Forest Gate police station, was sitting in the front talking to the driver about football. He glanced over his shoulder and noticed that Winston was getting a bit fidgety. "We're nearly there now, pal," he said placatingly.

Bale was a fair-haired Welshman with the flat nose and cauliflower ears of a former rugby player and the beer belly of a man who enjoyed a good drink. Straight after introducing himself, he had made a point of informing Winston that he and his colleagues were merely delivery men and that they wouldn't be having anything more to do with him once they'd dropped him off at the police station. In fact, the burly detective from the Welsh valleys had only spoken to Winston on one other occasion, just after they drove out of the prison gates, and that had been to enquire whether he had been raised as a Rastafarian or had converted in later life, and if it was true that Rastas grew long dreadlocks to denote the covenant that they had made with their God.

Winston had considered these questions so unbelievably stupid that he hadn't even bothered to reply. Yes, he was of Jamaican descent, and yes, he sported shoulder-length dreadlocks, but that didn't automatically make him a Rasta. As it happened, the way he wore his hair had nothing to do with religion – he just liked having dreads; they were his pride and joy.

Winston had retreated within himself almost immediately after that, and he had spent the remainder of the tedious journey lost in melancholy. Two short months had passed since those arseholes from the murder squad had put him behind bars but, to him, it felt more like two years. Winston had made two bail applications since being locked up – the first at the Magistrate's Court the day after he'd been charged, and the second at the Old Bailey, two weeks later.

Neither had been successful.

According to his wankstain solicitor, he couldn't make another bail application unless a substantial change in the circumstances surrounding his case occurred – like that was going to happen.

Depressingly, his trial wasn't scheduled to be heard at the Bailey until late August, which seemed a lifetime away.

But there was still hope, and if everything went according to plan, he would be a free man by the end of the week.

Winston had ostensibly been produced in order to be further questioned about drug-related offences – at least that's what the production order said, and what the screws at The Ville had been told but, of course, it was a complete lie.

He had been produced in order that he could escape.

As soon as the second bail application had been refused, Winston had started exploring other ways of getting out, and it hadn't taken him long to come up with a viable plan to regain his freedom.

He had set the wheels in motion in early December by having his puppet solicitor approach the drug squad with a cryptic suggestion that it might be in everyone's best interest if they arranged to visit him at The Ville as soon as possible.

His solicitor, Oliver Clarke, was a man with a serious drug dependency and far fewer ethics than most of the criminals he represented. At Winston's behest, he had claimed his client was in a position to provide them with all the information they needed to shut down a multi-million-pound drug operation being run by one of the UK's largest crime cartels. Clarke had also implied that Winston had enough dirt to put several influential cartel members away for a string of unsolved murders, all of which were drug-related. If the right deal were to be tabled, Winston might be willing to turn Queen's Evidence and testify against them.

Clarke had met with DS Frank Skinner, the detective who had run an unsuccessful operation against Winston's gang the previous year. Unable to resist such a juicy proposition, Skinner had booked a legal visit for the following week.

When they'd met, facing off against each other across a Formica prison table like a couple of poker players, Winston had laid it on thick for Skinner, who was, in his opinion, an ineffectual copper who spent his waking hours dreaming of glory that would never be his.

Winston had bragged that he could – if properly incentivised –

unquestionably help Skinner to put away some of the UK's biggest crime bosses.

Of course, Winston had absolutely no intention of selling anyone out. It wasn't that he had reservations about becoming a super-grass; he simply didn't possess a fraction of the information that he'd claimed to hold.

Following the initial contact, there had been three further visits to assess his suitability. Winston had worked incredibly hard during these interactions, sowing little seeds of hope here and there, manipulating conversations to make himself look good, and drip-feeding Skinner little titbits of information that resulted in the drug squad making a few minor arrests.

As soon as they started talking about producing him for a proper debrief, he knew that they had taken the bait. This was great news because security procedures inside HMP Pentonville were far too tight for him to attempt a breakout from within. An escape while being transported to a police station, on the other hand, was an entirely different proposition. Generally speaking, the police tended to use normal cars or mini-vans to collect prisoners in, and they usually only provided three escorts.

Of course, the police weren't totally stupid; for security reasons, they were never going to let him know the exact date and time that they intended to produce him in advance, but that didn't matter in the slightest. Once housed at a police station, he would have unrestricted access to his bent solicitor, who could then pass information about his return date to his associates.

Using his unscrupulous solicitor as a conduit, Winston had sent word to his nephew, Deontay Garston, to start organising the breakout. Within a week, Deontay had reported back that everything was in place. All he needed now was the details of Winston's return journey and the name of the police station he would be departing from.

After what seemed like an eternity, the people carrier finally pulled into the back yard of Forest Gate police station and drove around the back of the building to the custody entrance.

As it pulled up next to a caged-off area outside the redbrick building, Winston experienced a crippling bout of stomach pain. This was the worst so far, and it took his breath away. He leaned forward to disguise his discomfort, knowing that he couldn't say anything to his escorts in case they decided to return him to The Ville for medical treatment and reschedule the production for another date.

The pains had started a couple of days ago, but during the past twenty four hours, they had grown steadily worse. At first, he'd assumed it was either a minor stomach bug or something that he'd eaten, but when no one else on the wing complained about being ill, he had begun to fear it might be something far more serious.

Winston prayed that, whatever the ailment was, his body would hold on for a few more days before succumbing to it. That was all the time that he needed to break out of jail and flee the country.

To say that Detective Inspector Tony Dillon was unhappy was a massive understatement. The former competitive powerlifter was seething as he tried to digest the unsavoury news that Jack Tyler had just fed him. "I can't believe this," he said, not for the first time. "What do they think they're playing at?" As he spoke, he paced up and down Tyler's office restlessly, reminding Tyler of a caged animal.

"They must think they're going to get something really big out of him," Jack said from behind his desk. "It wouldn't be worth their effort otherwise."

Dillon grunted his disapproval and scrunched his shovel sized hands into fists. "That low life piece of shit probably thinks he can trade information for time off, even though he's looking at a life sentence for what he did."

During their pursuit of him two months earlier, Winston had shot one of their colleagues, Colin Franklin, in the chest. Had it not been for the fact that Colin was wearing his Met-vest, he would probably have died. As it was, Winston had gone on to shoot a young British Transport Police officer twice, and it was a miracle that the boy – PC Jenkins – had survived. He was still off sick, recovering from his injuries.

Jack shrugged. "According to Andy Quinlan, even if he doesn't get his sentence significantly reduced, he won't end up going into general population with all the other scumbags if he turns QE, and if he becomes a super-grass, he might not even serve his time in prison."

Dillon spun on him, the huge muscles of his neck straining against his collar.

"What do you mean?" he demanded, eyes narrowing to the size of slits. "Why should turning Queen's Evidence or becoming a super-grass guarantee him an easy ride?"

"It's not that, Dill. HMP wouldn't be able to guarantee his safety, which is why people who turn QE end up in segregation, and super-grasses normally end up being housed in police stations that no longer have a working custody suite, like the one at Woodford Green." Tyler snorted derisively. "Can you imagine that? He would be looked after round the clock, literally waited on hand and foot – it would be like he was staying in a bloody hotel."

Dillon's face darkened. "Don't tell me that," he said. "my blood pressure's already climbing through the roof."

Tyler stared at him with sympathetic eyes. "Well, I've spoken to George Holland, and he says there's nothing we can do about it. He phoned his oppo at the drug squad to see if he could find out what they're up to, but the man was unwilling to go into any detail for fear of –" he made air quotes "– compromising operational security."

After the call, Holland had wryly explained that the turn of phrase had been managerial speak for 'fuck off and mind your own business.'

Tyler was a pragmatist; he figured that if George Holland couldn't get to the bottom of it, then he and Dillon stood no chance. The trouble was, from the determined look on his square-jawed face, Dillon wasn't ready to throw in the towel just yet.

"I've got a mate – well an acquaintance to be precise – who works at the drug squad. His name's Frank Skinner, do you know him?"

Jack shook his head. The name didn't ring any bells with him. "Can't say I do," he said.

"We were on a Project Team at SO7 at the same time. He's a miserable sod, and a bit of a tosser if I'm completely honest, but he owes me. I'm gonna give him a discreet call and see if he can shed any light on this."

Jack considered this and concluded that it might be worth a shot. "Go for it," he said, and then decided to add a word of caution. "But remember this: we've done our bit. We arrested him and put him behind bars. If it's been decreed from on high that Winston is supergrass material, there's nothing we can do about it, no matter how unpalatable that might be."

Dillon's face sagged. "I know," he said, "and it makes me sick to my stomach."

CHAPTER TWO

Wednesday 5th January 2000

Claude Winston awoke in agonising pain. His body was covered in sweat, and he barely made it to the metal toilet in the corner of his cell before he threw up.

The room was spinning and he felt like he was going to pass out. The pain in his lower stomach was so unbearable that he couldn't even stand up straight. *No, no, no,* he thought, fighting off the panic, *this can't be happening. If I'm ill, the escape will have to be abandoned and I might never get another chance.*

He had no idea what time it was, but he could tell from looking through the thick frosted glass of his cell window that it was still dark outside. Winston staggered back to his cot and flopped down on the shiny blue plastic mattress. Perhaps it would pass if he just laid down for a while. He closed his eyes and tried to focus on his breathing, doing his best to ignore the searing pain in his stomach and right side.

Trish Raven was the early turn civilian gaoler at Forest Gate, and when she conducted the first of her hourly checks at seven o'clock that morning, she found Winston unconscious on his bed, his chest covered in vomit. For a moment, she thought that he had chocked on it and was dead, so completely still was he. Then, as she stood there, gagging at the smell and trying not to panic unduly because a death in custody had just occurred on her watch, he groaned out loud and threw up again.

Thank God! Trish thought, moving forward cautiously. She was so relieved that, if he hadn't been so smelly – and possibly contagious – she might actually have considered hugging him.

"Mr Winston, are you okay?" she asked. It was a stupid question, she realised because he obviously wasn't. When he didn't respond, she reluctantly moved closer to check his vitals. There was no time to don a pair of rubber gloves, and she hoped that whatever ailment he was suffering from wasn't catching.

"You really don't look too good," she said, seeing the film of sweat that covered his unnaturally grey face. He was burning up, too, and he didn't respond when she shook his shoulder, nor when she pinched his ear lobe. From what she could remember from her first aid training, that meant his GCS – Glasgow Coma Scale – score was very low and he required urgent medical treatment. "Shit," she said under her breath and rushed out to call the custody sergeant. He would know what to do.

―――

When DS Frank Skinner and DC Patrick Donoghue, his ginger-haired, freckle-faced sidekick from the drug squad, arrived at Forest Gate police station at nine o'clock that morning to start interviewing Winston, they received a nasty surprise.

"He's not here," the custody officer informed them without looking up from the record he was hurriedly updating in an illegible scribble that would have done most doctors proud.

The custody suite was heaving as half-a-dozen overnight prisoners were being prepared for the G4 security van to take them off to court, and a ripe odour of sweaty bodies mixed with farts and alcohol tinged breath pervaded the area they were congregated in.

"What do you mean, not here?" Skinner demanded, looking totally perplexed. In order to produce an inmate from prison, the station used to accommodate him had to be on an approved Home Office list, and one of the conditions of the production order was that he would be housed there, and nowhere else.

The custody sergeant smiled grimly. "He was rushed to hospital earlier with a suspected burst appendix. Luckily, Dr Mackintosh, the on-call FME, was already in the station when the gaoler found him unconscious in his cell and, after examining him, an ambulance was called straight away. The Duty Officer's not best pleased, though. Three officers from early turn had to go with him as escorts."

"Shit!" Skinner said, drawing the word out. He ran a calloused hand over the stubble on his dimpled chin as he considered the implications of this. He would have to notify his boss and the prison Security Governor, neither of whom would be any more pleased than the Duty Officer had been. "What hospital did they take him to?" he asked.

"The Royal London in Whitechapel," the custody sergeant said.

Skinner swore. His plans for the day, and possibly the week, had just been blown right out of the water.

"Let's get straight over there," he gruffly told his colleague.

As they headed for the door, he pulled out his chunky Motorola mobile phone and pulled the small extendable aerial up; he wasn't looking forward to the two calls he would now have to make, but there was no point in delaying them. Unfortunately, as there was no signal in the custody area, it looked like he would have to do just that. Cursing the stupid phone for having no signal, and Winston for having the temerity to fall ill on him, he slipped it back in his jacket pocket. He would try again when they were on their way to the hospital.

When they reached the car, a Vauxhall Vectra, Donoghue turned to Skinner. "There's no rush, is there?" he asked, rubbing his oversized stomach. "Only I was thinking we could nip off and get a bite to eat before setting off for the hospital. Sounds to me like they'll be taking Winston straight into surgery, so what's the point in us tanking over there and then having nothing to do but twiddle our thumbs for the next hour or two?"

Skinner gave him a look that would have curdled milk. "Get in the car," he ordered.

Donoghue's face sagged as he pressed the button on the fob to release the central locking. With a sigh, he lowered his lumbering figure into the driver's seat, which creaked under his weight. "Looks like breakfast will have to wait, then," he said, unable to hide his disappointment.

———

When Dillon arrived at the hospital at half-past-four that afternoon, he found a subdued looking Frank Skinner sitting alone outside a private room on the third floor. His potato-like head and square chin had about the same amount of dark stubble on them, and a fleshy hand that was festooned with gold rings was alternately rubbing one and then the other. The podgy fingers were stained yellow from nicotine, Dillon noticed, and the nails had been chewed down to the quick. Skinner projected an aura that was more akin to dodgy bookmaker than a cop, and Dillon felt confident that, beneath the shirt and tie, there would be a thick gold chain draped around his chavvy neck.

Opposite the bench on which the drug squad officer was sitting, two serious-faced uniform officers were standing guard outside the room's entrance, one either side of the door.

"What are you doing here?" Skinner immediately asked, glaring at him suspiciously. His voice was deep and raspy, a legacy from all the cigarettes he had chain-smoked over the years.

Ignoring the hostility, Dillon sat down next to him, forcing him to bunch up to make room.

"I phoned KF's custody suite to ask for you a little while ago, as you weren't answering my calls," Dillon said angrily, "and they told me I'd find you here. Imagine how surprised I was to find out from them that Winston had been rushed to hospital this morning, bearing in mind that you bloody well promised to give me an update if anything significant happened."

When he'd called Skinner the previous day, the drug squad man had been disingenuous over Winston. He'd started off by spouting the usual 'we've produced him as a matter of routine to see if he'll give us any TICs,' story, but Dillon had known that was complete bollocks and had told him so in no uncertain terms.

TIC is a police acronym for 'taken into consideration.' The process involves prisoners putting their hands up to the previously unsolved transgressions that they've committed over the years. In exchange for their full and frank confession, the police submit a report to the court requesting that these matters be taken into consideration when passing sentence for other offences, instead of also charging them with the additional crimes. The courts could still choose to impose consecutive – or back to back – custodial sentences for the offences being taken into consideration, but normally they were dealt with by means of a concurrent – served at the same time – sentence. In other words, a man charged with two burglaries but having a further ninety taken into consideration would only receive custodial sentences for the two charged burglaries; he wouldn't incur any additional jail time for the TICs, although these would be shown as guilty findings against him on the Police National Computer.

"No, honestly, we just thought he might want to get a few things off his chest as he's likely to be doing a fair bit of porridge," Skinner had insisted. He wasn't the brightest spark that Dillon had ever worked with.

"Yeah, right," Dillon had replied, making no effort to conceal his cynicism. A burglar, a car thief, even a street robber might want to clear their slate and ask for other offences they had committed to be taken into consideration, but not a class A drug importer or a man charged with two attempted murders.

From Dillon's perspective, the phone call had terminated most unsatisfactorily, with Skinner promising to get back to him if anything significant came out of the production or if there were any unforeseen problems. It had taken him less than a day to renege on his promise, and Dillon chided himself for being foolish enough to expect anything else from a shifty fat fucker like Frank Skinner.

"So, what happened?" Dillon asked, scathingly.

Skinner blew out his cheeks, spraying spittle everywhere. "Nothing bloody happened," he said petulantly. "The fucker's appendix ruptured before we could even speak to him. Peritonitis, I think they call it. Long story short, he's going to be hospitalised for quite a while, which means by the time he's ready to be discharged, the poxy production order will have expired and he'll have to go straight back to prison. If we want to speak to him, we'll have to go through the whole rigmarole of producing him again. It's a bloody disaster, mate." He thumped the chair next to him in frustration.

Serves you bloody right, Dillon thought, resisting the urge to smile smugly. "Has a risk assessment for the hospital watch been carried out yet?" he asked instead, noting that the uniformed officers were unarmed.

Skinner didn't like the tone of Dillon's voice, and he responded by folding his arms defensively, the way that small-minded people often do when put on the spot.

"Yes," he said, guardedly. "I've carried one out myself, in conjunction with the local Duty Officer. It's all been properly documented."

"Look, I'm not trying to teach you how to suck eggs," Dillon said, struggling not to lose his cool, "but have you considered requesting an armed guard. He's a nasty fucker and his gang has access to guns."

Skinner snorted at that. "Practically every villain in the country has access to firearms these days," he said, dismissively. "Don't worry, there will be three uniformed PCs with him for the duration of his stay. I'm happy that that's enough and, more importantly, so is the Duty Officer who's providing the staff."

Dillon didn't share his confidence. Unlike Skinner, he'd seen what Winston was capable of at first hand, and there was no doubt in his mind that armed officers were definitely warranted. By choosing not to go down that route, he felt that Skinner was making a big mistake. Cynically, he found himself wondering whether the decision was down to poor judgement or laziness. After all, getting the authority to deploy an armed guard involved a hell of a lot more paperwork than drafting in three lids from the local station do the job.

Skinner's tone became slightly more conciliatory. "Look," he said, pausing to smile indulgently, and looking like he was trying to pass wind. "It's not like he's a member of one of the Turkish or Albanian organised crime gangs we used to deal with at SO7, is it?"

Dillon scowled at him. "Meaning what exactly?"

Skinner spread his arms expansively. "Meaning it's highly unlikely that anyone would care enough about the twat to try and spring him out of here, even if they could."

Dillon could tell that there was absolutely no point in continuing the conversation. Skinner's narrow little mind was made up, and nothing he said was going to change it. "I really hope you're right, Frank," he said, standing up to go, "because if you're not, it won't be your life on the line when the shooting starts."

CHAPTER THREE

Thursday 6th January 2000

At precisely eleven o'clock that morning, two smartly dressed men carrying expensive-looking briefcases turned up at Winston's room and demanded access.

"Sorry," PC Stanley Morrison said, barring their way, "this man's in police custody and only authorised persons are allowed to visit."

The elder of the two, a white man in his mid-thirties with a spray-on tan and heavily gelled hair, smiled indulgently and produced a laminated badge, which stated that his name was Oliver Clarke and that he was a fully qualified solicitor working for a company called Cratchit, Lowe and Clarke.

"I'm Mr Winston's solicitor, and I'm here to visit him in that capacity," Clarke announced. Morrison was surprised to hear him speak in a coarse East London accent more becoming of a barrow boy than a solicitor. He had expected something much snootier from the man's flashy appearance, although now he came to think about it, maybe the unevenly sprayed-on tan should have given him a clue.

"This is my intern, Jeremy Peters," Clarke said, introducing the thin black man in his late twenties who had accompanied him.

Morrison eyed the studious ebony-skinned intern carefully. He certainly seemed respectable enough, so he probably was exactly who he claimed to be, but orders were orders. "Do you have a formal ID like this?" he asked, waving Clarke's laminate in his face.

"I'm sorry, I don't," Peters said, smiling apologetically. He was far better spoken than Clarke and Morrison got the impression that he had come from a wealthy background, attended a posh school and an even posher university.

Morrison stared at them indecisively. He had strict orders that any solicitor requesting access to the prisoner was to have proper identification. Otherwise, a check was to be made with the Law Society and a drug squad skipper called Frank Skinner was to be consulted before they were admitted. Morrison knew that getting the intern checked out with the Law Society would take time, and now that he thought about it, no one had actually said anything about interns. Were they even registered with the Law Society? Morrison suspected not. He decided that his instructions were ambiguous enough to give him some leeway in how he interpreted them and concluded that as long as the solicitor checked out, which he did, there was no need to worry about the intern accompanying him.

"Okay," he said, handing the ID back to Clarke. He opened the door and showed them in.

"I'd like to see my client in private," Clarke said, nodding towards the bored-looking cop sitting in a soft chair opposite the bed, reading a magazine about angling.

Morrison was uncomfortable with that. "We were told that he wasn't to be left alone," he said.

"He won't be alone," Clarke said, smarmily, "he'll be with us."

The man's flippancy riled Morrison, who didn't like solicitors much at the best of times. He opened his mouth to fire back a sharp retort but, before he could speak, Peters cut in, his tone conciliatory. "Officer," he said, "we're three floors up, and none of the windows have an opening big enough for a man of Mr Winston's considerable stature to squeeze through."

To make his point, he nodded towards the windows, which Morrison saw only had narrow top openers fitted. Winston had to be a good six-feet-five inches tall in his stockinged feet, Morrison estimated, and he easily weighed in at eighteen or nineteen stone.

"Besides," Peters continued, "the door has a glass panel in it, so you'll be able to see in from outside."

Morrison considered that, realised that the intern was right and that no harm could come of allowing them to speak in private, which they were allowed to do with their client anyway.

"Fair enough," he said, "but we'll be right outside, so no funny business." The last comment was addressed to Winston, who simply sucked through his teeth in response.

As soon as they were alone with their client, the two suited men pulled up chairs, sitting next to his bed with their backs to the door to prevent the officers outside from being able to read their lips. They were probably being a little paranoid, but it was better to be safe than sorry, especially given the nature of the discussion they were about to have. They both sat as close to the patient as they could, leaning in and speaking in hushed tones.

"How are you doing, uncle?" Deontay Garston asked. Now that he had dropped the phony accent he'd used while masquerading as Peters, he sounded every bit as much a local boy as Oliver Clarke.

"You've scrubbed up pretty well, nephew," Winston said with a chuckle. "The posh accent you put on was impressive. It certainly had the pigs fooled."

Garston allowed himself a modest smile of self-satisfaction. "I've been practising," he said.

"Mr Winston," Clarke cut in. "Just for the record, I'm not happy about having to lie to the police to get your nephew in here. If they had checked with the Law Society or my firm, I could have lost my job –" he swallowed hard "– or worse."

Winston sneered at the spineless toad. "Get over it," he snapped.

"You're being well compensated for getting the boy in to see me, so shut your mouth and do your job."

"My job is to represent you, not assist you to break the law," Clarke insisted edgily.

Winston ignored him. "So," he said to his nephew, "you know what we had planned for my return journey to Pentonville, is it still on?"

Garston glanced uneasily at the solicitor, unsure about how much information to reveal in front of him.

Winston waved this away dismissively. "Don't worry about him," he said, staring at the lawyer and loading the last word with contempt. "If he says anything to the filth, he'll be in as much trouble as we will." His voice became full of menace as he leaned forward. "You won't say anything, will you?"

Clarke couldn't hold his eye. Looking down at the floor, he gave a forlorn shake of his head. "No, I won't say a word," he confirmed, the modulation in his voice expressing a mixture of fear and shame.

Winston gave a satisfied grunt.

"What were you going to say?" he asked, returning his attention to his nephew.

"I think I've come up with an even better escape plan," Deontay declared. Out of the corner of his eye, he noticed Clarke cringe at the use of the word 'escape'. "Your being in here might actually work in our favour. If we can find a way to overcome the three cops outside your room, we'll have all the time in the world to make good our escape." Lying awake in bed the previous night, it had suddenly occurred to him that if they snatched Claude from a police car, and the cops had a chance to use their radios, they might only have a couple of minutes to make good their getaway before reinforcements started to arrive. If, on the other hand, they broke him out of here and secured the guards so that they couldn't summon help, they could well have upwards of an hour. It was a game-changing difference as far as their chances of success were concerned.

"No shit, Sherlock," Winston said scathingly. "The problem is, how are you gonna do that without them using their radios, and without alerting any of the hospital staff?"

Deontay smiled nervously. "I've already thought about that," he said. "I know a bloke who can source me some powerful sedatives. All I need to do is work out a way to administer them."

Clarke was looking thoroughly miserable now.

Winston rolled his eyes in contempt. "Just get a couple of shooters, and we can pop the fuckers," he said. "You don't need to make things more complicated than they need to be."

Deontay raised a cautionary finger to his lips, afraid that Winston was going to blurt something out loudly enough for the officers outside to hear. "Leave it with me, Claude, I've already got an idea of how this might work. I just need to recruit the right people to help me pull it off."

"Well, don't fuck about," Winston instructed harshly. "If they can get the infection under control and bring my temperature down, the doctor reckons I'll probably be fit enough to be released on Saturday. If not, it'll be Monday morning, straight after doctor's rounds."

"Don't worry, uncle," Deontay told him. "Before I leave, I'll introduce myself to the ward sister and make sure they know I'm your legal rep and give them a code word. That way, I'll be able to call in and get updates every day without arousing suspicion."

CHAPTER FOUR

Monday 10th January 2000

It was still dark outside her bedroom window when Melissa Smails awoke to find their black cat, Merlin, sitting on her chest, staring down at her with his big green eyes and purring loudly.

Meow, he said by way of greeting.

Merlin had recently taken to sleeping at the bottom of the bed, which she didn't really mind, but he had also taken to waking her up when he wanted his breakfast, which she was far less enthusiastic about.

As she lay there, she could feel the reassuring outline of her partner's large body pressed against her back, and she instinctively snuggled into him, siphoning off his body warmth. He was snoring loudly, and she elbowed him in the ribs, causing him to turn over. He licked his lips noisily, grumbled something in his sleep and then fell silent.

"Strewth, Merlin, why don't you ever wake daddy up when you're hungry," she complained, rubbing the residue of sleep from her bleary eyes. As if offended by the reprimand, the snooty cat jumped off of her chest and wandered out of the room with a haughty swagger.

That cat has definitely got a serious attitude problem, she thought as she yawned.

Craning her neck, Melissa – Mel to her friends – squinted at the glowing red digits of the clock-radio on her bedside table. Her heart sank when she saw there were only nine minutes left until the alarm was due to go off. She badly needed to pee, but if she got up to use the loo now there would be no point in returning to her lush warm bed afterwards, so she pulled the 15-Tog duvet tightly around her neck and rolled over, determined to stay put until the alarm sounded. Unfortunately, her bladder was having none of it. When you've got to go, you've got to go – right?

Mel, who had grown up in Australia, hated the harsh British winters; they were always cold and bleak and depressing, and it didn't matter what shift she was rostered to work at the hospital, it was always dark when she woke up and always dark when she went to bed.

Mel was down to work an 08:00 – 20:30 hours shift today, and she consoled herself with the knowledge that at least she would get to see a few meagre hours of daylight, unlike when she worked the dreaded 20:00 – 08:30 hours night shifts that came around all too frequently. When she was on those, her sleep pattern meant that several days could pass without her seeing the sun at all, and after a while, the perpetual darkness made her go a little cranky.

Thankfully, after today's shift, she had three whole days of glorious leave to look forward to. Dave, her partner of four years, was a paramedic with the London Ambulance Service. He was also going to be off, and they were planning to visit his parents in Cornwall for a couple of days, driving down first thing in the morning. It would probably be too cold to surf, even for a diehard like her, but she was looking forward to a brief respite from all the noise and pollution of the big city.

Despite needing to urinate, Mel was finding it harder than usual to drag herself out of bed today. It didn't help that the flat's ancient heating system had packed up on Boxing Day, and since then the place had been colder than an Eskimo's igloo.

Despite Dave phoning their tight-fisted landlord every day, there was still no sign of the tradesman the wanker had repeatedly promised to send around to carry out emergency repairs. That was probably because the boiler didn't even have a current safety inspection certificate; it didn't just need repairing – it needed replacing, and a job like that would cost the skinflint they were renting the flat from more money than he was prepared to part with.

Their six-month tenancy was up for renewal at the beginning of March, but they had already decided not to stay on. The heating debacle was just the latest in a long list of things that had gone wrong since they had moved in. Not only was the property riddled with damp and falling apart, but the drains also kept getting blocked up. On top of that, one of her neighbours was a bit of an oddball and the other one was – if the pungent smell wafting out of his flat and the steady stream of callers was anything to go by – selling drugs.

As much as Mel would have preferred to remain cocooned in her lovely warm duvet, she began to worry that if she didn't get up soon, she would end up wetting the bed.

Having delayed the inevitable for as long as she could, she timidly slid her feet down onto the cheap carpet, feeling around for her slippers in the dark and gasping as cold air engulfed her calves in its icy grip.

On Friday just gone, they had found an old electric heater in a utility cupboard while clearing it out. It was now plugged into the socket beside the bed, and Mel bent down and switched it on. She wondered why she was bothering; even when sitting directly in front of it, as she was now, the only way to tell that it was on was from the faint smell of burning it gave off.

Mel had showered before going to bed the previous night, so all she had to do now was slip out of her PJs into her work clothes, but she was dreading losing all the residual heat from her sleepwear while she swapped one outfit for the other.

As she sat in the dark, shivering, Mel's hand scuttled across the bedside table like an angry crab until she found the switch for the small lamp. Squinting at the sudden brightness that invaded the room, and unable to stand the cold any longer, she reached back onto the bed and snatched the duvet from Dave. "Sorry, sweetie," she said as she draped it over her shoulders.

Poor old Dave squirmed in his sleep and wrapped his arms around himself, but he didn't wake up. He was wearing his *Superman* pyjamas. Truth be told, he looked more like a 'Man of Stodge' than a 'Man of Steel', but she loved him anyway.

Before the boiler died, the flat's heating had been programmed to come on an hour before they were due to get up, which meant that Mel could hang her clothes over the bedroom radiator when she went to bed, knowing they would be lovely and warm when it was time to get dressed.

Without the benefit of central heating, Mel had been forced to find an alternative method of warming up her clothes, and her solution was – if she said so herself – pretty fucking ingenious. Picking up her unwieldy hairdryer, she turned the blower up to max and spent a few seconds running it over each item of clothing before putting it on, taking special care to ensure that her socks were toasty warm. Dave, who constantly astonished her by his ability to sleep through virtually anything, didn't even stir at the incredible racket coming from the rickety hairdryer as it rattled away in her hand.

When she was finally dressed in the dark blue uniform of a ward sister, Mel turned the bedside light and the electric heater off and gently re-covered Dave with the quilt, kissing him on the forehead as she tucked him in. As she closed the bedroom door on him, he was snoring contentedly.

Deontay Garston carefully spread two lines of fine white powder across the glass surface of a compact mirror that rested precariously upon the car's dashboard. Then he rolled a lottery scratch card into a small tube and inserted it into his left nostril. Bending forward, he inhaled the first line vigorously.

"Oh, man! That's good stuff," he told his three cohorts before repeating the process with the other nostril. Almost immediately, the tropane alkaloid began to take effect. Still sniffing, he turned to the scruffily dressed man sitting next to him in the driver's seat of the stolen car, a top-of-the-range Ford Scorpio.

"You're clear on what's expected of you, Mullings?" he asked again, despite having gone over the plan with the others more than a dozen times. He didn't care if he got on their nerves – there was a lot riding on this, and he was determined that everything would go smoothly.

"I'm cool, man. Don't worry," the drug runner cooed. He had a great big spliff on the go, which was probably why he was so mellow.

Garston turned his attention to the sultry black woman sitting stiffly in the rear. He had some lingering doubts about the hooker, but there was no doubting her loyalty to Winston. Besides, with the time restraints imposed on him, there just hadn't been a chance to recruit anyone else; and at least she knew how to use a syringe safely, which was more than any of the others involved in the escape could say.

She had a pretty face, with intelligent brown eyes, high cheekbones, and smouldering lips. It was a pity it was marred by the distinctive scar that ran down one side of it, all the way from her right ear to her chin. That would be remembered by anyone who got a good look at it. Hopefully, that wasn't going to happen.

"Ready Angela?"

She shrugged lethargically, "I guess so."

The lacklustre response angered him. He knew she was sulking because he'd refused to let her shoot up with heroin before the breakout, forcing her to make do with a few puffs from Mullings' joint instead. Garston reached into the back of the car and took hold of her wrist. "Just make sure that you don't let me down," he warned. "Fuck up today and you won't just have me to answer to, you'll have to explain yourself to Claude as well. Do you understand?"

Just to make sure she did, he squeezed her arm until she winced.

"Okay, okay!" she cried.

He waited a long moment before releasing his grip, taking more satisfaction than he should from the way she immediately cowered away from him.

He patted her bony knee and smiled at her. "That's a good girl," he said, patronisingly.

The last member of the team was a sullen-looking bald man in his mid-twenties. His name was Errol Heston, and he was a nightclub doorman who Garston occasionally used when he needed someone to rough up the punters who owed him money or encourage the hookers who were underperforming to work a little harder.

Garston was already beginning to experience a cocaine rush. A feeling of confidence and wellbeing surged through him, making him feel invulnerable. Any uncertainties he had about how things would pan out evaporated, and he knew that his brilliant plan would work like a Swiss watch.

"Let's get it on," he announced, opening the passenger door with a grin of hyped anticipation.

The car was parked in a no waiting area outside the entrance to The Royal London Hospital; positioned so as to ensure an easy getaway, but not so as to cause an obstruction to an arriving ambulance. The last thing they wanted to do was draw attention to themselves from the hospital security staff or the police.

He took a moment to scope out his surroundings. When he was satisfied that no one was paying them any undue attention, he removed his three-quarter-length Burberry and casually tossed it into the back of the car. Underneath, he wore a long white doctor's coat over a pair of surgical greens. An authentic NHS nametag was pinned to his chest, and it proclaimed him to be Dr P. W. Owusu. He didn't have a stethoscope, but hopefully, he'd be able to nick one from inside the hospital.

He glanced over at Angela, who had removed her jacket to reveal a nurse's uniform. "Kinky!" he said, giving her a lascivious smile as he ran his eyes over her breasts. It fell from his face when she didn't immediately respond. "Suit yourself," he said with a shrug of indifference.

Errol was the last one to get out of the car, and underneath his leather bomber jacket, he was dressed as a porter.

It was eleven forty as they approached the hospital entrance. According to the latest report from the nursing station, which he'd received earlier that morning when he'd called in posing as Oliver Clarke's intern, the police were sending a team to take Uncle Claude back to prison at one o'clock. Perhaps he was cutting it fine by leaving the breakout attempt until the eleventh hour, but he figured the longer he left it, the more complacent the cops would become.

"Guv, there's a phone call for you. I think it's the hospital." DS Steve Bull shouted as he poked his head through the doorway of Dillon's small office.

"Bloody hell, Stevie! Can't you take a message?" Dillon snapped. "I was just about to make an important call for the boss." He waved the telephone handset at Bull to emphasise his point.

Jack Tyler was going to be stuck at court for most of the day; he had a PCMH – a Plea and Case Management Hearing – listed at the Old Bailey this morning, and an appeal against sentence was scheduled to be heard at the Royal Courts of Justice at two-thirty. Before leaving, he'd asked Dillon to speak to the NPIA – which stood for the National Police Improvements Agency, although most coppers he knew thought the acronym ought to stand for 'No Point In Asking' – with a view to them recommending an expert in gait analysis for a trial that was due to commence in late February.

"Sorry, guv. They asked for you in person." Bull shrugged apologetically as if to say 'what could I do?' After delivering the message, he took his leave quickly, before Dillon could hurl abuse at him.

With a sigh of pure frustration, Dillon lowered the receiver and pocketed the crumpled sheet of paper Jack had given him. "Oh well, I didn't really want to speak to the NPIA anyway," he mumbled under his breath. Closing his door behind him, Dillon strutted into the main office and snatched up the telephone that Steve Bull was pointing to.

"Hello, Detective Inspector Dillon speaking..."

Melissa Smails genuinely loved her job at the RLH where, for the past two years, she had worked as a ward sister on a mixed-sex, short-stay surgical ward with a surgical elective admission unit. There were fifteen beds in total, catering for all of the surgical specialities. The patients currently under her care included people who had undergone complex surgical procedures, were receiving chemotherapy and radiotherapy, or required symptom control.

Mel's working day had begun, as always, with a detailed handover from the night shift, during which she had been briefed about each and every patient – especially the mysterious one being guarded by the police in a private room just along the corridor.

Although the clinical shift started at 8 a.m., Mel was ultra-conscientious and she always liked to arrive a few minutes early so that she could review the staffing and skill mix for the day; this helped her to effectively plan the nurse-to-patient allocation so that none of the nurses were inadvertently put in a situation that exceeded their skills or capabilities.

After the handover, there had been time for a quick cup of coffee, and then Mel had commenced her ward round and personally visited every patient under her care, chatting with some, simply exchanging a cordial greeting and a smile with others.

Throughout the morning, teams of doctors from the various surgical disciplines had carried out their ward rounds and checked on their patients' progress. It had been controlled pandemonium as usual, and she had presided over it like a fussy mother hen.

As Melissa wearily hung up the phone after fielding yet another lengthy call, she reflected that she had spent a disproportionate amount of her morning speaking to the hospital's bed manager and other ward managers trying to juggle beds for patients.

Mr Winston, it seemed, would be leaving them today. She'd uttered a silent hoorah when she'd received the news; not only was the man utterly obnoxious, but having all these policemen around, not to mention all these extra security precautions that had been put in place, interrupted the smooth flow of her ward, and she didn't like it.

She glanced at her watch. It was quarter-to-twelve. There was a bit of a lull going on at the moment, and she wondered if she'd have the time to scoot down to the hospital cafeteria and grab herself a fancy coffee and a bar of chocolate before it got busy again.

———

As soon as he cradled the phone, Dillon looked around the office, checking to see who was available. The place resembled a ghost ship;

Colin Franklin, Kelly Flowers, and young Dick Jarvis had accompanied Jack to the Bailey, and almost everyone else was out on action-led enquiries.

"Steve, what are you and George doing right now?" he asked. The only other people in the room were Dean Fletcher and Wendy Blake, two DCs who worked on the team's Intel Cell, but they were both swamped with work.

"Why?" Bull asked guardedly. It was like having a bad case of déjà vu because he knew exactly where this was leading.

"What are you doing?" Dillon repeated, impatiently folding his arms across his barrel of a chest.

Bull grimaced, sensing that he was about to be lumbered. "Some urgent enquiries for the boss," he said, hoping Tyler's name would be enough to deter Dillon from burdening him.

"Not anymore, you're not, mate. I've just spoken to a Consultant at the hospital. The drug squad boys are coming to collect Winston at one-o'clock and I want to make sure that he gets back to The Ville safely."

A look of despair appeared on Bull's slender face. "But the DCI wants this stuff completed before he gets back from court," he protested.

Dillon held up a large hand to stave off any further protest. "Don't you worry about that. I'll take full responsibility for dragging you away."

Bull groaned inwardly, wondering why Dillon was so desperate to stick his oar into something that no longer concerned him? "Winston's the drug squad's problem now," he argued. "Why are we getting involved?"

"Shame on you, Steve," Dillon scolded, wagging a righteous finger at him. "You know what that man's capable of. How could you say such a thing?" During Winston's arrest at Liverpool Street station in early November, the bastard had shot a BTP officer twice before turning the gun on Dillon. If it hadn't been for Tyler's timely intervention, just as Winston pulled the trigger, the conflict might have ended very differently. As it was, even after he'd been disarmed, Winston had put up a hell of a fight before finally being overcome and restrained.

Steve lowered his voice. "Jack won't thank you for poking your nose in, Tony," he warned. "Especially after George Holland told him in no uncertain terms that whatever's going on between Winston and the drug squad is out of AMIP's hands."

Dillon knew that Bull was absolutely right and that he ought to leave Skinner and his team to sort Winston out without any interference from him, but he had a really bad feeling about today.

Was he behaving irrationally? Steve obviously seemed to think so; he could tell that from the disapproving way that the team's most experienced DS was staring at him.

Dillon couldn't fully articulate why, but he was convinced that Winston would try to escape before the end of the day. After all, what did he have to lose? He was looking at a life sentence, which meant that he would be an old man by the time he was eligible for parole.

Maybe the drug squad officers were alive to this danger; maybe they had ramped up their security procedures accordingly – but then again, with Frank Skinner in charge, could he afford to take that chance?

Surely, having a few extra people around when Winston was moved couldn't possibly hurt?

As a compromise, Dillon vowed that he'd do his best to keep a really low profile and not piss anyone off.

"Bring the car around to the front," he said stubbornly. "I'll drag Georgie Porgie away from the phone and we'll meet you downstairs in a few minutes."

Bull knew that there was no point in arguing. Dillon was on a mission, and nothing anyone said was going to sway him. The big man had already crossed to the far end of the room and was looming over George Copeland, waiting impatiently for him to finish a telephone conversation.

Checking that he still had the keys to the Omega in his pocket, Bull grabbed his jacket and headed for the stairs, resigned to the fact that Tyler's enquiries would now have to wait until later. Hopefully, it wouldn't be too much later!

When George Copeland put the phone down, he turned to smile up at Dillon, who was now perched on the desk beside him. He was very much looking forward to his lunch break, which he intended to take in precisely twelve minutes time when the clock struck midday.

"How can I help you, boss?" he beamed.

"Grab your coat, Georgie boy," Dillon instructed, tersely. "We're going out."

George was crestfallen. "What! Aw, c'mon boss, I've arranged to take my lunch at twelve o'clock and I'm famished!"

"Never mind, George," Dillon said, glancing back over his shoulder. "You could do with losing a few pounds."

"Bloody hell," Copeland grumbled as he stood up and shoved his chair under his desk. Snatching an emergency cereal bar from his top drawer, he picked up his tweed jacket and followed obediently.

Helicopter pilot Peter Myers guided the HEMS aircraft into its final approach for a helipad landing on the roof of the Royal London Hospital in Whitechapel while his co-pilot, Daniel Reed, sat in the seat beside him, enjoying the ride.

The red Virgin MD902 Explorer Air Ambulance had become a familiar sight above the London skyline since Richard Branson's Virgin Group had taken over funding the project from Express Newspapers in 1997, and he was incredibly proud to be flying it.

The Helicopter Emergency Medical Service – HEMS – had been formed in 1986 in response to a report by The Royal College of Surgeons documenting the number of unnecessary trauma-related deaths that occurred following accidents, and criticising the poor levels of roadside care that seriously injured patients received in the UK. Originally created to serve the whole of South East England, the inaugural HEMS mission was flown in September 1989, and this involved ferrying human organs from Scotland to London for a surgical transplant. Of course, since then its role had changed drastically, becoming far more hands-on.

Surprisingly, the London Air Ambulance's arrival hadn't been heralded as a success by everyone. In 1990 a local newspaper called The East London Advertiser featured an article in which it was branded a 'disaster for local people' by Labour Councillor John Biggs, who was quoted to have said, 'The helicopter takes off and lands with a deafening noise drowning conversation and disturbing the peace of the people in the area.'

Fortunately, despite opposition from some quarters, the HEMS operation had thrived, and with the ongoing help of sponsors and other charitable donations, its team of highly trained doctors and paramedics continued to save lives on a daily basis.

The helicopter was returning from a serious road traffic accident that had occurred in Walthamstow. The casualty was a teenage boy who had been riding a moped in convoy with several of his friends; they had been racing each other along Forest Road, weaving in and out of traffic as they headed towards the college for another boring day of further education. The journey had ended in disaster when the rear of the moped clipped the front of a car it was overtaking as the inexperienced rider swerved to avoid a head-on collision with oncoming traffic.

By the time the HEMS bird arrived on scene, an ambulance and Fast Responder motorcyclist were already there, having been dispatched from the nearby ambulance station in James Lane at the back of Whipps Cross hospital.

Coming together under the supervision of Dr Pamela Bennett, they had all worked tirelessly for the best part of half-an-hour to stabilise the patient, who had suffered multiple injuries after being thrown from his moped. In addition to obvious breaks to both lower limbs and an unstable fracture to his pelvis, his abdomen had become distended and was covered in dark purple bruising, which was indicative of an internal bleed.

As the helicopter began its decent, Myers spotted the dedicated helipad ground crew waiting to receive the patient. As soon as they landed, the patient would be placed on a gurney and wheeled across the tarmac to an express elevator that went down to the accident and emergency department on the ground floor. A trauma team, consisting of A&E doctors, general surgeons, specialist trauma surgeons, and anaesthetists would be waiting to assess and then treat the young man once Pamela Bennett had completed her handover.

Myers toggled his mic. "Pam, we're coming in to land, and the ground crew's already on the tarmac awaiting our arrival." The ground crew included a two-man fire team; operating protocol specified that they had to be present on the helipad every time the helicopter took off or landed.

Bennet raised a thumb in acknowledgement. "Thanks, Pete," she said, looking up briefly.

The patient was barely conscious. Despite the oxygen they were giving him, his breathing was becoming increasingly laboured, and that concerned Bennett. She had given him as much pain relief as she could, but he was still in considerable distress. "Not long, now, my love," she said, soothingly.

The landing pad was directly below them now, and Myers eased back on the cyclic control, flaring the helicopter for landing, a technique that puts the aircraft in a 'nose up' altitude to increase drag and reduce momentum. A very experienced pilot, Myers bought the machine into a hovering position above the circular helipad, the centre of which was identifiable from the air by a large capital 'H' painted in red.

Seconds later, they were safely on the ground.

"Safe to exit," Myers told his passengers, and then he waved to Mike Cummings, the ground crew supervisor, who crouched a safe distance away, letting him know it was okay to approach the aircraft.

Cummings led the ground team and their trolley forward. The rear doors were opened and the patient was transferred onto the trolley and wheeled off under the strict supervision of Pamela Bennett.

Garston instructed his two subordinates to wait in the downstairs foyer while he carried out a final recce to confirm that the planned escape route was still viable.

He didn't go as far as actually visiting Winston's room, but he did travel the circuit they would need to complete in order to get there and then return to the car park. Everything went smoothly and he was satisfied that, providing they could overpower the three police guards before the alarm was raised, they would have no trouble getting Winston out of his room and safely away from the hospital.

On his return to the ground floor a few minutes later, Garston spotted a harried-looking porter pushing an empty wheelchair through the foyer towards him. Approaching the man, he raised a hand to get his attention.

"Excuse me, my good fellow, where can I get one of those things?" he asked, putting on his best public-school accent again, just as he had done when he'd posed as a solicitor's intern. For some strange reason, it always seemed to impress the lower classes. "I need to arrange for a patient to be taken for some x-rays, you see," he said by way of explanation.

The unshaven porter scratched his head. "Well, you can have this one if you like, doctor," he offered. "I can't help you myself as I need to be somewhere else, but I could call another porter to push it for you if you like?"

Garston smiled, taking control of the wheelchair. "Good Lord, no. You chaps have more than enough to do around here. Leave it to me."

What a bloody nice bloke! the porter thought to himself as he watched the slim doctor push the squeaking wheelchair away. Almost immediately, a nurse sashayed over to join him. As they headed towards the freight lift at the far end of the corridor, a stocky, bald-headed porter he hadn't seen around before lumbered over and took control of the wheelchair. It pleased him that another porter had offered to help the pleasant young doctor out. *Well done, mate,* he thought. With a final glance at the trio that predominately lingered on the nurse's calves, he smiled to himself and resumed his journey.

. . .

"Did you see how easily I sweet-talked that pathetic little man out of his wheelchair?" Garston boasted as they reached the doors to the freight elevator a couple of minutes later.

Angela didn't like Garston; she thought he was an arrogant show-off, and she wasn't remotely impressed by his antics. "You take too many chances," she criticised. "You should have sent Errol to get the stupid wheelchair. That's what porters do."

That put Garston's back up and he glared at her until she averted her eyes.

They waited for the lift in awkward silence.

When it finally arrived, Garston stormed in and poked the button marked 'three', the floor on which Winston was being held. Angela's abrasive comment had stung him and, after a few seconds of silent brooding, he turned on her. "In future, keep your worthless opinions to yourself," he warned, jabbing her in the sternum with his forefinger.

She responded by rolling her eyes at him, which infuriated him so much he couldn't even bring himself to speak. With an attitude like that, it was no wonder that someone had striped her face with a razor when she was younger.

With his anger still festering, Garston checked that the revolver he was carrying was properly concealed, making sure it could easily be reached when the time came.

When he ordered them to glove up, Errol fished a pair of rubber gloves out of his pocket and began inserting his large, calloused hands into them. To his annoyance, Angela raised her rubber-coated hands and wriggled them at him. "Already done," she said, smugly.

"Smart arsed cow," he mumbled. If he hadn't needed her for the breakout, he would have slapped the smirk from her face.

After what seemed like an age, the doors finally slid open on the third floor, announcing their arrival with a pleasant ping. Garston poked his head outside, cautiously checking left and right.

The corridor was clear and he signalled for them to step out of the lift.

"Right, you two," he said, pulling the flimsy white mask out of his pocket. "No fuck-ups from here on in or we're all done for." As he spoke, he carefully tugged his surgical mask up over the lower half of his face, making sure it covered him from the nose down.

The freight elevator they had used was located on the opposite side of the building to Winston's room, but the advantages of using it outweighed the lengthy walk they now faced. Firstly, its use was restricted to hospital staff so it didn't get half the foot traffic that the public access elevators did. Secondly, and perhaps more importantly, it was only about forty yards away from the exit that led out to where Mullings was waiting with the getaway car.

As they set off, Garston found himself hoping that none of the officers who'd been on duty last week, when he'd accompanied Clarke on his legal visit, would be around today. Even if they were, it shouldn't matter as long as he kept the mask on. He glanced sideways, checking that Angela had done the same and that her scar was properly concealed.

She had and it was.

Being a thicko, Errol had somehow managed to put his mask on upside down, and they were forced to make a brief stop so that Angela could sort it out for him. Garston used the respite to pour a thick line of coke along the back of his hand. Lowering his mask, he inhaled greedily until there was nothing left.

The insufflation brought with it a wonderful new sense of awareness, and by the time they were approaching Winston's room, with Errol pushing the annoyingly squeaking wheelchair beside him and Angela trailing just behind, a wonderful feeling of calmness had descended over Garston. He knew it was a cocaine-induced euphoria, but he really didn't care. They were going to pull off this incredibly audacious breakout, and they were going to do it without a single fucking hitch.

He stopped outside Winston's door, smiling at the stern-faced policeman standing nearest to him. The disinterested looking man was leaning against the wall, looking like he might nod off at any second. Thankfully, he wasn't one of the officers who'd been present last time. Neither was the short woman with the brunette bob who stood a few feet away, looking equally bored.

"Hello," Garston said with forced cheerfulness. "We need to whisk the patient off for a few last-minute tests before he's released."

"No problem," the male officer replied, stepping aside to let him in.

"Actually, he was rather aggressive towards me the last time I spoke to him," Garston said, affecting an air of concern, "so I was wondering if you two would come inside with me, just in case he gets any funny ideas."

"Do you have any reason to think there might be a problem today?" the female cop asked, responding to his question with one of her own.

Garston shrugged with uncertainly. "Well no," he said hesitantly, "but if the last time was anything to go by…"

While she didn't actually go as far as calling him a 'wuss', the female officer's scornful expression implied that that was exactly what he was. "Sorry," she said, looking anything but. "One of us has to remain outside at all times."

Garston frowned. This engagement wasn't going the way he'd envisaged it would. "But it would make me feel an awful lot safer if you both came in," he said, trying to pander to her ego. As he spoke, he noticed Errol's hand was casually drifting behind his jacket towards the revolver that was tucked into the rear of his waistband.

The brunette seemed impervious to his charms, and all he got for his efforts was a raised eyebrow that told him she wasn't going to put herself out for him. She was obviously a rug muncher, he thought, trying not to let his frustration show.

"Tell you what," the male officer said, looking hot and uncomfortable in his blue NATO jumper. "I'll come inside with you if it makes you feel safer, but Shazza will have to remain out here. And before we go anywhere, we'll need to radio in and get permission to move him to another part of the building."

Garston felt himself becoming flustered. "But –"

"It's part of the security protocol that's been agreed by the hospital hierarchy," the officer called Shazza said firmly.

Garston decided that he really didn't like her.

Snatching a quick glance through the glass pane in Winston's door, Garson spotted his uncle slouched on the bed, looking like the caged animal he was. Sitting in an armchair to the right of the door, the third and final police officer was browsing through a magazine. Garston immediately recognised him as the man who'd inspected Clarke's ID and then shown them into the room last Thursday.

Shit!

Garston felt his heart rate spike a little. He took a deep breath and told himself not to panic; everything would absolutely be fine as long as he kept the mask pulled up. He exhaled nervously, conscious that the police officers were picking up on his agitation and it was making them uneasy.

"We need to radio in where we're taking the prisoner and why we're going there," Shazza said impatiently, and her tone had gone from indifferent to downright hostile. Garston realised that the officers were starting to become suspicious, and that further attempts at subterfuge were almost certainly pointless. They had reached an impasse; he needed them to go inside and they had no intention of doing so. Fortunately, he had a contingency plan to cater for this.

His eyes flicked left and right, making sure that the corridor was still clear. It was, and with a heavy heart, he caught Errol's eye and nodded decisively.

Moving as one, both men drew their firearms and lunged forward to overpower the two officers. Garston grabbed hold of the male officer by the scruff of his neck and pushed him roughly backwards, knocking him off balance. Before the man could react, he jammed the muzzle of his revolver under the startled man's chin. Breathing hard, he glanced sideways and was relieved to see that Errol had pinned the female officer against the wall by her throat and had the barrel of his gun rammed against her temple.

Garston's drug-fuelled eyes flitted between the two terrified officers. "Keep your hands down by your sides and don't say a fucking word," he warned. "If either of you makes a move for your radios or shouts out a warning, you'll both be dead a second later."

Frozen with fear, both officers allowed themselves to be pushed flat against the wall. "Hurry," Garston hissed at Angela, knowing someone could walk by and discover them at any second.

With trembling hands, Angela relieved them of their radios. Then she removed the quick-cuffs from their utility belts. Starting with the male, she spun each of the officers around to face the wall. Pulling their unresisting arms behind their backs, she applied the rigid handcuffs to their wrists. She squeezed the ratchets as tightly as she could, ignoring the grunts of pain that followed.

Garston's voice was full of menace. "Right, you two, I want you to walk into the room as though everything is perfectly normal. We'll be right behind you. Remember, if either or you say a single word, I'll blow both your fucking heads off."

Angela was looking up and down the corridor anxiously. "Hurry," she pleaded.

With their hands secured behind them, the two cops were manhandled into Winston's room, with the barrel of a gun rammed into the small of their backs.

The police officer sitting by the bed looked up, startled when everyone bundled into the room. "What's going on?" he asked, confused, but unconcerned.

As soon as Angela closed the door behind them, Garston took a step backward and viciously clubbed the male officer across the side of the head, dropping him like a stone. A second later, his weapon was levelled at PC Morrison who was, by now, half out of his chair and going for his baton.

"DON'T MOVE!" Garston screamed. And then, a little quieter, "Do as we say and no-one gets hurt. If you cry out or try to use your radio, I swear we will shoot you all."

Being careful to keep out of the line of fire, Angela cautiously made her way forward and took control of Morrison's radio and handcuffs. The officer didn't even look at her; he was transfixed by the weapon now being pointed at him.

While Morrison was being dealt with, Errol ushered the female officer into the opposite corner of the room. He kicked her feet as wide apart as they would go and then made her stand with her forehead pressed against the wall. That done, he dragged the semiconscious male officer over to join her.

"Lay down on the floor next to your mate," Errol said, speaking for the first time since they had entered the hospital. He sounded like

Frank Bruno, and Shazza half expected him to finish the sentence with 'know what I mean, Harry'.

Still facing the wall, Shazza knelt down awkwardly and then tried to shuffle backwards on her knees so that she could create the room she needed to lie face down. She didn't do it fast enough for Errol's liking, so he grabbed her ankles and yanked them backwards, pulling her legs from under her with tremendous force. Shazza's chin smashed into the floor with a sickening thud, and she was instantly rendered unconscious by the force of the impact.

"You'll never get away with this," Morrison said, licking his lips nervously. He risked a quick glance over his shoulder at Winston. "Look at him. He's not even fit to walk unaided, so how are you ever gonna get him out of here?"

"Don't talk about me as if I'm not here, pig," Winston snarled at Morrison. Clutching his right side, he gingerly stood up from the bed and lumbered over to his nephew's side.

"Give me the gun," Morrison said, tentatively holding out his hand, "before you end up doing something that can't be undone."

Garston ignored him. "Lay down on the floor next to your colleagues," he ordered, pointing at the floor with the barrel of the gun.

"There isn't enough room," Angela told him. "You need to put him on the bed."

Garston immediately saw that she was right, but felt the way she had said it undermined his authority. Before the day was out, he suspected that he was going to have to do something about her increasingly disrespectful attitude. First, though, there were more pressing issues to worry about.

"Lay face down on the bed," he told Morrison.

The cop shook his head. "Don't be a prat," he said defiantly. "Stop this nonsense now, while you can."

Garston could feel his heart racing. Why the hell was the cop trying to be such a hero? And then it dawned on him that the policeman was deliberately stalling in the hope that someone would walk by and raise the alarm. Either that, or he was expecting his colleagues from the drug squad to arrive early and rush to his rescue.

He cocked the revolver.

"Last chance," he warned, trying not to let his hand shake, "or I'll shoot you in the gut and watch you bleed out." It was a bluff, of course. He had no intention of shooting anyone.

Thankfully, Morrison didn't know that, and he resentfully did as he was told. Once he was on the bed, Angela rushed forward and handcuffed his arms behind his back, conscious that the revolver was being still pointed at the officer's spine.

When that was done, she ran back to the two officers on the floor. Breathing hard from her exertions, she knelt down beside them and removed three syringes from her pocket. Each was filled with an ominous-looking brown liquid. She removed the cap from the first one, checked it for air bubbles, and then injected the semi-conscious officer. He groaned, took a deep breath, and then lapsed into a deep sleep. The female cop was still unconscious from where she had smashed her head into the floor, but they didn't know how long she would be out for so Angela injected her as well. Finally, she stood up and walked towards Morrison.

"Wait," Garston commanded. "Go outside and get the wheelchair first."

"But Errol could do that," She complained, and then realised that she had inadvertently said one of their names out loud in front of the policeman.

It was the last straw, and Garston was across the room in two steps. "You stupid fucking bitch," he snarled, backhanding her across the face so hard that she spun into the wall. "Now go fetch that wheelchair in here, right now."

Holding the side of her face, Angela staggered out of the room. When she returned, a few moments later, Garston was gratified to see a splodge of blood seeping through her facemask at the point where her mouth would be.

Walking over to the bed, Garston removed a pillowcase and unceremoniously tugged it down over the policeman's head. Satisfied that the cop wouldn't be able to see his face, he pulled the surgical mask down and smiled triumphantly at Winston.

"Not bad, eh?" he smirked, expecting to receive praise from his uncle.

"Not bad," Winston allowed. "But not good enough." With that, he shuffled forward and snatched the gun from Garston's hand.

Looking down at the revolver, Winston sneered derisively. "Are you seriously telling me that the best gun that you could get your hands on was a pathetic little twenty-two?"

Garson bristled at the spiteful jibe. He had originally sourced a couple of 9mm Browning hi-power pistols for the job, but the deal had fallen through and he only just about managed to find alternative weapons in time.

The revolver was a Brocock ME38. It bore a strong resemblance to the .357 Colt Python Magnums that were used by the motorcycle cops in the second *Dirty Harry* film, *Magnum Force,* although it didn't pack anywhere near the same level of stopping power.

Nonetheless, the Brocock had become extremely popular amongst London's criminal fraternity of late, mainly because it could be converted from a harmless replica airgun into a real firearm that discharged a .22 cartridge in less than ten minutes simply by using a household drill to bore it out. Winston might have a point about it not being the most powerful firearm on the black market, but Garston knew it would do the job it had been purchased for, and the dealer had even thrown in a free box of factory-made .22 ammunition as a bonus, which meant that they had fifty rounds to share between the two guns.

The manner in which his uncle was now staring down at the prone form on the bed started to made Garston feel uncomfortable. After all, Winston had previous for shooting coppers.

His fears were confirmed when Winston thumbed the hammer back and watched the cylinder rotate with a satisfied smile. Picking up a pillow, he placed it on top of the officer's head.

"What are you doing?" Garston asked, alarmed at the obvious implication.

Winston gave his nephew a look of distaste before burying the muzzle deep into the pillow and pushing down until it pressed against the back of the policeman's head.

Garston felt physically sick as he listened to the terrified officer hyperventilating. He obviously knew – or at least suspected – what was coming next.

"No, Claude, please wait…" Garston said, his voice filled with dread.

"We can't let him live," Winston responded matter-of-factly. "He knows Errol's name."

Garston raised his hands to stay his uncle. "Claude, please, no…"

Winston sneered, and then he squeezed the trigger. Although the pillow acted as a noise suppressor, the sound of the shot was still alarmingly loud within the confines of the room. Blowing smoke from the end of the barrel, he turned to address an ashen-faced Garston. "When you do a job, you do it properly. Let that be a lesson well learned, nephew."

CHAPTER FIVE

It was approaching midday as the battered green Omega pulled up outside the front of the hospital, blocking in a large, shiny black Ford that was parked in a chevroned off area clearly marked 'Drop Off Only – No Waiting.' The scrawny driver was tucked right down in his seat as if asleep, and it didn't look like he'd be moving off any time soon.

Parking spaces were clearly at a premium and there were none currently free. "Doesn't look like there's anywhere to park in here, so do you want me to stay with the motor while you pop inside?" Steve asked, hoping that Dillon would say yes.

"Um, no, wait here for the moment," Dillon said, opening his door. "I'll have a word with that bloke sitting in his car, see how long he's going to be."

As he sauntered over to the car, a Scorpio, he noticed that the engine was still running. With a bit of luck that meant that the driver would be moving off soon and wouldn't mind swapping positions with them, seeing as the cheeky sod shouldn't be waiting there anyway. He couldn't help noticing that the driver didn't fit the car. He was far too young, for one thing. And he was a scruffy bugger, too.

The Scorpio's lone occupant sat up as Dillon approached, and there was an aura of uneasiness about him that made the detective wonder if something might actually be wrong here. As he reached the driver's door it was immediately apparent that the lock had been forced. A screwdriver, or something similar, had been used. The damage was recent; he could see that the scratch marks around the lock were fresh.

Dillon's heart sank. *Please tell me this isn't what I think it is,* he prayed.

Putting on a mask of indifference, he tapped on the window, smiling in at the driver and hoping that his casual manner would put the man at ease.

"Yeah?" the young black man demanded cautiously, having lowered the electric window a couple of inches. It was enough. The car reeked of cannabis and there was a half-smoked joint in the driver's hand.

More importantly, Dillon could see that the ignition had been ripped out and the wiring spliced, confirming his suspicion that it was a stolen car.

Great!

Just what he didn't need – not today.

If he believed in that sort of thing, he might be tempted to think that this was fate's way of preventing him from making a nuisance of himself with the drug squad wallahs.

"Sorry to bother you, mate. I was just wondering how long you're going to be here, only there's nowhere else to park and I don't want to block you in."

"Oh," the man said, visibly relaxing. He looked around in a dilemma, trying to decide what to do for the best. "I'm waiting for some people, bruv," he eventually said. "I'm not sure how much longer they'll be."

Dillon smiled at him disarmingly while wishing that he could punch the little twerp's lights out for spoiling his plans. "Tell you what, I'll have a quick gander to see if there are any other spaces while you wait here. Back in a minute." With that, he straightened up and began walking towards the Omega. As soon as he turned away from the Ford his smile vanished, to be replaced by a look of consternation.

Steve Bull had been watching Dillon's interaction with the Ford's driver with mounting interest, and now he turned to Copeland.

"Shit!" he said, stretching the word out miserably.

"What's up?" George asked, frowning at the sudden trepidation in his friend's voice.

"I dunno," Bull said, glumly, "but we're about to find out." He powered down the electric window as Dillon reached them.

"We have a slight problem," the big man said, leaning in to address his colleagues.

Bull let out a disheartened sigh. "I figured as much. Go on then, what's wrong?"

"That Scorpio's a nicked motor."

Copeland naively craned his neck forward to get a better look.

"Don't be so bleedin' obvious, George," Dillon growled, placing a shovel sized palm on Copeland's forehead and pushing him back down into his seat.

"Ouch," Copeland complained, rubbing his head.

"How can you tell it's nicked?" Bull asked.

"The door lock's been jemmied and it's been hotwired. The driver's just sitting there, smoking cannabis – says he's waiting for some mates to come out."

Bull swore under his breath. "What do you want to do about it?" he asked. At this rate, he'd never get any of the tasks Tyler had assigned him started today – let alone finished.

"We don't wanna lumber ourselves with a crappy TDA, boss," Copeland piped up from the back. "Why not call it in and have the locals come and nick chummy? We can always wait here till they arrive so that he can't drive off."

Dillon shook his head. "We can't do that, George," he said, really wishing that they could. "It would look like we think it's beneath us. We'll just have to bite the bullet and nick him."

"Shouldn't we call for back up anyway?" Copeland persisted. "What if the people he's waiting for come out? It'll be a bit embarrassing if they see us and have it on their toes."

It was a good point.

Dillon expelled his breath in a long sigh of frustration. "Steve, get on the radio to the local nick. Tell 'em what we've got and request a couple of uniform units to back us up in case the driver's mates appear. Request a silent approach. George, if you cover the passenger's door, I'll take the driver's side. Steve, as soon as we're in position, drive across his path and block the little shit in."

Bull gave him a thumbs up. He couldn't answer because he was already on the radio, requesting back up.

Still rubbing his head, George joined Dillon outside, where his rumbling stomach earned him a look of disdain. "Sorry, but I'm hungry," he explained sheepishly.

Dillon walked back to the driver, bending down to get a better look inside. Hopefully, the car's central locking wasn't on.

"Sorry mate, no other spaces available. How long did you say you'd be?"

Before the man could reply, the Omega lurched forward, completely trapping the Ford in place. Realising that something was very wrong, the driver instinctively reached for the automatic transmission but, by then, Dillon had wrenched the door wide open and grabbed him by the scruff of the neck. "POLICE!" he yelled, pushing the startled man back into his seat so hard that he almost ended up with whiplash.

Mel had just come up the stairs after paying a brief visit to the Foyer Café on the ground floor. She was holding a polystyrene takeaway cup containing a large Cappuccino in one hand and a 100g bar of Dairy Milk in the other. She planned to consume them both at the nursing station while she added her shifts for the rest of the month to her diary and then updated the latest batch of patient records.

As she'd recently told Dumpling Dave during a campaign to persuade him to start going jogging with her and lose a few pounds, one of the benefits of training regularly was that she could treat herself to the occasional bar of chocolate without feeling remotely guilty. Dave hadn't been convinced. He was such a lazy sod that he wouldn't even run to catch a bus, let alone to keep fit. Needless to say, her attempts to get him out pounding the pavement with her had fallen on deaf ears.

As she emerged onto the third-floor corridor, she heard a loud bang. It had come from one of the rooms up on her left. The noise almost made her jump out of her skin, and if there hadn't been a secure lid on the coffee, it would have gone everywhere. It sounded like some silly sod had just let a firework off, but surely no one would daft enough to do that inside a hospital? Then again, she had seen plenty of people do far crazier things during her career.

Lips pursed in disapproval, Mel set off briskly in search of the culprit, determined to have them ejected for their irresponsible tomfoolery. The two uniform police officers she had passed on her way down to the café a few minutes ago were nowhere to be seen. *Bloody typical!* She thought, feeling more than a little miffed. The bloody cops had repeatedly gotten under her feet during the past week. Now – when they might actually have proved useful for once – the buggers had vanished into thin air.

When she reached Winston's room, she glanced through the door's glass panel and was surprised to see several medical staff in the room with him. There was a doctor she didn't recognise, a slim nurse and a bald-headed porter, both of whom were standing with their backs to her. Winston was out of his bed, standing amongst them and looking as surly as ever. There was a hospital issue wheelchair beside him, which suggested that the medical team were in the process of getting him ready for his discharge. Already angry about the firework, this only served to wind her up even more. As ward sister, they should have run this by her first as a courtesy. Then, as it occurred to her that they might have tried to do exactly that while she was off buying refreshments, she felt a twinge of guilt for having jumped to conclusions so hastily.

Pushing open the door, Mel poked her head inside to find out what their plan of action was and how long it would be before the bed became free again. She decided to ask them about the firecracker while she was at it. "I don't suppose you just heard a loud…"

The words died in her mouth as she spotted what looked like a gun in Winston's outstretched hand. Every head in the room whipped in her direction, and she saw shock and hostility in their eyes.

"What's going on?" she asked suspiciously.

"Get her," Winston snarled at the porter, who was standing with his mouth open, looking as guilty as a pubescent schoolboy who'd just been caught knocking one out.

Fortunately for Mel, it was only after Winston gave him a forceful shove in the back that the sluggish porter started to move towards her.

As she backed away, Mel caught a glimpse of the two officers who had been outside the room a little while ago. To her horror, they were both face down on the floor and their hands had been restrained behind their backs. As she stared down at them in shock, she felt, rather than saw, the porter extending his arm in her direction, his hand opening and closing in a grotesque parody of the claws on one of those stupid amusement arcade games.

Mel swatted his hand away and hurriedly took another step backwards. "Don't touch me," she warned him, her eyes darting back and forth between him and the gun in her patient's hand. At the same time, a voice in the back of her head screamed at her to turn and run while there was still a slim chance of getting away.

It was only as she retreated into the corridor on her third backward step that she became aware of the officer on the bed, and her eyes were immediately drawn to the big splash of red that occupied the spot where his head ought to be.

Mel felt her heart jump into her mouth.

"Oh my God," she whispered. dropping her coffee cup, which exploded on impact, sending a spray of hot liquid flying into the air.

Finally, survival mode kicked in, and Mel turned and sprinted along the corridor. The porter's heavy footsteps echoed off the walls behind her, but she had no way of knowing if he was a long way behind or right on her heels, and the uncertainty made the situation seem all the more terrifying. In the end, she risked a fleeting glimpse over her shoulder and saw the blurred shape of her pursuer about ten paces back.

An all-consuming shroud of fear engulfed her and, to combat this, she tried to focus purely on her running technique. All that mattered was getting her breathing right and forcing her arms and legs to pump rhythmically, the way they did at the athletics track when she was practicing for the relay race.

Breathe, pump those arms, breathe…Just keep going, a terrified voice in her head screamed, *and whatever you do, don't look back.*

The shell-shocked driver had been unceremoniously dragged out of the Scorpio and secured against the side of the car. Handcuffs were being applied in the rear stack position just as the first local unit arrived, its roof-mounted blue lights strobing brightly.

Already halfway through a search of the car's interior, George stood up holding a bag of white powder and a lady's compact mirror that had been found respectively in the front passenger footwell and on the dashboard.

"Boss, take a look at this," he said, waving the transparent, self-sealing bag in the air like a trophy. "Cocaine, I'd say. About an ounce of it." He placed both items on top of the car's roof and then delved back inside to see what else he could find.

"They're not mine," the driver said quickly. "Never seen them before."

When Copeland re-emerged a few seconds later, he was holding several sheets of folded paper in his hand, and staring at them in consternation. "Boss, I found these under the front passenger seat. I think you'd better take a look at them."

Frowning, Dillon leaned across the top of the car and took the papers that were flapping around in the wind from his outstretched hand. As he studied them, his face darkened.

"What are these for?" Dillon demanded, shoving the papers under the driver's nose.

The man squirmed uncomfortably. "They ain't mine either," he said. "Never seen –"

"Yeah, I get it," Dillon snapped, cutting him off. "You've never seen them before."

The driver shrugged. "Never seen anything else you find in there before either."

Steve appeared by his side and relieved Dillon of the prisoner. He led him over to the two uniformed locals and explained what had happened. To Bull's delight, one of them was a newbie probationer who was dead keen to have the arrest, which meant that all the AMIP officers would have to do was provide a brief statement of detention.

Bull heard his name being called, and when he looked around, he saw Dillon impatiently beckoning him over. As soon as he got there, Dillon passed him the three crumpled sheets of A4 paper that George had found.

"What do you make of these?" he asked.

Bull's forehead creased into a deep furrow as he studied the handwritten diagrams. "They look like rough drawings of the hospital, marking out all the entrances and exits, the location of the lifts, staircases and —" Bull's eyes widened. "Shit!"

"And the location of Winston's room on the third floor, the number of officers guarding him, and their shift changeover times," Dillon said, finishing the sentence for him.

In an instant, Bull's facial expression transitioned from confusion to shock. "I don't believe it," he said, disbelievingly. "Someone's really gonna try and break him out."

"Looks like it," Dillon said, and then turned to Copeland. "Anything else of interest in there?"

Copeland had a quick nose inside and then re-emerged, shaking his head. "Nah, doesn't look like it, just three coats on the back seat – two men's and one female from the look and size of them."

Dillon considered this. The driver was already wearing a winter coat, so unless one of the male coats had been brought along for Winston, there were currently two unidentified men and one woman wandering around the hospital, getting ready to break Winston out.

In his opinion, the optimum time to strike would be just as the drug squad officers were putting Winston into their car for his return journey to prison, but that wasn't scheduled to happen until one o'clock, which hopefully gave him a little time to prepare. If he could get armed officers in place before then, he should be able to thwart the escape and arrest everyone involved.

"George, get on the radio," he said, speaking quickly. "I think Winston's gang are gonna try and spring him from custody when he's taken back to prison. We need to get armed support in place before then, and we're gonna need enough officers to sweep the building. I think there's a little team roaming around the hospital waiting for the drug squad to move him."

Copeland's face blanched. "Bloody Nora," he said.

"Organise an RVP at the entrance over there, and as soon as the first Trojan unit arrives send them straight up to Winston's room. In the meantime, me and Steve are going up to warn the officers guarding him that trouble's brewing."

As soon as they checked on the officers guarding Winston, Dillon planned to get someone over to the hospital's CCTV room to review the footage of the Ford Scorpio arriving. With luck, they would be able to retrospectively track the suspects through the hospital and work out where they were. Once located, Trojan units could be sent to intercept them before the drug squad moved Winston.

Leaving Copeland to organise back up, Dillon and Bull sprinted into the hospital.

Errol was embarrassed by his pathetically slow response to Winston's command, and he knew it would all be on him if the slender, frizzy-haired woman he was now chasing along the antiseptic scented corridor managed to get away and raise the alarm.

In his defence, if he hadn't still been reeling from the shock of Winston executing a defenceless cop right in front of him, he wouldn't have been caught off guard when she barged into the room so unexpectedly.

The nurse was damn fast; he'd give her that. One moment, she'd stood riveted to the spot in shock, and the next she had taken off like Speedy bloody Gonzalez, slamming the door in his face on her way out. As he'd run out of the room after her, Errol had slipped in the puddle of spilled coffee and nearly fallen flat on his face. He must have twisted his ankle during the fall because with every stride he now took, a jarring pain shot up his left leg from ankle to knee.

Ten yards ahead of him, his quarry skidded to a halt, crashing into the wall by the ward's door with a thud that seemed to knock the wind out of her. He was rapidly closing the distance between them as her finger furiously jabbed at the little access pad, keying in the code to open the secure door.

"Come on, come on..." he could hear her saying breathlessly.

Her face was white with fear as she glanced back at him.

Smiling in triumph, Errol reached out to grab her.

Suddenly, there was a dull buzzing noise and, just as his fingertips brushed against her shoulder, the door popped open and she was through it in an instant.

"No," Errol shouted as the heavy wooden door closed in his face. He thumped it with his fist, and when that didn't work, he tried to shoulder it open. Then, in desperation, he stepped back and kicked the door with all his might, but the magnetic lock held firm.

The noise reverberated along the corridor, making almost as much noise as the gunshot.

"Get back here," he heard Garston screech, and when he turned around, he saw his boss had already wheeled Winston out of the room and was waiting impatiently for him to return. Angela's face was a picture of misery as she frantically waved for him to come back.

"Hurry the fuck up, you useless idiot," Garston raged. "We need to get Claude out of here before that woman summons help."

His head bowed in shame, Errol ran back to join them, wondering if his failure would put them all in jail.

The hospital foyer was teeming with people, and every single one of them seemed hellbent on impeding their progress as they ran towards the lifts.

"Move aside, please," Dillon shouted, brusquely. "Police officers coming through." That didn't seem to impress anyone, so he just shouldered his way through them instead.

They eventually reached a central hub where several corridors converged. It contained two elevators and a staircase. Unfortunately, both elevators were currently taped off, and a big sign next to them read: *'Closed for essential maintenance'*.

A large map of the hospital was mounted on the wall opposite the lifts, but the floorplan wasn't particularly easy to decipher. A red arrow pointed to a spot that read: *'YOU ARE HERE'*.

The two detectives stared up at the map, trying to orientate themselves. After a moment, Bull turned to Dillon in exasperation. "Please tell me you know the way to Winston's room because I can't make head nor tails of this."

If truth be told, Dillon wasn't terribly sure. On his last visit, he had entered the building from a different point. "I think this is the staircase we want to use," he said, sounding far from certain.

As he turned around, Dillon clattered straight into a group of visitors who had assembled directly behind him and were now engrossed in studying the map. Several of them were people he had shunted out of his path on the way here, and they gave him filthy looks.

"Excuse me," Dillon said gruffly, elbowing his way through the small gathering for a second time.

Cringing with embarrassment, Steve Bull skirted around a red-faced, obese man who was shouting very descriptive insults at Dillon's receding figure.

Completely oblivious, Dillon sprinted up the stairs, taking them two at a time, and he didn't slow down until he reached the halfway point between the second and third floor landings.

"You're like a bloody bull in a china shop," Bull complained when he finally caught up with him.

Without looking back, Dillon raised a forefinger to his lips. "Hush," he said, signalling for silence.

"That was rude, the way you barged..."

Dillon spun to face him. "Shut it, Steve," he hissed.

That did the trick. Bull glowered at him with barely suppressed anger, but he refrained from saying another word.

Winston glanced back over his shoulder in confusion. Errol had just pushed him straight past two lifts and a staircase.

"Where the hell are you taking me?" he demanded aggressively. He spun his finger in the air, indicating that they should turn around. "Go back. We need to get down as quickly as we can, not fanny around up here." He was extremely agitated that the nurse had got away, and he had already threatened to have them all shot if the escape failed because of it.

Errol hesitated and nervously glanced sideways at Garston for instruction. Angela said nothing; she was too scared to speak.

"Keep going," Garston ordered through gritted teeth.

Winston didn't like that. He wasn't used to being countermanded. "What are you playing at, boy?" he snarled.

Garson took a deep breath and tried to remain calm. "Those lifts are out of order in case you didn't notice the sign," he explained, struggling to keep his voice from rising. "Besides, we want the freight lift on the other side of the building. It'll bring us down right by the exit where the getaway car is waiting."

Winston considered this for a moment. "Fair enough," he allowed, "but for fuck sake get a move on 'cause as soon as the Old Bill arrives, this place'll be sealed off tighter than a nun's knickers."

Not wanting to piss Winston off any more than he already had by letting the nurse escape, Errol immediately started to walk much faster.

"Don't speed up," Garston said, placing a restraining hand on the faux porter's arm. "If we do, it'll only draw attention. Just keep walking nice and slow, like we belong here, and no one will give us a second look." At least he hoped they wouldn't. He couldn't ignore the possibility that the damned nurse might already have circulated their descriptions to hospital security.

Inwardly, Garston was struggling not to panic. Everything had been going according to plan until that stupid slut, Angela, had opened her big mouth, giving Winston an excuse to take over and run amok in his usual brutal fashion. The gunshot had jeopardised everything, but the situation might still have been retrievable if that lumbering fool, Errol, had reacted a little quicker and grabbed hold of the nurse before she'd reached the safety of the ward.

He calculated that it would take her colleagues a minute or two to calm her down and get some sense out of her. Then, they would have to call it in, and it would take the police several minutes to respond. If they could use that time to get down to Mullings and the getaway car, they could still be miles away before the law arrived. At least he didn't have to worry about their ride not being there when they reached the ground floor – it was probably the only part of the plan that hadn't gone wrong so far.

Dillon tip-toed up the last remaining steps to the third-floor landing with Bull sulking along behind. "Winston's room should be the fifth door from the end on our left if I remember correctly," he whispered. After listening for a few seconds, he cautiously poked his head around the corner and risked a quick look in both directions. Off to his right, he spotted a couple of hospital staff walking away from him in the distance, a doctor and nurse if he wasn't mistaken. There was a porter in front of them, pushing a wheelchair. Nothing suspicious there. To his left, there was no sign of anyone at all, which was surprising.

"That's odd, there's no one outside his room," he told Bull when he was safely back behind the wall.

Bull shrugged. "Isn't that a good thing?" he said.

Dillon shook his head. "No, Stevie, it's bloody well not. There should be a couple of cops standing guard outside, but there's no trace of them."

"Maybe they've just popped inside the room for a minute," Steve suggested.

"Maybe," Dillon allowed, but he didn't sound hopeful. "Come on, we'd better go and check it out."

CHAPTER SIX

The Plea and Case Management Hearing at the Old Bailey had finished earlier than expected, and they were out of the building by just after twelve. Colin Franklin and Dick Jarvis were feeling lazy, so they decided to take the easy option and pop over to Snow Hill police station for lunch.

Jack and Kelly were feeling a little more adventurous, so they elected to travel a bit further afield to eat. Before going their separate ways, they all arranged to meet up again outside the main entrance to the RCJ at a quarter-to-two, which would leave them plenty of time to speak to their barrister before the two-thirty appeal began.

The sky had darkened, heralding the approach of rain, and thick nimbostratus clouds were being blown across the heavens like a video being played on fast forward.

Wrapped in their warm winter coats, Jack and Kelly set off towards Ludgate Hill, from where they intended to take a brisk walk along Fleet Street to The Strand. However, by the time they reached Farringdon Street, the first drops of icy rain had started to fall, so when an invitingly warm bus came chugging along, they decided to take advantage of it. Two stops later, they found themselves standing opposite the imposing buildings of the Royal Courts of Justice.

More commonly known as the Law Courts, the RCJ housed the

High Court and the Court of Appeal. The large, grey, stone edifice had been constructed in the 1870s. Designed by George Edmund Street, it had been opened by Queen Victoria in 1882 and it remained one of the largest court buildings in Europe.

For a moment they just stood in silence, taking in the view.

"Impressive, isn't it?" Jack said, pulling his collar tight around his neck to keep the biting wind out.

"Amazing," she replied, staring up in awe.

The rain had turned into full-blown hailstones by the time that Jack ushered Kelly into a quaint little Italian place that he liked to eat at whenever he was up this way. It was situated almost directly opposite the RCJ's main entrance, which meant they wouldn't have to rush their meal, and they wouldn't end up getting too wet if the ghastly weather hadn't eased off by the time they left.

The restaurant was small, dimly lit and very cosy. As it was still early, there was only a smattering of people inside, so they had no trouble getting a table.

In the background, Dean Martin's voice could just about be heard crooning out the words to *'That's amore'*.

A smiling waiter with a mop of curly black hair that fell right down to his eyes and an aquiline nose steered them into a secluded, wood-panelled booth and handed over menus. She ordered pasta; he went for the pizza. As this was a working lunch, they decided against ordering alcohol, opting for sparkling mineral water, instead.

"We can stop off for a real drink after court if you want," Jack suggested. There were some fantastic little pubs dotted around the RCJ and nearby Temple, many of them hidden in little out of the way alleys and tiny cobbled side streets. *The Old Bell Tavern* and *Ye Olde Cheshire Cheese* in nearby Fleet Street were two examples that popped to mind. Then there was *The Seven Stars*, located just behind the RCJ, a great pub but also a stomping ground for the pinstripes of the legal profession, so perhaps not the place to go if they didn't want to be recognised.

Kelly pouted sadly. "Sorry, handsome, I'd love to but I can't. Got a gym class booked with the girls tonight, and I don't want to let them down, bearing in mind that I've already missed the last two through work."

"Another time, then," Jack said, feeling strangely disappointed. After a furtive glance around the restaurant to make sure that no one was looking, he reached across the table to squeeze her hand.

"Don't think I didn't notice you checking the room out before you did that," she said, pretending to be annoyed.

Jack blushed guiltily. "Sorry," he said, "but it wouldn't look very professional if someone spotted a DCI holding hands with one of his DCs while they were on duty."

Kelly smiled forgivingly. "It's okay," she said. "I'm only teasing."

He looked relieved. "I wouldn't want you to think that I was embarrassed to be seen out with you," he told her, because he really wasn't. In fact, Jack thought that Kelly was rather beautiful. She had flawless skin, symmetrical features, eyes he could happily lose himself in and a mouth he yearned to kiss every time he saw it. He wanted to tell her that, as far as he was concerned, she was a study in perfection, but that would have been far too gushy, and he wasn't a Mills and Boon type of guy.

A few minutes later, the waiter arrived with their freshly prepared dishes. Kelly sniffed the air appreciatively. "That smells delicious," she said as he placed her Carbonara on the table in front of her.

Jack's thin-crust Margherita was next, and the aroma was equally inviting. After providing them each with the obligatory sprinkling of parmesan cheese, their waiter bowed graciously. "Buon Appetito," he said, leaving them to enjoy their food.

"This really was a much better idea than eating lunch in a police canteen," Kelly said, tucking in with gusto.

Jack smiled indulgently at her. "And you're much better company than Tony Dillon," he said, imagining that his friend was, at this very moment, sitting in a stuffy police canteen with Steve Bull, eating crap food and talking shop.

Bull felt slightly apprehensive as they set off along the corridor towards

Winston's room. Unlike Dillon, he had always preferred cerebral challenges to physical ones; it was one of the main reasons why he'd chosen to pursue a career path as a detective. There was still no sign of the police guard that was meant to be stationed outside the door, and he was becoming increasingly concerned by this.

Dillon instinctively took the lead when they reached Winston's room, thrusting the door open and rushing in.

What he saw stopped him dead in his tracks.

"Sweet Jesus," he gasped.

"What is it?" Bull demanded, anxiously trying to peer over Dillon's shoulder. As Dillon moved aside, he caught a glimpse of the carnage inside the room.

It was enough.

It was more than enough.

Two cops – a male and a female – were lying face down on the floor with their hands cuffed behind their backs. Both had their eyes were closed, and neither was moving.

A third officer lay motionless on the unmade bed, hands also cuffed behind him. He was completely inert, reminding Bull of a discarded rag doll. A starched, white pillowcase had been pulled over his head, and even from the doorway, Bull could tell that it was stained a deep, wet red. There was a strong, coppery smell in the air, mixed with the residue of cordite to create an unpleasant tang that stung the back of his throat. He swallowed hard. "I think they're all dead," he said.

George Copeland was shivering from the cold as he stood next to the stolen Ford Scorpio. He tried stomping his feet in a vain effort to keep them warm, then rubbed his hands together vigorously and blew into them. He studied the ominous looking clouds above and wondered how long he had until the heavens opened up again. He deeply regretted not bringing his overcoat with him, but then he had expected to go straight into the hospital, not end up hanging around outside like a prize wally.

A dozen local officers had joined him and they were just awaiting the imminent arrival of two Trojan units before deploying into the hospital.

A station van had already collected the driver of the LOS, and he was on his way to the local nick with the probationer, who had volunteered to arrest him, acting as escort.

Two of the local PCs, Nick Bartholomew and Terry Grier, had worked with the AMIP team before, and George was aware that Nick had aspirations to join the department and had recently applied to become a Trainee Detective Constable.

"George," Nick said, turning to him with a concerned look on his face. "What floor did you say Mr Dillon was going up to?"

Copeland frowned. "The third floor – why?"

"It's just coming over the radio, there's been a fatal shooting up on the third floor. The informant's a ward sister called Mel something-or-other. Hang on mate there's more coming through now…" Holding the radio to his ear, he listened for a few seconds more. "Shit! It looks like the victims are police officers."

"Flippin' heck!" Copeland exclaimed. With a trembling hand, he fished his mobile out of his jacket and hurriedly started dialling Dillon's number.

Having heard the transmission, several uniformed officers started to rush inside, intent on reaching their stricken colleagues as quickly as they could.

It was noble but stupid.

"Stay where you are," George bellowed. "No one goes inside until Trojan arrives."

The uniform lads didn't look happy, but they grudgingly obeyed his instruction and came back to await armed assistance.

As he listened to the monotonous dialling tone, George became aware of sirens growing louder by the second. Hopefully, this augured the arrival of the Trojan units they were waiting for. "C'mon, boss," he said, staring imploringly at his mobile, "answer your bloody phone and let us know you're okay."

Dillon felt as though someone had just punched him in the stomach, knocking all the air from his lungs. For a moment, his mind flashed back to that dreadful night on the Central Line platform at Liverpool Street station in early November, where he'd stumbled across the young BTP officer Winston had gunned down while attempting to evade capture.

He waved Bull towards the unmoving man on the bed as he knelt down to check out the two officers on the floor. To his astonishment, they both had strong pulses when he pressed his fingers against the carotid arteries in their necks. "Can you hear me?" he asked the first one. There was no response. Unfortunately, Dillon didn't have a handcuff key on him, so he couldn't remove the manacles that were cutting deep, ugly grooves into the constables' wrists.

Behind him, a sharp intake of breath from Steve Bull caused him to turn his head. When their eyes met, Bull shook his head with grim finality, and the look of revulsion on his friend's face told him everything he needed to know.

The man on the bed was dead.

Dillon didn't know the deceased man, but that didn't make his sense of loss any less profound. He had been a fellow cop, a decent human being whose life had been dedicated to doing good. That it had been so cruelly snuffed out by someone whose very existence was a blight on humanity was a terrible travesty.

Resuming his examination, he gently shook each of the surviving officers by their shoulders, telling them to open their eyes. When that didn't work, he tried pinching their ear lobes, but even when he squeezed really hard it had absolutely no effect.

His phone started to ring, but he ignored it.

As carefully as he could, he rolled the male officer over onto his side, supporting his flopping head with one hand and checking him out for gunshot wounds with the other.

As he worked, he barked out orders. "Stevie, call the Yard and chase up that armed assistance," he instructed. "Trojan need to set up a perimeter around the hospital ASAP. Also, get Winston's description circulated. He's such a distinctive looking bastard that there's no excuse for anyone missing him."

As he turned the female officer onto one side to examine her for injuries, he spotted a thin silver key dangling from a fob on the front of her utility belt. Unclipping it, he set about removing her handcuffs and placing her in the recovery position, a process he quickly repeated for her colleague.

Dripping with the sweat of his exertions, Dillon stood up just as a frizzy-haired nurse in her early thirties appeared in the doorway. Her taut face was streaked with mascara.

"Who are you?" she demanded, her eyes darting nervously from one to the other. She sounded like an Aussie, Dillon thought, although her voice was so strained that he couldn't be totally sure. The athletic-looking nurse fidgeted anxiously while awaiting his reply, and he could tell that she was poised to run if the slightest thing spooked her.

"Police. I'm DI Dillon and this is DS Bull," he said, producing his warrant card from his pocket.

Bull was talking animatedly to the operator at IR, but having heard his name mentioned, he raised a hand in greeting.

"Thank God," the woman said, sagging against the door frame.

"What's your name?" he asked her, thinking she looked emotionally drained.

"My name's Melissa Smails, but everyone calls me Mel."

He indicated the two unconscious officers on the floor. "Mel, I need you to come in and examine my colleagues for me, but this is a crime scene now so you'll have to be really careful where you tread and what you touch."

"I understand," she said, nodding weakly. "I'll be careful."

Crossing the room cautiously, Mel knelt down and gave each of the officers a cursory examination.

It didn't take long. "I think they've been drugged with a powerful sedative," she told him when she'd finished. "I'll arrange for them to be moved somewhere more suitable so that we can get them checked out properly, but I don't think either is in imminent danger."

"Thank you," Dillon said, enormously relieved that the body count wasn't set to increase.

"How did you get here so quickly?" Mel asked as she stood on wobbly legs. "I only called this in a couple of minutes ago."

Dillon stared at her in confusion.

She let out a short, mirthless laugh. "You're not here because I called the police, are you?"

Dillon shook his head. "We were coming here to supervise Winston's return to prison."

"You're too late for that," she said, bitterly.

He didn't think she had intended it as a dig, but it stung anyway. "What exactly happened here?" he asked her.

Mel ran a trembling hand through her hair, brushing it away from her eyes.

"I was on my way back to the ward when I heard a bang. When I came to check it out, I found three people in here with Mr Winston – two men and a woman. They were all dressed as hospital staff, but I didn't recognise any of them so I'm guessing the clothing was just a disguise."

"Exactly how long ago was this?" he asked, staring at her intently. "Please think carefully."

Mel bit her lip. "I reckon four or five minutes tops. After I stumbled across them, the bald one chased me back to the ward. I... I was lucky to get away."

Her voice wobbled and, for a moment, Dillon thought she was going to break down and cry. Instead, she took a deep breath to compose herself and then continued. "As soon as I was safely inside, I dialled 999. The emergency services operator said help was on the way, and a couple of minutes later I saw you guys run in."

"Can you describe any of the people who were with Winston?" Dillon asked.

Mel nodded. She doubted she would ever forget the oaf who had chased her. His face would haunt her dreams for years to come.

"They were all black," she said, her voice quivering. "One was dressed as a doctor, one as a porter – that's the one with the bald head – and the woman was dressed as a nurse."

As she described them, Dillon realised that these were the very people he had seen walking along the corridor as he'd arrived. If he and Steve had reached the top of the stairs thirty seconds earlier, they would literally have bumped into them. He really wasn't sure how he felt about that – should he be relieved or angry that he had missed them by such a narrow margin?

"Did you see how many of them had guns?"

"The only one I saw with a gun was Mr Winston."

Dillon nodded, digesting this information. "How many lifts are there in this place?" he asked, turning his mind to how the suspects were going to get down to ground level.

Mel shrugged. "I dunno, five or six, I would imagine. It's a big hospital, after all."

He waved his arm to get Bull's attention. "Steve, this is Nurse Smails. She –"

"It's Sister Smails, not Nurse," Mel interrupted.

Dillon acknowledged the correction with a curt nod. "Sister Smails got a good look at the suspects. Can you take a description from her and get it circulated?"

Dillon's telephone rang again, and this time he checked the caller ID. It was George Copeland. Excusing himself from the others, he pressed the green button. "How are you getting on with that back up I asked for?" he demanded, tetchily.

Copeland ignored the question. *"Thank God you're alright,"* he blurted out with a huge sigh of relief. *"We heard that there were police fatalities up there and we were all worried."*

"George," Dillon cut in, "we're both fine, but the bastards who did this are still inside the hospital and we need to get ourselves organised, so just answer my question."

"Oh – er – right... *I've got a dozen locals with me,*" Copeland informed him, sounding a little flustered, *"and the first two Trojan units have arrived. There's several more on the way. Where do you want them?"*

Dillon pulled the map George had found in the getaway car from his inside pocket, where he had placed it for safekeeping. It was surprisingly detailed, and as he ran his eyes over it, he spotted something that he had completely missed the first time around.

"Oh, you stupid, stupid fucker," he said, slapping his forehead in exasperation.

"What have I done now?" Copeland demanded indignantly.

Dillon was mentally kicking himself for not studying the map properly earlier because the clue he needed was staring him right in the face. There was a freight elevator on the far side of the building, which, according to the map, would bring Winston's party out close to the spot where the LOS was parked up. He knew that was where they were heading because it was marked with a great big X.

"Not you, George. Me."

"*I don't understand,*" Copeland said, sounding confused.

There was no time to explain so Dillon didn't bother trying. "Listen carefully," he said. "Claude Winston's just escaped from custody. The bastard's armed, and he's killed one of the officers guarding him. He's heading for the freight elevator, which will bring him down near to where the LOS is parked up."

"What do you want me to do?" George asked, and Dillon could hear the uncertainty in his voice. The Yorkshireman had a lot of sterling qualities, but decision making wasn't one of them.

"Send three PCs up to me and take the rest – including all the armed support – over to that freight elevator. If you get a wiggle on, there's a slim chance you'll be there in time to meet him when the doors open and he steps out of that elevator."

"*I can do that,*" George informed him with malevolent glee. "*I've got six AFOs with me – let's see if Winston's still so fucking brave when he's facing someone who can fire back.*" If the vehemence in his voice was anything to go by, it sounded as if the normally placid exhibits officer was actually hoping Winston would be stupid enough to shoot it out with SO19.

"Wait – before you go, let me give you the descriptions of the other suspects," Dillon said hurriedly.

"*No need,*" Copeland told him. "*Information Room has just circulated them over the radio as an update from Stevie.*"

"George – be careful," Dillon warned. "As far as I know, Winston's the only one with a gun, but to be on the safe side, you should assume they're all armed."

George snorted down the phone at him. "*I'm half hoping they've all got shooters, truth be told. It'll give the AFOs an excuse.*"

When Dillon hung up, he saw that the Aussie nurse – or rather ward sister – had gone to organise help for the injured PCs.

Looking haggard after his lengthy call to Information Room, Bull turned to Dillon. "What now?" he asked as he pocketed his phone.

The friendly Cockney porter that Garston had earlier relieved of the wheelchair was standing in the freight elevator when they boarded it. He didn't recognise them at first because they were wearing masks, but then it dawned on him who they were and he became very chatty, asking far too many questions for Garston's liking. Thankfully, he didn't seem remotely concerned by the fact that they were wearing rubber gloves and facemasks, because that would have been awkward to explain.

"This is me stop," he informed them when the elevator shuddered to a halt on two. He gave them a warm smile as he pushed his gurney out of the lift ahead of him. "'Ave a nice afternoon," he chirped in parting.

"And you," Garston replied, woodenly.

"Bye," Angela muttered, giving him a little wave.

Errol just grunted. His left ankle was hurting like a bitch and it was starting to swell up, making his foot feel tight in his shoe.

None of them spoke another word until the doors had closed.

"Can't this fucking thing go any faster?" Winston snapped the moment the lift started moving again. He slammed his massive fist into the side in frustration, making both Errol and Angela flinch away from him.

"Just a few more minutes," Garston soothed, "and then we'll be out of here. The getaway car's waiting outside and it's ready to go." Despite his calm exterior, he was absolutely furious. Shooting the cop had been totally unnecessary and utterly stupid, and Winston's wanton display of aggression had put them all in the frame for murder.

The elevator finally settled on the ground floor and the doors slid open with agonising slowness. The rear exit was only about forty yards away and he could already see grey daylight through it.

"Get a move on," Winston growled in a voice so gravelly it sounded like he'd been gargling with broken glass.

Garston went out first to check that the coast was clear. A moment later, he signalled it was safe for Errol to push the wheelchair out of the elevator. Almost immediately he regretted having done so as a whole squad of police officers appeared at the other end of the corridor and started charging towards them like a small army storming a castle breach. At least four of them had what looked like chunky assault rifles clasped against their chests.

"There they are," their leader, a roly-poly shaped man in a tweed jacket, shouted as he pointed his pudgy finger at Garston and the others.

Garston's stomach constricted. They had been rumbled and the game was up.

CHAPTER SEVEN

Dillon was torn between going after Winston and remaining where he was to help Steve manage the scene. As the debate raged within his head, he gradually became aware of the clatter of fast-falling footsteps in the corridor outside. Within seconds, people were converging on the room from both directions. A doctor, two nurses and a man pushing a gurney from the left, three out of breath plods from the right. The two rival groups formed a bottleneck in the doorway, vying with each other to be the first inside.

"Wait there," Dillon bellowed at them all, holding up a restraining hand to prevent anyone from entering.

After telling Steve Bull to supervise the removal of the injured officers, Dillon stepped outside and ushered the three local officers – two of whom he was pleased to see were familiar faces – to one side. Having just run up three flights in heavy Met-vests, the poor bastards were all panting rather loudly.

"I don't get it, boss," Nick Bartholomew said by way of greeting. His cheeks were rosy red and a thin sheen had broken out across his forehead. "I thought Winston was banged up on remand. What the hell is he doing here?"

Nick had been on a temporary secondment to AMIP during the

night that Winston had been arrested, and he remembered all too well the mayhem that had occurred during the lengthy chase.

"Don't ask," Dillon said with a grimace, and then turned to a slim PC whose baby face bore the pockmarks of a recent outbreak of acne. The poor boy didn't look old enough to shave yet, let alone go out on patrol, and from the pristine look of him, Dillon guessed that he was a brand-new probationer fresh out of Hendon.

"Young man," Dillon said, pointing at him with a sausage sized finger.

The startled constable flinched and swallowed nervously.

"Yes, sir?" he replied in a high-pitched squeak that made Dillon question whether his voice had broken.

"I need you to stay here with DS Bull and guard the crime scene. Until a log arrives, record everything in your notebook."

"Yes sir," the boy responded timidly.

"Nick, get me to the freight elevator as quickly as you can. That's where Winston was heading for."

Bartholomew nodded. "Okay, boss. Follow me," and with that, he set off at a brisk trot, keeping an ear glued to his radio as he ran.

The Yard was now monitoring and recording Whitechapel division's radio channel, and they had linked it to the Force Main-Set so that officers responding from adjoining areas could also follow the incident. There was plenty of chatter going on, but nothing to suggest the officers downstairs had engaged the suspects yet.

———

"Get back in the lift," Garston said, frantically waving the others back the way they had just come.

"Now what?" Winston remonstrated with his usual belligerence.

"HURRY!" Garston screamed as the horde of cops swarmed towards them. As he watched, two of the lead shots fanned out from the others and dropped to their knees. At the same time, they raised their carbines and took aim. "STOP! ARMED POLICE!" they shouted in unison.

Garston ignored them; he knew they wouldn't open fire unless the fugitives pointed their weapons at them or at any passing civilians.

Because of the dodgy wheel, Errol was struggling to manoeuvre the wheelchair around, so Garston helped him manhandle it back into the elevator, with Winston still facing forward, towards their pursuers.

As soon as they were all back in the lift, Angela started pressing random buttons in the hope of finding the one that would make the doors close.

Garston swatted her hand aside and pressed 'CLOSE', and the doors immediately started to move inwards.

Several of the cops broke into an all-out sprint, hoping to bridge the gap before the doors could shut.

"That's it, pigs! Rush to your death," Winston screamed.

To Garston's horror, the man in the wheelchair cackled maniacally and began to raise his gun at the advancing officers. He wondered if his uncle was suicidal; if the idiot started taking pot-shots at the police, it would give them the excuse they needed to open fire.

"NO!" he yelled, placing a restraining hand on his uncle's arm.

Winston's dreadlock covered head swivelled in his direction, and the eyes were like burning orbs. If hatred was electricity, he would have been able to power the National Grid with that stare. He knew he needed to explain his intervention, but he couldn't say anything that might make him look weak.

"You need to save your bullets, Claude," Garston hurriedly said, hoping that would appease his uncle. "We might need them later."

The thick metal doors closed with a dull thud a nanosecond before the outstretched hand of the nearest policeman reached them. From the relative safety of the freight lift, they heard a frustrated officer shouting at his colleagues to find him something to prise them open with. Thankfully, as the lift began its climb, the clamour below quickly diminished.

Doing his best not to wilt under Winston's withering gaze, Garston leaned back against the cold metal wall and breathed a huge sigh of relief.

Suddenly, Winston grabbed hold of his arm and yanked it down until they were at eye level. His warm breath was rancid. "Now what do we do, boy?" he demanded, spraying spit all over his nephew's face.

Garston was taken aback by the raw malevolence. "Relax, Claude," he spluttered. "I - I'll get you out of here, I promise." He wasn't sure how he was going to do it, but right then he would have said anything to placate his lunatic relative.

Without warning, Winston jammed the barrel of the gun into Garston's stomach. "You'd fucking well better," he raged. "Nephew or not, if you screw this up, I swear I'll put a hole in you."

Recoiling in shock, Garston pulled his arm free and stood up straight. He opened his mouth to protest, but nothing came out. To hide his shame, he turned and faced the doors. As he stood there with his back to the others, he could feel Angela and Errol's questioning gaze drilling into the back of his head.

Garston's hand was shaking as he reached into his pocket for the map he'd bought along. Thankfully, he'd had the foresight to mark up an alternative escape route in case things went wrong and the main exits were sealed off.

To his horror, it wasn't there.

He started patting his pockets with the urgency of a man trying to put out a fire, but it wasn't in any of them. Then, with gut-wrenching clarity, he remembered; he'd put it down in the car's footwell to snort cocaine and hadn't picked it up afterwards.

"Shit," he whispered, feeling the blood drain from his face. Winston would kill him if the breakout wasn't successful, but how was he going to find another way out without the map?

———

Dillon hadn't realised just how big the Royal London Hospital was, and even though they were running at full pelt, it took ages to get all the way around to the other side of the building.

When they reached the freight elevator, there was no sign of Winston or his cronies. Annoyingly there were no stairs nearby, which meant they would have to wait for it to come all the way back up before they could go anywhere. Dillon glanced at the floor counter on the wall and then started jabbing at the call button impatiently. Each jab got harder and faster until his forefinger started to throb.

"Boss, you're gonna break the damned thing if you don't stop doing that," Bartholomew pointed out when he showed no sign of stopping.

Dillon responded with a truculent harrumph, but he withdrew his finger and flexed it gingerly. "I'll probably end up with RSI now," he announced, glumly.

According to the needle, the lift was stationary on the second floor, and he wondered if Winston was inside it at this very moment, gloating because he thought they were home and dry.

"I can't stand this waiting malarkey," Dillon growled, prodding the call button again for good measure.

"Will you please leave that poxy button alone," Bartholomew snapped, and then added a very polite, "sir."

Suddenly, the needle was moving again, and they watched in silence as it travelled all the way down to the ground floor. They waited with bated breath, knowing that if George had got his team in place, this would be the moment of truth.

Seconds passed, but there was no news of an engagement over the radio. And then, as the three men looked at each other in perplexity, the lift started to ascend. The needle travelled steadily upwards, making no stops along the way. And suddenly, with a gentle 'ping', the doors began to open.

"About bloody time," Dillon said, placing his hands on the slow-moving doors to pry them apart.

At which point, the world descended into chaos.

The unexpected sound of radio chatter as the lift's doors began to open on the third floor galvanised Winston into action. Assuming that the armed police they had encountered on the ground floor had somehow managed to get ahead of them, he was already raising the ME38 in his right hand in readiness for the shootout that must surely come.

Better to die than to go back to jail, he thought, grimly.

Ignoring the searing pain that the sudden movement caused him, and the horrible pinging sensation as a couple of his stitches popped, he lunged out of the wheelchair and swung the gun in a covering arc that stopped the three advancing officers in their tracks.

"STAY WHERE YOU ARE!" he bellowed, pointing the gun in their faces. To his surprise, none of them were armed. To his delight, the one in front was the same pig who had smashed his face up pretty badly the last time they'd met. He almost laughed at the startled expression on the man's gawping face.

His cruel features twisted into a malignant smile. Whatever else happened today, at least the pig would atone for the suffering he had put Winston through last year.

Powerless to do anything but watch, George Copeland had stood there as the lift doors slammed shut a heartbeat before the nearest SO19 officer could get his hands into the rapidly diminishing gap. They had come tantalisingly close to apprehending the fugitives, but in the end, as the saying went, a miss was as good as a mile.

Dillon would not be pleased.

George's idea of exercise was getting dressed in the morning and, despite the coldness of the day, he was perspiring heavily as he walked the last few yards to join the SO19 officers who had rushed ahead and were now waiting for him by the lift doors.

The senior Trojan officer came to meet him halfway. "Where's the nearest set of stairs?" he asked.

Copeland was still too breathless to speak so he just shrugged. He didn't know and, unfortunately, DI Dillon had purloined the hand-drawn map that he'd discovered during the search of the car.

One of the locals peeled away from the rest to join them. "I can take you to the nearest set of stairs," she offered, "but it's a bit of a trek from here."

Copeland shook his head, spraying little beads of sweat everywhere. Dillon wouldn't want them running around the hospital, chasing shadows. "No," he said firmly. "Let's regroup outside at the

RVP and start setting up a containment on all the exits. At least we know what the suspects look like now, so they won't find it easy to slip by us."

At least I hope they won't, he thought.

George noticed that the Trojan officer's head was tilted to one side and he had two gloved fingers pressed to his left ear. Either he'd developed acute earache or he was listening to an incoming transmission over the Trojan channel in his earpiece.

"My gov's just arrived," the Trojan officer announced a moment later, removing his fingers and straightening his head, "and there are two more ARVs just pulling into the hospital behind him."

"Let's go and meet them," George said, ushering the uniforms back towards the entrance. As he turned to follow them, he glanced over his shoulder and saw that the freight lift had stopped on the third floor. Was that because the suspects were getting out, or had someone else just got in, completely unaware that the lift's other occupants were armed fugitives who had recently murdered a police officer?

Dillon found himself staring down the barrel of a gun. Never a good place to be at the best of times, it seemed infinitely worse when the person holding the weapon was a confirmed cop-killer who hated your guts, had previously tried – but failed – to kill you, and had made no secret of the fact that he was desperate to have another go at ending your life.

Despite the shock, Dillon's reaction was instinctive and immediate. Without conscious thought, his left hand shot forward to seize Winston's right wrist in a vice-like grip, jarring the gangster's gun arm up towards the ceiling. At the same time, he lunged forward and attempted to bury his right elbow into the side of Winston's face.

Unfortunately, Winston saw the strike coming and he tucked his chin into his shoulder so that his deltoids absorbed most of the power. Nonetheless, the sheer force of the impact sent Winston staggering sideways into the wall of the elevator.

Inevitably, the gun discharged; its bark painfully loud within the tight confines of the metal lift. Thankfully, the sub-sonic round imbedded itself harmlessly into the overhead lighting instead of ricocheting into one of the lift's crouching occupants.

A natural-born brawler, Dillon had always enjoyed fighting at close quarters, where he could make the most of his considerable strength. It was one of the reasons he'd taken up Ju Jitsu in his early teens instead of Karate or Kung Fu, which were all the fashion back then thanks to the popularity of the Bruce Lee films and the iconic seventies TV series that featured David Carradine as a Shaolin monk called Kwai Chang Caine.

Still holding onto Winston's wrist, Dillon jammed his shoulder under his opponent's right elbow and yanked downwards to execute a vicious straight-armed lever lock.

Winston let out an agonised howl and shot up on tip-toe to avoid his arm being snapped in two. His fingers involuntarily sprang open and the revolver was propelled from his hand, landing on the floor directly in front of them. Thankfully, the hammer was down, so it didn't result in an accidental discharge.

Maintaining his grip on Winston's wrist, Dillon pirouetted inwards, wrapped his free arm around the gangster's wide waist, and executed a near-perfect hip throw that sent Winston sprawling over the top of the wheelchair to land on his back with a heavy thud. The lift floor vibrated in protest, and the gangster bellowed in pain as more of his stitches were ripped apart.

Without pausing for breath, Dillon quickly spun and kicked the gun out into the corridor, where it clattered noisily across the linoleum floor until it came to a halt in a corner. He would retrieve it once they had all the suspects detained.

At the edge of his peripheral vision, he saw that Bartholomew had moved forward to engage the man dressed as a doctor, while Terry Grier had his hands full trying to restrain the bald-headed brute who had chased the ward sister. With six people fighting three separate battles, it wasn't long before the combatants started getting in each other's way.

Over in a corner, Winston had dragged himself up onto his knees and, with one arm folded painfully across his midsection, he was now trying to summon the energy to rise to his feet.

"Stay down," Dillon warned as he advanced on him, and there was an undiluted air of menace in his voice.

Before he could reach the escaped prisoner, a feral woman launched herself onto his back and wrapped her legs tightly around his waist. Caterwauling like a demented banshee, she attempted to claw out his eyes with her frighteningly long nails.

Blindsided by the attack, Dillon just about managed to grab her flailing wrists in time to stop the talon-like nails from inflicting serious damage to his face. With her hands now nullified, Dillon's assailant screamed in primal frustration and started trying to bite his ear off.

Dillon bucked and twisted like a rodeo bull as he endeavoured to dislodge the demented creature before she could sink her teeth into his flesh. As much as it went against the grain to strike a woman – even one as vile as this – he quickly realised that if he didn't, there was a good chance he was going to end up disfigured.

Reaching behind his head, he scrabbled around until he found the woman's hair. Taking a firm grip with both hands, he violently extended his arms upwards until the elbows locked out. Hoisting her above his head as if he were performing a clean and press, Dillon threw her out of the elevator.

As she sailed through the air, the ululation of her scream denoted fear and rage. The shrieking came to an abrupt halt as she slammed into the corridor wall and slid down into a messy heap on the floor.

Dillon straightened up, gulping down air, to find Claude Winston staring up at him from the floor, where he still knelt, his beady little eyes filled with pain and hatred. Allowing himself a savage smile of triumph, Dillon marched over and hoisted him to his feet by the scruff of his neck. "You're nicked, sunshine," he said, gleefully.

"Get your grubby hands off me, pig," Winston snarled, ineffectually trying to pull away.

Dillon ignored him. The man was a spent force, almost doubled over in pain. Blood was now seeping through the fingers of his right hand as it protectively clutched his abdomen.

Dillon realised that the heavy landing from the hip throw had caused the stitches from his operation to burst open but he felt no sympathy; in fact, he hoped it hurt like hell.

With Winston now in custody, Dillon allowed himself to take in his surroundings properly for the first time since the elevator doors had opened. He was pleased to see that Bartholomew had control of his prisoner, and was holding the fake doctor's arm in a gooseneck, the most well-known of all the traditional police arrest holds.

Alarmingly, there was no sign of either Grier or the big bald-headed man he'd been grappling with.

"Where's Terry?" he asked.

"He went after the bald bloke," Bartholomew said between pants.

The deafening sound of the gunshot nearly caused all four men to jump out of their skins, and they turned as one to see the dishevelled nurse standing in the corridor, legs akimbo, pointing the still smoking gun at them. There was a hole in the ceiling above her head, and a great chunk of plaster now lay on the floor by her feet.

Dillon's heart sank. "You've got to be kidding me..." he said.

"D-don't move," the black woman ordered, holding the gun in both hands and squinting down the barrel.

She looked dazed, Dillon thought, wondering if she had sustained a slight concussion from hitting the wall. It was either that or she was a junkie in withdrawal.

"Put the gun on the floor," he told her calmly. "You're in enough trouble already, don't make things worse."

"Shoot the motherfucking pig!" Winston yelled at her. "Do it now – pull the trigger and end him."

Dillon saw her eyes anxiously flit from Winston to him as her forefinger tightened on the trigger. All it would take was five-pounds of pressure.

He held up a hand to stay her. "Wait," he told her, and just to be sure that she did, he thrust Winston's giant bulk in front of him and used him as a human shield. "If you try to shoot one of us, you might hit your mates."

Dillon glanced to his side and was relieved to see that Nick Bartholomew had followed his lead and was now using the doctor's body as a screen.

Shoving Winston forward in front of him, Dillon started to advance on the black woman.

"Stay still!" she screamed, taking a nervous step backwards to maintain the distance between them.

Dillon was so focused on the gun, and the shaking hands that held it, that he didn't notice the sly smile that slithered onto Winston's brutal face.

The next time Dillon pushed him forward, Winston let out a sharp cry of pain, swayed for a moment and then started to sag forwards.

"Shit!" Dillon cursed, convinced that Winston was about to pass out from his injuries. If he let Winston fall, he would lose the only protection he had against being shot, which was why, when the man's knees started to buckle under him, Dillon was left with no choice but to release his grip on Winston's shoulders and grab him around the waist to keep him in an upright position.

It was the moment that Winston had been waiting for. Summoning the last of his flagging strength, he rammed his head backwards with all the force he could muster, intent on smashing Dillon's face into a bloody pulp.

The average human being's reaction speed to visual stimulation has been calculated to be around 250 milliseconds, but that's under optimum conditions in an environment where the brain is only processing a singular event. When multiple stimuli are found to be present, reaction time usually shrinks to around 500 – 600 milliseconds or, in layman's terms, half a second.

Somehow, against the odds, Dillon managed to turn his head to the side, and while he wasn't quick enough to avoid the impact altogether, he did succeed in minimising it to a glancing blow against the side of his concrete-thick skull.

The collision was powerful enough to stun him momentarily, but it didn't do anywhere near the amount of damage that Winston had intended.

Having broken free from his captor, Winston tottered forward unsteadily. "Give me the gun, he shouted, hand outstretched.

Ignoring the pain, and the horrible ringing in his ears, Dillon hurtled himself forward to re-engage Winston.

"Stay where you are, pig," Winston warned, pointing the reacquired gun at his centre mass.

Still a good three strides away, Dillon had no choice but to comply. The left side of his head was starting to throb like a bastard. "This is starting to become a tiresome habit," he said, reaching up to rub it.

Grinning vengefully, Winston thumbed back the hammer. "Don't worry, this'll be the last time." To his disappointment, there was no fear in the detective's eyes, only defiance – not that it would do him any good.

"Got anything to say before I kill you, pig?"

Dillon nodded slowly. "Yeah, how's your hair growing back?" During November's arrest, Dillon had ripped out a huge handful of Winston's precious dreadlocks.

The leering grin vanished from Claude Winston's face, only to be replaced by a thunderous scowl, and he subconsciously raised a hand to his head as the painful recollection caused his scalp to start tingling.

Nick Bartholomew was standing a yard or so to Dillon's left, still hiding behind the bogus doctor. While not directly in the line of fire, he was still near enough to feel extremely uncomfortable, and he knew that once Winston had finished with Dillon, he would turn his attention on him.

Moving slowly, so as not to draw attention, Bartholomew felt for the canister of CS spray in the pouch on his utility belt. Without taking his eyes from the gun-toting psycho, he unclipped the Velcro fastening and removed it.

Nick knew that if he was going to make a move it would have to be very soon, while Winston's attention was still focused on Tony Dillon to the exclusion of everybody else around him.

The angle of attack was all wrong for what he had in mind, so Nick cautiously shuffled a half step to the left, dragging his unresisting prisoner with him.

To his enormous relief, Winston didn't seem to notice, and the fake doctor was so absorbed in what was going on between Winston and the detective that he didn't protest.

Bartholomew's legs felt like rubber, but he forced them to move again, propelling himself and his prisoner yet another step to the left. The can felt damp in his hand, clammy and uncomfortable. He could feel beads of sweat running down the side of his face, and his shirt felt unbearably sticky as it clung to his perspiring body.

It was all down to timing now, Bartholomew realised – well, timing and luck.

He was suddenly consumed by self-doubt. What if he dropped the canister at the vital moment, or missed with it altogether? He had never used the stuff in anger before. In fact, for all he knew, the canister might be out of date and not even work when he tried to use it.

During his Officer Safety Training sessions, the instructors had rammed home how unwise – stupid was the actual word they had used – it was to discharge CS in a confined space like this. Unlike pepper spray, CS didn't just target the person who was sprayed, it spread outwards, affecting anyone unfortunate enough to be standing within reach of the ever-expanding cloud like nuclear fallout.

Despite his considerable misgivings, Bartholomew knew that he simply didn't have a choice. He swallowed hard, knowing he was only going to get one chance at this, and that was going to be...

...*NOW!*

Roughly shoving his prisoner aside so that he could get a clear, unobstructed shot, Nick Bartholomew brought his right arm straight up, making sure that the CS was aimed directly at Winston's chest – *always aim at the centre mass and then work the stream upward till it hits the face,* he recalled his instructor telling him.

When he pressed the trigger mechanism with his thumb, he was relieved to see a concentrated jet shoot out of the cannister's nozzle. In a textbook display, it struck Winston's upper chest and then travelled upwards to soak the gunman's face.

Winston immediately raised his left hand to block the liquid, but it was too late. The CS had already started to affect the soft tissue of his mucous membrane, attacking the eyes, nose and throat. Letting out an agonised scream, he pivoted towards Bartholomew and angrily pulled the trigger twice.

Fortunately, Bartholomew was no longer there, and both bullets imbedded themselves harmlessly in a thick concrete wall, several feet off target, spewing out plaster fragments and generating a fine mist of dust.

Without the threat of the gun to hold him at bay, Dillon charged forward and, taking hold of Winston's gun hand in both of his for the second time that day, he wrenched it downward with savage force.

Winston dragged his sleeve across his face to wipe the disabling substance away, but that only made things worse. He couldn't open his eyes, and he was struggling to draw breath.

Weakened to the point where he could hardly stand, he was on the point of dropping to his knees when he realised that the CS was having an equally detrimental effect on Dillon.

"Nick, Nick, give me a hand," the detective spluttered, and there was an unmistakable urgency to his plea. "Drop the gun," Dillon coughed, tugging at his arm again.

"Never!" Claude Winston screamed. He clung to the weapon defiantly, as if it were a magic talisman, something enchanted, which – as long as he retained control of it – would guarantee his eventual success.

As Deontay Garston watched his injured uncle fight a hopeless battle against the hulking detective, Angela appeared by his side and placed a tentative hand on his arm. Her hair was bedraggled, her uniform was torn, and she looked totally shell shocked. "What should we do?" she implored, looking as vulnerable as a lost child.

Garston seriously considered grabbing Angela's arm and making a run for it. In his weakened state, Winston didn't stand a chance, and Garston knew that if they remained where they were for much longer, they would both end up in the clink with him.

A wave of pessimism flooded over him.

They were done for.

Without the map to guide them, he had no idea how to find the alternative escape route he'd been told about. Within minutes, all the hospital exits would be in lockdown, so even if they got out of their current predicament, it would only be a matter of time until they were run into the ground. Short of flying out of here, there was no chance of...

Wait a minute! Flying! Of course!

For the first time since the wave of armed officers had surged toward him on the ground floor, he experienced a fleeting glimmer of hope. Perhaps there was a chance after all, albeit a very remote one.

"Get yourself over to the lift and wait for me," he whispered to Angela. Ignoring her protests, and praying that she wouldn't desert him the moment he turned his back, he pulled a heavy leather sap out of his white coat and ran towards the uniformed policeman who had sprayed Claude. The man was now trying to help his muscle-bound colleague, who was struggling after being exposed to the CS gas.

Acting with a single-minded determination born of desperation, Garston charged straight up to Nick Bartholomew and viciously belted him across the side of the head with the cosh. It was full of lead shot and Bartholomew went down like a stone, landing groggily on his hands and knees.

Satisfied that the uniformed cop had been incapacitated, Deontay turned his attention to the two big men, trying to position himself for a clear shot at the detective. The CS was already starting to sting his eyes, and he wondered how long it would be before he was forced to withdraw.

The first ineffectual blow glanced off Dillon's shoulder, merely annoying him. The second swing, more through luck than skill, connected with the side of his neck, stunning him.

Before the policeman could recover, Garston wrapped a supportive arm around Winston's waist and half walked him, half dragged him towards the safety of the waiting elevator.

"Come on Claude, you can do it," he coaxed through gritted teeth. His legs were almost buckling under his uncle's gargantuan weight, but somehow Garston managed to keep going. "Close the doors, close the doors!" he ordered as soon as they were inside.

Angela did as she was bid, this time finding the correct button.

Releasing his uncle, Garston swivelled to see Dillon stumbling towards the lift, arms outstretched to block the doors. Clearly disorientated, the detective was swaying from side to side as though he was on the deck of a ferry during a rough channel crossing.

"Come on, come on!" Garston screamed as the doors finally began to move.

Stunned or not, Dillon was rapidly closing the distance between them, and Garston raised his sap in readiness to take another swing at him.

Dillon's equilibrium was all over the place; he stumbled, righted himself and carried on, but his floundering had cost him valuable time. Just as they were about to close, Dillon crashed into the doors and thrust both hands into the tiny gap.

"NOOO!" Garston cried, and immediately lashed out with the sap, hoping to break the cop's fingers.

Dillon saw the blow coming just in time, and he reacted by snatching his hands back.

With nothing to impede their progress, the metal doors came together with a soft jolt and the freight elevator began its upward journey.

CHAPTER EIGHT

Dillon leaned against the elevator door to steady himself. The right side of his neck ached like hell, and it was throbbing in unison with the left side of his head. He could hardly open his eyes and the floor under his feet seemed to be swaying up and down like a see-saw. He shook his head to dispel the dizziness, causing a small constellation of stars to explode in front of his eyes.

"Bollocks!" he raged, pounding the metal door with the bottom of his fist. Gasping for breath, and coughing like he smoked fifty a day, he looked around, taking in the chaotic farce in an instant.

Bartholomew was back on his feet, rubbing the side of his head as he staggered across to join Dillon.

"You okay?" Dillon asked. He reached an arm out to steady the junior officer and guide him away from the area contaminated by CS incapacitant.

"Yeah, I think so," but Bartholomew sounded far from certain.

Dillon studied his eyes; pupil dilation looked equal, which was a good sign. "How many fingers am I holding up?" he asked, raising two.

Bartholomew stared, squinted, and then stared some more. "Five," he eventually said. Seeing Dillon's eyes widen in alarm, Bartholomew broke into a lopsided grin. "I'm joking!" he said.

Dillon scowled at him for a moment. "That's not funny," he said.

Bartholomew shrugged. "It was a little."

Dillon laughed, which made him cough uncontrollably. When he finally got the hacking under control, he turned to stare at the smaller man, his expression thoughtful. "Listen, I'm very grateful for your intervention back there."

Tears streamed down his face as he spoke, but Bartholomew knew this was just a side effect of the CS and not an emotional outpouring of gratitude.

"You're welcome," he said.

In a moment of spontaneity, Dillon wrapped an arm around Bartholomew and dragged him in close.

Bartholomew winced as his throbbing skull was pummelled into Dillon's shoulder. "Please!" he squealed. Then quieter: "Please – don't be so grateful, boss. I don't think I can stand the pain!" Disentangling himself, Bartholomew sagged down on his haunches and rubbed at the bump on his head.

But Dillon wasn't listening. "We need to find out where Terry is," he said, dabbing at his eyes. "I won't be happy till I know he's safe."

Grier was exceedingly proud of the fact that he'd never lost a prisoner during a foot chase. Nor had one ever escaped from him once he'd actually laid his hands on them – at least not until today. The suspect had somehow got the better of him during the struggle in the freight elevator, and now his one-hundred-per-cent record was on the line.

To be fair, the bald man had a considerable weight advantage over Grier, which he'd used to good effect by slamming Terry into the side of the elevator so hard that it had taken his breath away. Temporarily winded, all he'd been able to do was place his hands on his knees and suck in one mouthful of air after another as he watched his burly prisoner decamp from the scene in futile anger.

By the time Terry had sufficiently recovered to set off after him, the bald man had opened up a big lead. And, thanks to the interference of the fake nurse who had just spitefully stuck out her leg and tripped him up, that lead was about to grow even bigger.

Landing heavily, Terry slid along the shiny linoleum surface on his hands and stomach. Somehow, without losing too much forward momentum, and with all the elegance of a foal standing up for the very first time, he managed to scrabble back to his feet and continue running.

Glancing back, he saw that the nurse had already turned her attention to DI Dillon, and she was now hanging from him like a kid being given a piggyback ride.

The bald man was bloody fast, Grier acknowledged grudgingly, but he was faster, and he was determined to make up the lost ground.

Grier temporarily lost sight of the suspect when he turned right at the end of the corridor, but he wasn't overly concerned by that. Unless his quarry nipped into a ward, which was unlikely given the fact that to gain entry you had to be buzzed through by someone inside, Grier knew that he would eventually come to the staircase that he and Bartholomew had ascended on their way up to join Dillon.

Grier allowed himself a brief smile of satisfaction when he regained sight of the fleet-footed fugitive a few seconds later, and another when he realised that he had substantially closed the gap between them. Relaxing into his stride, he focused on his breathing and visualised himself applying handcuffs to the man he was chasing.

As the pursuit continued, the bogus porter started glancing nervously over his shoulder every few seconds like a marathon runner desperate to cross the finishing line before his nearest competitor could overtake him. That was a good sign; if the fleeing man had any confidence in his ability to maintain his current speed over any distance, he wouldn't be wasting so much energy looking back.

By the time they reached the staircase, Grier had bridged the gap a little more. He tried to transmit on his radio, but the wire connecting the handset – the talking brooch as it was often referred too – had become detached during their earlier struggle. He attempted to slip the connector back into the socket but thought better of it after he almost tripped himself up because he wasn't paying enough attention to his footing.

They descended at a recklessly fast pace, taking the stairs three at a time, clinging to the bannister and blindly throwing themselves into each turn. Luckily, no one was coming the other way because a collision at that speed would have been ugly.

As he reached the ground floor, Grier spotted a bored hospital security guard leaning against a wall up ahead, and he shouted to the man to help him stop the fleeing suspect. The guard was short and middle-aged, with the figure of a man who had eaten too many doughnuts.

With a look of trepidation plastered across his face, the security guard moved away from the wall he'd been holding up, spread his arms wide and started shuffling from side to side like a Sunday league goalkeeper getting ready to try and save a penalty kick from David Beckham. His chubby face was scrunched up in fierce concentration as he clumsily attempted to wrap his arms around the suspect's waist, only to be shouldered effortlessly aside.

The bewildered guard was sent tumbling to the floor, where he rolled a couple of times before coming to an abrupt stop in a rather messy heap. For a moment, he lay there as unmoving as a bouncy castle that had just been deflated.

As Grier raced past a second later, he was relieved to see that the guard's only obvious injury was a dented pride.

Up ahead, the suspect barged through a glass plated exit door leading out into an area at the side of the hospital where the ambulances all parked up between calls. Once outside, he paused for a moment, head frantically turning left and then right as though trying to decide which way to run. A second later, the suspect disappeared off to the left, heading towards Raven Row and the back of the hospital.

Grier dodged past a nurse who had stopped to stare at him quizzically, zigzagged around an elderly couple, one of whom was using a Zimmer frame, and cannoned through the exit door after him.

The IRV that he and Bartholomew had arrived in was parked off to the right, blue lights still flashing, which probably explained why the fleeing man had opted to go left. Following suit, Grier immediately collided with a petite paramedic coming the other way. Manhandling her to the side as gently as he could, at the same time apologising profusely for his clumsiness, he set off towards Raven Row desperate to regain sight of the bald suspect.

By the time he reached the road, his quarry was nowhere to be seen. Cursing profusely, Grier ran into Milward Street, which was set almost directly opposite the rear of the hospital car park. He paused by another parking area that led through to Cavell Street, eyes scanning left and right. Surely, the bald man couldn't possibly have come any further than this?

Grier took a moment to reattach the loose cable into his radio and then strode purposefully into the middle of the car park. Being careful to avoid all the dirty puddles that had formed after the earlier deluge, he dropped flat on the floor as though he were about to do start doing press-ups.

His eyes traversed the cold, wet concrete floor from one side of the car park to the other, and his diligence was rewarded by a blur of movement beneath one of the SUVs parked nearest to the Cavell Street exit.

Springing back to his feet in triumph, he saw that the suspect was already up and running. The man's surgical mask had come off, and as he glanced back Grier was afforded a decent look at his face. Doing his best to commit it to memory, he set off in pursuit.

Now that he had the man clearly in his sights, he pressed the orange emergency button on his radio, which cleared the airwaves and gave him a few seconds of priority transmission. "Hotel Tango from 167, active message... chasing suspect concerned in a murder at the Royal London Hospital... Cavell Street towards Stepney Way... suspect is a bald-headed IC3 male... dressed as a hospital porter and wearing rubber gloves..."

Dillon and Bartholomew had retreated a safe distance from the CS contaminated area and, although his eyes were still streaming, Dillon was at least now able to open them without too much pain. From afar, he followed the slow progress of the needle in silent fury. It had now almost reached the top floor.

There were procedures in place to deal with a CS discharge inside premises, and he was waiting impatiently for a local supervisor to turn up and implement them so that he could get back to the business at hand.

"Where the hell is this skipper coming from?" he demanded of Bartholomew, "Greater Manchester?"

Bartholomew stopped rubbing his head long enough to shoot Dillon a sideways glance. "I'll get back on the radio, boss, but Mr Speed said he was sending someone straight up."

Ray Speed was the local duty officer, the Inspector in charge of Bartholomew's team, and he had now arrived to take charge of the incident.

So far, the lift had stopped twice on its way up, and Winston's party could have got out on either occasion, or they could still be inside, heading for the top floor. Regardless of where they alighted, Dillon knew they would eventually have to make their way back down via one of the other lifts scattered around the building. From what he'd seen of Winston, the man was in no condition to take on the stairs, which was good news because it bought him a little time to get organised.

Dillon and Ray Speed had spoken briefly on the phone, and they had agreed that their number one priority was setting up an exclusion zone around the hospital's perimeter with armed officers stationed at each of the exits. Until the building was in total lockdown there was no point in even thinking about going after the suspects.

Dillon's stomach churned at the thought. *God, the media's going to love this.*

The last time that he had gone up against Winston, the Central Line at Liverpool Street underground station had ended up being closed for several hours. This time, a major London hospital was going to suffer the same fate. While closing a train station had left a few night-time travellers disgruntled because their journeys had been interrupted, the implications of shutting down the Royal London were too horrific to even consider. Important surgical procedures might be delayed or even cancelled, and how would the busy A&E department, which was always stretched to the very limit, be affected?

Perhaps a better plan would be to order a withdrawal and let Winston out of the building; the risk of collateral damage if they tackled him inside the hospital was staggeringly high. Hopefully, there would be well thought out contingency plans in place for just such a scenario, and these would be implemented shortly, relieving Dillon of the burden of having to make such a troubling decision.

Bartholomew rushed over, holding his radio up. It provided a welcome distraction from the tumultuous thoughts crashing around inside Dillon's aching head. Hopefully, Nick was about to announce the imminent arrival of the skipper who was going to deal with the CS discharge.

"It's just come over the PR that Terry's chasing the one that got away in Cavell Street," he said, excitedly.

"Is back up on its way to him?" Dillon asked. At the back of his mind, there was a nagging fear that Winston might not have been the only one who was armed.

Bartholomew nodded and then winced at the pain the movement had caused him. "There are multiple units converging on his position as we speak. Don't worry, boss, Terry does decathlons for a hobby. The bastard won't outrun him."

When Terry Grier's urgent assistance call came out over their car's Main-Set, DS Susan Sergeant and DC Kevin Murray were driving along Commercial Road on their way back to AMIP HQ at Arbour Square, having spent most of the morning at a case conference with Senior Treasury Counsel at Inner Temple.

"That's just down the road from here," Susie said, pulling the car into the kerb opposite Watney Market so that they could get their bearings. "I think it's that side road up on the left," she said a moment later, gently raising the clutch to allow the Astra to creep forward so that she could get a better view.

As they drew closer, Murray pointed a skinny forefinger at a sign on the corner of the road. "Cavell Street," he read. "You're right."

"I usually am," Susie replied with a tongue in cheek grin.

Murray licked his lips in anticipation, reminding Susie of a reptile – or at least what a reptile would look like if it was capable of growing a goatee. "The lid must be chasing that bloke right towards us."

As she steered the car into Cavell Street, both officers instinctively released their seatbelts so that they could jump out quickly if the need arose.

Susie normally wore trouser suits and flat shoes to work, but she had uncharacteristically dressed in a skirt and heels today, wanting to make a good impression at the case conference. She was now ruing the decision, wishing that she had stuck to her normal attire. "It's Sod's Law that the one day of the year I wear a bloody skirt and high heels, I'll end up having to chase a suspect," she complained in her soft Irish lilt.

Murray grinned. "Tell you what, you stick to driving and leave any running to me."

Susie glanced sideways at the skinny man sitting next to her, wondering if she had misheard him. With his smoking, drinking and poor diet, Murray was hardly the epitome of health and fitness. Even in heels, she could probably outrun him comfortably.

There was a harsh crackle of static and then a transmission came over the Main-Set. *"MP to 167 Hotel Tango, please keep the commentary going..."*

Operators at Information Room always seemed so incredibly calm and composed, Susie thought. Of course, it could all be a front; for all she knew, they could all be running around NSY like a bunch of headless chickens.

There was more static. *"MP from 167, we're now in Stepney Way, heading towards Sidney Street..."* The chasing officer was breathing hard, but he sounded focused, and he was still clearly going strong.

"Shit!" Susan cursed, gunning the accelerator. The foot chase had veered off to their right well before reaching their position and it was now heading away from them.

Errol Heston had failed to put any distance between himself and the young policeman who was breathing down his neck, and fatigue was now setting in. His legs had grown so heavy that he could hardly lift them and his searing lungs felt ready to explode.

Knowing he couldn't keep this gruelling pace up for much longer, he thought about pulling the revolver on his pursuer, just to put the frighteners on him. The problem with doing that was if he fired the gun – if he literally just let off a warning shot in the air like they did in the movies – the police would twist it into something far more sinister and he would end up being charged with attempted murder. As it was, just carrying a loaded shooter would get him banged up for five years.

He could hear multiple sirens in the distance, and they were getting louder by the second. It seemed as though they were converging on him from every direction. He risked a glance over his shoulder and was horrified to see that the lanky cop was now only an arm's length behind.

Errol jammed on the anchors, jinked left, then right, and as the startled policeman drew level with him, he palmed the man off, sending him toppling straight over the bonnet of a parked car to land face down on the tarmac. He didn't have the energy to celebrate, so he just gritted his teeth and set off again.

Up ahead, a black London Taxi had just stopped to drop a fare off at the junction with Sidney Street. As he reached the cab, the driver looked out of his window dispassionately and said, "Sorry, mate, I'm about to finish for the day so I'm not taking any more fares."

Pulling the gun from his waistband, Errol yanked the driver's door open and rammed the revolver into the cabbie's frightened face. "OUT!" he screamed, looking back over his shoulder to make sure there was no sign of the cop who had taken a tumble.

The cab driver was aghast. "You can't do that," he spluttered indignantly. "This cab's my livelihood."

Errol grabbed hold of his shoulder and unceremoniously dragged him out.

The cabby tried to resist, but he was half Errol's size and about thirty-years older. "Gerroff," he shouted defiantly as he struggled to disentangle himself from the bigger man's grip.

Ignoring his protests, Errol gave him a firm shove that propelled him away from the cab and left him lying in a crumpled heap on the wet pavement.

Errol slid behind the wheel and slammed the door shut. The seat was too close to the steering wheel for comfort but he didn't have time to adjust it. Slamming the selector into drive, he jammed his foot to the floor and the cab lurched off towards Commercial Road.

"Wanker!" the cabby yelled after him, running into the road and shaking his fist at the man who had just deprived him of his wheels.

Despite the bitter coldness outside, Errol left the driver's window down to let in some much-needed fresh air. *Maybe, if I'm really lucky,* he thought as he adjusted the rear-view mirror, *I might actually pull this off.*

Officers were now turning up in their droves. As each new cluster arrived, Ray Speed gave them a thirty second briefing and quickly deployed them in a loose perimeter to secure all the exits. Their orders were simple: visual containment. No one who even vaguely fitted the description of the three suspects was to be approached without SO19 support.

There were already four Trojan units on scene, and now their duty officer, call-sign Trojan One, had arrived. His name was Inspector Pat Connors, and Dillon knew him from way back.

Dillon quickly assembled all the AFOs and briefed them fully, noting how grim they became when they were told how their fellow officer met his death. He felt it said much for their training and professionalism that none of the twelve firearms officers present made a single comment.

Connors started by making tactical deployments of his four three-man teams. Their mission was fundamentally one of containment and support while they awaited the arrival of more ARVs and a level-one-response team from their training facility at Lippits Hill in Loughton.

Connors agreed with Dillon that, in the short-term, the only thing Winston and his gang would be thinking about was getting away from the hospital as quickly and quietly as they could, and they would apply all their energy to making sure that happened without further incident.

From a policing perspective, the problems would start when they realised that they were trapped inside. At that point, they would start to panic – and that was when things would get interesting.

Connors knew from bitter experience that one of two things would happen once the gang worked out that they had no way out. They would either accept defeat and lay down their weapons, or they would adopt a siege mentality and start taking hostages.

With Claude Winston running the show, Dillon knew that the former scenario wasn't a realistic option, and with a heavy heart, he confided his fears to Connors.

"I really hope you're wrong," Connors said, looking grim, "because when that happens, more often than not, people tend to start dying."

CHAPTER NINE

Susie gunned the sluggish Astra along Stepney Way, wishing that the clunking diesel engine had a little more oomph in it. She suddenly became aware of a siren and, glancing in her rear view, she saw that an Immediate Response Vehicle had just turned into the road. While still a little way behind, it was coming up on her at a great rate of knots, roof bar strobing a dazzling blue, headlights flashing alternately, first left and then right. The yelping of the two-tones steadily grew in volume until the noise became deafening.

Susie was desperate to find a space big enough to pull into in order to let the gung-ho response driver by, but there were no gaps anywhere. The driver, who obviously didn't realise they were police officers responding to the same shout as him, was furiously pointing towards the nearside, trying to make her understand that he wanted her to give way.

"I bloody well know," she shouted at the mirror, "but there's nowhere for me to pull into, you tosser."

"Temper, temper," Murray chided, earning himself a fierce look of rebuke.

He squirmed in his seat, withering under the intensity of her glare. "Alright," he said defensively, "there's no need to go all premenstrual on me."

"Oh, shut up you cretin," Susie snapped. If she hadn't been driving at speed, and therefore felt the need to keep both hands firmly on the wheel, she would have slapped him around the head for making a comment like that. Not that it had surprised her in the slightest; Murray was a racist, sexist, homophobic misogynist, and he had a gift for insulting just about anyone he came into contact with. The staggering thing was that he genuinely seemed to have no idea how unpleasantly inappropriate he was virtually every time he opened his mouth.

Susie finally spotted a large enough gap up ahead, and she pulled into it to let the IRV pass. Instead of blatting past her, the IRV drew level and stopped, its crew giving her daggers. The driver wound down his window angrily, and she could tell that he was about to have a go at her for having got in his way. Already angered by Murray's premenstrual comment, she had no intention of allowing this dickhead to let off steam at her.

Susie scowled at them. "We're AMIP," she shouted, "and don't you dare bloody moan about me blocking your way because I pulled over the first chance I got. You must have the forward vision of a mole if you think otherwise."

The driver looked like he was about to reply, but then he saw the fire blazing in those pretty green eyes, thought better of it and simply nodded.

Murray nudged her elbow. "Susie..."

"What?" she demanded, ready to punch him if he made another stupid remark.

Murray pointed, and as she followed his finger, she caught sight of a uniformed officer sprawled in the road between two parked cars.

They sprang out of the car and rushed to help him. As they assisted the officer to his feet, she recognised him at once from his AMIP secondment during the Whitechapel murders of the previous year.

Murray also recalled Grier. "Terry! Bloody hell, mate. Are you alright?" he asked, running his eyes over the taller man with uncharacteristic concern.

The young PC nodded brusquely as he brushed himself down. "I'm fine," he said, looking more embarrassed than hurt. "Just a few cuts and grazes to my hands and knees."

The IRV pulled level with them. "Which way did he go, Tel?" the operator shouted.

Grier pointed straight ahead, towards the junction with Sidney Street. "He went that way. He's only got a few seconds ahead of me. If you hurry, you might still catch him."

The IRV operator nodded, and as it shot off, the driver gave Terry a thumbs up.

Murray led Grier back to their car. "Jump in the back, mate," he said, half guiding him, half pushing him in.

Once everyone was inside, Susie set off after the IRV, only to see that it had now stopped at the junction, having been flagged down by an irate looking white man in his early sixties who had run out into its path, waving his arms like a nutter.

"What the fuck's going on here?" Murray said, irritably. "Why have the lids stopped to speak to that twat when they're supposed to be after a murderer?"

The man he was referring to was jabbering away to the IRV operator in a clear state of agitation, and as he spoke, he kept pointing towards Commercial Road. Suddenly, he jumped into the back of the IRV, which then rocketed off in the direction he had indicated.

"Well, I wasn't expecting that," Murray said, scratching his head.

Not having a clue what was going on, Susie tucked into the IRV's slipstream and followed behind.

The mystery was solved moments later as the IRV's operator broadcast an update over the Main-Set. "*MP, MP, active message, Hotel-Tango-Two-Three...*"

"*Hotel-Tango-Two-Three, go ahead, MP over...*"

"*MP the IC3 male suspect that 167 was chasing has now car-jacked a black London Taxi cab at gunpoint, and he was last seen heading along Stepney Way towards Commercial Street within the last minute...*"

The IRV operator proceeded to broadcast the cab's registration and Taxi licence number. "*We've got the owner on board, and we're searching the immediate area, but all units are to approach with caution.*"

When they reached the junction with Commercial Road, the IRV turned right and started bombing along the outside of the traffic.

"No point in us trying to follow him without blues and twos," Susie said. "Let's have a punt the other way." With that, she turned left and set off towards Limehouse.

By now, over thirty officers had attended the assistance call at the hospital, and there were still more en route. Two carriers of TSG had just turned up, and they were being deployed to manage crowd control. Trojan units from Central and South London were being drafted in for the armed containment. Even a DPG Ranger unit from Central London was responding.

The debacle had been formally declared a major incident, and a senior member of the hospital administration staff had been sent to obtain a set of blueprints and floor plans to enable the police to co-ordinate their search and any subsequent evacuation. No decision had been made regarding evacuation yet, but one would be called for soon. With a gunman running loose in the hospital they had to consider the safety of the patients, staff and the public above all else.

Inspector Connors decided to use an ARV parked at the front of the hospital as his forward control point, from which to co-ordinate the deployment of resources with Ray Speed.

Divisional Chief Superintendent Charles Porter was en route, and he would take on the role of Gold once he arrived. Unfortunately, he was travelling from Area HQ at Edmonton in North London, where he'd been attending a Borough Commander's meeting, so it was going to take him a while to get there. Until he formally assumed control, Speed was the man in charge and he had adopted the call-sign of Silver.

While they were waiting for the floor plans to arrive, one of the hospital's security team came forward and asked to speak to whoever was in charge. He looked like a man with a lot on his mind.

"What is it?" Dillon asked. He didn't welcome the intrusion, which he suspected would just be another gripe about how long the hospital was going to be closed. He had already fended off a couple of those.

"I'm sorry to bother you," the man said, "but I've just received an alarming call from the HEMS team upstairs. The call was cut off mid-flow, but before the line went dead, they said someone was trying to force their way inside, and I wondered if it might be connected to what you're dealing with."

Dillon's eyes widened. "I thought the HEMS was in a secure area that couldn't be accessed by the public."

The security officer nodded. "It is," he confirmed, "but if they waited outside and jumped someone who was about to swipe themselves in, there would be no way of stopping them from inside."

Dillon paled. If the fugitives gained access to the helicopter facility, they might force the pilot to airlift them from the building.

Dillon turned to Nick Bartholomew. "Do you know how to get up there?"

"Well yeah, of course, but..."

"No buts. Take us up there, right now," Dillon ordered, looking across to Pat Connors for support.

He was rewarded with a firm nod of agreement "I'll have to come with you, Tony, to provide armed support," Connors said. He spoke into his lapel microphone, informing the other members of his team (they worked on an independent radio channel) what was happening, then he signalled for another shot who was standing up by the hospital entrance to come over and join them.

"I'll stay here and hold the fort," Speed said, "but let me know the moment you have an update."

"I will do," Dillon promised.

They were joined by an intimidating looking man in sunglasses who carried a carbine across his chest. "Tony, this is Eric, one of the best shots on the team," Connors said, making the introductions.

"*The* best shot," Eric, a shaven-headed man of about forty, corrected, and Dillon could imagine hawkish eyes narrowing behind his wraparound sunglasses. He nodded casually at Dillon and Bartholomew in turn and then checked that his magazine was seated properly.

"We need to get up to the HEMS team on the seventeenth-floor,"

Connors explained to the newcomer. "There's a possibility that our suspects are trying to break into their base."

Eric merely raised an eyebrow. He was clearly not an overly talkative chap, Dillon realised.

The four men: Dillon, Connors, Eric and Nick Bartholomew, started up the stairs towards the hospital entrance; their mission to find and secure the helipad on the hospital rooftop.

Peter Myers left his helicopter, having ensured that it was ready to go at a moment's notice. You never knew when the warning claxon was going to sound or a call was going to come in requiring immediate action. Mike Cummings walked beside him.

"Right, I'm going down into the mess room for a cup of rosy and some nose-bag," Cummings declared with a huge grin. He was a rotund man who enjoyed his job immensely. "You coming?" he enquired casually.

Myers smiled back and then blew into his hands to stave off the cold. "You bet. I could murder a hot drink right now." As they approached the entrance to the muster room, it suddenly burst open in front of them.

Two men, one of them dressed in operating room attire, emerged. They looked ruffled, out of breath and in a big hurry. The doctor – at least he looked like a doctor – was supporting the other man, who appeared to be in considerable pain.

"What the hell?" Cummings mouthed, stopping in his tracks. Who did these people think they were? Didn't they know that it was a secure area, for authorised persons only?

A third person appeared behind them, this one a dishevelled looking female wearing the uniform of a nurse. She was sweating profusely and her hair was as lank as it would have been had it just been put through a mangle. There was a large scar running down one side of an otherwise attractive face.

Cummings raised his hands to stop them. "Excuse me folks, but you can't come out here. It's off-limits to anyone who doesn't have the proper authority," he explained, wondering how they had bypassed security.

Winston lunged forward, grabbing hold of the supervisor's overalls. "Here's my authority, motherfucker!" He rammed the muzzle of the pistol under Cummings's' chin, forcing his head back.

Cummings instinctively recoiled. Whimpering in fear, he stared up into the hate-filled, watering eyes of the hulking brute. "Please!" he begged, raising both hands submissively, "don't hurt me."

"Shut up," Winston growled, now jabbing the gun into the side of his face and grinding it into his flesh.

A cry of pain escaped Cummings quivering lips.

Ignoring him, Winston turned to Peter Myers. "You – can you fly that thing up there?" He nodded at the helicopter sitting majestically on its pad.

"Well, I..." Myers stalled, trying to buy them some time. Surely someone in the control room would see what was going on and call the police?

"Don't fuck with me, man!" Winston screamed. He rammed the gun deeper into Cummings' cheek to emphasise the point, eliciting another cry of anguish.

"Pete, Please!" Cummings implored, knowing that his life hung in the balance.

Myers raised his hands in defeat. He was wearing a HEMS jumpsuit with four stripes on his sleeve; he could hardly pretend to be anything other than a pilot. "Okay, okay, you win. Yes, I can fly it."

Winston grunted. "And do you need him to help you?" he asked.

"No."

Winston allowed himself a cruel smile. "Good." He released his grip on Cummings, who staggered back, almost fainting with relief.

As the ground crew supervisor leaned towards Myers for support, Winston lashed out, pistol-whipping him across the side of the face. With a dull thud, Cummings dropped flat on the floor, his hands flailing uselessly as he fell. Myers could only stare on in disbelief. There had been no warning. There had been no need.

"You bastard," Myers said through gritted teeth, his fists clenching and unclenching helplessly by his side.

"Let's move it, man," Winston gestured up the ramp with the handgun, pointing it towards the helicopter.

Leaning into the wind, the party of four made their way over to the aircraft. Garston and Angela got in first, moving as far over as they could. Winston gestured for Myers to board next. As the pilot opened the cockpit door, Winston placed a hand on his arm, pulling him near.

"And remember, no funny business," he warned.

Myers grunted unhappily. He would do as he was told. He wasn't paid to be a hero.

When they were all aboard, Myers began the pre-flight safety checks, working his way methodically through the list as every good pilot should. He was praying that the police would arrive and stop the flight before it became airborne.

Winston glared at him with menace. "Come on, man. Let's go!" he demanded impatiently.

"I'm going as fast as I can," Myers snapped back. It was a lie, but the man with the gun didn't know that. "I have to do the pre-flight checks or we could all end up dead, okay!"

He glanced across the rooftop at his injured friend, who was sluggishly trying to pull himself up off of the cold tarmac. "Starting her up," Myers said, hitting the switches. Both engines immediately came to life. The four rotor blades began to turn, slowly at first but quickly gaining in momentum. He keyed the radio toggle. "Heathrow from Helimed 27, seeking permission to leave the Royal London. Flight plan to follow, over."

"Turn that radio off," Winston ordered, leaning forward to prod the pilot in the back with the gun.

Myers glanced over his shoulder angrily. "Listen, chum, I have to speak to them. If we don't get clearance to lift off, we could end up climbing straight into the path of another aircraft and then we're all dead. Now let me get on with my job."

"Helimed 27 from Heathrow ATC, what's your tasking code and direction for your flight, over?"

There were three different tasking codes for the air ambulance. The first, Alpha, meant that it was going on an operational flight, for example deploying to an incident or transporting a patient from the scene to the hospital. The second, Echo, was typically used to denote that the aircraft was returning to base having finished its Alpha tasking. The final code, Zulu, indicated that the aircraft was undertaking a training or maintenance flight.

"Er, Heathrow, I have three passengers onboard holding me at gunpoint, and I'm being ordered to fly them away from the hospital to evade arrest, over."

There was a long silence.

"*Helimed 27 from Heathrow, can you repeat, over? I must have misheard because it sounded like you said you were being hijacked.*"

"You heard correctly," Myers responded, tetchily. "And these people don't play nice, so I'm taking off or getting shot. What's it to be?"

More silence. And then a strained voice said, "*Helimed 27, that's all received. Take off at your discretion. Climb to fifteen-hundred. VFR one-kilometre.*"

VFR – Visual Flight Rules – are the regulations under which a pilot operates an aircraft in good visual conditions, as opposed to flying that relies on instruments. In order to fly under VFR, the pilot must be able to see outside the aircraft for a minimum safe distance, navigate visually from landmarks, and be able to visually avoid all land and air obstacles that might be encountered during the flight – these included skyscrapers, telephone poles and, of course, other aircraft.

There is a requirement for some VFR aircraft, like the one Myers was flying, to be equipped with a transponder in order to assist Air Traffic Control to identify it on radar, thereby providing separation to IFR – Instrument Flight Rules – aircraft.

Myers checked to see that the tail was clear before applying more power, pulling up on the collective and lifting the helicopter into the cold grey afternoon sky. The wind was picking up, and the aircraft was buffeted as he hovered it above the landing pad, while the pilot looked around to make sure that nothing was in his intended path.

"Okay Mr Gunman, where am I taking you?" Myer asked.

"Just head for Barking in East London, man. I'll tell you more when we're on our way," Winston shouted to be heard above the engine noise, not realising that the headset he had donned had a sophisticated built-in communication system. "And don't tell those motherfuckers on the radio."

"But they need to know…" Myers began, but his protest was cut short.

"Just do as you're told, you dumb fuck," Winston barked, cutting him off angrily. "Stop making pony excuses and fly this damn thing." He was already beginning to feel queasy as the aircraft was rocked back and forth by the strong wind.

"Fair enough," Myers replied, and the aircraft commenced a turbulent climb as he set a course for Barking.

Winston had always suffered badly from travel sickness and, within seconds, he was looking around urgently. "Quick, somebody find me a sick bag," he gagged. "I think I'm gonna puke."

The radio was chattering away furiously, with the base controller demanding to know what was going on. Myers ignored him, glancing over his shoulder to study his captors.

"So, where exactly do I take you?" he asked conversationally, as though this was an everyday occurrence.

"Head for the East Ham ski slope, please," Garston instructed. His pallor was almost as grey as Claude's. "And we would all be extremely grateful if you would try your best to keep this *thing* flying smoothly."

He tried to distance himself from his uncle as the larger man threw up again. The acrid smell, which seemed to impregnate everything around it, was revolting, and the sight of the green bile oozing out of the corner of Claude's mouth made Garston want to wretch.

As soon as they emerged onto the bitterly cold roof, two-hundred-and-eighty-feet above the streets of East London, they heard the unmistakable sound of the helicopter powering up.

"Over there," Dillon said, pointing in the direction that the sound was coming from. He made to set off towards the ramp, but Connors blocked his path. "Stay behind us," the Trojan Inspector ordered firmly.

Dillon found this very frustrating, but he nodded his acceptance.

The landing pad loomed above them like a giant trampoline. A large red sign prohibited entry for unauthorised personnel. They proceeded slowly, ready to take cover if they came under fire. As they reached the top, Dillon saw the red Air Ambulance had passengers in it, and was about to lift off.

His stomach knotted.

"Look!" Connors shouted, pointing towards a man in blue overalls who was staggering across the tarmac like a drunk, holding the side of his head protectively. He appeared to be locked on a collision course with the helicopter's tail.

A unique feature of the MD902 Explorer is that it's equipped with NOTAR technology. The acronym stands for no tail rotor system. In other words, instead of having a big spinning tail rotor like most other helicopters, the MD902 expelled air out of its tail at one-hundred-and-twenty miles per hour to stop it from spinning.

"Shit, shit and double shit!" Dillon cursed, breaking into a sprint. The engine noise increased substantially as he closed on the aircraft, closely followed by the SO19 Inspector, who was calling for him to come back.

Eric stoically dropped to his knee and raised his carbine ready to provide covering fire if it became necessary.

Ignoring the tremendous downdraught, Dillon grabbed hold of Cummings and quickly dragged him to safety. For a moment, as he stood there shielding his face with his hand, he thought he caught sight of Winston inside the cabin, but he couldn't be sure, having only snatched a brief glimpse of the man's side profile. Moving forward again, he waved his arms and shouted at the pilot to switch off his machine and get out, but his voice was smothered by the roar of the turbines.

And then the helicopter lifted off. It hovered directly above them for a short time; tantalisingly close, but for all intents and purposes it might as well have been a million miles away.

Dillon stared up, blinking away the storm of dust particles that battered his face; whisked up by the powerful gust of wind the aircraft had generated.

"They haven't even seen us, the bastards," he shouted above the noise.

The realisation suddenly hit him hard.

Winston had done it – he had got away.

Dillon felt painfully impotent as he stood there, desperately wishing that there was something – anything – he could do to make the helicopter land, but there wasn't. As he watched, the aircraft began to climb, shrinking in size as it gained height. "Holland's not gonna be very happy about this," he told himself, feeling utterly despondent.

A hand rested heavily on his shoulder. "Come on, Tony. There's a lot to be done."

"I'm coming Pat," Dillon acknowledged gravely. He gave the disappearing helicopter one last look and then shook his head in despair, which only served to aggravate his injured neck.

They crossed the windswept tarmac in silence, descended the ramp, and then followed the markers until they found the control room.

Dillon desperately needed to know whether the Met Air Support Unit had either of its aircraft up. If either India 98 or 99 could establish visual contact with the HEMS bird before it came down, it might be possible to track the rogue helicopter from a distance and guide ground units in to intercept the hijackers as they landed. It was a long shot, which was why he also needed to find out whether ATC relied purely on radio communications or if they had any other means of tracking the HEMS helicopter.

Was it fitted with a transponder, for instance?

If so, could ATC track it from the ground?

His contingency plan, if the ASU were unable to help, relied upon ATC being able to monitor the aircraft's descent on radar or by transponder or by whatever means they used while directing ground-based units towards the general area it was coming down in. This would be a lot more haphazard, requiring IR to muster sufficient resources to flood a large area in the hope that one of the ground units would be able to reach the helicopter before the hijackers decamped.

If neither plan was viable, they were well and truly screwed.

As Connors disappeared into the control room, Dillon paused at the door and glanced back up into the cold, unwelcoming sky. It had started to rain again, reducing visibility, but in the distance, he could just make out the fading red shape of the air ambulance, its anti-collision lights flashing brightly as it flew over the city towards the east.

The three-man crew of India 99 were drinking tea in the operations room at Lippitts Hill when the call to scramble came through to them via MSS – the message switching system employed by the Met.

Sergeant Phillip Webber, the senior officer of the watch, read it carefully. "Ruddy heck!" he exclaimed, reading the telex again to make sure that he hadn't made a mistake. "Jon, Keith, let's scramble! We've got a really hot one, this time." They ran the short distance to the aircraft, which had just finished being refuelled.

Jonathan Danvers, their civilian pilot, started the Squirrel up, running through the pre-flight checks with practised ease. Webber briefed them both on the hijacking while this was being done.

Within minutes they were airborne and racing towards the red air ambulance's last known location.

"How fast can that thing move?" Dillon asked Mike Cummings, who sat nursing a bruised and lacerated face. Someone had found him a bag of ice, and he was pressing this into his jawline without enthusiasm. The man appeared to have a mild concussion, but he had repeatedly refused to go and get himself treated until he knew that the pilot was safe.

Cummings shrugged. "It'll do about a hundred-and-fifty miles per hour in a straight line, and we pride ourselves on being able to reach any point inside the M25 within fifteen minutes."

Dillon grimaced. "That's too damn fast for my liking," he said acidly. "How long can it remain airborne?"

Cummings scratched his head as he considered this. "Well, if memory serves, it carries 564 litres of fuel and it has a range of 328 nautical miles on a full tank," he said.

"That's right," Daniel Reed confirmed. He had been in the toilet when the helicopter had been taken, and he was racked with guilt for not having been there to support his friend and colleague, Myers.

"And has it got that much fuel in it now? I understand you only returned from a call-out a little while ago."

Reed nodded. He was a short man in his mid-thirties with dark brown hair, a big nose, and delicate hands. "More or less. We wouldn't want to be caught with our pants down if an emergency came in, would we?"

"Great. So, they could be two hundred miles away from London in an hour's time?" Dillon said, thinking that the situation was just going from bad to worse.

Reed nodded again, miserably this time. "I'm afraid so. Look, I do hope Peter's going to be okay?"

"So do I," Dillon said, unable to hold the other man's eye. Knowing Winston's form as he did, he didn't rate the pilot's chances at all.

A concerned looking colleague came over, apologised for interrupting, and handed Cummings a steaming hot mug of tea. Accepting it gratefully, he smiled a thank you at her as she left.

Dillon stood up to leave. "Thanks, you've both been a great help," he said. "Don't stray too far, we may need to speak to you again."

"Don't worry, I'll be right here if you need me," Cummings promised, taking a tentative first sip of his tea.

"Likewise," Reed said, standing up to shake the detective's hand. He had a surprisingly strong grip, Dillon noticed.

Leaving Cummings to enjoy his brew in peace, Dillon wandered over to Pat Connors, who was on the phone to Information Room, seeking an update on the ASU deployment.

"Any news, Pat?"

Connors shook his head wearily. "Sorry mate, nothing yet."

Dillon didn't know what to do next and, as a man of action, he hated this unfamiliar feeling of impotency; it made him feel weak and indecisive. Realistically, though, there was nothing he could do now but wait for Holland to arrive and pray that, by the time he did, there would be some good news to pass on.

This investigation would now become a top priority case for the murder squad detectives. Cop killers automatically jumped to the front of the queue for manpower and resources. It was the same the world over.

He bitterly recalled his parting words to Frank Skinner when they had been sitting outside Winston's room last week, arguing over whether or not armed support was necessary. *I really hope you're right, Frank, because if you're not, it won't be your life on the line when the shooting starts...*

A cold stab of guilt pierced his heart as he asked himself the unpalatable question: should he have made more of an effort to get Skinner's decision overturned.

I guess we will never know, he thought morosely.

He hadn't seen Skinner or his lackey, Donoghue, yet, but when he did, he planned to vent his considerable displeasure on them.

His phone rang and he answered it anxiously, hoping it would be Jack Tyler.

It wasn't.

It was Steve Bull, calling to update him that the two officers who'd been guarding Winston had now been removed from the scene and were now undergoing treatment. Alarmingly, neither had regained consciousness yet and blood tests were being rushed through to establish which sedative they had been injected with.

Dillon thanked him and hung up. Thirty seconds later the phone rang again. Hope flared that Tyler was finally responding to the messages he had left.

It was Steve Bull again, calling him back to let him know that DCS Holland had arrived and was at the third-floor crime scene.

"Tell him I'll come straight down," Dillon said.

"*Mr Holland says for you to remain up there, boss,*" Bull said. "*He'll come up as soon as he's finished down here.*"

"Am I in his bad books?" Dillon asked. There was a long, strained silence, and he guessed that Bull was unable to speak freely because of his close proximity to Holland.

"Never mind," Dillon said, feeling dejected. "I think I can probably work out the answer to that one for myself."

With that, he hung up.

The control room suddenly felt cloyingly hot. Ignoring the bitter cold, the icy rain, and his throbbing neck, Dillon ventured back outside to get some much-needed fresh air.

The helipad towered above the streets of London and, even in the rain, the view it afforded was incredible. Under different circumstances, he would have enjoyed soaking it up, but today he might just as well have been standing in an unlit coal bunker for all the pleasure it gave him.

With a heartfelt sigh, he pulled out his Job issue Motorola mobile phone and extended the small aerial. He might as well try calling Tyler again, although he wasn't overly hopeful of getting a response. He dialled the eleven digits from memory and pressed the green button.

"Tony, they've found the air ambulance!" Connors shouted from inside the building. His voice was brimming with excitement.

Dillon immediately pocketed his phone and ran back to join his SO19 counterpart. "Where?" he demanded tensely.

"Wasteland near Canning Town. We've got ground units inbound as we speak."

"How did we find it?" Dillon asked. The adrenaline surging through his veins was making him feel jittery like he'd overdosed on caffeine, and it was all he could do to remain still.

"India 99 spotted collision lights flashing on the edge of their horizon. It was too far away for a visual ID, but they were convinced it was another helicopter. They tried to establish radio contact with the unidentified bird but got nothing in response. Naturally, 99 gave chase, but they lost sight of it after a few seconds. By then India 98 was inbound from South London. The bad guys must have heard all this activity going on over the radio and decided to put down."

Dillon let out a low whistle. "So, they didn't actually see it land?"

Connors shook his head. "No, but all available ground units were ordered into the area it was last seen in while India 99 continued to search for it from above. They've just radioed in to say that they'd spotted the air ambulance in a large area of wasteland in Canning Town."

"Do they have a visual on the suspects?" Dillon asked, holding his breath and hoping against all the odds that they did.

Connors shook his head again. "No, afraid not."

"What about the pilot? Is he okay?"

"The local area car should be on scene any second now," Connors told him as they crowded into the cramped control room.

Dillon dry washed his face and swallowed hard. He was starting to feel sick with anticipation. "I've got a bad feeling about this, Pat," he confessed. He was aware of Cummings and Reed standing close beside him, their faces etched with worry.

"Yeah, me too," Connors said quietly. "What did your gov'nor say when you called him?"

"Jack? I haven't been able to reach him yet."

Both men stared at the radio in the Trojan officer's hand, willing it to end the painful suspense and put them out of their misery.

"Come on, come on…" Dillon whispered under his breath. Not for the first time, he prayed that no one else would get hurt today.

CHAPTER TEN

Detective Chief Superintendent George Holland stood in the doorway of the hospital room, looking down at the unmoving form on the bed with great sadness. He was a middle-aged man with fair hair and a craggy, unreadable face. Underneath the white coveralls, he wore his customary dark suit and red braces, and his burgundy tie and pocket handkerchief matched perfectly.

After a quick word with Steve Bull and the Crime Scene Manager, a petite blonde called Juliet Kennedy, he emerged from the room and walked a short distance over to where Ray Speed stood. Speed was engaged in a subdued conversation with a uniformed colleague whose face appeared numb with shock.

The newcomer's name was Russel Percival, and he was the operations Chief Inspector from Forest Gate division, where the deceased officer had been based. Percival was a weak chinned man in his early fifties, and he had the soft-centred look of someone who had spent most of his career avoiding any form of confrontation.

Holland knew the type only too well, and he suspected that Percival was a shiny arse who had spent most of his career hopping from one administrative role to another, polishing a succession of comfy chairs with his posterior. To Holland's surprise, he asked to be admitted to the room so that he could see Winston's butchery for himself, but this was a crime scene now, so Holland refused him access.

"How well did you know PC Morrison?" Holland asked as he slipped out of the plastic overshoes to reveal a pair of black Oxfords that were so shiny, they would have impressed a drill sergeant.

"Not well, sir," Percival replied, "but, by all accounts, he was a very good officer."

Percival's proximity to the murder scene was clearly making him uncomfortable, so as soon as Holland removed the white Tyvek coveralls, he steered the man further along the corridor to spare him from having to listen to the Crime Scene Manager and Steve Bull discussing the logistics of body removal and the timescales for getting the special post mortem arranged.

On first impressions, Percival seemed far too timid to be a cop, but Holland cut him some slack as this was clearly the first murder scene he had ever attended. He knew the man would be going through inner turmoil, battling against intense emotions that hampered the ability to remain calm and process information with detached professionalism.

It was never easy to separate oneself from the inevitable anger and frustration that occurred after a colleague had been killed, or to banish the overwhelming desire for revenge and focus purely on getting the job done. This was especially true when the perpetrator had escaped and was still free, seemingly laughing in the face of justice and decency.

Inevitably, Holland found himself wondering about the people that Morrison was leaving behind, the people he had loved and shared experiences with.

Was he married?

Did he have children?

Regardless, he was still a mother's son, and a grieving family would now have to cope with the unimaginable pain and loss of a sudden bereavement. Holland had attended so many similar scenes over the years that he had become all but immune to them, although he still remembered his first murder scene, when he had reacted in much the same way that Percival was reacting now. The main difference between them was that he had been a probationer at the time, not a Chief bloody Inspector.

Holland placed a gentle hand on Percival's shoulder and was surprised to feel the man flinch at the contact. "Look, Russ, there's nothing more you can do here," he said. "The two PCs who were with Morrison are still out for the count, so you might as well head back over to Forest Gate."

Percival stared at him uncomprehendingly for a moment before nodding slowly, and it was obvious that he was struggling to get a grip. "Yes, yes, I think you're probably right," he said, sounding a little punch-drunk.

The cynic in Holland suspected that Percival couldn't wait to get away from the ugly chaos of the hospital and return to the safe familiarity of his cosy office.

"I'll need to arrange for Occupational Health to be called out."

"Why would you want OH called out?" Holland asked, staring at him quizzically.

Percival started to get flustered. "W-well..." he stammered, and then ran a finger around the inside of his collar, as if it had suddenly become too tight, "I - er – I think the officers on Morrison's relief ought to be given an opportunity to speak to an OH advisor before coming on duty tomorrow, don't you?"

Holland's lips compressed into a thin angry line. In his day, people just got on with life; nowadays, they couldn't even tie their bloody shoelaces without receiving input from some quack spouting a load of meaningless psychobabble. When he spoke, Holland's tone was harsh. "Russell, before you get yourself too caught up in all that OH crap, can I trouble you to make the necessary arrangements to inform PC Morrison's next of kin?"

Percival's already harried face blanched. "Of course, sir," he said, somewhat hesitantly, "unless you'd rather have one of your chaps do it?" There was an imploring look in his eyes as he asked the question.

"I wouldn't," Holland said, staring at him unblinkingly.

Percival nodded gravely, accepting there was no room for negotiation. "Very good, sir."

Holland shook the junior officer's extended hand, which had a grip that was every bit as weak as his chin. "I'll let you know how things go here in due course," he promised.

Once Percival had left them, Holland turned to Speed. "Well, Ray, as the suspects have made good their escape and the hospital's been reopened to the public, I don't suppose Charlie Porter still plans to grace us with his presence?"

Speed grinned. "That's right, sir. He called me a little while ago to say that, as everything is now under control, he was diverting to Whitechapel. I'll have the dubious honour of briefing him upon my return."

Holland smiled wryly. "Lucky you," he said.

———

When Errol reached the junction with Commercial Road, he made a left and set off towards his home turf. He knew it was only a matter of time until the dispossessed cabbie flagged down a passing police patrol and reported the carjacking, and he wanted to put as much distance as possible between himself and the area in which it was taken.

At least the owner wouldn't be able to phone the theft in as his mobile was currently poking out of a cup holder in the centre console next to Errol. The poor old sod wasn't having a good day, Errol reflected with a mirthless smile. In that respect, they were kindred spirits.

Despite the rain, the early afternoon traffic was flowing relatively freely for a change, and he didn't hit a single red light until he reached the intersection where Commercial Road bisected Burdett Road to the left and West India Dock Road to the right.

Willing the lights to change, he kept shooting nervous glances along West India Dock Road towards the imposing redbrick building that was Limehouse police station. He could see there were a half dozen police vehicles parked in the road outside, and the last thing he wanted was for one of them to pull away and notice him. The old J registration cab had no go in it, and he doubted it would be able to outrun a battery-operated mobility scooter, let alone the Old Bill.

Interlocking his fingers, Errol placed both hands atop his bald pate. He screwed his eyes shut and started rocking back and forth in the driver's seat, releasing his breath in a low moan of anguish and wondering how he had ever allowed himself to get muddled up in something as terrible as this. As soon as he had discovered that nutter Winston was involved, he should have just walked away.

It was all Sonia's bloody fault – he had only agreed to do this job because the money he was being paid would finance the flash Caribbean beach wedding that she had been dreaming about – nagging him about, more like – for years. If he went away for this, he thought bitterly, he would make sure the ungrateful cow understood that it was all her fault; if she had been content with a simple registry office ceremony like any other girl, he wouldn't have ended up in this train crash of a situation. But no, Sonia had filled her otherwise empty head with illusions of grandeur, and now, because of his desire to please her, his freedom was on the line.

His head was spinning as he tried to plot his way out of trouble. Trouble was, he was more of a doer than a thinker – all brawn and no brain, as Deontay was fond of reminding him – and his mind remained stubbornly blank.

Errol decided that his first priority was to dispose of the cab, and he knew a patch of wasteland in Canning Town that would be a perfect place to dump it in.

Once the cab was taken care of, his next priority would be to dispose of the gun. That, he decided, would go straight into the Limehouse Basin. Deontay would be pissed; guns were a very tradable commodity on the streets, and he'd made it clear that he wanted the revolver back once the job was done. Errol couldn't afford to worry about that anymore; the others had probably been nabbed back at the hospital, so now he had to think about saving his own skin and making sure that he didn't end up standing in the dock with them.

As soon as he got home, he would take all his clothes off and burn them. Once that was done, there would be nothing left to tie him to the botched breakout. None of the others would grass him up, he was reasonably confident of that, and Sonia would alibi him if the Old Bill ever came snooping around. She was a good girl – a bit dim, perhaps, but very loyal – and she would lie for her man, telling the Filth that he'd been at home with her all day.

A sudden blur of movement off to his right caught his eye, and when he turned to check it out, he was surprised to see a mass exodus occurring at Limehouse police station. Officers were running out of the front and jumping into cars as though they were contestants in a race. Engines were starting up, blue lights were flashing, and cars were wheel spinning away from the kerb.

"What the fuck…?"

His heart in his mouth, Errol instinctively slouched down in his seat, trying to make himself as small and inconspicuous as possible.

"Where the hell is Jack Tyler?" Holland thundered.

Dillon shrugged helplessly. "I don't know, boss. I've been on to the Police Room at the Bailey, but apparently, the PCMH finished earlier than anticipated. I've spoken to Colin Franklin and Dick Jarvis, but they had lunch over at CP4, while Jack and Kelly went elsewhere. Either they're somewhere where they can't get a signal or neither of them has remembered to switch their phones back on since leaving court. Colin said they're all meeting up again outside the RCJ at a quarter to two for the appeal. If we haven't reached him by then, he'll get Jack to call straight in."

Holland grunted, clearly unimpressed. Dillon knew he expected his senior officers to be contactable at all times. "It might just be that there's no signal where they're getting lunch," Dillon said lamely.

If Holland had heard him, he gave no indication. "How the hell did this happen, Dillon, tell me that? Three officers overpowered. A good man dead. What a bloody waste." Holland found himself becoming angrier as he spoke. "I've called DCI Quinlan's team out to take point on this. They dealt with the original investigation last year after you and Jack arrested Winston, and they're due to go in the frame in a couple of days anyway, so it makes perfect sense."

Dillon bristled at that. "Hold on a minute, sir!" he protested angrily. Although he understood why it had been operationally necessary, it still rankled that Holland had made them hand the case over after they arrested Winston back in November, and he was desperate to retain this latest investigation.

Holland raised a finger in warning. "Don't 'hold on a minute' me, DI Dillon." There was an edge to his voice that told Dillon he was skating on thin ice. "I understand how you feel, but you can't have this case."

"With all due respect…"

Holland held up his hand, and there was a finality to the motion that cut Dillon off mid-sentence.

"Enough. Tony, write your statement up and hand it over to DCI Quinlan when he arrives. Got it?"

Dillon was positively seething. "Yes sir," he said through teeth gritted so hard that it made his jaw ache. Somehow, he managed not to say anything he might later regret.

The latest downpour was almost over. What had begun as torrential rainfall had fizzled out to an inconsequential drizzle, and for the first time all day, the clouds seemed to be clearing.

They had driven all the way along Commercial Road to the junction of Burdett Road without seeing any trace of the stolen Taxi, and Susie was on the verge of giving up and turning around when Terry Grier suddenly lunged forward from the rear seat and pointed.

"Look," he said, excitedly, "isn't that our LOS cab waiting at the lights?"

Sure enough, the stolen cab was sitting in the nearside lane directly ahead of them. Murray checked the registration number against the one that the IRV had broadcast a few minutes earlier just to be sure. The vehicle only had one occupant, a bald-headed black man.

"Is that the bloke you were chasing?" Murray asked Grier.

Grier nodded excitedly." It certainly is," he said. With hope resurgent, he reached for the door handle; maybe he would get to keep that one hundred per cent arrest record after all.

"Stay where you are," Susie Sergeant snapped, her green eyes boring into him via the rear-view mirror. "He's got a firearm, remember?"

Grier huffed like a disappointed child, but he obediently sagged back in his seat, his young face a mask of frustration.

"Don't worry," Susie said, recalling how enthusiastic she had still been as a probationer, "once the cavalry arrives, you can have the arrest."

Susie suppressed a grin as Grier's face lit up like a kid whose parents had just told him that they were taking him to an ice cream parlour and then onto his favourite toy shop.

At that moment a convoy of police vehicles came zooming through the junction, the various wail and yelp settings of their two-tones competing with each other to create a painful cacophony of sound. Susie counted them as they sped by: two area cars, two IRVs, a station van, and a TSG carrier.

"Something big must be going down somewhere," Grier said, staring at the procession in awe.

Murray raised a contemptuous eyebrow. "Is it bigger than a murdered police officer?" He shook his head emphatically. "I don't think so, and anyway, if it's that important, why isn't it coming out over the main-Set?"

Susie groaned. "The power button's a bit temperamental on this old heap," she said, glancing down at the unit in the dashboard. "Sometimes it turns itself off."

Swearing at the inconvenience, Murray leaned forward and tapped the button but nothing happened. He tried again, this time holding it in with a skeletal finger. After several seconds, the speakers crackled and came back to life, and it rapidly became apparent that something big was, indeed, going down. Virtually every available unit in the area was converging on a remote section of wasteland where the hijacked HEMS air ambulance was believed to have put down.

In the distance, and off to their right, Susie spotted India 99 hovering high above the ground, and she guessed that it must be directly above the spot that everyone and their dog was currently breaking their necks to get to.

"What do we do?" Grier asked as the lights changed to green and the cab moved off, spewing out a giant cloud of diesel from its exhaust. "You can't just interrupt –"

Although Murray genuinely liked Grier, his default setting was to react stroppily when anyone told him what he could or couldn't do. "Can't I?" he bristled. "Just watch me."

Murray snatched the mic out of its cradle and pressed the PTT – press to talk – button. "MP, MP from Metro Sierra Nine-Three, active message." He used the designated HAT Car call sign as their vehicle was a general-purpose pool car, and as such it didn't have a unique call sign of its own.

The operator responded immediately, sounding as cool as a cucumber. *"Metro Sierra Nine-Three please change to Channel Five as we already have an ongoing incident in progress..."*

Channel Five was normally reserved for units needing to have car-to-car or car-to station conversations, but it was occasionally used as a live channel when there was already an incident running elsewhere.

Murray was defiant. "Negative, MP," he said, shaking his head to emphasise the point as if the Information Room operator could see him. "We're in Commercial Road heading towards the Blackwall Tunnel Northern Approach, just passing Burdett Road on our left, and we're behind the LOS taxi cab containing one of the gunmen involved in the murder of a police officer at the Royal London Hospital. We need immediate armed assistance to stop the vehicle and detain the driver."

He glanced over his shoulder and gave Grier a satisfied smirk. "I think that trumps whatever else is going on," he said triumphantly

The operator at the Yard was having none of it. *"Change to Channel Five,"* he insisted, and then added, *"Any armed units able to assist Metro Sierra Nine-Three please also change to Channel Five."*

―――――

Kelly felt a little bit like a lovestruck schoolgirl. During the meal, she'd been unable to resist sneaking occasional furtive glances across the table, and every time her eyes had settled on Tyler, another tingle of excitement had washed over her. She could honestly say that she'd never felt this way about anyone before, and she desperately wanted to ask him if he felt the same, but after Dillon had told her about his messy divorce and how it had left him so relationship averse, she knew she couldn't, in case it scared him off.

Before she'd met Jack, Kelly had sworn never to become romantically involved with another cop. In fact, she'd once told her sister that she'd rather die a spinster than marry a policeman. Mary had struggled to understand her attitude, but then, unlike Kelly, she had no idea just how disastrous relationships between cops could be. They were great when they worked, but more often than not they ended in tears, and when that happened working relationships were invariably compromised, and everyone around the former lovebirds suffered from the inevitable toxicity of the fallout.

The saying: *don't shit on your own doorstep or you'll have to live with the smell* might be a little crude, but it was certainly apt when it came to Job-related romances.

And yet, despite her well-known antipathy towards police relationships, Jack Tyler had won her heart without even trying, and she now ached to tell him that she loved him, but she knew she would have to be patient and wait until she was sure he was ready to hear the L-word.

As if by magic, their attentive waiter appeared the moment they finished eating. "Can I get you anything else?" he asked, smiling at each of them in turn. "Some coffee, perhaps?"

"Just the bill, please," Jack said, checking his watch. It was getting on for one-forty, and they needed to make a move.

The crew of Barking's area car, Kilo-Four, found Myers slumped in the cockpit of his aircraft. There were two bullet holes in the plexiglass windscreen. The front of his face, they saw as they opened the door, was covered in blood. Miraculously, when they examined him closer, they found that he was still breathing. Other units were scouring the vicinity for the three suspects, but they seemed to have vanished into thin air.

"Look at his helmet!" one of the officers exclaimed in surprise. As they gently eased Myers out of his seat, they saw the blackened gouge that furrowed the side of his helmet in a diagonal line, from his right temple to the base of his skull.

"Shit! I think he's been shot!" the older of the two officers proclaimed, reaching for his radio to summon medical assistance.

Thankfully, it had stopped raining by the time they emerged from the restaurant, although the temperature seemed to have dropped even lower and the wind was picking up. "I wouldn't be surprised if we had snow by the end of the week," Jack said, staring up at the dull afternoon sky.

"I hope not," Kelly said, pulling her collar up and shivering with cold.

Tyler was tempted to wrap his arms around her and give her a crushing embrace to warm her up, but he couldn't take the risk of someone they knew spotting them behaving intimately. If it became common knowledge that they were seeing each other, Holland would probably insist that Kelly be moved to another team. That would mean them working different rotas, and it would lead to them seeing far less of each other than they did now. It would also cost him one of his best officers.

With the hijacked HEMS helicopter now secure on the ground, and the pilot no longer in imminent danger, Murray had been instructed to switch back to Channel One.

Upon doing so, the channel operator informed them that India 99 was diverting to assist them, leaving the ongoing search for Winston and his two cronies to the numerous ground units that had flooded the area.

Seemingly oblivious to the fact that an unmarked police car was sitting on its tail, the stolen cab was happily chugging its way along East India Dock Road at a steady thirty-mile-per-hour. It was still heading towards the A12 and the Blackwall Tunnel Northern Approach.

Less than a mile behind, three Trojan units were racing through afternoon traffic in an attempt to catch it up.

Inside the battered Astra, Murray continued to provide a detailed radio commentary.

The game plan was to try and stop the LOS before it reached the turn off for the BTNA, which wasn't far that away.

East India Dock Road had widened to two lanes in each direction, with a set of metal railings separating the two streams of traffic. They were coming up to another busy intersection, and beyond that, on their left, was the slip road for the northbound A12, which led to Bow and Hackney.

"If they're going to intercept him before he reaches the BTNA, they're going to have to put a bit of a spurt on," a worried-looking Grier said, staring out of the rear window to see if there was any sign of the Armed Response Vehicles.

Murray squeezed the PTT. "MP, we're still eastbound in East India Dock Road, just coming up to red ATS at the junction with Cotton Street." ATS – Automatic Traffic Signals – were police speak for traffic lights. "The bandit's in lane one of two," he continued, "brake lights now showing. Stand by..."

A moment later, the cab stopped with its nose straddling the white line, and Susie coasted to a halt just behind it. "Make sure he can't see you using the radio," she warned Murray.

"What a good idea," he said, acerbically.

Traffic from Cotton Street, which was off to their right, was now filtering its way through the yellow box junction in front of them. Because of the light phasing up ahead, there was already a bit of a tailback, even though East India Dock Road, from this point onwards, widened from two to four lanes.

The Main-Set suddenly crackled into life. "*MP from Trojan Five-Oh-Three, can I have a quick talk through with Metro Sierra Nine-Three, please?*" It was one of the approaching Trojan units, asking to speak directly to them.

"*Trojan unit, make it brief, MP over,*" the IR operator responded.

"Metro Sierra Nine-Three from Trojan Five-Oh-Three, we're only thirty seconds away. Can you punch up so that your car is literally almost touching the back of the cab? If the lights don't change, we're going to put in the hard stop where you are now."

Susie's eyes immediately shot to her offside wing mirror. Sure enough, the trio of Trojan units was zooming along the outside of the traffic, and they were mere seconds away. Although their headlights and blue lights were flashing, their sirens were switched off for a silent approach. There was something predatory about the sight; it was like watching three big white sharks clearing a path through a shoal of smaller fish.

Murray glanced at Susie apprehensively and was rewarded with a decisive nod.

He pressed the PTT. "Received by Metro Sierra Nine-Three. Moving up now."

As he spoke, Susie gently allowed the clutch pedal to rise, letting the clunking Astra creep forward until it was virtually kissing the cab's rear bumper. "Stand by for the fireworks to start," she said quietly.

Murray gave his latest update. "MP from Metro Sierra Nine-Three, the suspect's still stationary in lane one at red ATS, with us directly behind. Lane two is still clear. We have Trojan units inbound and we're handing commentary over to them."

"Metro Sierra Nine-Three from MP, that's all received. Stand by. Trojan Five-Oh-Three, Trojan Five-Oh-Three, what is your ETA, MP over...?"

"MP from Trojan Five-Oh-Three, we're just arriving on scene, and we're moving straight in to execute the hard stop. A MP unit, remain in your vehicle until we call you forward."

"Received," Murray acknowledged and then turned to look at the others. "Like they even needed to say that," he said.

Things quickly got interesting from that point onwards.

The first Trojan vehicle, a marked Vauxhall Omega, shot down the outside and swerved across the front of the stationary Taxi, blocking its path. The timing was perfect as a second later, the lights started to change. Three SO19 officers alighted quickly and immediately brought their weapons to bear. The driver brandishing a Glock 17 Self Loading Pistol, nimbly moved around the ARV's bonnet, kneeling down and using it for cover. From that position, he could cover the front of the target car, and he had a clear shot at the suspect through his windscreen.

The front and rear passengers were each carrying Heckler and Koch G36C carbines, a short-barrelled semi-automatic weapon chambered to fire the powerful 5.65 rifle round. As they thumbed the selector switches from 'safety' to 'fire', both were shouting, "ARMED POLICE, SHOW ME YOUR HANDS!" repeatedly as they closed in on the driver, positioning themselves so that they wouldn't get caught in a crossfire if the situation deteriorated into a firefight.

The second ARV, a liveried Eight Series Rover, pulled up level with the Taxi, and again the two nearside passengers were out of the vehicle in an instant, drawing down on the suspect with their carbines before he could react. More shouts of "ARMED POLICE, SHOW ME YOUR HANDS!" filled the air.

The final ARV, another Omega, stopped behind the AMIP Astra, slewing diagonally across the two lanes in order to stop any vehicles following behind them from accidentally straying into the sterile area around the hard stop. While the driver turned to face oncoming traffic, his two compatriots rushed forward to provide additional firepower to their colleagues.

Two local Panda cars had also attended via Cotton Street, and they now closed off the junction, effectively creating an exclusion zone around the armed interdiction.

CHAPTER ELEVEN

As Tyler and Flowers crossed the road, they spotted Colin Franklin and Dick Jarvis standing outside the RCJ's main entrance. Colin rushed forward to meet him as he ascended the steps that led up to the court.

"Boss, have you spoken to Mr Dillon yet?" he asked, and there was an underlying sense of urgency in his voice.

"No," Jack said, "not since this morning. Why?"

Franklin's expression was unusually serious, and Tyler started to feel concerned. Had something bad happened?

"He's been trying to call you for ages," Franklin said. "Apparently, it's all gone pear shaped at the hospital and Claude Winston has escaped."

Tyler felt his jaw drop open. "He's done what?" he demanded.

"You need to phone Mr Dillon," Franklin said. "It's really bad. One of the local officers guarding him was shot and killed during the breakout."

"Oh, my God," Kelly said. "Is it anyone we might know?"

Franklin shook his head. "The name's not been released yet," he said. "Mr Quinlan's team has taken the job."

Jack's face darkened. "Colin, you and Dick go inside and find our Treasury Counsel. Tell him that I'm outside if he needs me. Explain that a job has just broken and that I'll join you all as soon as I can." He turned to Kelly. "You'd better go in and find the victim's mum. I don't want her being left in the lurch." Kelly was the Family Liaison Officer for the case they were here for, and she had made arrangements to chaperone the victim's mother, who had insisted on being present during the appeal. Kelly had done her best to deter her, explaining that it was just legal arguments and that no witnesses would be called to give evidence, but the grieving woman was having none of it.

As soon as he was alone, Jack pulled out his phone and promptly swore. He had forgotten to switch it back on after coming out of The Bailey. How had he managed that, he wondered?

As soon as the phone powered up, he saw there were numerous missed calls, voicemails, and text messages, all from Tony Dillon.

"Shit," he said, and immediately started dialling the big man's number.

The call was answered after the first ring. "*Where the bloody heck have you been?*" Dillon snapped at him by way of greeting. There was an air of desperation in his voice, and Jack was immediately wracked with guilt.

"Sorry, Dill," he said, sheepishly. "Been having a bit of a problem with my phone." The problem being, he decided to omit, was that it hadn't been turned on when it was meant to be.

The excuse didn't wash. "*Kelly been having the same problem, has she?*" Dillon asked. His tone was acid.

Tyler felt himself blush. "Look, I'm really sorry mate," he said, avoiding the question, "but I'm here now. Tell me what's happened?"

Dillon gave him the main headlines, and then vented his frustration at how things had turned out. He clearly blamed himself for not being more insistent that an armed guard be put in place for the duration of Winston's hospital incarceration.

"It's not your fault," Tyler said, angry that his friend felt responsible for something he had absolutely no control over.

The simple fact of the matter was that the drug squad skipper in charge of the production had carried out a thorough risk assessment in conjunction with the host borough. They had jointly concluded that Winston was only a medium risk and that, even though he had previously had access to guns, there was no current intelligence to suggest that he remained a firearms threat, or that his criminal associates had the means or the desire to facilitate a breakout. Dillon had made representations in the strongest possible terms that Winston ought to have armed officers guarding him for the duration of his hospital stay but, ultimately, he had no power to enforce his recommendations.

Dillon clearly didn't share Jack's view. *"I'm not so sure that the dead officer, or the two beat cops who've been drugged, or the seriously injured pilot would agree with you,"* he said. *"Winston's disappeared into thin air and, if the drug squad has any idea where he might be, they ain't saying. One of the twats who turned up to collect Winston this afternoon had the temerity to tell me he that couldn't share any information with us unless it's cleared at a higher level. I nearly knocked him out when he said that."*

Despite the seriousness of the situation, Jack had to smile. He suspected the drug squad officer had been sent on his way with a flea in his ear. "Can't you just ask your mate? What was his name, Frank Skinner?"

Dillon gave a derisive snort. *"Turns out that Frankie boy isn't quite the mate I thought he was. He's the fucker who's refusing to pool information."*

When the marked police car swerved in front of him at the traffic lights, Errol's heart nearly burst straight out of his chest.

He had been sitting there wracking his brains, trying to figure out a way to explain the mess he'd gotten himself into to Sonia, but no matter how hard he tried, he couldn't see any way of avoiding her wrath. She was a feisty cow at the best of times. She would hit the roof when she found out what he'd done, and then she would probably hit him.

When the funny South Park song had started playing on the radio, he'd turned the volume to max and sung along heartily to take his mind off of his predicament for a couple of minutes. The blaring music, he now realised, must have blocked out the noise of their approaching sirens because he hadn't heard them coming.

With the windows all steamed up by condensation, he hadn't seen them either, not until it was too late.

In the back of his mind, there was a vague recollection that black Taxi cabs were meant to have an amazing turning circle, and he decided that there would never be a better time to put that to the test.

Without even checking his mirror, he grabbed the gear selector and rammed it up a notch, moving it from neutral into reverse, and then he gunned the accelerator for all he was worth. He could clearly hear police officer shouting at him as they spilled out of the car and ran towards him, although most of what they were saying was muffled by Mr Hanky singing *The Christmas Poo* song.

The cab jolted backwards, but only about an inch, and then it came to an abrupt halt. He tried revving the gas pedal but nothing happened.

"What the fuck…?" Looking back over his shoulder, he saw that some stupid ginger-haired woman had stopped so close that there couldn't have been more than a fag paper's worth of gap between their bumpers.

Fucking women drivers, he fumed. It was the sort of dumb thing that he was always telling Sonia off for doing; that woman of his just didn't have any spatial awareness.

Ignoring the muffled shouts from outside, he dragged the selector down into drive and spun the steering wheel as far as it would go to the right. He was dimly aware of two coppers standing right outside his window, pointing at him, but the side windows were too heavily misted for him to take in any detail. The good thing about the fogging, he realised, was that it would prevent the pigs from getting a detailed look at his features.

As the cab lurched forward, it almost collided with the side of the big police car blocking its path. So much for the cab's fabled turning circle. He considered ramming the car, but it was too big and heavy, and it was so close that he would never be able to gain the momentum needed to shunt it out of the way. He had already tried and failed with the car behind, which was much smaller.

As a feeling of utter desperation swept over him, he knew he had an unpleasant choice to make – use the gun or be arrested. If he could intimidate them into backing off with the revolver, he could jack the police car in front and make good his escape in that.

He knew he would be crossing a line if he brandished the gun, and that there would be no going back once he did so. But what alternative was there?

Wishing there was another way, Errol reached over and snatched the revolver from the gap between his seat and the armrest, where he had wedged it for safekeeping.

The weight of the heavy gun in his hand was strangely reassuring. Adopting his hardest expression, the one he'd copied from watching the pugilist, Lenny Maclean, and now used when he was about to rough a punter up, he turned to face the policemen.

As he swivelled the gun around to point at them, he noticed two very disturbing things in quick succession: Firstly, there were a lot more cops out there than he'd realised – he counted six, but suspected there might be even more. Secondly, and far more importantly, they were all carrying big 'fuck-off' guns, and every single one of them was pointing straight at him. Bizarrely, it had never occurred to him that any of the cops trying to arrest him might be armed.

"Shit!"

PC Keith Cash was twenty-nine-years old. He had been a policeman for eight years, the last two of which had been spent on SO19. Unlike some of the other guys in the unit, Keith had no previous military experience and, before joining the Job, he had never even seen a gun in real life, let alone handled one. He wasn't a 'gun nut' and he didn't get a thrill or a buzz from carrying a firearm around. He had elected to become an Authorised Firearms Officer in order to save life, not take it, and although he had been required to draw his weapon countless times over the last two years, he had never fired a single shot in anger. He had been hoping to go through his entire career without ever having to do so.

Cash had been the front seat passenger in Trojan Five-Oh-Three, the Omega that had stopped directly in front of the Taxi. He had been the first of the three man crew to get out of the car, and since taking up a static position by the driver's door he had been incessantly screaming instructions at the black man who was in sitting in the driver's seat to stay still and show his hands. He was reaching the point where his voice was starting to become hoarse.

Overhead, he heard the distinctive whup, whup, whup of the helicopter arriving, and on risking a quick glance upwards, he saw India 99 was now hovering above them. It would, no doubt, be filming the incident, and it might even be transmitting the images back to Information Room at The Yard in real-time.

The suspect had no intention of coming quietly, that much had become very apparent. His first reaction had been to try and shunt the unmarked GP behind them out of the way. Fortunately, its driver, a pretty girl with strawberry blonde hair, had followed the instructions he'd given her over the Main-Set earlier, and she had stopped with her front bumper kissing the bandit's exhaust pipe.

The suspect had then tried to whip the Taxi around the front of the Omega, but that had also failed. Now, instead of doing the sensible thing and surrendering, he was frantically scrabbling around for something inside the car, below Cash's line of sight.

The fool was wilfully ignoring the chorus of shouts to sit still and show his hands, and although the radio inside the cab was playing ridiculously loudly, the man must have been able to see that he was surrounded by armed officers.

The hairs on the nape of Cash's neck stood up. During SO19's relentless training sessions, he had rehearsed scenarios like the one now unfolding in front of him many times, and in each and every one, the suspect had invariably pulled a gun on them and opened fire. Of course, this wasn't a training scenario at Lippitt's Hill; this was real life, and it might pan out very differently, but Keith knew that if he hesitated when the time came, as he had done several times during training, he or a colleague could end up every bit as dead as the divisional officer who had been fatally shot at the hospital.

"FACE THE FRONT AND SHOW ME YOUR FUCKING HANDS," he screamed for the umpteenth time, praying that, on this occasion, the man in the cab would actually heed his words and comply with the instruction.

And then they reached the endgame, and the suspect was spinning around to face him, rapidly bringing his right hand up as he moved.

It was as though someone flicked a switch and the world suddenly moved into slow motion. Keith's colleagues were still shouting, but their words now seemed painfully drawn out and distorted to him.

As the suspect's hand appeared from beneath the door, Cash's brain processed that it was holding a big black revolver with a barrel approximately four inches long.

"GUN!" he yelled at the top of his voice, at the same time sighting his weapon on the suspect's centre mass and taking up pressure on the trigger.

Now that the moment of truth was finally here, a tremendous sense of calmness descended over Keith Cash. He had often wondered what he would do if he ever found himself standing face to face with a gunman and had a split-second to decide whether or not to end the man's life. He had secretly feared that he would be found wanting at that moment and that he would be unable to pull the trigger, even if doing so would save the lives of countless others.

Now, though, his training kicked in, and he instinctively weighed up the danger to himself and his colleagues, concluding that non-lethal force would be insufficient to nullify it.

Knowing that it was him or the gunman, and holding an honest belief that his life was in imminent danger, Keith Cash did the only thing he could – he fired two well-placed rounds into the car.

His colleague, Lucy Cornwall, who had been the rear passenger in the ARV with him, had reached the same conclusion and, at almost exactly the same time, she had discharged her carbine, also firing two rounds.

As the window shattered inward, and the man inside the cab was driven backwards by the force of the bullets entering his torso, the world around Keith Cash sped up again, and suddenly there was frantic movement everywhere.

As he took a step backwards, stunned by what had happened, his AFO colleagues rushed forward to pull open the driver's door and drag the unresisting suspect out of the cab. After making sure that he had no other firearms on him, they immediately commenced emergency life support. Their driver, Danny Marsh, was on the radio, requesting an ambulance and HEMS. Although the helicopter was out of service, they still had a fleet of fast response vehicles in which expert medical support could be deployed.

Lucy appeared at Keith's side, looking every bit as shaken as he felt. "Why did he do that?" she asked in a daze. "He must've known how it would end."

Keith could only shrug helplessly. He had been wondering exactly the same thing. "Perhaps he wanted suicide by police?" he suggested lamely, referring to the phenomenon in which a suspect deliberately behaved in a threatening manner in order to provoke a lethal response from law enforcement. From his training, Cash knew that this situation fit the profile perfectly. The man on the floor had committed a murder and was facing life imprisonment. Perhaps, when he realised the game was up, he decided that he would rather die than endure long-term incarceration, especially if he had only recently been released from another lengthy prison sentence and couldn't bear the thought of going back inside.

Keith felt a flicker of anger as he considered this. He and Lucy would have to live with what they had just done for the rest of their lives, and if it transpired that the bastard had tricked them into killing him as an alternative to going to jail, that would just make him feel ten times worse.

There are three main areas of UK law covering the use of force. The first is Common Law, which allows someone to use reasonable force in order to prevent crime, carry out a lawful arrest, or recapture someone who is unlawfully at large. The second is Section 3 of The Criminal Law Act, which allows the reasonable use of force in the prevention of crime and in the defence of oneself or another, or in the protection of property. Lastly, there is Section 117 of The Police and Criminal Evidence Act, which allows a constable to use reasonable force in the lawful execution of any power, such as when they are making an arrest or carrying out a search.

Regardless of the legislation relied upon to justify their actions, officers were required to demonstrate that the force was both reasonable and necessary in all the circumstances – in other words, it had to be proportionate to the threat posed. Keith was well aware that the fatal use of force would be subjected to the most intensive scrutiny. After what had just happened, he and Lucy would be placed on restricted duties – desk-bound, in other words – until the Complaints Investigation Bureau and the Independent Police Complaint's Commission had finished their respective investigations and had declared the incident a 'clean shoot'. That could take a very long time, he knew, and if CIB and the IPCC decided it wasn't a 'clean shoot,' then he and Lucy could find themselves gripping the rail – a police euphemism for standing trial – for murder or manslaughter. And the Job hierarchy wondered why rank and file officers were so opposed to routine arming of all officers?

Once the scene was secured, everyone involved would be taken straight to Leman Street police station for the Post Incident Procedure. Apart from the officers involved, there would be CIB, Police Federation representatives and a legal advisor present.

In accordance with established procedures, after the PIP debrief, the officers would make initial notes of the incident. They would then be sent home and would not make their individual full written statements until their return to duty in two days' time.

"We did the right thing, Keith," Lucy said, placing a reassuring hand on his arm and giving it a little squeeze. "We had to take the shot."

He nodded. "I know we did," he replied. "It was him or us." He just hoped that if the suspect dies, the CIB and IPCC would see it the same way.

CHAPTER TWELVE

It was almost 5 p.m. when Tyler and the others arrived back at Arbour Square. The appeal at the RCJ had been heard, and the presiding panel of senior Judges had decreed that they would deliver their judgement in three weeks' time. Until then, there was nothing more that the enquiry team could do, and so the case could be put on the back-burner for a little while.

The office was practically deserted when Tyler and the three DCs who had accompanied him walked in. "Deano, where is everyone?" Jack asked.

Dean Fletcher, the lead researcher on his Intel Cell, was hunched over his desk, his stern features locked in fierce concentration as he ham-fistedly typed up a report. A radio was playing classical music in the background, and it sounded depressingly dull to Jack, like something you'd hear at a funeral parlour.

Dean turned to look at them over the top of his reading glasses. "The team's been seconded to assist Mr Quinlan with the cop killer," he explained gruffly. "Everyone else has gone over to his office for a briefing. Me and Wendy have been given a tonne of research to crack on with, but we can just as easily do that here as in there, and as it's much quieter here, we decided that we might as well stay where we are."

Jack nodded towards the radio, which was playing Tchaikovsky's Serenade for Strings 1st movement. "Are you sure they haven't all just fled the office to get away from that din?" he asked with a crooked grin.

Dean stiffened. "Can't beat a bit of classical music, guv," he insisted.

Not if you're looking for something melancholy to listen to while you slit your wrists, Jack thought.

Just then, Wendy Blake, Jack's other researcher, walked through the door carrying two mugs of steaming hot liquid. Her face brightened when she saw Tyler. "Hello, guv," she greeted him warmly. "Didn't know you were back. Do you want me to make you a hot drink?"

Jack shook his head. "Very kind of you to offer, Wendy, but I'd better not."

He looked at Franklin, Jarvis, and Flowers in turn. "I think it's probably best if we all drop our stuff off at our respective desks and then pop straight over to Andy Quinlan's office to see if we can do anything to help out."

———

"So, I know you've already been through this separately with Andy Quinlan and George Holland," Jack said, "but I want you to tell me what happened."

He was sitting behind his desk, nursing a cup of coffee that Wendy had insisted on making him the moment he returned from Quinlan's office. Dillon, Steve Bull, and George Copeland were sitting on the other side, facing him. Like Jack, they had also benefited from Wendy's kind offer to make them a brew.

Dillon nodded. "Okay," he said with a resigned sigh. "It all started when the hospital phoned to say that Winston was ready for collection. By the time we got there, the breakout was already in progress, and the three PCs guarding him had been overpowered: two drugged, one dead." Dillon paused for a moment, and when he resumed speaking his eyes bored into Jack's, imploring his friend to believe him. "There was nothing we could have done to save that officer. Nothing."

"No one thinks otherwise," Jack said.

Dillon shrugged as if to suggest he didn't care what anyone else thought as long as Tyler believed him. "Anyway, we were lucky enough to spot the getaway car parked in the hospital grounds when we –" he gestured to include Copeland and Bull "– arrived, and we arrested the driver."

"It was Mr Dillon who spotted the car, not us." Steve cut in. "Isn't that right, George?"

"Yeah, that's right, sir," George said. "Not that we wouldn't have seen it ourselves," he added quickly.

"We were in a no-win situation," Dillon said flatly. "It was all happening too fast. George and some AFOs tried to nab Winston and the other three as they came out of the freight elevator on their way to the getaway car, but he spotted them and jumped back in the lift. Then me and Nick Bartholomew almost got him on the third floor, but he got away again. From there on in, it all went horribly pear-shaped." Dillon rolled his neck and then grimaced at the pain it caused him. He had been checked over by a doctor, who had advised him to go sick, but he had ignored the advice and dosed himself up with strong painkillers instead

"Anyway, you know the rest. The cavalry arrived and SO19 set up a perimeter. We were getting ready to evacuate when we were informed that someone was trying to break into the HEMS facility on the roof. I went up there with Nick Bartholomew and Pat Connors, a gov'nor on the ARVs, but we were too late. The bastard had already taken off." He shrugged again as if to say: what more is there to tell.

"I see," Jack said, stroking his chin thoughtfully and feeling the rasp of a day's stubble on his fingers.

It was always easy to speak with the benefit of hindsight, but if Skinner had followed Dillon's advice in the first place, and posted a more formidable deterrent, Winston would still be in custody, and PC Morrison would probably still be alive.

As it was, Dillon, Steve, and George had stumbled across an armed breakout and they were lucky to have escaped unharmed. They had done their best under the most testing of circumstances, and they had almost succeeded in recapturing Winston.

Nick Bartholomew had probably saved Dillon's life, and his efforts had earned him a minor concussion. After being checked out at the hospital, he had been sent home against his wishes to rest. To his credit, instead of worrying about his own health, the only thing on Nick's mind had been finding a way to be temporarily seconded back to AMIP when he returned to duty in a few days' time. Dillon had promised he would speak to Ray Speed to see if it could be arranged.

Terry Grier had also done incredibly well, pursuing the bogus porter out of the hospital, alone and unarmed. The male – they still hadn't established his identity – had undergone extensive emergency surgery after being shot by the ARV crew who had finally stopped him, and the last report stated that he was somehow clinging to life by the thinnest of threads. His chances of surviving the day were considered slim at best, but miracles happened.

There was no point in trying to dissect what had happened now, Jack decided pragmatically. It would all come out during the post investigative debrief when every aspect of the investigation would be reviewed. Right now, he needed his team to be fully focused on getting on with the job and recapturing Winston.

"Right, I take it that you've already completed your MG11s?" Tyler asked.

"Yep, our statements are already in Andy's MIR," Dillon confirmed.

"Okay. I've spoken to George Holland. DCI Quinlan's team has taken PC Morrison's murder. However, as we don't have a live job at the moment, our team will be assisting them until further notice. I promise I'll do my best to ensure that you three get the chance to be in on Winston's takedown, if and when we find the bastard, but in the meantime –" he looked at Bull first and then Copeland, "I need you two to go and put yourselves at Mr Quinlan's disposal."

"You got it, boss," Bull said. He stood up and grabbed Copeland's arm, jerking it hard. "Come on, George. We've got places to go and people to see."

"Have we?" Copeland asked, confused.

"I'll explain on the way," Bull told him. George could be a bit slow on the uptake sometimes.

When they were alone Dillon turned to Tyler. "I'm really sorry,

Jack. I feel like I've tarnished your reputation. You know that you're Holland's golden boy. He thinks very highly of you and I wouldn't want to spoil that."

"Dill, you're being silly. You said it yourself: you were in a no-win situation. You nearly achieved the impossible anyway. Now stop berating yourself. God, how many times have you said that to me over the years, um?" Jack stood up and walked around the side of the desk.

"We've had the debrief, now it's time to move on. We've got a lot of work to do and I don't want to see you moping around feeling sorry for yourself, especially when it's not warranted." Tyler placed a hand on his friend's massive shoulder.

"Thanks, Jack," Dillon said. "Look, I know none of this is my fault, but I keep thinking that if I had kicked up more of a stink about Winston having an armed guard this might not have happened."

"Dill, you did kick up a stink, but ultimately it wasn't your decision to make. Besides, I've managed to take a sneak peek at the drug squad's risk assessment. They did take into account the fact that he was detained in possession of a firearm, and that he had shot two police officers immediately prior to arrest – but that was then and this is now. He's a drug-dealing pimp, not a cartel leader, and there was no intelligence to suggest that he or his known associates currently had a firearms capacity. Realistically, it would have been nigh on impossible to justify deploying armed officers, even if the drug squad had concurred with your view." That was true, at least on paper, but if he or Dillon had been tasked with writing the assessment up it would have read very differently, and it would have concluded that an armed guard was necessary.

Dillon considered that for a moment and then nodded. "Fair enough. So, what do we do now?"

"Has the getaway driver said anything yet?" Tyler asked.

Dillon laughed. It was a harsh, humourless sound. "He's been interviewed, made no comment, and is looking at being charged with TDA and possession of Class A drugs as holding charges."

"Have they searched his drum yet?"

"Yeah, they carried out a Section 18 search at his flat before he was interviewed. I think they were half hoping to find Winston hiding there, but that was never going to happen. They recovered some more drugs and some drug paraphernalia, but nothing significant."

Section 18 of PACE – the Police and Criminal Evidence Act 1984 – allowed the police to search any property occupied, owned or controlled by a person in custody for an arrestable offence for evidence connected to that offence or similar offences without first having to obtain a warrant.

"Did he have a phone on him?" Jack asked.

"He did. Obviously, it's been seized."

"Good. Let's get call data and cell site applications submitted. If any of the numbers he's been in contact with today mirror his movements up to the point where he arrived at the hospital, they might belong to the two suspects who are still adrift and we can look at pinging them to see where they are now. Also, let's get an urgent research package started to see if any of his known associates fit the profile of our mysterious doctor, nurse or the fake porter that SO19 took out."

As soon as the man who had been shot was out of danger, a set of fingerprints would be taken and rushed up to the fingerprint bureau at NSY. If he croaked, the same thing would happen. Ironically, knowing what they now knew, the risk assessment had been ramped up and he was under armed guard at the Royal London ICU.

"On that note, do you know if the bloke who was shot had a mobile on him? If he did, we need to do the same thing with his phone."

"I believe he did, but I'll check with Susie Sergeant afterwards."

"And what about the LOS Ford Scorpio? Has it been taken to Charlton for a forensic exam?"

"That I don't know," Dillon said.

"It needs to be properly examined, Dill," Jack said. "I reckon there's a very good chance our unknown suspect's fingerprints and DNA will be all over that car." He frowned, recalling something that he'd overheard Bull and Copeland discussing earlier. "Wasn't a bag of drugs and a mirror found in it? Or am I just imagining that?"

Dillon's mind flashed back to the scene and George holding up a bag of white powder and a lady's compact mirror. "You're right," he said. "With everything else going on I had forgotten about that."

"Surely there'll be fingerprints and DNA on those?" Jack said.

Dillon seemed excited by this. "I'll have a word with George, and get them fast-tracked up to the lab. Also, there were several jackets in the car. We're bound to be able to get wearer DNA from those."

"Make sure you let Andy know all this, so he can document what needs to be done in his Decision Log."

When Dillon left, Jack was pleased to see that the spring was back in his friend's step and that he seemed less burdened than he had when the meeting started. Maybe the pep talk had helped, or maybe it was just the fact that Jack had given him some actions to occupy his mind. Either way, it was better than seeing Dillon torture himself over something that wasn't his fault.

Jack walked out into the main office and switched the TV on, hoping to catch the main news. Unfortunately, the closing credits were already rolling, but he decided to hang on for the regional BBC bulletin to see what that said about the incident.

Sure enough, the show opened with a tantalisingly brief segment on the murder of a police officer and the killer's dramatic escape in the hijacked air ambulance. The presenter promised there would be more on that story later, but viewers would first have to endure lacklustre pieces about a James Bond look-alike contest, a local authority that had painted some yellow lines around a row of parked cars and promptly ticketed them, a dog that could sing, and an inner London school that was in deep shit with OFSTED because of its sub-standard performance figures.

Jack decided to give it a miss.

He meandered along the corridor until he came to the main office for Andy Quinlan's team, where he stopped and peeked through the door. Where his own team's office was deserted, Andy's was a buzzing hive of activity. There wasn't a spare seat anywhere, and officers were talking animatedly on telephones, hurriedly typing reports up on their computers, filling out forms and generally rushing around trying to get the job done. It was always like this when a new job broke – manic, but with a great sense of purpose. He loved it, and he was a little disappointed that Andy had got to keep this job, even though it made perfect operational sense, seeing as he was about to go into the frame anyway, and he had been the SIO for Winston's original arrest last year.

Jack found himself at a bit of a loss. Although his team was assisting Andy's, there was nothing for him to do. An investigation only required one DCI, and he could hardly start peering over Andy's shoulder every few minutes; it would look like he was trying to muscle in and take over. With a heavy sigh, Jack turned around and wandered back to his office. He would call Andy for a quick chat, just to see how he was getting on, and then he would head off home. Dillon would let him know if anything exciting happened.

They were holed up in a little one-bedroom flat just off Star Lane in Plaistow. It was situated in the basement of a run-down, Victorian terraced house that had been divided into three separate accommodations.

The flat was currently being sub-let by one of Garston's drug runners, an anemic rat-faced white boy whose name was Rodney Dawlish, although pretty much everyone who knew him called him Rodent. The unflattering nickname had come about as a result of his unfortunate resemblance to a sewer rat. It wasn't just the protruding upper front teeth or the pointy nose and bushy side-whiskers; it was also his furtive and twitchy mannerisms and the way that he didn't so much walk as scurry along.

Garston had rung Rodent while the pilot was preparing the helicopter for take-off, and he had ordered the boy to meet them at the edge of the wasteland in which they had subsequently forced the pilot to land. From there, Rodent had driven them straight back to the cramped little flat in his clapped-out Rover 216 hatchback.

Had everything gone smoothly, Garston would have driven Winston straight out of London to the safe house he had rented near the Sussex coast; it was a tiny cottage in the middle of nowhere, surrounded by marshes and well away from prying eyes. Then, after laying low for a couple of days, Winston would have been slipped onto a fishing boat during the hours of darkness and smuggled across the channel. However, following the brawl in the elevator, it had quickly become apparent that Winston wasn't up to an arduous journey, so he had been forced to recalibrate his plan and call on Rodent's services instead.

Garston planned to review the situation in the morning, but right now the most important thing was that they were off the streets in a safe location unknown to the police.

Garston took himself on a quick tour of the pokey little flat. In addition to the single grungy bedroom, it consisted of a small living room, an even smaller kitchen, and a mold-infested bathroom with an avocado suite that had gone out of fashion years ago. The rickety toilet was lacking a seat, and there were some horrendous brown stains at the bottom of the bowl. Unbuttoning his zip, he found himself hoping that he wouldn't need to do more than take a piss while they were there.

After flushing the chain and rinsing his hands, Garston looked around for a towel, but there was none to be seen. Wiping his hands on his trousers, he joined the others in the living room. It was inexcusably messy, and it stank of last night's Indian takeaway.

"Sorry. Been meaning to clean the place up, but just haven't got around to it yet," Rodent said, clearly embarrassed.

With Angela's help, Garston led Winston along the narrow corridor into the bedroom. He noticed how her tone of voice and demeanour immediately became deferential and compliant in his uncle's presence, and it grated on him that she was yet to show him this same degree of respect, although he had to admit that her attitude had marginally improved since he'd given her the slap at the hospital.

After undressing him, they laid him down on Rodent's bed, but it was too small for his giant frame. The middle of the thin mattress sagged down almost to the floor when he laid on it, and the springs creaked and groaned under his weight.

Garston spotted some nasty looking stains on the bedsheet, but he didn't say anything and Winston was too ill to even notice. As they covered him in a thin, grimy quilt, his feet and ankles protruded beyond the mattress and hung uncomfortably over the end of the bed.

When Angela peeled back his dressing, she was shocked to see that only about a third of his stitches remained intact. The rest had popped, and the inflamed wound had already started to leak.

Leaving Winston to rest, the others retired to the living room. Rodent was given an impromptu shopping list and sent out to get some supplies, including paracetamol and fresh bandages from a nearby chemist in Barking Road.

When Rodent returned, about forty minutes later, Angela was given the unpleasant task of washing the wound with warm salt water and then changing the dressing. She applied two whole packets of steri strips, but most of them quickly came undone.

Winston complained throughout, and he threatened to hit her more than once if she didn't start taking greater care.

The chemist had advised Rodent that if the patient was in considerable pain, he could alternate between paracetamol and ibuprofen, and that would allow him to take pain medication every two hours.

When Angela had finally finished administering to Winston's needs, Garston instructed Rodent to give her have a wrap of Brown as a reward. She hungrily snatched it from his hand and retreated to the bathroom to shoot up.

After injecting the smack, Angela returned to the living room and crashed out on the imitation leather sofa. Before long, she had slipped into a fitful slumber.

While Rodent put the kettle on, Garston turned on the TV. To his horror, the breakout was plastered all over the news. As he watched, the screen filled with a custody record photo of Claude Winston, taken when he was charged with the two attempted murders back in November. The usual *'this man is armed and extremely dangerous, and should not be approached by the public'* rhetoric was quoted by the newsreader.

Ignoring Angela's snoring, Garston buried his head in his hands and asked himself: *what the fuck was Claude thinking?* How could his barbaric uncle have been stupid enough to think he'd get away with killing a defenceless cop in cold blood.

If the bloodthirsty idiot had just left everything to him, they would all be safely ensconced in a remote little Sussex cottage right now, chilling out as they waited for their contact to come and collect

Winston for his night-time jaunt across the channel. Once in France, he would have been free to jump on a plane to Jamaica and disappear forever.

Hopefully, Garston could still make that happen. While Rodent had been out shopping, he'd spoken to his fisherman contact. The man was still willing to help, but he was now demanding more money. Winston wouldn't be fit to travel for a few days, and they had agreed to leave the passage across the channel until the end of the week. Until then, they would rest up here and let Winston recover.

Logistically, now that Winston was public enemy number one, and his ugly mug was being plastered all over the television, it was going to be much harder to move him. The trip to the coast would have to be made under the cover of darkness, and he would have to hide Claude away in the back of a van.

By tomorrow, the story would be all over the papers and everyone would know what his stupid thug of an uncle looked like. Garston considered asking Claude to chop off his precious trademark dreads. That would make him marginally less conspicuous. Somehow, though, he just couldn't see the cantankerous bastard agreeing to that.

As much as he hated the grubby little flat, Garston didn't feel that he could trust either Angela or Rodent to take care of Winston without supervision, so he resigned himself to staying there with them, at least for the first night.

His mind turned to Errol. He'd tried calling him, but the idiot's phone just rang until the answerphone kicked in. Then he'd made the mistake of ringing Errol's other half, Sonia – a brassy woman with an attitude to match – only to have the stroppy fat bitch give him a massive ear-bashing, ranting that she hadn't heard from Errol all day and promising that he was in big trouble when he finally showed up.

There had been a worrying segment on the news about a man being shot and seriously injured by police following an armed incident in East India Dock Road, but they hadn't revealed anything about the man's colour or identity. Nor had they disclosed any further information about the incident.

Surely, that couldn't be anything to do with Errol – could it?

CHAPTER THIRTEEN

Tuesday 11th January 2000

The briefing in the conference room at Arbour Square was due to kick off at eight o'clock sharp, and Jack only made it with a couple of minutes to spare.

The room was crammed full of people when he entered, and although he knew most of them, there were a few that he didn't recognise. He assumed they were detectives drafted in from the host borough to assist with the enquiry. It wasn't uncommon for AMIP to do that, especially with a major enquiry like this one.

At the front of the room, five chairs had been arranged to face the assembled officers. Quinlan sat front and centre, nervously adjusting the Joe Ninety spectacles that gave him such a professorial look. Nearer to fifty than forty, there wasn't a single strand of grey visible in Quinlan's shiny mop of black hair, which made Jack wonder if he secretly dyed it to keep it that way.

The matronly figure of DI Carol Keaton and DS Susie Sergeant occupied the two seats to his left, and DCS George Holland sat on his right, leaning back in his chair while he chatted with Quinlan.

Holland had absent-mindedly tucked his thumbs under his trademark Gordon Gekko braces and was currently pushing the elastic outwards in a style reminiscent of the TV comedian, Bobby Ball.

Does he ever take those things off? Jack asked himself as an irreverent image of Holland, tucked up in bed at night, pyjama bottoms held aloft by his braces, popped into his head. He quickly smothered the childish snigger that was brewing before it could reach his lips.

Quinlan waved him over and directed him to take the empty chair next to Holland. "We're about to kick off so you'd better get a move on," he whispered.

The mood in the room was sombre, business-like, but then they were here to hunt for a cop killer so it was hardly an occasion for joviality.

Dillon was sitting in the front row, almost directly opposite Tyler. He looked as fresh as a daisy, even though he'd probably had less than half the amount of sleep Jack had. Splendidly turned out as always, he didn't appear to be any the worse for wear after being whacked with a lead-filled sap the day before. Jack could only marvel at his friend's recuperative powers, knowing that almost anyone else would have gone sick. It really did confirm the old adage; no sense, no feeling.

The rest of Jack's team were mingled in amongst Quinlan's, and – unlike Dillon – they all looked pretty knackered. After speaking to Kelly earlier, Jack knew that most of them hadn't finished work until well after midnight, and had only managed to grab a few hours of sleep before dragging themselves back in this morning. He'd experienced a little twinge of guilt on hearing that because, while they had all been busy grafting, he had been relaxing at home, enjoying his Indian takeaway, treating himself to a bottle of Peroni, and watching one of his favourite James Bond films on VHS.

After checking his watch, Holland stood up and cleared his throat. "Right, there's a lot to get through, so let's crack on." Conversation amongst the waiting officers had been subdued anyway, but now it petered out until there was absolute silence.

"Yesterday, just after midday, PC Stanley Morrison, a forty year old officer based at Forest Gate police station, was shot dead at the Royal London, killed by a single bullet to the rear of the head. The fatal shot was administered while he was lying face down on a hospital bed with a pillowcase over his head. He had been handcuffed by that stage and posed no threat."

As he considered his next words, his face visibly clouded with anger. "Make no mistake, this was a cold-blooded execution carried out for the killer's personal gratification." Holland paused a moment to let that sink in. "PC Morrison was on duty with PCs Alec O'Brien and Sharon Lassiter, and they were providing a hospital watch on a man called Claude Winston, a drug dealing pimp who's been on remand at HMP Pentonville since last November, having been charged with the attempted murder of two police officers."

There was a collective intake of breath from those who were unfamiliar with Winston's history.

"A joint risk assessment had been carried out by the drug squad, who were producing Winston, and the Duty Officer at Forest Gate, who was providing the staff to watch over him. They concluded that an armed guard was unnecessary. On paper, I cannot fault that decision," Holland said, but his acerbic tone made it abundantly clear that he didn't agree with it.

"On January fourth, that's last Monday, the drug squad produced Winston to Forest Gate on a three day layover. However, before they could interview him, his appendix burst and he was rushed to the Royal London Hospital for surgery."

"Pity he didn't croak on the operating table," Kevin Murray piped up from his second row seat, "or get gunned down by SO19 during the escape like his mate."

A mumbled chorus of assent echoed around the room, and even Tony Dillon, who couldn't abide Murray, nodded supportively.

"I agree," Holland said, holding his hands up to quieten them down, "but unfortunately he didn't. Winston was discharged yesterday morning, and arrangements were made to transport him back to Pentonville at one o'clock. However, with the help of three associates, two males and a female, he managed to escape in spectacular style less than an hour before he was due to be collected."

"How did they know Winston was being moved, guv?" Dean Fletcher asked.

"We're not sure they did know," Holland said.

Quinlan chimed in with his opinion. "I'm inclined to think they would have waited until he was in the car before springing him if they'd known he was being moved. That's how I would have done it."

"Let's concentrate on the known facts and leave the speculation till later," Holland said, looking around tetchily. "As I was saying, PCs O'Brien and Lassiter were standing guard outside the room, while PC Morrison sat inside with the prisoner. The suspects, one dressed as a doctor, one as a porter, and one as a nurse, forced them into Winston's private room at gunpoint. They restrained O'Brien and Lassiter using their own quick-cuffs and then drugged them before shooting Morrison."

Murray's hand shot up, interrupting the flow of Holland's briefing.

"Yes, Kevin?" he said, clearly annoyed at the distraction.

"Boss, have you got any idea why they merely drugged O'Brien and Lassiter but shot Morrison?"

It was actually a reasonable question, Jack thought, which was unusual from Murray. Normally, his contributions were limited to telling crass jokes and making smutty innuendo.

Holland shook his head. "I don't. We know they could just as easily have sedated him as they did the others because we found a syringe full of what we suspect will turn out to be ketamine on the floor next to the bed. I know DI Dillon has a theory. I suppose now is as good a time as any to share it with you all. Dillon?"

Dillon stood up and looked around the room. "For those of you who don't know me, I was one of the officers who arrested Winston back in November. The man is as nasty as they come and, in case you haven't already worked it out, he hates police officers. I think that after the gang drugged O'Brien and Lassiter, but before they got around to injecting Morrison, they made the mistake of giving Winston a firearm. Had they done this earlier, I suspect that we'd probably have three dead colleagues on our hands instead of one."

Dick Jarvis raised his hand. "But why risk the noise of the gunshot alerting hospital staff?" he asked in his frightfully posh accent. "Surely it would have been more prudent to drug him like the others?" Dick was the youngest person on Tyler's team and the most recent addition.

A graduate entry, he was still a little wet behind the ears, and the wanton brutality of the people they had to deal with on AMIP still surprised him at times.

Dillon shrugged. "You have to understand that Winston isn't rational. If Morrison resisted when they went to inject him, or if he said something disrespectful, or if he even looked at him in a manner he didn't like, that would be reason enough in Winston's eyes."

The room had gone deathly silent as the detectives digested Dillon's words, and Jack could tell from the thoughtful expressions on their faces that every officer present was mentally putting themselves in Morrison's place and imagining what he must have gone through. And for what? The killing had not only been senseless, it had been totally avoidable.

"It's a sobering thought, and an indication of how dangerous the man we're hunting is," Holland said, indicating for Dillon to sit down again. "We know they planned to leave the hospital in a stolen car, but when Mr Dillon and his two colleagues turned up unexpectedly, Winston had to radically alter his plans. There's no denying that the gang were incredibly lucky; one of the suspects made good his escape on foot while the other three managed to make their way to the roof and hijack the HEMS helicopter. That was found on wasteland in Canning Town a short time later, and we think it only put down there because India 99 and India 98 were rapidly converging on it. I'll hand over to Mr Quinlan to take you through the investigation from that point onwards."

"Thank you," Quinlan said, standing up and self-consciously fiddling with his glasses. "Killing a policeman obviously wasn't enough to satiate their bloodlust because, after landing, the fugitives shot the pilot, a man called Peter Myers. Fortunately, they waited until they'd alighted the aircraft to open fire on him and, as luck would have it, the plexiglass windscreen deflected both bullets. One shot missed entirely, the other gouged his helmet. Although he was rendered unconscious by the impact and he sustained a nasty concussion, no permanent harm appears to have has been caused."

"Was he able to shed any light on where they went afterwards?" Steve Bull asked. He was sitting next to Dillon in the front row.

Quinlan shook his head. "No, Steve. As I said, he was badly concussed and we haven't been able to speak to him yet, but that'll be addressed as a priority today, and hopefully, he might be able to provide some useful information. Perhaps, I could ask you to look into that for me?"

"Of course," Bull said, wishing he'd kept his gob shut.

Another hand shot up in the third row. "I think I'm going to ask you all to hold back on your questions until I've finished," Quinlan said, waving the man's hand down. He smiled reassuringly at the man who was now looking rather embarrassed. "Don't worry, I promise you'll get another chance to ask your question, but I want to complete my overview first."

He cleared his throat. "So, as I mentioned earlier, one of the suspects made good his escape on foot. He then carjacked a London Taxi outside the hospital, but this was later spotted by DS Sergeant and DC Murray, and they followed it along East India Dock Road until SO19 arrived and carried out a hard stop just shy of the slip road to the Blackwall Tunnel Northern Approach. Instead of surrendering, the suspect pulled a gun on them and promptly got himself shot. Unfortunately, despite making it through surgery, he passed away during the night."

"Not exactly a loss, is it boss?" Murray said, earning himself a look of disapproval from George Holland.

Quinlan carried on as if no one had spoken. "A wet set was taken from him at the hospital during the early hours and rushed up to NSY for urgent comparisons. Do we have a result back yet?" The question was addressed to Susie Sergeant.

"Yes, boss," she said, consulting her blue daybook. "The deceased is an IC3 male called Errol Heston, a low-level thug with petty form for possession of cannabis, a couple of ABHs and some public order offences. Basic research hasn't revealed any obvious connection between him and Winston."

Quinlan thanked her. "So, where are we as far as the investigation is concerned? Well, we've already seized all the CCTV from inside the hospital, and I'm hoping its footage will yield clear facial shots of Winston's, as yet, unidentified accomplices before they donned their masks. The getaway car's been impounded and will be forensically examined later today. Hopefully, that will give us the unknown suspect's fingerprints and DNA. The car itself was stolen from Beckton train station a couple of hours before the escape, and we'll combine local authority CCTV and ANPR to backtrack its movements between those times."

Every time a vehicle passes an Automatic Number Plate Recognition camera its details are run through the database to see if there are any interest reports on it. If there are, for instance, because it's shown as being stolen, concerned in crime, making off without payment – which basically means that the driver has driven out of the garage without paying for their petrol – or it's marked up as having no insurance, the hit is flagged up to local patrols for them to be on the lookout for it. However, as the car hadn't yet been reported stolen, there were no reports on the Ford Scorpio, which meant a retrospective search would have to be carried out on NADAC - the National ANPR data centre – to see if it had passed any of the system's cameras without triggering an activation.

"The getaway driver, Mullings, had a mobile on him. We've requested call data, cell site and billing information from that. As DI Dillon suggested last night, there's a good chance Mullings will have been communicating with the others involved in the breakout by phone. We might be able to link them all by calls made between their phones or by their handsets mirroring each other's route on the way to the hospital. If we get any matches, the plan is to ping the outstanding phones and see if we can narrow down their current location. A pound to a penny says that the two unknown suspects are still with Winston, so if we find them, we also find him."

Quinlan looked around the room until his eyes came to rest on Juliet Kennedy, who was dressed as though she were about to go out on a dinner date. The Ilford born Crime Scene Manager had a reputation for always being glammed up, even when processing the most gruesome of scenes. "Where are we with forensics, Juliet?" he asked.

"Record photography on the room where PC Morrison was shot has been completed, and it's been forensicated for fingerprints, DNA and fibres. I'm not overly hopeful that we'll get anything out of that if

I'm honest, Andy. The suspects were gloved up and wearing surgical masks. However, the syringe that was found on the floor by the bed might give us something. I very much doubt that they intended to leave that behind, and it might well yield prints or DNA. Obviously, the contents of the syringe will be tested and compared to whatever chemicals were in O'Brien and Lassiter's blood. The hospital thinks it was probably a strong dose of ketamine or something similar, but we'll have to wait and see. The Ford Scorpio's over at Charlton. That'll be examined today. The bag of white powder and the compact mirror that George Copeland found in the Ford Scorpio is being rushed up to the lab this morning, as are the coats that were also recovered inside. I think there's a really good chance we'll get DNA and prints off those. The SPM is being carried out at one p.m. today over at Poplar mortuary. Who's going to that, by the way?"

Any suspicious death required a Special Post Mortem examination to be carried out by a Home Office Forensic Pathologist, and the process normally took between four and five hours to complete.

"Carol's the DI who'll be attending, and Kevin Murray's the exhibits officer," Quinlan informed her, pointing at each of the officers as he spoke.

"Carol, can you make sure a pathologist's briefing document is prepared before you go, and I'll meet you there at about twelve-fifty," Juliet said.

"I'll get it done straight after the meeting," Carol Keating, a no-nonsense woman who reminded Jack of the late Hattie Jacques, promised.

Quinlan's eyes roamed the room until they came to rest on a tall, stick insect thin, DC with a thick bush of unruly brown hair that resembled a bird's nest, a huge beak of a nose, and eyes the size of saucers. "Dazza, how are we getting on with the CCTV?" Quinlan asked.

"Not as well as I'd like," Darren Blyth informed him in his thick Mancunian accent. His voice was surprisingly deep, which wasn't at all how Jack had expected him to sound.

"It's all been downloaded for us by the hospital but, typically, it's not in a compatible media format to play on our antiquated system.

I've got a tech specialist coming over from Newlands Park later today to run it through a programme that'll supposedly convert it. If that works, we should be able to view it and produce some stills later today."

Quinlan didn't look happy, but there was nothing he could do about it. "Let me know as soon as we can view the footage please, Darren," he said. "Susie's going to be conducting further interviews with Gifford Mullings, the getaway driver, at midday and it would really help if we can play a CCTV compilation of the hospital footage to him."

"Actually, Andy, I've got a bloke on my team who's a bit of a geek," Jack said, leaning across to address Quinlan. "He might already have some software that can assist you. Reggie?"

Tyler scanned the room for DC Reg Parker, a cherubic looking man in his mid-thirties.

"Over here, boss," Reggie said from several rows back. He raised a hand and waved to help Tyler zone in on him.

"Reggie, can you have a gander at this CCTV for Mr Quinlan, see if you can work your magic on it?"

"Will do," Parker said, "but I can't promise anything."

"I'd be obliged if you would try anyway," Quinlan said, smiling encouragingly. "It might save us a lot of time."

"I'll get straight on it after the meeting," Reggie assured him.

Quinlan paused to look around the room before continuing. "Statistically speaking, absconders from custody don't tend to remain at large for terribly long before being recaptured. The good news – from our point of view – is that all Winston's assets were seized when he was charged last year, so he won't have ready access to large amounts of cash, which means he'll be completely dependent on others to help him. He's likely to be holed up somewhere local while he tries to work out what to do next. With that in mind, today's plan is to visit all his known associates and start putting pressure on them. I want them left in no doubt that we're going to make all of their lives a living hell until we've recaptured Winston."

Quinlan's jaw set determinedly as he looked around the room making eye contact with as many detectives as he could. "If anyone you speak to even remotely resembles the mysterious doctor or nurse, have their phones straight off them and get a statement from them outlining their movements for yesterday. Don't take any shit; if anyone fails to cooperate fully, nick them on suspicion of being involved. I want the word getting out that we're not messing about."

Jack was impressed. Andy wasn't normally the pushy type, but this morning he was coming over as a real ball-breaker.

Quinlan held up an A4 sized manila file. "The Intel Cell has put together a detailed list of the people we want seen and the questions we want asked. After the briefing, you'll be divided into teams, and I want all these people blitzed today. Susie, anything from you?"

Susie Sergeant had been appointed as Case Officer for the investigation, and when she stood up her green eyes smouldered with a desire for justice. "Our job is to uphold the law, which means remaining professional and impartial even though the people we're hunting have killed one of our own. That said, we need to let them know that our gang is bigger than theirs, so as the gov'nor has already indicated, we will be imposing a zero-tolerance policy when we engage these people. We're not taking any lip; we're not being fobbed off. We need to get information, and they need to know that we are going to keep cranking up the pressure until we get it. Once the briefing's over, grab a quick brew from the canteen and then come straight back up to the office to collect your respective taskings from me."

Quinlan thanked her, and then, as promised, he took questions from the assembled officers, starting with the man who had raised his hand earlier, an officer who had been seconded in from Forest Gate. Unbelievably, all he'd wanted to know was what the operation was called and, more importantly, the overtime code.

"It's Operation Alabama," Quinlan informed him. All murder investigations were recorded on HOLMES – Home Office Large Major Enquiry System – and the machine-generated random titles for each account that was opened. Last year it had been English towns and cities; this year it looked like they were going with North American towns and cities. "You don't need a code, just put that down."

When the Q&A session finished, he gave them fifteen minutes to grab a drink and pop to the loo.

"One last thing," Holland bellowed as the assembled officers started to rise. They all sank back into their chairs and the room became quiet again. "The people we're after are extremely dangerous, so take proper precautions out there today. Take your personal protection equipment with you. Wear your Met-vests. Make sure you have fully charged radios and phones, and please make sure that you update DS Sergeant or the Intel Cell when you arrive and when you leave each address so that we know you're safe. The last thing we want is for anyone else to be harmed, and we need to keep track of where everyone is so that we can send help if it's required."

CHAPTER FOURTEEN

It was almost 10 a.m. when Winston finally awoke. Garston had been checking in on him every half hour since seven, but he had decided not to wake his uncle, figuring that the more rest he had, the better he would feel. Besides, Claude was a lot easier to handle when he was comatose.

Angela should have been sharing the work, but she was still fast asleep in the lounge, and when he'd left the room a few moments ago she had been laying on the sofa with her mouth and legs both open in a most unladylike fashion.

Much to his irritation, the hooker had been prone to outbursts of gibberish in her sleep, and at various stages throughout the night, she had suddenly sat bolt upright, shouted out something unintelligible, pulled a distressed face and then flopped back down again to continue her restless slumber. He had lost track of the times she had disturbed him by doing that.

Rodent had been out most of the night, selling drugs, and hadn't returned until just after 3 a.m. Slinking into the cramped living room as quietly as he could, he had uncomplainingly curled up on the floor in a sleeping bag he had put aside before going out.

While he hadn't been noisy, he had been gassy, and the room soon grew thick with the rancid smell of his farts.

By default, Garston had been left with the lumpy armchair and, as a result, his back was now in agony from where a protruding spring had been poking into it all night.

With the flat's central heating system up the spout and his winter jacket left in the getaway car, Garston had been forced to requisition one of Rodent's tatty old coats to use as a makeshift blanket. Unfortunately, the flimsy garment had proven woefully inadequate, offering next to no protection against the bitter cold that had seeped into his bones throughout the night.

"What time is it?" Winston asked, looking around the room in confusion. He tried to sit up but immediately winced in pain.

"Let me help you," Garston offered, but as he moved forward to assist, Winston shrugged him off angrily.

"I can manage," he snapped, struggling himself up into a sitting position. He glared at Garston as though the pain was his fault.

"This place is a shithole," Winston complained after taking in his surroundings properly for the first time since they had arrived the previous day. "And it's freezing cold." He pulled the blanket up under his chin and hugged his arms across it. "I'd be warmer in fucking Siberia."

Garston shrugged. *I wish you were in Siberia*, he thought.

"Best I could do in the circumstances," he said.

Garston was cold too, and he was sorely tempted to point out that if Winston hadn't shot the cop, they'd have all spent the night in a cosy little cottage down by the coast, with central heating that worked and comfortable beds. Instead, between the discomfort of the broken chair, the arctic conditions of the flat and Angela's frequent outbursts, Garston had hardly managed to grab any sleep at all, and to top off the experience, his poor aching spine felt as though one of his vertebrae would snap if he made any sudden moves. Of course, it would've been unwise to mention any of this to his selfish uncle so he just kept quiet.

"I'm hungry," Winston snapped, scowling at him petulantly. "Get me some food."

Biting his tongue again, Garston turned to leave.

"Wait. I need a leak, so get Angela to sort out the food while you help me into the toilet."

Forcing his face to remain impassive, Garston turned to face his uncle. "Your every wish is my command," he said with an elaborate bow.

"Don't take the piss," Winston growled, and promptly threw a lumpy pillow at him.

Garston sidestepped the cushion, shook his head in despair, and walked out of the room.

"Where d'ya think you're going?" Winston shouted after him. "I need that pillow!"

"Get it yourself," Garston mumbled under his breath as he closed the creaking door behind him.

As he trudged back to the lounge to wake Angela up, he heard Winston clamber out of bed, complaining about having to retrieve his own pillow. When the cantankerous bastard yelped in pain, Garston allowed himself a petty smile of satisfaction.

He checked his phone in case the fisherman who was going to smuggle Winston to France had called him, but he hadn't. Sonia had though. He had a series of missed calls from her. He pulled a face; she was probably ringing to shout at him again because Errol had finally turned up and had confessed everything to her like the weak-willed idiot he was. Garston couldn't face dealing with her ranting at him right now; he would call her back later.

Angela hadn't moved since he'd left the room, so he impatiently shook her arm until she stirred, and then yanked her up into a sitting position.

"Aaargh!" she cried, confused and disorientated.

"Get up," he demanded, venting a tiny portion of the anger he felt for his uncle on the confused prostitute.

Wrapping her arms around her body and shivering with cold, Angela stared vacantly ahead; a pale-faced zombie with dark rings under bloodshot eyes.

"Claude's hungry. You need to sort him out some breakfast, and when that's done, you'll need to clean his wound and change his dressing."

Angela sluggishly pulled her knees up to her chest. Sniffing back the snot that was trickling from her nose, she groaned as though she were about to die and let her forehead sag onto her knees.

"Are you listening to me?" Garston demanded, shoving her shoulder so hard that she nearly toppled off the edge of the sofa.

Returning her stockinged feet to the floor, Angela wiped her nose along the length of her forearm and sniffed some more. "Leave me alone, I don't feel well." The words were spoken so softly that they were almost inaudible, but the sentiment of self-pity they conveyed came through loud and strong.

Garston's eyes narrowed. When he spoke, his voice was thick with scorn. "Fucking useless whore, pull yourself together and get on with it. When you've done as I've told you, I'll sort you out something to make you feel better."

Angela gave him a wild-eyed stare and then ran a trembling hand through her dishevelled hair. "I need something now. I feel terrible."

That was the trouble with using addicts; once the drugs wore off and the downer began to kick in, they were unable to function properly or to think about anything apart from where they were going to get their next fix from.

It was pathetic.

Garston regarded her as though she were sub-human. "I promise I'll make you feel a whole lot worse if you don't get a fucking move on," he warned her.

Even in that state, Angela knew a threat when she heard one. "Okay, okay," she said through lips that were dry and cracked. "Just give me a minute to get my shit together."

In the corner of the room, the hood of the sleeping bag was pulled back and Rodent's bleary-eyed face appeared from within and he started scratching at the whiskers on his face. "Anything I can do to help?" he asked, groggily.

Garston nodded. "Make sure this worthless slag gets its sorry arse into the kitchen to rustle up some breakfast while I help Claude into the bathroom. If she isn't in there by the time I return, I'll hold you responsible." With that, he turned and stormed out of the room.

By half past ten, Winston had been toileted and fed – three slices of burnt toast with lukewarm beans splashed over them, and a mug of steaming hot tea to wash it down - and his wound had been washed. Garston hadn't said anything while it was being cleaned, but he was worried about the state of it, and as soon as she finished applying the new dressing, he signalled for Angela to follow him out of the room.

"Do you think his wound might be infected?" he asked her as they walked back into the kitchen where Rodent was leaning against the worktop and shovelling cereal into his mouth.

Angela's shrug was listless. "I dunno," she replied, and from the lacklustre expression on her face, Garston could tell that she didn't much care either.

"I don't think it should be that red or swollen," Garston continued, "and I don't think it should be leaking all that blood and pus you had to wipe away either."

Angela merely shrugged again, and Garston immediately felt the urge to slap her.

"It didn't smell very nice," Angela quickly added after seeing the look on his face. It was her first useful contribution to the conversation.

Garston hadn't noticed the smell, and on hearing this, his brow creased into a worried frown. Even he knew that a foul-smelling wound was a clear sign of infection.

"Why don't you pour some alcohol over the wound and set fire to it," Rodent suggested enthusiastically. "That's what they do in the films when someone's been shot."

Garston stared at him incredulously. "What are you talking about, you idiot? Claude hasn't been shot."

"Yeah, but an open wound's a bit like a gunshot, innit? I've got a bottle of Russian vodka hidden away for special occasions. It was a Christmas present from me nan, but you can use a drop of that if you like, and I could heat up a screwdriver to seal the wound."

"What a ridiculous thing to say," Garston snapped. "What we need to give him is antibiotics, not third-degree burns."

The angry rebuke didn't seem to deter Rodent. "Well, it always works in the films," he persisted, "so there must be something to it."

Garston slapped him across the top of the head. "I told you, he hasn't been shot; his surgical wound has opened up and might be infected."

"I was only trying to help," Rodent said, rubbing the top of his skull dejectedly. He looked like he was going to cry.

"He needs to see a doctor," Angela said, filling the kettle with water. "Those steri strips Rodent got us yesterday aren't strong enough to hold his wound together. It needs re-stitching."

"Impossible," Garston said with a firm shake of his head. And then a thought occurred to him. "I don't suppose you know anyone with medical experience who might be willing to help us on the quiet, do you?" he asked. "Obviously, it would have to be someone whose discretion we could rely on and not someone who'll go straight to the Old Bill and sell us out."

Angela thought about this for a little while. "Well," she said, dragging the word out, "if you're really desperate, I suppose you could always ask Horace Cribbins. He'd be able to stitch Claude's wound up."

Garston's eyes widened in disgust and he shuddered. "Horace Cribbins? The bloke who likes shagging dead bodies?"

"So the rumour goes, but he was never charged with it."

Garston snorted. *I haven't been charged with most of the crimes I've committed,* he thought cynically, *but I've bloody well done them all the same.*

Horace Cribbins had worked as a mortuary assistant in his younger days, preparing the bodies for post mortem and then sewing them up afterwards. The story went that he had been sacked for having sexual relations with some of the corpses. No one knew if it was true or not, and as Angela had pointed out, he had never been charged, but he had been dismissed under a dark cloud, and in Garston's book there was no smoke without fire. These days, old Horace worked as an embalmer at a funeral home, preparing bodies for burial or cremation.

"Claude's wound needs to be stitched up," Angela said pragmatically. "You said so yourself. We can't exactly take him back to hospital, so unless you fancy having a go with a needle and cotton, what alternative do we have?"

He would certainly know how to stitch up a wound, Garston thought, reluctantly seeing some merit in the suggestion

"Do you think he would be willing to help out?" he asked, struggling to overcome his natural revulsion at the thought of using the services of a man like that.

"We could ask him," Angela said.

"Do you know where he lives?"

Angela nodded. "He lives nearby, with his elderly mother."

Garston shuddered. "How very Norman Bates," he said drily.

Ting-a-ling-a-ling.

The old-fashioned bell above the door jangled like wind-chimes as Rodent entered the chemist shop in Barking Road.

Less than ten minutes after slapping him around the head, Garston had sent him out to get further supplies, medical stuff for Winston and food and blankets for the rest of them. He felt undervalued; no matter how hard he tried, or how helpful he endeavoured to be, no one ever seemed remotely grateful. As far as Deontay Garston was concerned, he was just a dumb gofer, a minion whose opinion and feelings were completely irrelevant.

The frumpy pharmacist he'd spoke to yesterday was nowhere to be seen. Instead, a plain-looking beanpole of a girl with long brown hair stood behind the counter. She wore black-framed glasses with thick lenses and a smattering of freckles dotted her face. She was dressed in a thick, tan coloured turtleneck jumper and pleated red skirt. She was a little geeky, he decided, but he found that strangely alluring. There was something vaguely familiar about her, although he couldn't put his finger on what it was. He walked up to the counter and hesitantly removed the crumpled shopping list from his jeans pocket. Perhaps it was just that she reminded him of a taller, slimmer version of Velma Dinkley from the Scooby-Doo cartoons.

"Morning," she said cheerfully. "How can I help you?"

"Er, I've got some errands I need to run for a ... for a friend. Do you have any..." he ran his eyes down the list, "...iodine?"

"Of course," she said, walking over to a shelf and picking up a bottle. "Here we are," she said, holding up the 20ml bottle. "Iodine tincture for wounds, cuts, and abrasions," she read aloud. "I think we've got a cream version too if you would prefer?"

Rodent shook his head. Garston hadn't said anything about a cream. "No, a bottle's fine."

She raised an enquiring eyebrow. "Anything else?"

"Er," Rodent consulted the list, feeling flustered by her steady gaze. "I need dressings and bandages for a wound, enough to last for several days."

Her eyes narrowed. "How big is the wound?"

Rodent didn't know. He hadn't seen it. "About six-inches long," he said, guessing.

"That's a big wound. Has your friend seen a doctor?"

"Of course," Rodent said quickly.

"And didn't the doctor give this friend of yours enough spare dressings and bandages to last until their next appointment?"

"Well..." Rodent began, but couldn't think of anything else to say so he just stood there awkwardly.

Taking pity on him, the girl removed the list from his hand and studied it. "Go and wait by the counter," she told him kindly. "I'll be back in a minute when I've got all the things you need."

"Thank you," Rodent said, relieved that she hadn't asked any more questions.

Leaning against the counter, he watched her flit gracefully around the aisles scooping up various items. She was wearing brown knee-length boots, he noticed. Sensible in this weather. He couldn't shake the feeling that he knew her, but she didn't look like the type of girl who would hang around the streets with wasters like him.

As he glanced down at the chair she had been sitting on when he'd entered, he caught sight of a folded newspaper. It was that morning's edition of *The London Echo*, and to his surprise, a mug shot of Claude Winston defiantly stared up at him from the front page. He leaned over the counter and picked up the red top, letting it unfurl so that he could read the headline.

'*EVIL COP KILLER UNLAWFULLY AT LARGE*', it proclaimed.

"Terrible, isn't it?" the girl asked, making him jump. He hadn't noticed her approach.

"What is?" he asked, confused.

"What that bloke in the paper did to that poor policeman yesterday," she said, indicating the newspaper with her brown eyes.

"Oh, yeah, right," Rodent said, handing her the newspaper. She placed it on the counter and turned to face him.

"You don't recognise me. Do you?" she asked, returning to the staff side and ringing up his purchases on the till.

"You do look familiar," he confessed, "but I can't think where I know you from."

"You're Jimmy Dawlish's kid brother, aren't you?"

"That's right," he said, wondering how she could possibly know that.

"Ronnie, isn't it?"

"Rodney," he corrected her. "Do you know Jimmy, then?" She looked far too young to have been one of his girlfriends – and way too smart. Jimmy had always preferred girls who had no opinions of their own and unquestioningly did as they were told, and Rodent couldn't imagine this one fitting into that category.

She grinned. "My name's Jenna Marsh, Kevin Marsh's younger sister."

Suddenly, everything made sense. Their brothers had been best mates for years. They had gone to the same schools, the same borstals, and the same prisons.

"We were in the same class at primary school," Rodent said as the memories came flooding back. "I remember you now," he said excitedly. "You always had your head buried in a book."

Jenna chuckled. "Nothing's changed," she told him. "What about you? You were always a bit of a loner as I recall, and I always thought you looked sad."

Nothing's changed with me, either, he thought.

"I'm doing okay," he said glumly. "Got a job and everything." He wasn't really sure if selling drugs counted as a proper job, but at least he was earning an income and not on the dole.

Jenna frowned. The last time anyone had mentioned Rodney to her had been a couple of years ago, and it hadn't sounded like things had been going well for him.

"A friend of mine went to the same secondary school as you," she said, "and I seem to recall her telling me that you left before taking your GCSEs. Surely that can't be right?" Jenna had studied for those exams as though her life had depended on passing them all, and her efforts had been rewarded with a series of straight-A grades. She had then repeated the feat with her A levels. Although she had now taken a gap year to get some life experience, she intended to go to university in September to study medicine. Because she was so driven to succeed in her studies, Jenna struggled to comprehend that some people didn't feel the same way about academia.

"I did," Rodney said, smiling to mask his embarrassment. "You know," he said trying to pull off a carefree shrug. "School wasn't really for me and I wanted to get out into the real world and start earning a crust."

Jenna didn't know at all. "But didn't you miss all your friends?" she asked. She had made so many during her secondary school years and she missed them all terribly now that she had left.

"Not really," he told her. "The other kids all thought I was funny."

"Funny ha-ha or funny crazy?" she asked with a mischievous twinkle in her eye.

Rodent shrugged again, awkwardly. "Bit of both, probably," he said with a lopsided grin.

Her face turned serious, and her big brown eyes seemed to bore into his, catching him completely off guard. They were beautiful eyes, he decided, feeling his throat go dry. Unlike his elder brother, Rodent didn't have a lot of experience with girls and he felt totally tongue-tied in her presence.

"Listen," she said, leaning in conspiratorially even though no one else was there. "This friend of yours with the wound, if he's hurt himself doing something illegal, or if he's been attacked by someone from a rival gang, he should still go to the hospital and get proper medical treatment."

Rodent shook his head adamantly. "It's nothing like that," he said, wilting under the intensity of her questioning gaze.

Jenna's face softened, and she placed a hand on his forearm, causing his pulse rate to spike. "I'm not trying to pry," she assured him. "It's just that I remember when Kevin slashed his arm wide open the night him and your brother broke into that Jewellers in Ripple Road. He didn't go to the doctors for days, and by the time he did, it was badly infected. Nearly lost his arm, he did, the stupid sod."

Rodent remembered it well. Despite the doctors calling the police, and Kevin being nicked for the burglary, he hadn't grassed Jimmy up.

Jenna removed her hand, and he immediately found himself wishing that she hadn't. The contact had been... comforting. It wasn't often that someone showed Rodent kindness, or touched him in a manner that didn't constitute an assault.

"Look, he hasn't been stabbed, and he hasn't hurt himself breaking into a shop," he told her uneasily. "He had an operation in hospital last week but his stitches have popped and we need to change the dressing. That's all."

"That explains why all those packets of steri strips were on your list," she said, "but I'm not sure they'll be strong enough to hold a surgical wound together."

Rodent shrugged his shoulders indifferently. He didn't know and didn't much care. He was just the delivery boy.

"Don't you think your friend should go back and get himself checked out?" Jenna persisted.

"He can't," Rodent said without thinking, "not with the Old Bill looking for him."

Jenna's eyes narrowed, but before she could enquire further, the doorbell trilled and two middle-aged women walked in, talking very loudly. They made straight for the counter.

"Morning, Jenna, love," the bigger of the two women said. Underneath her black hairnet, all Rodent could see was row after row of pink curlers. It was as if a huge colony of big fat slugs had taken up residence in her hair.

"Morning, Elsie," Jenna replied without taking her eyes from Rodent.

"I need something for my grandson's verruca," Elsie said, seemingly unaware that Rodent was even there. "And while we're here," she confided, "poor old Maud needs some ointment for her piles, don't you Maud?"

Maud, a slimmer version of Elsie, minus the hairnet, laughed unashamedly. "I do, dear." She leaned forward conspiratorially. "Giving me some right jip at the moment, they are. Been itching like a bastard all morning."

Rodent and Jenna exchanged glances as if to ask each other: *Did she really just say that?*

"No worries," Jenna said. "Just let me finish serving this gentleman and I'll get you some haemorrhoid cream, Maud."

Gentleman! Rodent thought. He'd never been called that before. Blushing, he handed over the money for his purchases and waited for Jenna to give him his change.

"It was nice to see you again after all these years," Jenna said with a warm smile. "Feel free to pop in and say hello any time you're passing."

Rodent grinned like he had just won the pools. "I will," he promised. With an embarrassed wave, he turned and started walking towards the exit.

"Rodney," she called out after him.

He turned; an expectant look plastered across his face. *Please let her ask me to stay and talk for a little while longer*, he prayed.

"Y - yes?" he stammered.

Jenna pointed to two large carrier bags sitting on top of the counter. "Don't you think you should take your supplies with you?"

"Oh," he said, unable to hide his disappointment. "Yeah, of course. Mustn't forget me supplies."

"I don't want to interrupt you two lovebirds," Maud said, reaching behind for a scratch, "but if you could get me that cream for my piles, I really would be very grateful."

CHAPTER FIFTEEN

Garston had come up with an idea for getting Winston some replacement antibiotics, and he was annoyed with himself for not having thought of it sooner.

The contact who had sourced the uniforms they'd worn during the breakout – and still wore as they had no other clothes to change into – had once boasted that he could get his thieving hands on most things medical. Garston decided it was time to put his claim to the test. He dialled a mobile number and waited impatiently for his call to be answered.

"*'Ello...?*" a wary voice answered after the seventh ring.

"Flogger, that you?"

"*Who's asking?*" the gruff voice was thick with suspicion.

"It's Deontay Garston, you Muppet."

"*Deontay! Hello mate, what can I do for you?*" The man's tone became friendly, jovial even.

"Do you remember telling me that you could get your grubby mitts on every kind of medical supply that I could possibly imagine?"

"*Yeah,*" Flogger responded cautiously. "*What is it you're after?*"

"I need a couple of weeks supply of antibiotics. Can you help?"

"*Is that all? Piece of piss, mate. What type do you need?*"

Garston didn't know. He'd asked Winston before making the call, but his idiot uncle had never bothered to read the name of the pills he'd been prescribed or check the dosage. "Not sure, but they need to be strong. I'm after something that could be given to someone fighting off an infection after an operation."

"*Okay, let me make a call, see what me contact says. I've got your number. I'll call you back in five.*"

When five minutes turned into fifteen, and there was still no word from Flogger, Garston began to get impatient. He was on the verge of chasing the supplier up when his phone rang.

Caller ID showed a withheld number.

"What?" he said.

"*Deontay, me ol' mucker, it's me, Flogger.*"

"You were only meant to be five minutes," Garston complained.

"*Sorry about that,*" Flogger said, amiably. "*Me contact was otherwise engaged so I 'ad to wait.*"

Garston sucked his teeth. "I hope what you've got to tell me was worth the delay."

"*Course,*" Flogger purred. "*Me contact reckons you want either a penicillin or cephalosporin based prophylaxis. I can get a couple of boxes of that for you in six days.*"

Garston was dumbfounded. "Six days? Six fucking days! He needs them now, not next week, you wanker."

"*Well, I can't 'elp that,*" Flogger said, defensively. "*Me usual provider's gone and sodded off to Cuba for two weeks in the sun, so I've 'ad to use a backup, and the geezer's a little bit slower at getting me the pharmaceuticals.*"

"Are you seriously telling me that I've got to wait until next Monday? Surely, you can source me some antibiotics from somewhere else? It's urgent. I need them today."

"*Well...*"

Garston could almost hear the cogs turning in his shifty associate's mind. Flogger wouldn't want to lose a sale, and he wouldn't want to look bad in a repeat customer's eyes.

"*There might be a way,*" Flogger said with some hesitance, "*as long as you're not too fussy about what type of antibiotics you end up with.*"

Garston thought about this for a moment, Surely, it didn't really matter? Antibiotics were antibiotics regardless of the brand. "I don't care what you get me, as long as they do the job," he finally said, massaging his temples as he spoke.

"*In that case,*" Flogger told him with renewed confidence, "*I think I can help you, but I've gotta warn you, I'm gonna 'ave to call in a favour and it ain't gonna come cheap.*"

Gaston rolled his eyes. Flogger was a greedy git, and he was trying it on because he knew he had Garston backed into a corner. Of course, from his perspective, he would simply see it as good business, an entrepreneur exploiting a client's need to increase his profit margins. Garston didn't like it, but what choice did he have?

"Not a problem," he said through gritted teeth, "as long as you don't get too greedy and start taking the piss."

"*As if I would!*" Flogger had the cheek to sound indignant, as if his professionalism had just been maligned. He quoted a price and added his commission. "*Let me know where you're staying and I'll get 'em dropped off to you this evening.*"

"No," Garston said. There was no way he was going to reveal his location to Flogger, just in case he put two and two together and decided to sell the information to the cops. "Let's meet on neutral ground."

"*Alright, then,*" Flogger said, "*what about that place we used last week when I gave you the uniforms?*"

"That'll do nicely," Garston said. "What time?"

"*How does seven o'clock tonight sound?*"

"Sounds good," Garston said, and hung up.

After being removed from the helicopter, Peter Myers had been rushed by ambulance to Newham General Hospital in Prince Regent Lane, Plaistow. He had regained consciousness not long after arrival and, although the subsequent brain scan had been satisfyingly clear, the doctors had decided to keep him in overnight for observations as a precaution.

When he'd been reassessed by the consultant this morning during doctor's rounds, the consensus had been that he was still suffering from the effects of a severe concussion and wasn't yet fit enough to be discharged. To Myers's disappointment, it was now looking like he was going to remain hospitalised for yet another night.

Upon his arrival at the all-male observation ward, Steve Bull dutifully reported to the ward sister, a stern-faced battle axe called Brenda Tierney, and requested access to the patient. During the brief conversation that followed, he found her to be marginally less friendly than a rabid Rottweiler.

Glowering at him with undisguised hostility, Tierney made it abundantly clear that Myers wasn't well enough to provide a statement yet and it would be better all-round if Bull could come back the following day. Bull flashed her his most charming smile, explained the urgency of the situation, and then insisted on speaking to the pilot there and then. As a compromise, he promised that he wouldn't stay long. The battle axe had grudgingly relented, but not before making it crystal clear that she didn't want her patient's recovery impeded by a drawn-out visit from the police. Vowing to chuck him out after fifteen minutes, regardless of where they were in the proceedings, Tierney stood aside to allow him temporary access to the patient.

Steve Bull found the pilot sitting comfortably in a soft chair beside his bed. He was so engrossed in a newspaper that he didn't even notice the detective approach. At least three other tabloids were stacked on a table next to his bed, along with a bottle of Robinson's Barley Water, a box of tissues and the obligatory bag of grapes.

Bull calculated that Myers was in his mid to late thirties. He had a wiry, muscular frame, and Bull's first impression was that this was a man who took very good care of himself. Myers was taller than Bull had expected, with slender, well-manicured hands and a mop of jet-black hair that showed no sign of greying, unlike Bull's thatch of brown, which was going greyer by the day. A large gauze strip was plastered across his right cheek, but other than that, Myers appeared in pretty good health.

"Peter Myers?" he asked, producing his warrant card. "I'm Detective Sergeant Steve Bull from the murder squad. If you're up to it, I was hoping we could have a little chat about your ordeal from yesterday?"

"Yes, of course," Myers said, lowering the paper. "Pull up a chair."

Bull purloined a chair from the next bed, which was empty at the moment.

"How are you feeling?"

Myers treated him to a melancholy smile, which accentuated the crow's feet at the edge of his eyes. "Lucky to be alive."

"You are lucky. Very lucky," Bull agreed.

Myer's demeanour became intensely serious, and the change made him look haggard. "Believe me, I know. The staff here couldn't really shed any light on what happened, but I've been reading all about it in the newspapers. I can't believe they shot a policeman before hijacking my helicopter. It's ghastly. Have you caught them yet?"

"No, unfortunately not," Bull said, shaking his head with regret, "but we're working flat out and we won't stop until we do."

They lapsed into an awkward silence, which Myers filled by pouring himself a large glass of barley water.

"How's Mike Cummings doing?" he asked a few moments later. "The last time I saw him, he was being pistol-whipped by the man who tried to shoot me."

"He's fine. Bit concussed, like yourself."

Myers smiled. "That's good to hear. I was really worried about him."

Bull fidgeted in his chair, unsuccessfully trying to get comfortable. "So, what about you?" he asked. "How badly were you injured?"

"Well, apart from having the headache from hell and this," he gently tapped the gauze square on the side of his face, "I'm a bit shaken up but otherwise okay"

"What happened there, if you don't mind me asking," Bull said, pointing to the injury on the pilot's face.

Myers grimaced. "When that bastard started shooting at me, a huge shard of plexiglass exploded out of the windscreen and imbedded itself in the side of my face. A couple of inches higher and it would have taken my eye out. It needed several stitches, but I'm told it'll be fine." His tone suddenly became light-hearted. "At least when it eventually heals, I'll have a genuine war wound to tell all the girls about so I guess it's not all bad." The accompanying grin seemed a little strained.

"Wouldn't have thought you'd need it as a chat-up line, what with being a helicopter pilot," Bull said, smiling back.

Myers leaned forward and lowered his voice, as though he were about to let Bull in on a closely guarded secret. "Sounds sexy, I know, but really I'm just a glorified chauffeur." He sat back in his chair and tapped his cheek. "But with this – well it's the badge of a man who's seen frontline action, and I'll wear it with pride."

His laugh was surprisingly carefree, but it didn't fool Bull; he'd dealt with enough trauma victims over the years to recognise that the banter was merely a smokescreen to disguise how chewed up the pilot felt inside.

Bull glanced over at the nursing station and was unsettled to see the battle axe staring back at him. Quickly averting his gaze, he checked his watch and realised that nearly five minutes of his allotted time had already passed.

"What can you tell me about the hijack?" he asked, getting down to business. He could almost feel Tierney's beady little eyes burning into the back of his head, but there was no way he was going to risk a second look.

Myers' shoulders slumped as though he'd just received a terminal diagnosis. He took a deep breath and blew out his cheeks. "Mike and I were heading for the crew room when three black people came barging out. Their leader was a fearsome looking brute of a man. I'm a bit of a short-arse at five foot nine, but Mike's nearly six foot tall and he towered over him. He was built like a tree trunk, and he had dead eyes that seemed to suck in light and reflect nothing back..." Myers voice tapered off as he replayed the incident in his head.

"Go on," Bull coaxed him after a moment's silence.

"...When he looked at me, I felt like he had already made up his mind to kill me and was looking forward to it. He..." Myers choked, cleared his throat and then licked his lips. "Sorry. He had shoulder-length dreadlocks that were blowing in the wind. I remember he was virtually doubled over with pain, clutching his stomach like he'd been shot. In fact, at one point, I thought I glimpsed blood on his fingers, but that could just have been my imagination."

Steve Bull furiously scribbled notes in his daybook; acutely aware that his writing – not terribly easy to understand at the best of times – rapidly deteriorated whenever he started rushing. He hoped he'd be able to decipher it all later and wouldn't be left with reams of embarrassing gobbledygook.

At some point in the future, Myers was probably going to have to attend an ID parade to try and pick out his attackers from a line-up. In accordance with Code D of PACE, a witness's first description had to be served on the suspect's solicitors before a parade could be held, and the sooner it was recorded, the more credence it was likely to be given, which was why Steve Bull had brought along three First Description Booklets. He only hoped he would have time to fill them in before Brenda the battle axe turfed him out.

Myers had stopped speaking again and he was clearly struggling to go on. After a moment, he reached for his glass with trembling hands and gulped down several mouthfuls of barley water. "Sorry," he said again, "my mouth's suddenly gone as dry as a bone."

"Take your time," Bull encouraged softly. "I know it's hard, but you're doing really well."

"It's very kind of you to be so gracious," Myers said. "However, truth be told, I suspect I'm not doing very well at all." With a wan smile, he raised the glass to his lips and drained the remainder of its content.

"At first, I thought the chap who was supporting him was a doctor," he continued a moment later. "He wore greens and a path lab coat, and he even had a hospital nametag pinned to his chest. There was a slim woman with them. She was dressed as a nurse. Sorry, I couldn't make out her face as she had a surgical mask on, and I'm embarrassed to say that all I remember about her was that she had nice legs."

"Do you think you would be able to recognise the two men again?" Bull asked.

Myers nodded emphatically. "Couldn't forget their ugly mugs if I tried, especially not the Neanderthal with the dreadlocks."

"So, what happened next?" Bull asked, waving for Myers to continue with his account.

Myers thought for a moment, then picked up the story where he'd left off. "Mike challenged them. Next thing I know, a gun's being rammed into the poor sod's face and I'm being forced to airlift them from the building."

"Can you describe the gun? "Bull asked.

Myers shrugged. "Not really. It was black, and it had a long barrel. I think it was similar to what they used in the old cowboy films, where bullets are inserted into the round bit in the middle, not into the handle like the more modern weapons the police carry."

"You took them to some wasteland in Canning Town," Steve said. "Can you remember anything they said during the journey that might help us to work out where they went afterwards or what they plan to do next?"

Myers considered this carefully. "While I was running the pre-flight checks, I became conscious of the doctor making a call on his mobile. I couldn't hear what he was saying because of the noise from the rotors, but after we took off I heard him telling his associates that someone was going to meet them and they were going to spend a couple of days at his house until he could sort out getting the big man out of the country." Myers suddenly grew excited. "He called him uncle! I've just remembered, the doctor repeatedly called the big man uncle."

"Are you sure?" Steve asked, making a note in his daybook and underlining it three times.

"Positive," Myers said.

This was an exciting development. In theory, if he was related to Claude Winston, it ought to make it much easier to identify the man dressed as a doctor. Of course, the expression could just have been used as a mark of respect. He knew that Turkish males often referred to their elders as uncle, even when there was no familial tie but, as far as he was aware, there was no such custom amongst Afro-Caribbean communities.

"That's really helpful," Bull said. "Anything else?"

"Well," Myers said, scratching his head in thought, "I might have misheard, but I could have sworn he referred to the person who was meeting them as Rodent. I must have misheard, but it definitely sounded like Rodent."

Bull made another note. "When did you say you heard them saying all this?" he asked.

"During the flight."

"I don't understand," Bull said, frowning in confusion. "You couldn't hear what was being said during the phone call before take-off but you managed to overhear bits of their conversation during the flight when it would have been even noisier. Can you explain how?"

Myers nodded. "The open faced helmets we wear are all fitted with internal comms. Out of habit, I donned mine before starting the pre-flight checks, but they didn't put theirs on until we were about to take off. At some point, one of them must have somehow activated their microphone. I think it was the girl; she seemed to spend most of the flight staring out of the window while the other two huddled together to talk. I think that's why I only caught snippets of what was being discussed rather than being privy to the whole conversation."

That made sense. "So, what happened after you landed?" Bull asked after checking his watch again. The battle axe had just sentried past them, and he sensed that she was literally counting down the seconds until she could evict him.

Myers's face darkened. "It's all a bit of a blur, I'm afraid. The two men were arguing. The big one was unhappy about something and the doctor was trying to get him to calm down. It was only when I heard the big man say something about 'not leaving any loose ends' that I realised they were arguing about what to do with me. A car pulled up... It was a small Rover, I think..."

Bull held up a hand to stay him "Do you mean a Metro?" he asked.

Myers shook his head. "No, a 214 or 216, red in colour. Anyway, a skinny white boy with ridiculously bushy sideburns running down the side of his face got out, couldn't have been older than nineteen or twenty... As the doctor ushered the brute with the dreadlocks towards it, the evil bastard spun and pointed the gun at me. I tried to duck down, but the flight harnesses held me firmly in place, effectively making me a sitting duck..."

Myers was struggling to speak; his breathing had become increasingly laboured and little beads of perspiration were erupting from every pore in his face.

Bull became aware of the mean faced battle axe striding towards them. "Go on," he whispered urgently. "We're nearly finished, and you'll feel better if you get it off your chest." He wasn't sure that Myers would, but he couldn't go back without hearing the last bit.

Myers nodded and then wiped the moisture from his brow. He stared at his glass longingly but it was empty. "I'm told that two shots were fired at me," he said, "but I only saw one muzzle flash. After that, everything went black. What I do recall is the doctor pushing the big man's gun arm up at the last moment. Do you think he was trying to save my life?"

Before Bull could answer, the scary ward sister was looming over him. "Right, that's it. Time's up. On your bike, sonny Jim."

———

When the phone rang, Garston assumed it would be Flogger calling him back about the antibiotics, but when he checked the caller ID his heart sank. It was Sonia again. He took a deep breath and pressed the green button with his thumb. "Hello Sonia," he said, readying himself for the verbal onslaught that was sure to follow.

"*YOU BASTARD,*" she screamed at him. "*You got my poor Errol killed. How could you do that to him? He trusted you!*"

"What the hell are you on about?" Garston spluttered, reacting as though he had just been slapped. If it hadn't been for the indescribably raw pain in her voice, he might have thought she was drunk.

Sonia couldn't speak, but her sobbing spoke for itself.

"The last time I saw Errol he was alive and well," he promised her, neglecting to add that he'd been running for his life, with the Old Bill hot on his heels.

"He's dead... my poor baby's dead..."

Garston's throat suddenly went dry. "I don't understand," he said lamely, but it didn't take him long to join the dots. Errol was the unnamed man he'd heard about on the news – the one who had been shot by the police during the incident down by the BTNA yesterday afternoon.

A piercing howl escaped Sonia's lips, and her pain washed over him like a tangible entity. "*He's fucking dead, Deontay. The police... those motherfuckers shot him yesterday...*" she broke off, wracked by giant sobs. "*... I thought he was gonna pull through, but he didn't...*" a long pause while she struggled to catch her breath. "*...My poor baby died during the night, all alone with tubes sticking out of him and an armed guard sitting by his side instead of me.*"

Garston slumped down in the lumpy armchair, shocked. "I don't know what to say," he stammered.

"*Tell me the truth, Deontay,*" Sonia demanded, and he could tell she was on the verge of hysteria. "*Were you with him when this terrible thing happened? Was he helping you spring that horrible fucking uncle of yours from the hospital?*"

"What makes you think I had anything to do with it?" Garston hissed at her. As much as he felt for Sonia's unspeakable loss, he couldn't afford to have her mouth off like that.

For a long moment, she was unable to reply. "*I'm not fucking stupid,*" she eventually told him, squeezing the words out between sobs. "*Errol wouldn't tell me what he was up to yesterday, other than to say he was doing a job that would pay for our wedding...*" her voice choked off as the implication of what she said hit her.

There would be no wedding.

There would be no future together.

"Why would you assume he was working for me?" he asked petulantly. "Errol did jobs for lots of people."

"*Yeah, well lots of people didn't have their waste of space shit cunt uncles bust out of hospital yesterday, did they?*" she yelled defiantly. "*I know you been running his business while he's been inside, so don't insult my intelligence by claiming you had nothing to do with his escape.*"

Errol had always said that Sonia was a firebrand and that there was no stopping her once she got herself wound up. Garston decided to try and steer the conversation away from Claude's escape.

"Listen, Sonia," he said gently. "I swear to you that Errol wasn't with me when he got shot. Until you just called, I had no idea what had happened. I promise you I'm not responsible for your man getting shot." *Well, not directly responsible*, he mentally corrected himself. "And as for Claude, well I'd be grateful if you kept your thoughts about me being involved in that to yourself."

He hung up, feeling drained.

After giving the matter some thought, he decided not to mention Errol's death to the others just yet. It would only complicate things. He was worried about Sonia, though. If she started shouting her mouth off that he had been involved in his uncle's escape, it wouldn't take long for the Old Bill to get wind of it and came looking for him. With that in mind, he dialled the number for his fisherman friend in Rye to confirm that everything was still on to get Winston out of the country before the weekend.

CHAPTER SIXTEEN

Beeeeeeeeeeeeeeeeeeeeeeep!

After what seemed like minutes, but was in reality only seconds, the irritating noise finally stopped, signifying that the tape was running. The red light on the twin-deck recorder started to flash, indicating that the equipment was working properly.

"Right, this interview is being tape-recorded. It's exactly twelve midday on Tuesday the eleventh of January two-thousand. We are in interview room number two at Whitechapel police station. My name is Susan Sergeant and I am a Detective Sergeant attached to the Area Major Investigation Pool based at Arbour Square. I am going to ask everyone present to identify themselves, starting with my colleague, DC Murray."

Murray sniffed, and then fidgeted in his seat. His underpants had become wedged in the crack of his arse and he was very uncomfortable. "DC Kevin Murray, also attached to AMIP at Arbour Square," he said between wriggles.

Susie glanced across at Mullings, who stared back sullenly; scrawny arms folded across a pigeon chest in defiance. He was trying to act tough but she could smell his fear. Unfortunately, she could also smell the rancid blend of aromas from his shoeless feet and unwashed armpits. The room was windowless and stuffy, and there was nowhere for the offensive pong to go but up her nose.

"No comment," Mullings said.

Susie groaned at his stupidity as she stared at him, unimpressed. "The interview hasn't started yet, Gifford. This is the bit where we tell the tape who we are." She gave his solicitor an imploring look and the man leaned in and whispered something to his client.

"My name's Gifford Mullings," the prisoner said after sucking through his teeth.

Susie nodded her thanks to the smartly dressed solicitor with the unevenly sprayed on tan, inviting him to speak with a flourish of her hand.

"I'm Oliver Clarke, a solicitor from Cratchit, Lowe, and Clarke. I'm here to advance and protect the rights and entitlements of my client and ensure that the interview is conducted fairly –"

And to bleed the legal aid coffers dry, Susie thought cynically. Out of the corner of her eye, she could see Kevin Murray tugging at the cheeks of his trousers, and it was very off-putting. Luckily, with the interview table between them, neither Mullings nor Clarke could see what he was doing, although they might have wondered about the strange faces he was pulling.

"– and to that effect, I will interrupt if I feel the line of questioning is inappropriate or unfair or not in accordance with the Police and Criminal Evidence Act of 1984."

Susie then went on to caution Mullings. When she'd finished, she asked if he understood what the caution meant.

"Course I do," he said smugly. "I've probably heard it more times than you have."

There was no arguing with that.

"Gifford," Susie began, "yesterday, you were charged with the offences of taking and driving a vehicle without consent, otherwise known as TDA, and possession of Class A drugs. Is that correct?"

Clarke sat forward in his chair. "Do you intend to question my client further in relation to matters for which he has already been charged?" he challenged.

Supercilious twat, Susie thought. She made a point of addressing her answer to the prisoner, not the solicitor, which immediately wound Clarke up a treat. "While serious enough in themselves, Gifford, these matters pale into insignificance in comparison to a murder charge, which you are now potentially facing. Do you understand that?"

"I ain't murdered no one," he said with a cocky grin. "You got Jack shit on me, know what I'm saying?"

"I do," Susie said, smiling sweetly at him. "However, since you were interviewed in relation to the TDA and drugs, new evidence has come to light that I'm going to put to you today."

Doubt flickered across Mullings's eyes and he squirmed in his seat uncomfortably. "Bullshit," he said, but there was a note of concern in his voice.

"We now have CCTV of the stolen car you were driving arriving at the hospital, and the three people you were carrying getting out, dressed in hospital uniforms."

"So what?" Mullings said with forced nonchalance, but he was starting to look on edge.

"Are you prepared to name the three people you drove to the Royal London Hospital yesterday?"

"No comment."

"Who's the male dressed as a doctor?"

"No comment."

"What about the woman dressed as a nurse? What's her name?"

"No comment."

"What about the bald man dressed as a porter?"

"No comment."

"Come on," Murray said, "You must know him? Looks like the lead singer from the seventies funk band, Hot chocolate, but without the snazzy moustache." He did an impromptu dance move in his chair and sang a couple of lines from the hit song, *You sexy thing*.

Mullings stared at him as though he had gone mad. "No comment."

"Did you take these people there willingly or were you acting under duress?" Susie asked, returning to her questioning.

Mullings seemed insulted that she should infer anyone might be able to make him do something against his will. "No comment," he said, angrily.

"We also have extensive CCTV of these same people moving through the hospital on their way to the room Claude Winston was being held in," she continued.

"Never heard of him," Mullings said.

"Don't be stupid," Murray said, impatiently. "We can prove you've been working for him as a low-level drug runner for a couple of years."

"Officer, there's no need to call my client names," Clarke interjected, eyeing the rake-thin detective with disdain.

"It was a statement of fact, not an insult," Murray responded tartly.

"We also have CCTV of the three people you brought to the hospital leaving with Claude Winston a short time later, after they had fatally shot one of the officers guarding him and drugged the other two," Susie said.

Mullings shrugged. "Even if that's true –"

"It is true," Murray snapped. "We're going to play you the footage soon. We made that obvious in the written disclosure we served on you prior to the interview. Didn't your spray tanned solicitor bother to go through it with you before we started?" He turned on Clarke accusingly, his face a mask of contempt.

Clarke's orange face turned the colour of puce. "How dare –"

"Mr Clarke," Susie said, and her eyes were burning with anger, "Please tell me that you went through the disclosure with your client."

Clarke opened his mouth to protest, but the withering look she gave him stopped him in his tracks. "I – I ..."

"Don't just sit there spluttering," Mullings blurted out. "Do something! These motherfuckers are trying to fit me up with some serious shit I didn't even do."

"That's just it, Gifford," Susie said patiently, "Under the law governing Joint Enterprise, driving them to the hospital to break Winston out makes you a party to everything that subsequently went down inside, regardless of the fact that you were outside at the time. When your so-called friends killed that officer, they made you as guilty of his murder as if you had pulled the trigger yourself. So, you see, to paraphrase your earlier comment, your mates are the ones responsible for landing you in 'some serious shit,' not us. My advice – if you really were just a getaway driver – is talk to us and tell us everything you know. That way, the Crown Prosecution Service will be able to make an informed decision on the most appropriate charges to bring against you. Otherwise, I suspect there's a very strong likelihood that you will be jointly charged with murder when all the evidence has been gathered."

Suddenly looking more like a frightened schoolboy than a hardcore gangster, Mullings stared bug-eyed at Susie, then at Clarke and then down at the table.

"Shit!" he said despondently.

"How very eloquently put," Susie said.

―――

Jack was sitting in his office at Arbour Square when his landline rang. He was just finishing off an e-mail, and then he was going to pop over to Quinlan's office to see how the manhunt for Winston was progressing.

"DCI Tyler speaking."

It was Steve Bull with an update from Newham General. *"Boss, I've just finished speaking to the pilot, Peter Myers, and I've got some interesting stuff you need to hear."*

"Steve, you should be telling Mr Quinlan this, not me," Tyler chided him gently.

"Sorry boss," Bull said, sounding a little sheepish. *"Force of habit, I guess. I just spoke to Tony Dillon and he said to let you know straight away. Shall I phone Mr Q instead?"*

Jack grinned and reached for a pen. "No, give me what you've got. I'm going over to see him in a minute, so I'll pass it on and he can call you back if there are any ambiguities."

Bull fired out the salient headlines: there was a possibility that Winston was the phoney doctor's uncle; a call had been made from the helicopter to someone called Rodent; they were going to stay at Rodent's place for a few days until they could get Winston out of the country; Rodent had been driving a red Rover 214 or 216; Winston was the one who had shot Myers.

"That's excellent work, Stevie. Well done. As soon as he's released,

I need –" Jack realised what he'd said and paused "– or rather Mr Quinlan will need Myers to be key witness interviewed on tape."

A key witness was someone who had witnessed a serious indictable offence or events that were closely related to it, or had received a confession from the culprit. Clearly, apart from having witnessed his own attempted murder, he was the main witness for the hijack and he also provided key evidence of Winston fleeing the murder of the police officer.

"Did he say he would recognise any of them again?" Tyler asked.

"*Yep. He's confident he'd be able to pick out both men in a line-up, but not the woman – she had a surgical mask over her boat race.*"

That was a pity. After the office meeting, Reg Parker had managed to install an update that had allowed them to play the CCTV they had retrieved from the hospital. With nothing more constructive to do, Jack had stood over his shoulder as he forwarded through it to make sure it all played okay. He had seen most of the compilation footage that Reggie had burned off for Susie Sergeant to play the getaway driver, Mullings, during the interview, and he had noticed that the woman either had her back to the camera or her mask on in all the close-range shots. Although there was some footage of her facing towards the camera from afar, it was a bit grainy, and he wasn't overly confident that anyone would to be able to identify her from it.

"I hope you completed first description booklets for each suspect while you were there," Tyler said.

Bull made a point of tutting loudly to demonstrate his disappointment that Tyler had felt the need to ask such a stupid question. "*WELL...DUH!*" he said indignantly, and Jack grinned as he pictured him rolling his eyes theatrically.

"*And I don't mind telling you that I had to risk life and limb to get them,*" Bull said pointedly. "*Honestly, the ward sister was a right old dragon. She only allowed me fifteen minutes with Myers, but I hadn't filled the forms in by that point so I refused to leave until I had. She threw a proper tantrum, and at one point I thought she was going to drag me out by the scruff of my neck.*"

Tyler laughed. "She sounds pretty scary," he agreed.

"*Scary? I'm not kidding you, if Errol Heston had gone after her yesterday,*" *instead of Melissa Smails, she would probably have ripped both of his arms off and then beaten him to death with them!"*

"I'm sure you were very brave in the face of great adversity," Jack said with a chuckle, "but I don't think it quite merits a Commissioner's Commendation, do you?"

"*You wouldn't be saying that if you'd seen her*," Bull said, also laughing.

As soon as the call finished, Tyler grabbed the brief notes he'd taken and made his way along the corridor to Andy Quinlan's office.

Arbour Square was virtually deserted now that all the other teams had migrated to their new base of operations at Hertford House, a building within a gated complex in Barking that was formerly owned by the Gas Board. It was to be the new home of the Homicide Command's East London satellite, or SO1(3) to use its departmental title. Placing homicide investigations under the purview of Specialist Operations, and making them a pan London Command instead of area-based, as Area Major Investigation Pools were, had come about following the recommendations of the MacPherson Report published the previous year. The budgeted workforce total – or BWT – for the command was also being drastically increased and recruitment had already begun to strengthen the teams.

Jack had already visited his new office on the building's first floor; it was modern and spacious, and it even had air conditioning. He had no doubts that it would be a great place from which to run major enquiries.

As bastions of the old guard, his and Andy Quinlan's teams had been left behind to man the fort until the new facility was up and running. All things being equal, they were due to join their colleagues at Hertford House before the end of the month, at which point Arbour Square, with all its magnificent history, would be closed down.

Rumour had it that the site was to be sold off for development and that the cells that had once held the infamous Kray twins and suspected Provisional Irish Republican Army terrorists would be turned into trendy flats for yuppies.

He gave a quick rap on Andy's door and walked in without waiting for an invite. "Fancy popping out to grab a bite to eat?" he asked. It was almost one o'clock and he was starving.

Quinlan was hunched over his desk, pen scribbling frantically as he added the latest entry to his decision log. The room was so stifling hot and stuffy that Jack was surprised Andy's glasses hadn't started to steam up.

"Greetings!" Quinlan said, lowering his pen. Although in his late forties, his boyish smile made him appear much younger. Running a hand through the mop of black curly hair atop his head, he stood up and strode over to a percolator on the filing cabinet next to the door.

"Haven't got time, I'm afraid, but let me make you a cup of coffee instead."

"Go on then. White, two sugars," Jack told him, taking a seat opposite his desk. "It's like a bloody sauna in here," he complained. "You need to open a window."

"Can't," Quinlan explained ruefully. "It's stuck, and as we're moving out shortly, maintenance won't send anyone along to fix it."

While Andy did the honours, preparing the coffee, Jack updated him on the news from Newham General.

"That's very interesting indeed," Quinlan said, returning to his desk and handing Jack a freshly prepared brew. "I'll get the Intel Cell straight onto it."

"Hopefully, there'll be a clear connection to Winston and his nephew on the system," Jack said. "And this Rodent character has to be local. With a bit of luck, he'll be easy to identify."

"Let's hope so," Quinlan said. "Actually, I've had a positive development, too." He reached into his second drawer and pulled out a prepacked sandwich. "You don't mind if I stuff this down my neck as we speak, do you? Only I'm Hank Marvin!"

Jack smiled inwardly. Like Dick Jarvis, Andy Quinlan was terribly well-spoken, and expressions like Hank Marvin – Cockney rhyming slang for starving – just didn't sound natural coming from him.

"Knock yourself out," he said. He knew what it was like when you were in the early stages of a job and had to eat what you could when you could. He watched as Quinlan eagerly tore the supermarket wrapping off and pulled out one half of a sorry looking sandwich.

Jack caught a whiff of rotten eggs. "Phwoar," he said, turning up his nose. "That smells like someone just let off a stink bomb. Are you sure it's okay to eat?" He picked up the packaging, which told him the offending article was meant to be egg mayonnaise. "This says 'best before 11th January'," he told Quinlan. "That's yesterday."

Quinlan sniffed it, wrinkled his nose, and then took a tentative bite. "I didn't get time to eat it yesterday, but those dates are only a guide. I'm sure it's fine."

Jack looked at him in alarm. "You're not telling me it's been left in your desk drawer all night, are you?" he asked incredulously.

Quinlan nodded. "It tastes fine," he said, taking another bite.

Jack shook his head in disbelief. Was Quinlan mad? The radiator was literally next to his desk, and it was belting out enough heat to make him perspire after only a few minutes in the room. What would it have done to the bacteria in the sandwich overnight?

"Seriously, mate," he warned, "I really wouldn't eat that if I were you."

Quinlan grinned. "I can assure you I ate far worse in my university days," he boasted. "I've got the constitution of an ox."

Tyler hoped he was right.

"So, what's your development, then?" he asked, trying not to breathe in the sulphurous odour of Andy's lunch.

"Two minutes before you came in, I had a call from fingerprint bureau at The Yard. We've got a match on the syringe we found in the hospital room."

"That's brilliant news," Jack said.

"I know," Quinlan said, munching away happily. "It's a thumbprint belonging to an IC3 female called Angela Marley. She's got a long list of petty convictions, mainly for drugs, shoplifting and prostitution. And get this, her long-time pimp is none other than Claude Winston."

Jack let out a low whistle. "So, the net begins to tighten."

Oliver Clarke, his artificially tanned face impassive, sat through the machine's irritatingly long beep and the boring introductions that preceded the second interview getting underway in earnest.

He studied the pretty strawberry blonde with the soft Irish accent as she cautioned his client and recapped what had happened during the first interview. She pointed out that they had taken a brief break at his request, in order for him to confer with his solicitor, and she confirmed that he was happy they had been given sufficient time for Clarke to properly advise him.

Clarke smirked at that. They had had ample time – after all, how long does it take to say, 'Keep your mouth shut and say nothing?'

Clarke decided that DS Sergeant had a very sexy voice; it was reminiscent of Maureen O'Hara, the Irish American actress who had played John Wayne's fiery love interest in the 1952 classic, '*The Quiet Man*'. His father had loved that film, but then his father had loved every picture that John Wayne had ever appeared in.

Clarke guessed that she'd be about five-eight in her stockinged feet, which was only three inches shorter than him. Beneath the jacket of her blue pinstriped business suit, he imagined a pair of firm boobs – probably contained by a sports bra – straining to break free. He thought about her bottom, which he had ogled when they had risen for a break. As a rule, he preferred women with pear shaped bums, whereas Sergeant's was tighter and rounder, not that he would have kicked her out of his bed because of it.

He was generous like that.

During the first interview, he'd noticed that if the light caught her at the wrong angle it could make her hair appear more ginger than blonde, but he'd always had a bit of a soft spot for ginger mingers so that was fine with him.

Her most striking feature, he decided, was the dazzling green eyes that changed vibrancy in accordance with her mood; they blazed with fire when she became angry and thawed to ice when she was asking questions.

Sergeant was currently wearing a pair of black-rimmed glasses, which gave her the scholarly appearance of a stern-faced schoolmistress; it was a look he found deeply arousing. He wondered what she was like in the sack, and if she'd be up for anything kinky. Before he could stop himself, his mind had conjured up a fantasy in which she had handcuffed him to the bed and was about to straddle him. The image triggered a lascivious smile, and he quickly dry washed his face to mask it; DS Sergeant was a woman of the world, and if she spotted him staring at her like that, she would know there was only one thing on his mind, and that it wasn't the interview.

As he looked up, his eyes locked with DC Murray's, and the skeletal detective with the goatee beard and scruffy suit glowered at him loathingly.

Awkward! he thought, realising that Murray had caught him mentally undressing Susan Sergeant. He tried to defuse the situation with a 'busted, but you can't really blame me?' grin, but Murray was having none of it.

Averting his eyes, Clarke realised that he would have to be more careful in the future. The sour-faced detective didn't miss much; his eyes were sharp, and his tongue was even sharper.

Most police officers were inherently wary of rubbing a solicitor up the wrong way, but Murray seemed hellbent on doing exactly that, and it had put him on the back foot.

Clarke suddenly became aware that DS Sergeant had stopped speaking and everyone was looking at him.

"Is that right?" she asked him impatiently.

"Sorry?" he spluttered, realising that he had become so wrapped up in his thoughts that he'd zoned out of what was going on around him.

DS Sergeant was not impressed. "Your client said you're going to read out a prepared statement from him – is that right?"

Mullings wasn't too happy about his lapse in concentration either. "You need to get your ears cleaned out, bruv," he chipped in.

Murray smirked at him as though he had just won a small but important victory.

Clarke could feel himself becoming flustered. "My apologies," he said, hurriedly rummaging through the papers on his lap until he found the document he'd written on his client's behalf during their consultation.

"Yes, a prepared statement. Here we go..." He cleared his throat and then began reading. "This is a prepared statement written by my solicitor but dictated by me, Gifford Mullings. I have asked my solicitor to read it out on my behalf. I will then be exercising my right to remain silent and will reply 'no comment' to all questions asked from that point onwards. I want to make it abundantly clear that I –"

"Use that word a lot, do you, Gifford?" Murray said, interrupting the solicitor. "Do you even know what abundantly means?" he scoffed.

"If I might be allowed to continue without further interruption," Clarke snapped, absolutely livid with Murray for disrupting his flow.

Murray shrugged the rebuke off. "Just confirming that it was something he would normally say and not words you've put into his mouth," he said with a saccharine smile.

Clarke's features contorted with rage, but he knew he had to tread carefully because he had put words into Mullings's mouth. In fact, he had written the prepared statement off his own back while Mullings read through the sports section of The Sun.

"As I was saying," he said through gritted teeth, "... I want to make it abundantly clear that I had no idea my friend and his two associates were planning to break Claude Winston out of custody when I drove them to the hospital yesterday. Had I known what they intended I would not have allowed myself to become involved. I was told that Mr Winston was being discharged after an operation and that they wanted to take him home in style, which is why they had stolen a top of the range car. I was there as a chauffeur, not as a getaway driver. I do not know the names of two of the three people who were in the car with me. The only one whose name I do know is my friend, Errol Heston. I'm sure he will vouch for me if you ask him." Clarke looked up and smiled triumphantly at Sergeant, who completely stonewalled him. It was clear from the frosty stare she was giving him that she didn't believe a word of it.

He didn't care what she thought. What he'd told them was complete bollocks, and everyone in the room knew it but, with Errol dead, the police would struggle to refute anything in the prepared statement. He cleared his throat again, feeling that he had regained the upper hand. "That concludes Gifford Mullings' prepared statement," he said piously. "I sincerely hope that you will now respect my client's wishes, and refrain from asking him any more questions."

Mullings nodded, seemingly impressed. "Can I go home now?" he asked.

"Not gonna happen," Murray said flatly. He turned to face Clarke, regarding the man as though he was something unpleasant that he'd just trodden in. "Your client can sit there and say as much or as little as he wants, I don't really care one way or another. Not only are we entitled to ask him any questions that we feel are relevant, we also have a sworn duty to the victim and his family to do exactly that, and for that reason, we intend to continue the interview as planned."

Clarke made a show of huffing and puffing and protesting on his client's behalf, but it was all gamesmanship and the police officers knew it. The bottom line was that Mullings was completely fucked. He was going to be charged with a Joint Enterprise murder; the only question was would it happen later today or would they grant him technical bail while they assembled all the outstanding statements, forensic evidence and CCTV at their leisure.

If they granted technical bail in regards to the murder, Mullings would still be remanded in custody for the TDA and drugs offences. When the poor naive fool had asked about his prospects of bail at Magistrates Court, Clarke had advised him not to hold his breath. The truth was there was no way in hell he was getting bail, not with his previous offending history. Mullings already had several convictions for failing to appear at court. Coupled with the fact he was looking at an imminent murder charge, it made him a considerable flight risk. Clarke reckoned there was more chance of persuading DS Sergeant to participate in one of his sexual fantasies with him, and getting DC Murray to pay for their hotel room than there was of a Magistrate granting Mullings bail.

CHAPTER SEVENTEEN

Dean Fletcher popped his head around Tyler's office door. "Sorry to interrupt," he said, looking over the top of his reading glasses, "but I thought you might be interested to hear that I've found out where Angela Marley is living."

"Excellent," Jack said. "Have you passed on the good news to Mr Quinlan?"

"Not yet," Dean said. "You're my boss, not Mr Q, so I wanted you to be the first to know. Well, the second if you count Mr Dillon."

Jack couldn't help but smile. Throughout the day, his team had been calling him with updates on the actions they had been given by Andy's MIR. They all knew that this went against protocol, and they should either be reporting back to a supervisor on Andy's team or calling it into his MIR, but they also all knew that, with his team seconded, Tyler had been left twiddling his thumbs with not a lot else to do. The fact that they were reporting back to him first was their way of keeping him involved, and it was very touching.

"Much appreciated, Deano," he said, "but you really should be telling Mr Quinlan or one of his supervisors this, not me."

"Don't care," Dean said with belligerence. The researcher tended to see things very much in black and white, and the way he approached work tended to reflect this. "We should have had this job. No disrespect to Mr Q or his team, but we nicked Winston the first time around and I'll bet you a pound to a penny it'll be somebody from our team who lays hands on him this time, too." He said this as though he considered it to be a point of honour.

A thought occurred to Tyler. "Is there a secret agenda going on here that I need to know about, Deano?" he asked, narrowing his eyes suspiciously.

"I don't know what you're talking about, guv," Fletcher said, shrugging nonchalantly. "But, if it was secret, I could hardly tell you, could I?"

Smartarse! Jack thought. But he had a point.

"You know, a more suspicious man than myself might wonder if there was some skulduggery going on to make sure that our team arrest Winston and his associates before Mr Quinlan's people can lay their hands on him, just to make a point that we should have been given the job in the first place."

Fletcher's visage remained as enigmatic as ever. "As if any of us would do that."

Tyler raised a cynical eyebrow. "As if," he echoed, thinking that Fletcher must be a superb poker player because his face was impossible to read. "But, if you did, I don't think it would be too hard to work out who the ringleader was."

There was no doubt in his mind that, if they were up to anything, Tony Dillon would be the one orchestrating it, but he would have had no trouble roping in the likes of Bull, Fletcher, and Parker.

Fletcher fidgeted impatiently. "Don't mean to be pushy, but I've got still a shed load of research to get through, so do you want to hear the update or not?"

"Come on then," Jack said, unable to resist. "Tell me everything."

Fletcher came in and pulled up a chair. He had printed out a couple of A3 sized maps and he gave one copy to Tyler and kept the other for himself. "Right, guv," he said, pointing to a house he had circled with a red felt tip pen. "This is a squat in Vicarage Lane, E15. The rear garden backs onto a similar house in Evesham Road."

Jack looked up. "So?"

"So, I've found several reports linking Angela Marley to this address over the past few months. She gave it as her home address the last time she was arrested, back in December, and a bail enquiry was carried out to confirm that she did actually reside there. Also, there's a CRIMINT entry from the local beat bobby, dated January second, when he spotted her entering the address at sixteen-hundred hours with an unknown IC3 male he believed to be a punter."

CRIMINT is the Met's searchable intelligence database, where all information reports relating to criminal intelligence are stored.

"I don't suppose the address has been searched recently?" Tyler asked.

Fletcher nodded. "Yep. A Section 18 was carried out there by the TSG in late November when another prostitute called..." he paused to check his notes, "...Lolaksi Agarwal – aka Lola – was arrested for possession of half-a-dozen wraps of cocaine. Nothing was found, but the TSG skipper had the brains to complete a floor plan of the address in case it was ever spun again."

Tyler nodded, impressed.

"Oh, and I forgot to mention," Dean said. "The name Angela Marley sounded vaguely familiar. I couldn't think why at first, but then it came flooding back to me so I ran her details through the Operation Crawley account on HOLMES and..." He paused for dramatic effect.

"And...?"

"And, as I thought, she's a hooker from Claude Winston's stable, and she was with Fat Sandra Dawson and Tracey Phillips on the night that the Phillips girl was murdered." Tracey Philips had been slaughtered on Halloween of the previous year. Operation Crawley, the randomly generated name that HOLMES had allotted for the ensuing investigation, had proved to be somewhat challenging, and it was a period in his career that Tyler would never forget.

"Well done, Deano, that really is very interesting. Tell me, do you have any information about any of the other occupants of this squat yet? I don't suppose anyone called Roddy or Rodent lives there?"

"Not that I can see, but I've only just started my research. There was an interesting CRIMINT from last June where the body of a working girl was found in an upstairs room by a new arrival. Everyone thought the deceased had moved out the previous week, but it turned out she hadn't; she'd overdosed and then crawled into a corner to die."

"Sounds like a charming place," Tyler said, screwing his face up in disgust.

"It's not the Hilton, that's for sure."

"Have you got anything else?"

"Nope. I've only had time for a quick look so far, but I'm gonna delve through the system properly once I let Mr Q know."

"What about this Rodent character? Who's researching him?"

"Wendy's been working on that, guv. Don't think she's getting very far though, at least not yet."

As soon as Dean had left, Jack picked up his mobile and dialled Kelly Flower's number to see if she could shed any light on what the team – or at least a clique within it – were up to. Maybe, he conceded, they weren't up to anything and he was just being paranoid.

"Are you free to speak?" he asked when she picked up.

"*Yeah, go on. Me and Colin are on our way to put the squeeze on another one of Winston's mates, not that it's got us anywhere so far.*"

"Ah, I wanted to ask you something, but in private."

There was a pregnant pause. "*Okay...*" she eventually said, and he could hear the cogs turning as she tried to work out what it was. "*In that case, I'll have to ring you back a bit later.*"

"It's nothing important," he reassured her. "I'll speak to you later."

They had broken from interview in order to let Gifford Mullings eat his lunch at a recognised mealtime in accordance with PACE.

After they booked the prisoner back in with the custody officer, the gaoler came straight over and handed him a hot meal, and then led him back to his cell to eat it. It didn't look particularly appetising, and it smelled like it had been badly burnt.

"Can't you give him something better than that?" Clarke complained, eying the stodgy meal the canteen had prepared as though it were a can of overcooked Pedigree Chum, which, knowing the canteen, Murray suspected it might well have been.

"I mean, does that gloop even qualify as food?"

"He gets the same food as we do," Susie said, "only we have to pay good money for ours."

Clarke wasn't convinced. "If this was an internment camp instead of a police station, I reckon the Red Cross would be up in arms by now. That pile of lumpy gruel you just gave my client would definitely contravene the Geneva Convention."

Murray became antagonistic. "Well, if you don't like it, why don't you put your hand in your pocket and treat your poor hard done by client to a MacDonald's or something?" He sneered at the look of horror that appeared on the solicitor's face. "Thought so. You're quick enough to complain, but you're not so keen to fork out any of your own money on the little scumbag, are you?"

Clarke spluttered, his face turning red. "How dare you!"

"Oi, Gifford," Murray shouted after the departing prisoner. "Your solicitor has kindly said that if you don't like the canteen food, he'll pop out and get you a Mackey Dees. You can have whatever you want, no expense spared."

Clarke stared at the detective with undisguised hatred. "I never –"

"Thanks, bruv," Mullings said, returning to the custody desk and contemptuously tossing his food onto it. "This stuff smells like shit."

"Maybe you should try it first," Clarke said quickly.

"You try it, bruv," Mullings said, turning his nose up at the suggestion. "I'll have a Big Mac, large fries, and a strawberry shake."

"They do a nice apple pie too, if you fancy a dessert," Murray told him.

"For real," Mullings said, nodding approvingly. "I'll have one of them as well. How long you gonna be getting it, bruv? I'm famished."

Murray smiled sweetly. "Yeah, you'd better hurry up," he said. "He's a growing lad."

Clarke nodded, knowing he could hardly refuse his client without losing face. "Very well," he said curtly. "I need to phone the office anyway, and feed the meter. Don't want the council clamping my brand-new Jag, do I?"

After escorting Clarke out of the station, Murray decided to take advantage of the enforced break and pop over to the nearest tobacconists to get himself a packet of fags. He was feeling rather pleased with himself for getting one over on the Tango-faced brief. The smarmy bastard deserved to be taken down a peg or two.

There was a queue in the shop, and Murray tapped his foot impatiently as the Indian proprietor worked his way through them with all the speed of a handicapped slug. Three scruffily dressed schoolkids stood directly in front of him, laughing and giggling and generally being a nuisance. Checking his watch, he considered coming back later, but he didn't' know when he would get another chance, so he waited in line, trying his utmost to ignore the noisy urchins in front of him.

After what seemed an age, but was in reality only a few minutes, the shopkeeper finally got around to serving the brats, and Murray breathed a sigh of relief.

It was almost his turn.

He wondered what delights the little horrors would waste their pocket money on. With any luck, he thought bitterly, all the sugar would make their teeth rot.

"How much are these, mister?" the first of them asked, holding up a bag of Skittles.

"What about these," the second chimed in, thrusting a packet of Rolo chocolate caramels in the Indian man's face.

While they distracted the shopkeeper, their mate started jamming packets of sweets up his jumper, as bold as brass.

When Murray saw this, he smiled. It was shoplifting, plain and simple, and he should probably have nicked them for it, but he had done similar things – worse things actually – as a youngster.

Discreetly removing his warrant card from his pocket, he slid it in front of the little tealeaf's face and placed a firm hand on his bony shoulder. Leaning forward menacingly, he whispered, "Be a good lad and put that lot back or you'll be spending an afternoon in the cells with all the kiddy fiddlers and rapists."

The boy froze on the spot, his face draining of colour. "I wasn't going to keep them, mister," he lied, hurriedly replacing the items as he spoke.

"Of course, not," Murray said, grabbing hold of the boy by the scruff of the neck. "Now get your scabby mates and piss off so that I can get served."

The boy nodded fearfully and quickly marshalled his two protesting friends out of the shop.

Murray smiled at the shopkeeper, who eyed him with undisguised suspicion, no doubt wondering what he'd just said to the poor innocent children to send them scurrying out of the shop without spending any money.

This twat probably thinks I'm a paedophile, Murry thought, wishing he'd kept quiet and left the boy to his own devices.

Ignoring the dubious looks the man behind the counter was giving him, Murray purchased a packet of twenty B&H, a giant bag of cheese and onion crisps, a can of full-fat Coke and a large bar of chocolate. If the proprietor did suspect that Murray was a child molester, he certainly didn't let it stop him from making a sale.

Murray considered grabbing a little something for Susie while he was there, but then decided against it. She was a big girl, and if she wanted food, she could get it herself.

As he left the shop with his little bag of goodies, he caught sight of Oliver Clarke standing in the side road opposite. Unaware that he was being watched, the solicitor was tenderly caressing the bonnet of a gleaming Racing Green Jaguar.

"Fucking perv," Murray muttered to himself.

While waiting for a suitable gap to appear in the fast-moving traffic, he saw Clarke remove a pile of loose change from his trouser pocket and start drip-feeding it into the meter beside his car. With a final loving stroke of the car's roof, Clarke set off in the direction of the nearest MacDonald's.

Murray didn't bother rushing back. Instead, he walked straight by the police station's entrance and carried on until he reached the park entrance a little further along. Despite being wrapped up in a winter coat and thick scarf, he was absolutely bloody freezing, but after having spent most of the morning in a smelly interview room with the odious solicitor and his pongy client, he badly needed some fresh air to clear his head so he decided to brave the cold for a little longer.

He found an unoccupied park bench, sat down and lit up a

cigarette. Letting out a smoke-filled sigh of contentment, Murray pulled his collar up, leaned back and watched the world go by.

Unsurprisingly, there was hardly anyone else around. In fact, other than a skinny woman walking a shivering Chihuahua along the footpath, and a bearded man who was being dragged towards her by a powerfully built English Bull Terrier, he had the park all to himself.

The Bull Terrier was a mean-looking bastard, with piggy eyes and a set of teeth that wouldn't have looked out of place in the mouth of a Great White shark. Apart from a splodge of brown on one side of its face, the dog's coat was white, and he was reminded of Bullseye, the dog owned by Bill Sykes in the film *Oliver!*

The woman with the little Chihuahua must have realised that the dogs were locked on a collision course because she suddenly did a quick about-turn and started heading back the way she'd come, dragging the confused animal behind her.

Wise move, Murray thought. *That evil-looking fucker would eat your scrawny mutt for breakfast.*

Stubbing out the cigarette, Murray ripped open the bag of cheese and onion crisps and started stuffing them into his mouth. He was just tipping in the dregs when the Bull Terrier appeared beside the bench, sniffing at his food and licking its lips. He was on one of those extendable lead things, and his owner was lagging way behind.

"Sod off, you ugly git," Murray said, shooing him away with his hand. "You're not getting anything from me."

The dog stopped sniffing, growled deep in its throat, and then abruptly squatted next to his foot and began to defecate.

"Really!" Murray said, drawing his feet away to avoid them being crapped on. He turned on the bearded man, face flushed with anger. "Your dog's got the whole park to take a shit in, so why are you letting him do it right next to me?"

The man shrugged apologetically. "I'm awfully sorry," he said, blushing with embarrassment. "I'm looking after him for my neighbour while he's on holiday. Only been gone a couple of days and already I can't wait for him to come back."

The dog had finished its business and was now jumping up at the bench, trying to steal Murray's chocolate bar from the plastic bag.

"Can't you control the damned thing?" Murray complained, snatching the bag away before the dog could get a good grip on the chocolate.

"I'm trying," the man grunted, fighting a losing battle to bring the dog to heel, "but he's very strong and incredibly stubborn. He just doesn't listen to a word I say."

Murray was gobsmacked. "Well try harder," he ordered. "You can't go around letting your dog shit on people's feet."

"I'm really sorry about the poo," the man said, sounding crestfallen. "Did any of it land on your shoes?"

Murray quickly checked. "No, but that's not the point, is it? Look at the mess he's made. Kids play in this park."

"Don't worry," the dog walker reassured him, "I'll pick it straight up." He reached into his coat pocket and produced a clear plastic bag. "I always come prepared."

Steam was coming off the turd, and the smell wafting up was worse than some of the decomposing corpses he had dealt with. "Oh my God!" Murray said, fanning his nose. "What are you feeding him on? Dead rats?"

The bearded man grinned sheepishly. "Bronson can be a bit stinky at times, can't you boy?" he said, reaching down to ruffle the Bull Terrier's neck fur. "If you think that's bad, imagine how I feel, being stuck in the same bedroom with him every night."

Glancing down at the dog, who had grown bored and was now sitting next to his temporary master, Murray suppressed a shudder. "Rather you than me," he said.

Holding his breath, Mr Beardy bent down to scoop up the dogshit and then, trying not to get any over his hands, clumsily tied the bag as tightly as he could to keep the rancid smell locked inside.

"There, all done," he said, holding it at arm's length. He looked around, trying to locate a bin, but there were none in sight. "Oh dear," he moaned. "Looks like I'm going to have to carry this all the way home." The bag was sagging under the weight of its unpleasant content, and he was clearly worried that it might not survive the journey.

He eyed Murray imploringly. "Don't suppose you know where the nearest bin is, do you?"

"No, I bloody don't," Murray snapped, wondering why Mr Beardy was still standing there like a gormless idiot. Perhaps he was hoping that Murray would offer to dispose of it for him.

Not much chance of that happening, Murray thought, scoffing at the very idea.

But then he had his Eureka moment.

His watch said it was almost 4 p.m.

Garston moved away from the bay window and let the curtains slide together. It was growing steadily darker outside and the street-lights had just come on, bathing the street in a pale-yellow glow. The intermittent rain that had been falling all day had started again, and this time it was coming down with more intensity.

According to Rodent, who had called him in a panic a few minutes earlier, the police were out in strength, visiting anyone and everyone who knew Winston and putting pressure on them to reveal where he was holed up.

He'd told Rodent not to worry, but the news had left him feeling vulnerable.

Winston had spent his whole life screwing over people on both sides of the law and, as a result, he didn't have many friends. Not only was he despised by rival dealers; he was disliked and feared by almost everyone who worked for him, and Garston knew it was only a matter of time until someone found out where he was staying and phoned Crimestoppers.

Being cooped up in the same tiny flat as Winston and Angela was sending him stir crazy. His uncle had been in a foul, confrontational mood all day, and the whore had been whining non-stop because she was going through withdrawal and needing a fix to take the edge off.

He was almost at the end of his tether, and he decided that as soon as Rodent returned from Tesco, where he been sent to stock up on food, he would borrow the boy's car and shoot back to his place for a change of clothes and a shower.

Angela had been easy enough to deal with. When her whinging had finally become too much, he'd simply given her a bag of smack and allowed her to shoot up. Since then, she had been asleep and out of his hair.

His uncle was a different proposition altogether. The man was insufferable. Nothing anyone said or did pleased him, and all he wanted to do was argue and pick fault.

Out of the kindness of his heart, he'd taken Winston a mug of coffee and a cheese and pickle sandwich about an hour ago, and the ungrateful swine's response had been to moan that there was too much milk and not enough sugar in his drink. Then he'd thrown a strop because he'd wanted ham, not cheese. After kicking up a huge fuss, he'd devoured the sandwich in four bites and demanded more. When Garston had told him there was no more bread, he'd gone into one, threatening to break Rodent's legs for not having a better-stocked larder.

Garston had been sent back to the kitchen to forage through almost empty cupboards in search of something else for him to eat. He'd reported back that the only two options available – unless he wanted Garston to cook him the mummified remains of the mouse he'd found in a trap – was a mug of oxtail flavoured cup-a-soup or a king-size bag of cheese and onion crisps. Winston had opted for the crisps, but he'd made it clear that he would have preferred salt and vinegar.

After he'd eaten, Angela had been allowed in to bathe and change the wound. Throughout her ministrations, Winston had cursed at her clumsiness and criticised her inability to do anything right, and she had left the room in tears, having been reduced to a bag of nerves.

Finally, back in the lounge, and indescribably grateful to have escaped from his uncle's energy-sapping negativity, Garston had switched the TV on and flopped down in the armchair with the dodgy spring.

That had only served to depress him more. The policeman's murder at the hospital, along with the subsequent helicopter hijacking, was still being featured on every news bulletin, and all the unwanted publicity Winston was receiving was going to make it very hard to move him when the time came. It had even displaced the manhunt for the soap star who had strangled his girlfriend as the top story.

There were no significant updates regarding the shooting near the BTNA, except to announce that the suspect had now died, the next of kin had been informed, and the Independent Police Complaints Commission had been informed.

Just thinking about the logistics of getting his uncle down to Sussex made Garston feel physically sick. He groaned and buried his head in his hands. Massaging his throbbing temples with his fingers, he could feel the blood pounding in his ears as a nagging stress headache began to set in.

"How the fuck am I going to move you from here to the coast when your godawful face is being splashed across the telly every five minutes?" he asked the grainy colour image of Winston that now filled the screen.

It stared back at him malevolently.

Resisting the urge to throw the remote at it, he stood up and strode back to the bedroom. He found Winston sitting up in bed, arms folded angrily across his huge chest. "What?" he demanded, petulantly.

Clearly, this wasn't a good time to have a rational conversation with his uncle, but then, when was? Sitting on the edge of the bed, Garston took a deep breath. "Claude," he began delicately, and then hesitated, wondering if it might be wiser to wait until his uncle was in a marginally better mood.

"WHAT?" Winston shouted, making him flinch.

"Maybe we should talk later," Garston said, making to stand.

Winston grabbed hold of his wrist and pulled him close, grimacing at the pain the sudden movement had caused him. "If you're gonna run my business while I'm away, you'd better grow a pair of balls and stop acting like a fucking pussy, because I'm telling you, unless you do, you won't last five-fucking-minutes in this game. Now, what do you want?" He released his grip on Garston and leaned back against the pillows.

Garston swallowed hard. "You're right, Claude," he said, trying to keep his voice level. "I'm going to give it to you straight. There's no way we can move you at the moment because your hairstyle is just too distinctive. What I propose is that, before setting off to Rye on Thursday night, you to let me shave off your dreadlocks. That would really change your appearance and it might give us a fighting chance of getting there without being spotted."

To his surprise, Winston laughed heartily. "I was wondering when you would work up the courage to ask me that," he confided.

Garston was confused by this reaction. He'd been expecting an outburst of pure rage. "I don't get it. I thought you'd be really angry," he confessed.

Winston shook his head. "I'm not angry, boy. What you're asking makes perfect sense."

"So, you'll let me do it, then?" Garston asked. He hadn't been expecting that.

"No," Winston said, still laughing. "There's no way in hell that you're doing that. And just so we're clear, I would rather cut your head off than my dreadlocks, and if you bring it up again, that's exactly what I'm gonna do. Now, be a good little boy and fuck off."

CHAPTER EIGHTEEN

Tyler ambled along the corridor, intent on having a quick word with Andy Quinlan before setting off for home. It was only 5 p.m. but there was nothing more for him to do at the office so he'd decided to call it a day. It looked like Kelly was going to be working silly hours again, so he figured he would be all alone for a second night on the trot. He couldn't justify having another takeaway – that would be too much of an overindulgence – so perhaps he'd stop off at the supermarket and get himself one of their freshly cooked chickens, and then treat himself to another Bond film. *Thunderball* would do very nicely.

The door was ajar and Andy's office was empty so Jack went looking for him. He wasn't in the MIR or the main office, and no one had seen him for a little while. Curious. Maybe he was in the loo, but Jack wasn't so desperate to talk to him that he was prepared to check in there.

Returning to his own office, Tyler logged off his computer and put the docket he had been reading back in the filing cabinet. He was just slipping his jacket on when his mobile rang.

"DCI Tyler," he said, slipping his man bag over his shoulder and flicking the switch to kill the lights.

"...*Jack*..." It was Andy, but he sounded like he had his head in a bucket, and he was out of breath as though he had been sprinting.

Tyler stopped in his tracks, frowning. "Andy...?"

"*BBBLLLUUURRRGGGHHH!*"

As if the retching wasn't bad enough, the unmistakable sound of projectile vomit splashing all over the toilet turned Tyler's stomach, and he instinctively snatched the phone away from his ear in revulsion.

After a few seconds of heavy breathing and low moaning, Quinlan was back on the line. His voice sounded pitiful. "I think that egg sandwich must have been off...I can't stop throwing..." the sentence was interrupted by another violent bout of sickness.

"Jesus!" Tyler said, looking at the phone in horror. Quinlan was obviously in the toilets with his head stuck down a bowl, and he wondered if he should go in and help. But what could he do? Besides, if there was one thing that Tyler couldn't stand, it was the smell of puke.

He recalled that Susie Sergeant was a trained 'First Aider at Work', so he decided to find her and turn her loose on Quinlan. That would either kill him or cure him, he thought wryly.

"*Sorry...*" Quinlan said when he came back on the line. "*Listen, Jack, I'm gonna have to go home but I can't leave poor Carol running a Cat A enquiry. Would you mind taking over for a ...*" Quinlan threw up again, so loud and so hard that Tyler was afraid he'd ruptured something internally.

"Bloody hell mate," he said, worried. "You really don't sound good. Do you want me to call out the FME?"

"*No point,*" Quinlan moaned, sounding very weak. "*I just need to let it run its course and then rest.*"

He was probably right, but Jack didn't want him being left alone in that state. "I'll get someone to drive you home," he said, thinking that they would need to make sure they had a bloody big bucket with them.

"*Thanks*," Quinlan said, breathlessly. "*Listen, can you step in and take over as SIO until I come back to work? I know it's a bit of a liberty for me to ask...*"

"Don't be silly," Tyler said. "I haven't got anything on the go so it's no trouble at all."

"*You're a star,*" Quinlan said, and then chortled mirthlessly. "*Come to think of it, are you sure you didn't poison me just to get me out of the way? I know how much you and Dillon wanted this job.*"

Jack laughed. "You poisoned yourself, you brainless wally. I told you not to eat that sandwich, but you wouldn't listen. So much for you having the constitution of an ox."

"*I do have the constitution of an ox,*" Quinlan insisted. "*A very sick ox.*"

It turned out that Susie Sergeant was unavailable to do her Florence Nightingale routine as she was still tied up interviewing Mullings. Luckily, one of the DCs on Andy's team had also gone on the course, and between them, she and Jack managed to get Quinlan out of the toilet and into the first aid room.

Returning to his office a few minutes later, Jack phoned Holland to let him know that he was temporarily taking over the investigation. *Thunderball* would have to wait for another night.

There was no reply, so he left a voicemail for the boss to call him back.

That done, he went straight into Quinlan's MIR and asked his Office Manager to give him an in-depth briefing on where they stood with the investigation.

Quinlan's OM was a fair-haired man in his late forties called DS Tom Wilkins. For some bizarre reason, Wilkins had a thing about wearing bow ties instead of regular ones, and today he wore a burgundy number with a swirl leaf pattern. His accent betrayed his Lancashire origins, and his weathered complexion suggested that he was a man who liked spending time outdoors. Wilkins had a fairly high-pitched voice, and when Jack closed his eyes it was just like listening to George Formby.

"As far as I'm concerned boss," Wilkins beamed, "everything's tickety-boo."

Jack frowned disapprovingly. "Not sure PC Morrison or his grieving family would say things were tickety-boo," he pointed out.

That wiped the smile from the OM's face. "No, no, of course not," he said, looking down at the floor, embarrassed. "What I meant was, from an evidential perspective, we're doing really well. We're only one day into the investigation and we already know who three of the four people involved in helping Winston to escape are. We've gathered all the CCTV from the hospital, and it's fantastic. We've got the baddies arriving, going in, and then hijacking the helicopter a short time later. Basically, their every movement inside the hospital is captured on tape apart from the murder itself, but that happened in a private room."

Jack grunted. "When I spoke to Reg Parker earlier, he was hoping that the scene outside Winston's room and the fight with Tony Dillon might have been caught on camera too. Do you know if he's managed to access that footage yet?"

The OM nodded solemnly. "Aye, he has, and it's chilling to watch. The jury will probably convict them on that alone."

"I'd like to see it if possible," Jack said.

"If you pop into the CCTV viewing room and speak to Darren Blyth, he'll play it for you. You can't miss Darren, he's a deep-voiced Manc, and he looks like someone stuck an owl's head on the body of a scarecrow."

Tyler smiled at the apt description, recalling Blyth from that morning's meeting.

"I'll do that, thanks. What about key witnesses? I've had an update about the pilot, Peter Myers, but what about the ward sister and the two drugged officers?"

"Yes, the ward sister, Melissa Smails, was key witnessed on tape this morning."

This basically meant that the whole statement taking process was completed in an interview room with an audio or videotape running, and it was done this way to prevent defence counsel from trying to infer that the witness had been primed or fed things to say.

"She's gonna be great in the box, from what I hear," Tom Wilkins said. "She's been looking after Winston for the best part of a week so she knows him by name and by sight, which eliminates any need for an ID parade. Also, she's confident she could pick out both the fake doctor and Errol Heston in a line-up. I was reading through the First Description booklets a little while ago, and she has done a really good job describing them."

"We don't need to worry about Errol Heston now he's brown

bread," Jack said. "I don't suppose his involvement is going to be contested by anyone."

"Especially as we recovered his gun," Tom Wilkins said.

"Do we think it had been fired?" Jack asked.

Wilkins shook his head. "According to the SO19 officer who made it safe at the scene, all five rounds were still in the cylinder and there was no sign of recent discharge. It'll have to be confirmed by the lab, but it fits in with what we already suspected – that Winston's the shooter."

"What about the fake nurse, Angela what's-her-name? Will Sister Smails be able to pick her out in a line-up?"

The OM shook his head. "Marley had her surgical mask up the whole time that Smails was in the room with her. It doesn't really matter; Marley left us a beautiful thumbprint on the unused syringe that was found near PC Morrison."

Tyler nodded. "I think we'll also get her wearer DNA off the coat that she left in the getaway car," he said.

"Yes, I'm sure we will," Tom Wilkins agreed. "Oh, and we've also got a statement from a real-life porter called Sidney Stevens who bumped into them a couple of times in the hospital, once on the ground floor on their way in, and then again in a freight lift as they were trying to get Winston out. Mr Q didn't want him treated as a key witness though."

That made sense. Although he'd witnessed them in the building, he hadn't seen the offence and they hadn't said anything incriminating in front of him.

"What about the two drugged officers?" Jack asked. "Have they come around yet?"

Wilkins nodded. "Yes, thankfully. They're being kept in for another night of observations but we should be able to get them statemented tomorrow morning. The detective who spoke to them at the hospital told me he was really impressed with the amount of detail they both remember, and their evidence will be powerfully compelling stuff."

Jack raised an eyebrow. If their recall was that good, he doubted that ketamine had been used on them. In his experience, people who had been given that particular drug struggled with their recollection when they came around.

"Will they be able to pick any of them out?" Tyler asked.

"No, afraid not. All three suspects were wearing surgical masks for the duration of the encounter."

"Pity," Jack said, disappointed. "Did they say who shot PC Morrison?"

"No, they were both out cold by the time that happened, and they didn't even know their mate was dead until someone told them."

"Please tell me the news was broken gently."

"As gently as you can break news of that nature," Wilkins said with a grimace.

Jack winced. Tom was right; there was no easy way to tell someone that their friend had just been executed. He turned his mind to the weight of evidence they had accrued so far. With the CCTV, witness testimony, fingerprint for Marley and the wearer DNA he fully expected to get from the coats of all three suspects, it was already looking like a pretty solid case.

"Any developments on the phone data yet?" he asked.

"Haven't heard anything on that," Tom admitted. "Reggie Parker was appointed as our phones man, so maybe you should have a word with him. Of course, it's possible that the applications have been slightly delayed because Mr Q wanted him to get the CCTV up and running first."

"I see," Tyler said. Reggie would be his next port of call after Darren Blyth, he decided.

"We've had people pounding the pavement all day, pressuring every lowlife dealer, addict, and hooker we could find, not to mention putting the squeeze on Winston's rivals, but so far we've drawn a big fat blank."

"Realistically, that was never going to be a quick fix," Tyler said, "but if we keep pushing, chances are that something will give further along the line."

"I hope you're right," Tom said. He didn't sound overly convinced.

After leaving the MIR, Tyler made for the CCTV viewing room, which seemed a rather grand title for a space that was, in reality, not much bigger than a broom cupboard. Inside, he found the owlish Darren Blyth and his own Reg Parker huddled together over a TV monitor. Both were giggling like naughty schoolchildren. They were so engrossed in what they were doing that they hadn't even heard him enter.

"Play it again," Reg sniggered. "I just want to make sure that flicker's gone."

Still laughing, Darren pressed rewind. "My pleasure," he said. There was a brief whirring noise and then a click. Blyth then pressed the play button and the screen came to life.

Jack tiptoed closer, intrigued. Parker had a reputation as a mischief-maker, so he had no doubt that the team's resident prankster was behind whatever was going on.

The theme to the 1978 Christopher Reeve *Superman* film started to play just as a freeze-frame image of a long, sterile-looking corridor came into view. The door to the RLH freight lift could be seen in the top right corner of the picture. As the music continued, with Darren humming along in tandem, words started to appear on the screen, written in white block capitals. They appeared one after the other, like the title sequence at the start of a movie:

Is it a bird...?
Is it a plane...?
No, it's a flying nurse...!

The words faded as the film started rolling. Almost immediately, a dishevelled black woman, clad in the uniform of a nurse, came hurtling out of the lift like a rocket. She had to be at least seven feet off the ground, and she was travelling at considerable speed, both arms flailing as she cartwheeled through the air. Both men erupted into laughter, and Darren started clapping his hands.

"Brilliant," he said as the woman landed on the floor in a heap. "Fucking brilliant!"

Tyler cleared his throat and both men spun around guiltily.

"Boss!" Parker exclaimed nervously. "I didn't hear you come in." As he spoke, he sidled in front of the monitor to block Tyler's view while his co-conspirator scrabbled to press the stop button.

"What are you up to?" Tyler demanded, acting like he didn't already know.

"Nothing," Parker said with forced innocence. The blush that started at his neckline quickly spread upwards, turning his cherubic face the colour of a stop sign.

"You're a terrible liar, Reggie," Tyler scolded, "and a bloody menace." A smile creased his face. "Now, play it again so I can have a proper look."

Parker's shoulders sagged in relief. "It's only a joke," he said. "Just a little something I put together for the enquiry team."

"If that footage gets into the wrong hands it'll cause havoc," Tyler warned them. He dreaded to think what a red-top newspaper like *The London Echo* would do with that if they got their mitts on it. "And be a little circumspect about who you show it to. I don't suppose close colleagues of PC Morrison would find it terribly amusing."

"No," Parker agreed, "but they might enjoy seeing one of their mate's killers thrown across the hall like a rag doll."

He had a point, Tyler accepted, but even so. "Just be careful who you show it to," he warned, "and don't lend that tape to anyone else under any circumstances. Capisce?"

Parker nodded obediently. "Yes, boss."

After the light relief of watching Dillon play 'toss the fake nurse', Jack instructed them to show him the footage of the suspects overpowering the two officers outside Winston's room. As Tom Wilkins had claimed, it was indeed chilling to watch, and no one seeing this could possibly be left in any doubt that all three suspects – the doctor, the nurse, and the porter – were equally complicit in the breakout, and, therefore, equally responsible for PC Morrison's death.

The dramatic footage of Melissa Smails fleeing the room, pursued by the burly porter, was no less shocking. As she glanced back over her shoulder, the look of abject terror on her face was perfectly captured by the camera.

"I can't imagine how terrified that poor girl must have been," Tyler said.

Reggie permitted himself an evil laugh. "Still, he got his comeuppance in the end, didn't he?" he proclaimed happily. "An ounce of lead through the forehead, courtesy of SO19."

They played the fight scene at the freight elevator next. Unfortunately, because the camera was mounted in the hall, most of the action went unseen. When the bit where Angela Marley was thrown out of the elevator came on, Blyth started humming the *Superman* tune and, out of the corner of his eye, Tyler caught Parker suppressing a grin. He wondered if he should confiscate the clip Reg had made before anyone else saw it? But knowing Reggie, the slippery sod would only make another one behind his back.

"Right, Mr Parker," he said after viewing the CCTV. "We need to discuss what progress you've made with the TIU and how they're getting on with our telephone enquiries." The Telephone Investigation Unit was based at New Scotland Yard, and they liaised directly with the various service providers to obtain telephone related data for police enquiries. "I want you in my office in five minutes time to walk me through all the applications you've made and any results that have come in during the day."

That wiped the smile off Parker's face.

As he walked back to his office, smiling at the *Superman* clip despite his better judgement, his mobile rang.

It was George Holland.

After explaining that Andy Quinlan had attempted to commit suicide by eating an out of date egg mayonnaise sandwich that had been left in a drawer next to a boiling hot radiator all night, he got down to business.

"I need urgent oral authority to commence covert surveillance on an address in Vicarage Lane, E15. It's a squat where Angela Marley lives. She's been identified as the suspect who was dressed as a nurse." An image of her sailing across the hall to the theme of *Superman* flashed into his head unbidden.

"*Why not just send an arrest team around to scoop her up?*" Holland asked.

"The problem with doing that is that we don't know if and when she's going to be there. At the moment, she doesn't know that we've identified her, but if we rock up and she's not inside, word will spread like wildfire and she'll go to ground, plus our mysterious doctor will undoubtedly hear about it and do likewise."

Holland considered this. "*Very well, but get the paperwork over to me ASAP, and in light of Andy being indisposed, I suppose you'd better join me for the press conference at Whitechapel.*"

"Press conference?" That stopped Jack in his tracks. "What bloody press conference?"

"*The one that starts at 6 p.m. You've just about got enough time to get here if you pull your finger out.*" ***

The interviews with Mullings were finally over; all the evidence had been put to him in the presence of his orange-faced solicitor. Predictably, the churlish getaway driver had mostly no commented every question they'd asked him, even the innocuous one about whether he'd enjoyed his MacDonald's.

It had been decided that they would grant him technical bail in relation to the murder to avoid putting themselves under undue pressure. After conferring with Jack Tyler – it hadn't been an easy conversation, what with the car's two-tones blaring in the background as he was whisked across East London for a press conference that he was unlikely to make in time – Susie had broken the news to Mullings.

"So why can't I go home then, if I'm being bailed?" he'd demanded.

"Oh, go on then, as you've asked so nicely," Murray told him.

Gifford Mullings could hardly believe his ears. "Really?" he asked, suddenly all smiles.

"Of course not, you moron," Murray said harshly. "We've already explained this to you several times. You've been charged with TDA and possession of Class A drugs with intent to supply. You have a nasty habit of skipping bail when it's granted. You're a flight risk and an idiot."

"I'm pretty sure being an idiot isn't a good reason to oppose bail," the custody sergeant, who had been eavesdropping, chipped in.

"Exactly," Mullings said triumphantly. "You can't refuse me bail just cause I'm stupid, innit."

Susie sighed in exasperation. "Gifford, your solicitor will explain it to you before he leaves, but the long and short of the story is you're going to be staying here overnight and then you will be taken to the Magistrates Court tomorrow morning."

"Where I'll get bail?" he asked.

"No!" Murray snapped in exasperation.

"Why not?" Mullings demanded.

Murray looked like he was in danger of punching the prisoner.

Susie Sergeant placed a restraining hand on his scrawny arm and turned to Clarke. "As soon as a formal charging decision is made regarding the murder, we'll let you know," she said.

Clarke scowled at her. "Reading between the lines, it seems to me that you've already made up your minds to charge my client," he said. "Even though it's blatantly obvious that the only thing he's guilty of is making some poor choices about who he befriends."

Susie smiled, disarmingly. "Not my decision to make," she said, although there was no doubt in her mind that he would be charged with the Joint Enterprise murder.

"He's guilty of making a poor choice in solicitors too," Murray whispered in Susie's ear just loudly enough for Clarke to hear.

Leaving the solicitor to have a final consultation with his client, Susie and Murray retired to the small CID office they'd purloined and gathered up their belongings. Susie tried to call Tyler back, but his phone had been switched off. She was tired and hungry, and couldn't wait to put her feet up for a few minutes. Not that there was any danger of that happening for a while. When they got back to Arbour Square, they still had all the custody paperwork to tidy up and submit to the MIR.

They returned to the custody suite fifteen minutes later in order to thank the custody sergeant for his assistance and leave a contact number in case there were any issues overnight.

"Is Mr Clarke still in with his client?" Susie asked.

The custody sergeant shook his head. "Left a few minutes ago. Couldn't wait to get out of here from the look on his face. Mullings was still asking why he couldn't have bail when he was taken down to the cells."

They made their way out to the front office and were just about to leave when Oliver Clarke stormed through the door, holding his right hand out in front of him as though it were infected with something horribly contagious.

"Bastards," he seethed. "Bloody animals!"

Susie walked over to him, curious. "Is anything the matter, Mr Clarke?" she asked, looking down at his hand, which was covered in a thick brown substance. And then she caught a whiff of it and recoiled. "Is that shit on your hand?" she asked, horrified.

"Yes, it bloody well is," Clarke fumed, his face contorted with rage. "Some horrible little oik has smeared dog shit all over the door handle of my beautiful Jag. When I went to open it – well, look. It's everywhere."

Susie had to bite her lip to stop herself from smiling. It was undoubtedly a prank by local yobs who were jealous of someone having a big flash car, but he was such a smug bastard that she couldn't help but be pleased by his reaction.

"Do you want to make a report of criminal damage?" she asked. "I can get the station officer to take it if you do."

"What's the bloody point?" Clarke snapped. "I've already checked, and there's no CCTV coverage. You lot aren't going to waste your time following something like this up so reporting it will just be a paper exercise."

"In that case, we'll say goodnight," she said. "I would shake your hand but..." she let her words trail off. There was no need to state the obvious.

A devilish grin had lit up Murray's face. "I wouldn't have shaken your hand even if it had been clean," he said, winking at the solicitor.

Leaving Clarke to rant and rave, Murray followed Susie through to the back yard. If the solicitor thought this was bad, Murray couldn't wait to see his reaction when he discovered the large dollop of dog shit that had been placed inside his precious chariot's exhaust pipe. When that heated up, it would produce an aroma that would cling to his car's interior for weeks to come.

"You seem particularly pleased with yourself tonight," Susie observed, having noticed the skip in his step as they crossed the yard towards their pool car. It was quite out of character, and her eyes narrowed with suspicion. "Anything I should know about?"

"No," Murray said with a carefree shake of his head. "Just feeling satisfied after another gratifying day of solving crime and keeping London safe."

CHAPTER NINETEEN

Tyler didn't like press conferences much at the best of times, but this one promised to be a real doozy. It was being held in a cramped conference room at Whitechapel police station. The media circus had turned out in full force, and it had now reached a point where it was oversubscribed and there was no more room inside for the stragglers who were still arriving in dribs and drabs.

"I'm quite happy to let one of the reporters take my place," he whispered in Holland's ear.

"Nice try," Holland replied, "but you're not going anywhere."

Having made it to Whitechapel by the skin of his teeth, Tyler now found himself sitting at a long table that had been draped in a layer of thick blue cloth embroidered with the MPS crest. To his immediate left sat George Holland. Beyond him, Charles Porter, the ambitious Borough Commander, was busily preening himself so that he would look his best for the public.

Behind them, providing a more aesthetic view than the room's drab wallpaper, a set of large concertina screens with the Met's 'Making London Safe' logo plastered all over them had been unfolded to provide a corporate backdrop. Directly in front of them, on the other side of the table, an intimidating line of cameras bore down on them, ready to capture any mistakes that they made on film.

"I didn't realise this was being recorded," Jack whispered, nodding at the TV cameras. He shook his head at his own naivety. "I thought it would just be a few reporters."

He'd already caught sight of Terri Miller, the *London Echo's* star reporter. She was sitting in the middle of the front row, pen poised like all the other journalists. The sight of them all clustered together, licking their lips in hungry anticipation, reminded him of a big cat enclosure moments before feeding time.

The pretty brunette, looking resplendent in a stylish and vibrant two-piece red suit and dark blue silk blouse, had had the temerity to smile at him like they were old friends when he'd entered the room a few moments ago.

She seemed to have conveniently forgotten how, in her desperation to get a story about the New Ripper, she had thoughtlessly trounced her way through a major crime scene back in November, contaminating vital evidence. Her buddy, the clumsy photographer who had helped her, was also there, standing amongst her fellow snappers and chatting away as if she didn't have a care in the world. He struggled to remember her name. Was it June or Julie? It was definitely something like that.

Having manhandled the grey thatch atop his head into some semblance of order, Chief Superintendent Charles Porter now turned his attention to his bushy eyebrows, using a spit laden forefinger to flatten them down. When he was finally satisfied with his appearance, he leaned back in his seat and started cleaning his glasses with a white handkerchief, squinting like Mr Magoo as he did so.

Tyler leaned in conspiratorially and indicated Porter with a flick of his eyes. "I hope he's not being allowed to speak this time?"

Holland grimaced as he recalled the last press conference that they had done together, in which Porter had gone off-script and started ranting at a serial killer on live TV. Porter's tirade had infuriated the man they were after so much that he'd struck again the following evening.

"No, he's only here as a courtesy because he's the Borough Commander and the hospital is on his ground. He's been told in no uncertain terms that he is not to engage with the media."

"That's a relief," Jack said. He hadn't had an opportunity to discuss the impending conference with Holland and he was feeling woefully unprepared. He raised a hand to shield his mouth in case anyone from the media was a lip reader. "Please tell me we're not going public with the fact we've identified the fake nurse?"

Holland gave an almost imperceptible shake of his head. "No, we keep that to ourselves," he said, following suit and covering his own mouth. "We will, however, formally announce the death of Errol Heston and link him to the hospital murder."

"That makes sense," Tyler agreed. The media had already begun openly speculating that the man who had died during a shootout with armed officers near the BTNA might have been involved in the earlier breakout. Officially releasing the man's name couldn't hurt the enquiry. In fact, throwing them a few titbits might keep the newsies off his back for a little while and allow him to get on with the job in peace. The last thing he wanted was to have rogue elements of the press breathing down his neck at every turn, the way they had during the Whitechapel murders.

"Are there any next of kin here?" Jack asked. He looked around but didn't see anyone who obviously fit the bill.

Holland shook his head again. "No, they were informed of the press conference but declined to come. I'm glad. I hate having to watch a victim's loved ones being subjected to all those heartless questions."

On the stroke of six, the Press Liaison Officer called for everyone's attention, and the briefing commenced.

Holland looked suitably solemn as he leaned forward to address the cameras, arms resting on the table in front of him, fingers gently interlocked.

"Yesterday afternoon a career criminal called Claude Winston escaped from the Royal London Hospital in Whitechapel, where he had been receiving treatment for a ruptured appendix. He was assisted by four people, three males and a female. During the escape, Police Constable Stanley Morrison was fatally shot in what can only be described as an abhorrent act of mindless violence. Two of his colleagues were also injured, but they are expected to make a full recovery. Three of the suspects made their escape by hijacking the HEMS ambulance and forcing the pilot, Captain Peter Myers, to fly them to a section of wasteland in Canning Town. However, two of the gang involved were not so lucky. The driver of the getaway car was arrested by detectives at the scene. Another member of the gang fled the building on foot and then carjacked a vehicle at gunpoint."

Cameras were clicking frantically as he spoke, and the repeated bursts of strobing flashes were giving Jack a headache.

Lucky none of us are epileptic, he thought, squinting against the constant glare.

"The stolen car was subsequently spotted, and armed officers carried out a controlled stop in East India Dock Road, near the slip road that leads to the Blackwall Tunnel Northern Approach. Unfortunately, during the incident that followed, the suspect, who I can now formally name as Errol Heston, a twenty-eight-year-old black male from East London, was shot. Tragically, despite receiving emergency treatment at the scene and undergoing extensive surgery at hospital, Mr Heston passed away as a result of his injuries during the early hours of this morning."

Tyler studied the gaggle of reporters. Their pens were scribbling so frantically that it wouldn't have surprised him to see smoke start rising from the paper they were writing on. Unlike most of the others, Terri Miller was holding up a small recorder, and her eyes were aglow as if she sensed another great story was hers for the taking.

Holland paused to draw breath before continuing. "I want to appeal to the public for their urgent help in locating Claude Winston. We know he's still in London, and we think he will probably be in need of medical assistance. At the time of his escape, he was taking strong antibiotics to battle a post-operative infection, but he fled the hospital without his medication. He also became involved in a physical struggle with officers who tried to detain him at the scene, and it is quite possible some of his stitches will have burst open as a result. If you work in a doctor's surgery or chemist, and anyone has come in to obtain medical supplies in what you consider to be unusual circumstances, please get in touch with the Incident Room directly, or phone Crimestoppers anonymously. Additionally, I'm confident that someone out there knows where Winston and the two fugitives who helped him are currently holed up, and I appeal directly to these people. Please, help us to recapture this extremely dangerous man and put him back behind bars before he harms anyone else."

Jenna Marsh sat in her living room eating her tea from a tray precariously balanced on her lap. She had arrived home from work a few minutes ago, announcing that she was tired, had achy feet and was absolutely famished. Her mother, Violet, had anticipated this, and she had a plate of sausage, mash and baked beans ready and waiting for her ravenous daughter.

As soon as Jenna had kicked off her boots, she had raided the fridge for a cold can of Coke to wash it all down with and then carried the lot into the living room to enjoy her scoff in front of the telly.

Their dog, a little Westie called Basil, was sitting by her feet, hoping to scavenge a few scraps.

"How was it today, love?" her dad asked, switching the TV on and flopping down in his favourite armchair to watch the BBC news at six. It had become a bit of a ritual over the years, all sitting down together for the early evening news, and they still did it whenever they could.

Violet had followed her in from the kitchen and was now relaxing next to Jenna on the sofa with her ever-present bundle of knitting and a nice hot cup of tea.

It never ceased to amaze Jenna how her mum could happily sit there for hours at a time, stitching away like an automaton, making scarves and jumpers that, more often than not, ended up being donated to charity shops.

Jenna shrugged indifferently. "It was okay," she said, pouring a liberal dose of tomato sauce over her sausages.

The presenter was updating viewers about a story that had broken the previous day in which seven young fishermen were feared drowned after their scallop dredger, The Solway Harvester, had disappeared off the Scottish coast during a force nine gale. Its last contact had been with a sister vessel called Tobrach-N at 17:50 local time, at which point the crew had said they were going to seek shelter from the weather at Ramsey in the Isle of Man. This afternoon, the announcer regretted to inform them, a boat using sonar equipment had found the wreck of The Solway Harvester in about forty feet of water, eleven miles southeast of the Isle of Man. There was no trace of the crew.

"Poor blighters," her dad said, shaking his head sadly. "What a terrible way to go." Seafaring stories always grabbed his attention because his grandfather's ship had been sunk while he'd been serving with the Merchant Navy during World War Two.

The next segment featured an update on the hunt for soap star Craig Masters, who had gone on the run in the early hours of New Year's Day after strangling his society girlfriend and well-known fashion model, Katie Cunningham.

Basically, the update was that there was no update, and the police appeared to be completely stumped as to where he was hiding out. There had been reported sightings in Brighton, Devon, Northumberland and even one as far afield as Aberdeen, but they had all turned out to be red herrings. "How can they be having trouble finding a bloke that famous?" Violet said, looking up from her knitting. "He must have one of the most recognisable faces in the blooming country."

"I saw a face from the past today," Jenna told them, shovelling food into her mouth. "Do you remember a boy I went to school with called Rodney Dawlish? Kevin used to hang out with his older brother, Jimmy."

Her mum's face immediately adopted a disapproving scowl. "That boy was rotten to the core. He led my poor Kevin astray, got him into all sorts of trouble." She simmered in silence for a moment, and then her face scrunched up in concentration. "I don't remember him having a little brother, though."

"Well, he did," Jenna said, "and I went to school with him. Anyway, Rodney came into the shop today. First time I've seen him in years."

In a voice dripping with bitterness, she said, "No doubt he's turned out to be just as big a waste of space as Jimmy."

"Actually, he seemed to be a nice guy," Jenna said, feeling obliged to leap to his defence. "He was collecting some medical supplies for a friend and he said he has a job, so he can't be all bad."

The next news segment took viewers to a live press conference at Whitechapel police station, where officers were appealing for witnesses in the hunt for another murderer who was on the run.

"Shush, you two. I want to listen to this," Jenna's dad, Alfie, told them.

Jenna pulled a face at him, and her mother rolled her eyes. He didn't like anyone talking when the news was on, said it spoiled his enjoyment.

A craggy-faced, middle-aged detective was speaking, his face suitably serious. The caption that appeared at the bottom of the screen read: Det. Ch. Supt. George Holland.

"I want to appeal to the public for their urgent help in locating Claude Winston. We know he's still in London, and we think he will probably be in need of medical assistance. At the time of his escape, he was taking strong antibiotics to battle a post-operative infection, but he fled the hospital without his medication. He also became involved in a physical struggle with officers who tried to detain him at the scene, and it is quite possible some of his stitches will have burst open as a result. If you work in a doctor's surgery or chemist, and anyone has come in to obtain medical supplies in what you consider to be unusual circumstances, please get in touch with..."

Jenna's fork stopped halfway between the plate and her mouth as her stomach suddenly constricted and her appetite vanished. "Oh no," she said as she recalled Rodney's visit to the chemist, the items he had purchased, and the things he had told her in conversation...

'*...Look, he hasn't been stabbed, and he hasn't hurt himself breaking into a shop,*' Rodney had said. '*He had an operation in hospital last week but his stitches have popped and we need to change the dressing. That's all...*'

An operation... like a burst appendix?

And then she recalled his response after she'd enquired about his friend going back to hospital to get himself checked out?

'*...He can't, not with the Old Bill looking for him...*'

An icy chill ran down Jenna's back and she closed her eyes, suddenly feeling very sick. *Oh, I pray I'm wrong,* she thought, telling herself not to jump to hasty conclusions.

"What's the matter, dear?" her mum asked, eyeing her with concern.

"Shhh," her father chastised, too engrossed in the story to drag his eyes away from the screen.

Jenna didn't dare voice her fears to her mum; she had such a downer on the Dawlish family that she would interpret Jenna's suspicions as concrete proof that Rodney was indeed every bit as bad as his brother.

"Nothing," she whispered, so as not to invoke her father's displeasure. "I've just remembered something I have to do."

While Jenna Marsh and her parents were watching the BBC news in the warmth and comfort of their home, Angela Marley was sitting on a low wall outside a detached house in Barking, shivering with cold and bracing herself against the cruel wind.

Every bone in her body seemed to ache from where she'd been thrown out of the freight elevator the previous day, and she felt that she really ought to be tucked up in her bed back at the squat, not stuck out here freezing to death.

Having left her own coat in the getaway car, Angela had been forced to borrow a tattered old Parka from Rodent, which she now wore over the skimpy nurse's outfit.

She was acutely conscious that the slap she'd received from Garston as punishment for blurting Errol's name out had left her face in a bit of a state; a mottled, hand-shaped, bruise covered one side of it and her bottom lip was all swollen and split, making it painful to speak. Fortunately, it was so dark that someone would have to be standing right next to her in order to notice.

Where the hell is the old perv? she asked herself, gritting her teeth to stop them from chattering. Standing up, she tried slapping her scrawny arms around her body to generate some heat, but it didn't help in the slightest, and after a few seconds she gave it up and sat down again.

She was incensed by Garston's callous disregard for her safety; he should have sent Rodent to recruit the old man, or – better still – come himself, not send an unescorted woman to do the job. When she'd attempted to lodge a protest, Garston's flippant response had been to point out that Cribbins only shagged dead girls, adding that as long as she kept breathing, she should be perfectly safe.

She hadn't found his disparaging remarks remotely funny.

Not for the first time, she wondered why she continually put herself in danger. The answer, of course, was as simple as it was obvious: money and the promise of free drugs. God knew she needed as much as she could get of both. What she raked in from being on the game was never enough; nor was the extra income she cobbled together from a doing bit of random shoplifting or robbing the female Vietnamese DVD sellers who floated through the area every now and again.

Besides, that could be dangerous; the last woman she'd tried to turn over had brought a minder with her, and the fucker had chased Angela down the road with a meat cleaver.

She knew Garston didn't give a toss if anything happened to her. In his eyes, she was a worthless, expendable whore. She hated the way that he looked down his nose at her as if she had willingly ended up as a drug addict, like it was a career choice or something – not that he was the only one who did that; the police, her punters, the staff at the needle exchange, even the pious little nurse practitioner who performed free health checks at The Sutton Mission, they all looked at her the same way.

When she'd been younger, Angela had been as full of dreams and aspirations as any other kid, but life was fucking cruel, and sometimes it forced you down a path you would rather have avoided.

She hadn't even reached puberty the first time that her step-father skulked into her bedroom during the middle of the night. What he had forced her to do after quietly closing the door and slipping into bed beside her had made her young skin crawl. Afterwards, as she lay there sobbing, he warned her not to say anything, that no one would ever believe her, and that she would only get into trouble for making things up – and he had been right. Her alcoholic mother had been more interested in the contents of a gin bottle than her daughter's welfare, and when, after weeks of inner turmoil, Angela eventually found the courage to tell her, she dismissed her accusations of abuse as the malicious ramblings of a spiteful girl who just wanted to cause trouble for her family.

When Angela timidly broached the subject again, a couple of weeks later, the woman who had bought her into this world, and who was supposed to love and protect her, had given her a severe beating for making up stories. Angela had kept quiet after that, choosing to suffer the repulsive nocturnal visits in silence rather than risk her drunken mother's wrath again.

At school, her behaviour had gradually deteriorated; she became disruptive in class and repeatedly got into fights with other children, often over the most trivial things. Her teachers came to consider her a problem child, a delinquent, and they were quite happy when she started bunking off.

By that stage, Angela had come to feel totally isolated; she was all alone in the world, with no one to turn to and no one to help her. As soon as she reached sixteen, she had run away from a home that felt more like a prison and started sleeping rough. It was better than living with the constant fear of being raped; the indescribable dread that every night time noise heralded the approach of a man she loathed and detested with every fibre of her being.

One evening, as she was walking through the park on her way to a squat she had started dossing down at, she was approached by a local dealer who offered her a freebie. He promised that the magic chemicals would bring contentment and happiness; a brief respite from the pain and misery that was her day-to-day life.

With nothing to lose, Angela had given the Golden Brown a try. Getting hooked had been that simple.

The second sample the dealer had supplied her with had also been free, but not the third. Having reeled her in, he was now demanding cold hard cash in exchange for his merchandise. Angela didn't have any money, but she needed the gear, so she nicked some electrical goods from a nearby Woolworth store and swapped them for the smack.

Shoplifting financed her fourth and fifth purchases as well, but by then the store guards had grown wise to her and had barred her from most of the local shops.

On the sixth occasion that she sought out her dealer, she hadn't had any drugs for a few days, and she was clucking badly. It was a horrible new experience, as unpleasant in its own way as the abuse she had suffered from her step-father. She was desperate for a fix when she met up with him, and with no other means of paying for it, she had performed oral sex in exchange for heroin. It had been the first step down a very slippery slope. That had been a lifetime ago, but she still relived the horrors every night in her dreams and she suspected that she always would.

Tearing her mind away from the past, Angela glanced up and down the road again, flinching as the wind lashed at her face.

According to an advert she'd found in the local Yellow Pages, the funeral parlour Horace Cribbins worked for closed at six p.m. It was only a few minutes' walk from there to his house, so why was she still stuck out in the cold at a quarter-past, desperate for a piss, and still waiting for the deviant wanker to arrive?

She wiped her nose on the sleeve of Rodent's coat. She wasn't sure if it was just running because she was so cold or if she was beginning to go into withdrawal.

"Can I help you miss?" A quiet voice said beside her.

Angela hadn't noticed anyone approach and she almost jumped out of her skin. She spun around to see a white man in his late fifties or early sixties staring at her with intense curiosity. Of medium height and a little overweight, he was dressed in a black cashmere coat, underneath which he wore a dark suit and tie. He had a thick shock of white hair that was neatly combed back, and a kindly face that could have belonged to any doting grandfather – as long as that grandfather enjoyed having sex with the corpses of young girls.

"For fuck sake, you nearly gave me a heart attack," she shouted at him as she sprang to her feet.

"Forgive me," he said, bowing apologetically, but Angela was so shaken by his sudden appearance that she hardly noticed the gesture.

As her heartbeat returned to normal, Angela took a moment to appraise the seemingly inoffensive man standing before her with his hands clasped behind his back. Something about Horace Cribbins made her take an instant dislike to him. Was it the blue eyes that brimmed with intelligence but were cold and remote? Or the thin cruel lips that were suggestive of a sadistic nature? No, she decided, it was the dark aura that enveloped him like a death shroud.

Angela had good instincts, and right now they were telling her that this man was dangerous and that she should tread carefully so as not to upset him. "I'm sorry for swearing at you but you made me jump," she told him, sounding contrite and avoiding eye contact.

"Apology accepted," Cribbins said, magnanimously, "but I would still like to know why you're sitting on my wall."

Angela shuffled uncomfortably from foot to foot. She was busting for a pee and standing up had made it even worse. "Before I explain, I don't suppose I could pop inside and use your loo, could I?" she pleaded.

Cribbins eyed her dubiously. "I don't think that would be a good idea. After all, I don't know you. For all I know, as soon as I open my front door a horde of your friends could jump me and pillage my house."

It was a fair point, Angela accepted. There had been a spate of aggravated burglaries around Christmas time, where people calling door-to-door on the pretext of collecting for charities had done exactly that. She had read all about it in the papers.

"I hate to sound unladylike," she said, hopping faster, "but if I don't get to a toilet, fast, I'm going to piss myself."

Cribbins studied her for a long moment, no doubt evaluating just how much of a threat she realistically posed, and then his face softened and he nodded reluctantly. "Very well, but I live with my elderly mother and I don't want her being disturbed."

He opened the squeaky gate and indicated for her to follow him along the path to the street door. After keying them in – and looking around suspiciously to make sure that no one had followed them – he showed her into the hall.

He was obviously doing well for himself, Angela reasoned, because the house was very lavishly decorated. Black and white Victorian checker tiles covered the floor, and a red Petrouchka flock wallpaper hung from the walls. There were several period paintings too, and in their ornate frames, they all looked like the real thing rather than cheap prints, not that she was any kind of expert. After closing the door, he threw his keys into a bowl on a washed oak console table and started to remove his coat.

"The downstairs convenience is the first door on your right. I'm going to have a quick word with my mother. If you finish before I return, wait here until I come for you."

That sounded a bit ominous, but right then all she could think about was getting into the toilet before she had an accident. "Okay," she said, already unzipping the Parker as she dashed off towards the loo.

When she emerged a few minutes later, feeling much better now that her bladder had shrunk back to its normal size, she was startled to find him standing in the hallway, waiting for her with his arms folded.

There were no pleasantries. "I believe you owe me an explanation," he said pointedly.

"Alright," she said, wondering how the unusual request was going to go down. "My friend came out of hospital yesterday following an operation. Unfortunately, he did something that caused most of his stitches to come undone and, for reasons I can't really go into, he can't go back to the hospital." She took a deep breath and released it slowly. "So, we were wondering if you'd be willing to help us out by coming over to where he's staying and stitching him up? For a fee, of course," she added hastily. "We're not expecting a freebie."

Cribbins snorted. "You must be misinformed, dear girl. I'm an embalmer, not a doctor."

"I know," Angela said. "I also know that you used to be a bloody good mortuary technician and that you're as capable of stitching a wound up as any doctor is."

His face had darkened at the mention of his previous occupation, and the transformation made him appear quite sinister.

Angela swallowed hard.

No one knew she was here, apart from Garston, but he wouldn't report her missing if she failed to return.

"What you are suggesting would be quite illegal, young lady," he said sternly. "Why would I want to do something like that?"

"You'd be very well compensated," she said, trying to make the proposition sound as appealing as possible.

Unimpressed, Cribbins waved a hand around the hall. "Does it look like I'm in need of money?" he asked.

"Well, no..." she admitted, quickly trying to think of another angle, "but my friend is very well connected and he would be in your debt if you helped him out. It never hurts to be able to call in a favour from a man like that."

Cribbins raised an eyebrow. "And who exactly is your friend...?" he asked, loading the final word with scorn.

She shook her head emphatically. "Sorry, I can't tell you that."

His cold, unblinking stare unsettled her. "Young lady, I keep abreast of what's happening in the world. Given the timing of your request and the circumstances you've outlined, I'm inclined to suspect that your friend is the man who shot the police officer yesterday. Would my deduction be correct?"

Angela almost laughed at him. *Deduction? Who the fuck does he think he is? Sherlock Holmes?*

"Look," she said, trying to be diplomatic, "I can't discuss anything more with you unless you agree to help. I'm not being difficult, but it's easier for everyone if we keep it like this."

Cribbins was silent for a while, and she could see that he was deep in thought, no doubt trying to work out how he could exploit this situation to his own advantage.

"Very well, describe the wound to me," he said.

"He had a burst appendix," she told him. "It's a big scar because they had to check his entire stomach cavity and remove a load of puss."

"A big scar?"

"Yes."

"Is it bigger than the one on your face?" he asked, smiling cruelly.

Angela self-consciously raised her hand to her face. "Yes," she said, her voice hard as flint. She could tell he was waiting to see if she would look away, or at least turn her head to hide the scar from his view, but she didn't. Looking him straight in the eye, she described the wound, the inflammation, the unpleasant smell and the state of the remaining sutures.

He seemed disappointed that his barb hadn't had more of an effect, but Angela hadn't survived all these years on the game without learning how to block out the spiteful insults that were intended to make her feel even more worthless than she already did.

One of the first lessons she'd learned was that lashing out at those less fortunate than themselves, whether verbally or physically, always made pathetic men like Horace Cribbins feel better about themselves.

The embalmer considered what she had told him. "Sounds like he has an infection. He'll need antibiotics."

"All in hand," Angela said.

"So, apart from receiving a fee for my services and being owed a favour by a wanted felon, can you think of any other reason why I should help your friend out?"

Angela shrugged. "Not really, but after the disgraceful way the police treated you when you lost your job at the mortuary, I would have thought you'd jump at the chance to stick two fingers up at them."

Cribbins actually smiled at that. "Maybe I would," he said. "Give me the address and I'll stop by after nine o'clock tonight. The streets should be a lot quieter by then."

"Really?" Angela had been so sure he was going to decline that she'd already started concocting excuses to justify her failure to Winston and Garston.

Cribbins nodded, all smiles. "Yes, really," he confirmed.

"That's wonderful, but you can't tell anyone," Angela warned him. "Claude's the most wanted man in London at the moment and there are plenty around here who would sell him out if they got wind of where he's staying."

"Don't worry," Cribbins assured her as he showed her to the door. "I'm a man of discretion. I won't tell a living soul."

Angela's relief was palpable. "Do I need to get any special supplies in?" she asked.

Cribbins shook his head. "I already have everything I need. Just tell me the address."

CHAPTER TWENTY

After finishing her tea, Jenna made an excuse that she was going to pop round to a friend's house for a little while. She slipped her boots and winter coat back on, and then set off for the council flat in Lawrence Street where the Dawlish family had resided for as long as she could remember.

It was a ten minute walk from her place in Percy Road, and she spent the time in quiet contemplation. Oblivious to the world around her, she tried to process all the information that she had pieced together, hoping against hope that she was wrong about Rodney and that he wasn't helping the escaped prisoner.

Ignoring the biting wind that numbed exposed skin and ruffled hair, Jenna wondered if she was just wasting her time. After all, she hadn't seen him for years and she had no idea if Rodney even still lived with his parents, but that was the only lead she had. Surely, even if he no longer resided there, they would know how to put her in touch with him?

The flats in Lawrence Road were two storeys high, and the Dawlish family lived up on the top floor. Jenna found an unlocked security door, climbed a urine-scented staircase and strode purposefully along the landing walkway. Stepping across a children's bike that had been blown over by the strong winds, and then ducking under several makeshift washing lines, one of which had an old-fashioned pair of woman's bloomers dangling from it, she counted down the numbers until she found the address she was looking for. There were lights on inside, and as she rapped on the solid wooden door, she could hear the muffled sound of a TV playing inside.

Was that the theme to *EastEnders*?

"Who is it?" an unfriendly female voice shouted from the other side of the door. It sounded slurred, as if the owner were drunk.

"Mrs Dawlish?" she said tentatively, "My name's Jenna Marsh. I used to go to primary school with your son, Rodney. I was hoping to have a word with him."

Silence.

"Mrs Dawlish?" Jenna called again, firmer this time.

"Rodney ain't 'ere so sod off."

"It's very important, Mrs Dawlish," Jenna persisted. "Do you know when he'll be back?"

Jenna listened to the woman shuffling about behind the door, sighing and swearing as she tried to unlock it. After what seemed an age, the door opened inward and Rodney's diminutive mother was standing there swaying. She was barefooted, and the faded jeans and rumpled T-shirt she wore were heavily stained. Jenna got the distinct impression she had been wearing them for several days at least, probably sleeping in them too from the look of it.

Jenna was quite shocked by Mrs Dawlish's unkempt appearance. The woman she remembered from her childhood had always looked so prim and proper, and she had always gone to great pains to ensure her children were well turned out.

In sharp contrast to her previous high standards, the tangled hair of the woman standing before her was sticking up as though she had just been dragged backwards through a thicket. The accusing eyes that struggled to focus on Jenna were rheumy, the skin on her face was blotchy. Mrs Dawlish's lips sagged along one side as though she had recently suffered a stroke, and the teeth were in a terrible state, with a number missing.

What was left of a bottle of vodka hung limply from her left hand, the clear liquid sloshing against the sides every time she moved.

Jeanna was so startled by the transformation that she just stood there, unable to speak.

Mrs Dawlish burped drunkenly and then tottered sideways until she came to a halt against the doorframe. "Rodney don't live 'ere anymore," she said, and then burped again.

Jenna instinctively took a backward step, afraid that Mrs Dawlish was about to throw up over her. She tried not to wrinkle her nose in disgust, but the smell wafting off the poor woman was so rancid that it was making her eyes water.

Her breath was like death; catching a sudden whiff of it, Jenna fought back the urge to gag.

"Do you know where I can find him? Please, Mrs Dawlish, it's important."

The woman shrugged, and in so doing nearly fell over. "Dunno," she slurred, and her face morphed into a mask of sadness. "Bastard never comes to see me anymore."

"I'm sorry to hear that," Jenna said, "but I need you to concentrate for a moment and tell me where he lives."

Mrs Dawlish waved the bottle in the air as she spoke. "Should be livin' 'ere with me, but 'e ain't, is 'e?" Her shoulders slumped and she started to sob. "I got no one left now," she said. "Kevin's banged up inside again, worthless little shit that 'e is, and their father... after all I done fer 'im. After givin' 'im the best years o' me life, the heartless git buggered off with another woman. Thought me precious little Rodney would've stayed with 'is dear ol' mum, but 'e turned out to be just like the others, only out fer 'imself."

As the drunken rambling continued, the woman became increasingly hard to follow, and Jenna soon realised that she wasn't going to get any sense out of Mrs Dawlish tonight. She would have to come back again in the morning. Hopefully, the poor woman would have sobered up a little by then and would be slightly more coherent.

"Okay, thank you, Mrs Dawlish," she said, turning to leave. "Maybe I'll pop by again tomorrow and see if you've been able to remember where Rodney is living these days."

Mrs Dawlish wasn't listening. "Never even visits me, the worthless sod," she said, tearfully venturing onto the walkway outside her flat. "Shame on 'im. 'E only lives in Star Lane. Not exactly like 'e 'as to travel far to see 'is poor ol' mum, is it?"

Jenna stopped in her tracks and spun around. "He lives in Star lane?" she asked, wondering if she had heard correctly.

"Course 'e does," Mrs Dawlish mumbled. She flopped against the wall for support. "Got 'imself a flat in one of them 'ouses opposite the park. All independent now, doesn't need 'is poor ol' mum any longer."

Jenna strode over to her. "Do you know what number he lives at?" she asked, grabbing hold of the woman's skinny arms and shaking them.

"Gerroff me," Rodney's mum shouted, pulling free. "'Ow would I know that? Never even been invited round there, 'ave I?"

Jenna stared at her for a long moment, wondering if she could wheedle any more information out of Mrs Dawlish. Probably not, she decided. With a sigh, she gently placed her hands upon Mrs Dawlish's shoulders and steered her back into her flat.

"You should try and get some rest," she told the woman. "And it might be an idea not to drink any more of that tonight," she added, nodding at the vodka.

It might also be a good idea to have a shower and clean what's left of your teeth, she thought as Mrs Dawlish closed the door behind her and went back to watching *EastEnders*.

Jenna had nothing to lose, so she decided to make a little detour along Star Lane on her way back home. As poor old Mrs Dawlish had said, it wasn't far away, and while she had no idea what number Rodney lived at, there was always a possibility of bumping into him in the street.

Jenna passed beneath the A13 flyover and waited for the traffic lights to go red before crossing the busy Barking Road. She made her way into Manor Road, following it around past the perimeter of Malmesbury Road Park.

Turning into Star Lane, with the park on her right, she walked slowly, staring into each of the properties she passed like a burglar canvassing the area, only instead of being on the look-out for valuables she was searching for Rodney Dawlish.

Why am I even bothering to do this? she asked herself. *I haven't seen him for years and it's not as though he means anything to me. Why don't I just go home, phone the police and tell them what I know? If Rodney's not involved, he won't have anything to worry about.*

But instead of returning home, as common sense dictated, she plodded on with her breath forming little clouds of condensation around her head as she walked.

She was surprised at how many people left their curtains wide open at night, allowing anyone passing by to see inside their homes, and she felt like a bit of a pervert for spying on them while they unknowingly went about their business.

There was something pitiful about Rodney that made her feel strangely protective towards him, and it wasn't just the fact that he was a bit simple. Clearly, he wasn't a saint, far from it, but she suspected that he was basically a good person at heart. The trouble was, he had no one to look out for him and he appeared to be easily led.

She didn't want to see his naivety getting him into trouble, but beyond confronting him about her suspicions, Jenna had absolutely no idea what she was going to do if and when she found him. Hopefully, he would simply laugh at her and tell her that she'd got the wrong end of the stick.

That would be a huge and very welcome relief.

But what if Rodney really was helping this horrible Winston character, and he wasn't the sweet and innocent person that she thought he was? If that turned out to be the case, what she was doing could have dangerous repercussions for both her and her family, and that was a sobering thought.

Feeling a little out of her league, Jenna decided to return home and call the police. As much as she wanted to help Rodney, she realised that she had acted without thinking things through.

Jenna was so wrapped up in her thoughts that she stepped into the road without looking properly, failing to spot the car that had just pulled away from the kerb until it screeched to a stop with its front bumper inches away from her legs. The driver, a slim black man in his late twenties, wound down his window and shouted at her angrily.

Jenna was too stunned to say anything, but she was really surprised by the man's outburst. She appreciated that he was probably in shock, having nearly run her over, and she accepted that it would have been totally her fault, but he had been wearing the surgical greens of a doctor. Surely someone like that should have responded with a little more decorum?

Maybe he'd reacted like that because he spent his working life trying to repair the broken bodies of mindless idiots like her who stepped in front of moving cars without looking?

Feeling lucky to be alive, Jenna cut through the park to Avondale Road and then into Percy Road and home.

Standing in the hallway, she hovered by the telephone, dithering over whether to call the police now or wait until the morning.

"That you, Jen?" her mother called from the kitchen.

That clinched it; Jenna would wait until the morning when no one else was around. Otherwise, her parents would overhear her making the call, and then they would want to know why she was phoning the police. She couldn't face an interrogation like that - not tonight. And besides, if she told them, she would only have to put up with her another bout of her mum droning on about what a terrible lot the Dawlish family were and how Rodney's elder brother had led her poor Kevin astray.

Deontay Garston placed both hands on the peeling green paintwork of the pub's main doors and pushed them open. The creaking hinges were badly in need of a little oil, but the racket coming from inside easily overpowered their feeble protest.

The pub's interior was dim and it took Garston a few moments for his eyes to acclimatise.

The bar was busy, with a three-deep line of customers spanning its circumference. Everyone seemed to be talking as loudly as they could, not only competing with each other but also going up against the music blaring out of the jukebox. The two harried-looking bartenders were buzzing from one side of the bar to the other, struggling to keep up with demand.

His eyes sought out Flogger and, after a few seconds, he spotted his distinctive form hunched in a corner booth at the far end of the building. He'd chosen a spot right beside the entrance to the men's toilets; it was the ideal location for a piece of shit like him.

In Garston's youth, this had been a classic East End pub with great character, a handful of loyal regulars and very little passing trade. Unfortunately, after struggling to make ends meet for several years, the traditionalist landlord had finally been forced to sell out to one of the big breweries who had immediately refurbished and rebranded the old boozer to make it more appealing to the masses.

Although it had retained the original's name, the new *Rose and Crown* had none of its predecessor's charm; the traditional East End accoutrement had been replaced by tacky – some would say kitsch – décor, and the overpriced beer the brewery insisted on serving was mediocre at best. Furthermore, there were no locals anymore, just a bunch of yuppies and Hooray Henrys.

Garston didn't like it at all.

Slipping through a wall of punters, Garston crossed the well-trodden, sticky floorboards and slid into a seat opposite Flogger.

"Sorry I'm late," he said.

After he'd nearly mown down the four-eyed bitch who'd stepped off the pavement right into his path, he'd driven home, changed his clothing and showered. He had collected some money and a few other things before setting off to meet Flogger.

Flogger shrugged. "Don't worry about it," he said magnanimously, which took Garston by surprise. As far as Flogger was concerned, time was money, and delays of any kind bit into his profits.

"I'd offer to buy you a beer," Garston said with a wan smile, "but I'm not queuing for half an hour to get to the bar."

"Already taken care of," Flogger said, and he nodded to a young man with a quiff of oily black hair, greasy skin, and a beaked nose who was leaning against a door marked 'Staff Only'. Dressed in the corporate uniform of a bartender, the man acknowledged him and disappeared inside.

"Me nephew," Flogger explained proudly. "Better than waiting in line with all the plebs."

Garston studied the man who sat opposite him.

Flogger – no one seemed to know his real name – was freakish to look at. He had a lumpy bald head that resembled a Maris Piper potato, gigantic ears stuck out at right angles, saggy jowls, and a triple chin, and the lenses of his black-framed glasses were so thick that they made his rheumy eyes look about five times larger than they actually were.

Garston detected a faint accent, possibly Jewish but definitely Middle Eastern. The supplier wore a long winter coat over a thick, round neck jumper – at least Garston thought that it had a round neck; buried under so many chins it was rather hard to tell. Flogger had the calloused hands of a manual worker, but his liver-spotted fingers were adorned with expensive rings, suggesting he wasn't short of a bob or two. Studying the well lived-in face, Garston decided that if Flogger was a day under sixty, he must have had a very hard paper round.

Flogger looked at him and smiled serenely, revealing two rows of tombstone-like yellow teeth. He leaned forward, beckoning Garston to do likewise. "Let me tell you a joke," he said amiably. "A gorilla walks into a bar and asks for a scotch on the rocks. He hands over a brand new ten pound note to pay for it. 'Well,' the savvy bartender finks to himself, 'surely, this gorilla won't have a clue how much a shot of whiskey actually costs,' so he pours out the spirit and pushes it across the bar along with fifteen pence in change. Making conversation a little while later, the bartender says, 'You know, we don't get a lot of gorillas in here.' The gorilla looks at him and replies, 'I'm not surprised. At nine pounds and eighty five pence a shot, I certainly won't be coming back.'" Flogger burst into laughter, exposing a mouth full of dull fillings.

He seemed disproportionately amused by the story, Garston reflected, not even bothering to smile.

"You know why I like that joke?" Flogger asked, still chortling away. "The bartender reminds me of me, that's why."

"A slippery fucker with no morals?"

"No, an entrepreneur with an eye for making money."

Before Garston could respond, the young man that Flogger had signalled to earlier reappeared and he came over carrying a serving tray that contained two foaming pints and a shot of JD.

"Your drinks, uncle," he said, carefully placing a pint glass before each guest. The whiskey chaser was also for Flogger, Garston saw.

"Thank you, Joseph," Flogger said, reaching for the beer. "Me friend 'ere is paying for 'em."

Garston rolled his eyes but dutifully reached for his wallet. *Should have seen that coming*, he told himself.

"L'Chaim," Flogger said, gulping down a mouthful of beer and sighing appreciatively.

"Cheers ears," Garston said, following suit. As soon as he'd said it, he realised he had made a faux pas. *Probably not the best choice of expressions to use when you're sitting opposite a man whose lugholes could rival Dumbo's*, he thought, smothering a smile in his beer glass.

Thankfully, Flogger didn't seem to notice.

"Did you get the stuff I asked for?" he enquired the moment the bartender was out of earshot.

Flogger paused with his glass halfway to his mouth. "Course I did," he said indignantly. "Gave you me word, didn't I?"

Garston held out an impatient hand. "Forgive my rudeness but I'm in a rush."

Flogger drained the remainder of the glass in a single gulp, made an elaborate show of wiping his mouth on the back of his hand, and then casually reached under his seat. After fumbling around for a moment, the hand reappeared carrying a paper dispensing bag. From inside this, he removed two small white boxes with printed labels on them.

"There you go, two weeks' worth of antibiotics as promised," he said, sliding them across the table for Garston to inspect.

Garston picked up one of the boxes and weighed it in his hand before reading the label. Almost immediately, his brow furrowed and he looked up at Flogger in disbelief. "Are you having a bloody laugh?" he demanded.

Flogger's face was the picture of innocence. "I don't know what you mean," he insisted, scooping up the whiskey chaser and eyeing it with anticipation as he swirled the amber liquid around in the glass.

"These are fucking horse pills!" Garston raged. He read from the packet. "It says here, 'Take as directed by the vet!'"

"You told me you didn't care what I got you as long as they did the job," Flogger pointed out defensively.

"Yeah, I know, but I was expecting human medication," Garston said, shaking the box incredulously. "I can't give him pills that are intended for animals."

"Why not?" Flogger asked with a mischievous grin. "From what I 'ear, Claude Winston's a proper fucking animal, so I would 'ave thought these pills were ideal."

Struggling to contain his anger, Garston leaned across the table. "This is taking the piss, and if I tell Claude what you've given him and what you just said about him, he'll hunt you down and slit your fucking throat, and you know I'm not exaggerating in the slightest."

Subconsciously raising a hand to his Adam's apple, Flogger swallowed hard and squirmed uncomfortably in his chair. Winston's reputation for violence was well known.

"Listen, me ol' mucker," he said, trying to sound reasonable. "I give you me bleedin' word that these will do the trick. An' I ain't lying, I really did 'ave to call in a big favour to get 'em for you. I can't get you anything else until the weekend at the earliest so, I'm afraid, it's these pills or nothing." He sat back and shrugged. "Tell you what, I'll even waive my commission as a sign of good faith."

Garston shook his head. "You're putting me on the spot, you know that?"

"Take the pills. I promise they'll make 'im better, and that's all that matters," Flogger said. "Don't tell Mr Winston that they're animal antibiotics. What 'e don't know won't hurt him."

Garston considered this. He was stuck between a rock and a hard place; it was either these or nothing.

"Did you actually speak to a vet to see if these were safe for human consumption?" Garston asked, starting to come around to the idea.

Flogger shifted uncomfortably. "I asked me contact, who works for a vet, which is virtually the same thing, and 'e swore they were okay."

Garston felt like he was losing the will to live. He dug out the money they had agreed on over the phone, deducting Flogger's standard commission before tossing it onto the table.

After taking a final swig, Garston raised his half-finished pint in a farewell salutation. "If Claude starts to neigh like a fucking horse, I'm coming after you," he warned.

CHAPTER TWENTY-ONE

Having endured the onslaught of questions that had been fired at him during the press conference, Tyler made a beeline for the door the moment it concluded, deftly swerving an approach from Terri Miller, who was angling for an exclusive interview, in the process. Desperate to return to Arbour Square and crack on, he had dragged Steve Bull away from the canteen and sneaked out of the building before anyone else could waylay him.

Holland had a meeting scheduled at NSY with Kim Daily, the DCI from West who was leading the manhunt for Craig Masters, and he accompanied them into the rear yard.

"Bit late for a strategy meeting isn't it?" Jack said, wondering why they weren't leaving it until the morning.

Holland's laugh was devoid of humour. "I've got to brief the Commissioner about it first thing in the morning," he said, "so I need Kim to bring me up to speed tonight."

Jack was surprised to hear that. At the end of the day, ignoring the fact that the victim and perpetrator were both famous, this was a simple domestic; one scene, one victim, one suspect and one key witness – the neighbour. They already knew who all the players were, and surely it was only a matter of time until they found Masters?

"Why's the Commissioner taking an interest?" he asked.

"Because Katie Cunningham's father is a Viscount, and the family are distant relatives of the Queen, and because her uncle is a Tory MP, that's why. This one has become political; the Commissioner is getting pestered by influential people, and the grief he gets from them is filtering down to me and Kim."

"I'm sure Masters will be caught soon enough," Jack said. "Being that famous will work against him. He won't be able to go anywhere without being recognised."

Holland pulled a sour face. "He seems to have managed okay so far," he pointed out.

Immediately upon his return to Arbour Square, Jack asked Steve Bull to crack on with the paperwork for the surveillance operation on the squat where Angela Marley resided.

Having pushed the meeting back twice already, he finally sat down with Reg Parker and Tony Dillon to go through the phones. It was eight o'clock by then, and Kelly Flowers had kindly done a pizza run for the team.

"Can't believe you resorted to poisoning Andy just to get this case," Dillon said, tucking into his Hawaiian.

The comment appealed to Parker's macabre sense of humour and he chuckled evilly.

"What makes you think I didn't sprinkle a little something on your food, too?" Jack asked, his mouth full of Margherita.

"I reckon I'm safe," Dillon replied with confidence. "You wouldn't have anyone to nag if you poisoned me."

"How is Mr Q?" Reg asked, taking a bite from his pepperoni. "Last I heard, he was still kneeling before the porcelain throne and doing the liquid scream."

Dillon's face turned pale. "Fuck sake, Reggie, I'm trying to eat!"

"Sorry boss," Parker said with a wicked grin. Dillon could be such a wimp at times. He'd shrugged off yesterday's assault with the lead-filled sap as though it was nothing, but talk about a decomposing body or someone being sick and his stomach curdled.

"Alison was taking him home," Ryder said. "Poor sod looked like a seasick ghost." Alison was Andy's wife. He'd declined the offer to have a colleague drive him home, preferring to entrust himself into the care of his wife.

"I reckon he'll be Être crevé for a few days at least," Dillon said. "Probably given himself Salmonella or something"

"He'll be what?" Jack asked.

"Être crevé," Dillon repeated, pronouncing the words slowly. "It's French for 'to be flat, to be dead.' It's what they say when they're bedridden."

"I didn't know you spoke frog," Reggie said, impressed.

"There's a lot you don't know about me," Dillon boasted. "I am an enigma, a man of mystery a –"

"Will you please shut up and let me eat my pizza in silence," Jack said, cutting him off mid soliloquy.

"Reckon they'll be fishing carrots out of trap one for days to come," Reg said, glancing at Dillon out of the corner of his eye to see if he'd bite.

"If you say another word about being sick, DC Parker, I'm going to scrub all the overtime you've earned over the past couple of days off your duty sheet," Dillon warned. He could play dirty too if that was how Reg wanted it.

"That's a bit harsh," Reg said, but he took the hint.

After they had finished off their food, they settled down to business. Parker gathered a bundle of forms and began going through them one by one.

"I'm going to be talking about four phones," Parker said by way of introduction. "They are all unregistered pre-pays and they all became active a couple of days ago. Let's start with the phone Gifford Mullings had on him," he said. "The number ends in 973. This phone has only had contact with two other numbers, one ending in 777 and the other in 321. I think it's safe to say these are the phones being used by the unknown doctor and Angela Marley. In interview, Mullings claimed Errol Heston was his mate, and that he'd recruited him for the job, but Errol's number isn't stored on his phone and he's had no contact with it."

"What does Errol Heston's number end in?" Dillon asked.

"His handset ends in 651," Reggie said.

"If they're using unregistered burners, it looks like the gang are aware we can use their phones against them," Tyler suggested.

"It does," Reggie agreed. "The call data for Gifford's handset is boringly predictable: a handful of incoming calls from the 777 number during the day before the breakout; a couple of incoming calls from it on the morning of the breakout. Nothing since the arrest."

"Any contact with the 321 number?" Dillon asked.

"There's one very short call from Mullings to 321 on the morning of the breakout, otherwise zilch."

"What about cell site data for Mullings?" Jack asked.

Reg placed an A3 printout of a computer-generated street map on Tyler's desk. "As you can see from the marks I've made on this map, this is the route that Gifford's phone took during the day of the escape." He traced it with his forefinger in case they couldn't see the bright red line that he'd drawn on the paper. "It shows the location of each of the cells the phone came into contact with, along with the precise times that the phone was pinged," Reg explained.

"You can see for yourself that Mullings' phone was pinged in the Beckton area, where the Ford Scorpio was nicked from, a short time before migrating towards the cell covering the RLH."

"How does his cell site data compare to the others?" Jack asked.

Reggie smiled. "Ah, now this is where it starts to get a little more interesting."

"Oh, good," Dillon said, drolly, "because I was in danger of falling asleep."

Reggie produced more A3 maps in quick succession.

"This is the cell site map for the 777 number."

Before they could look at it properly, he produced the next map.

"This is the map for the 321 number, and this..."

He slapped another map on top of the others, "...is the number for Heston's 651 number."

"You're going too fast," Dillon complained.

Doing the worst Inspector Clouseau impression that Tyler had ever heard, he announced, "Do not worry, Monsieur. Allow me to present my pièce de résistance..." With an elaborate flourish of his hand, Parker produced a sheet containing the merged data, which overlaid the routes of all four phones. "Voila." Thankfully, at that point, he dropped the terrible French accent.

"As you can clearly see, the phones mirror each other perfectly, indicating they were all together in the build-up to the breakout. At that point, the two unaccounted for phones – the ones ending 777 and 321 – headed off towards Canning town, presumably in the hijacked helicopter."

"Looks that way," Tyler agreed.

"Call data-wise, the 777 phone is easily the most active of the four burners," Reg informed them. "It's obviously the ringleader's phone. It rang all the other burners at various times yesterday morning, but the only one it called after the breakout was Errol's. In fact, there were spasmodic calls from 777 to Errol's 651 burner right up until midnight."

"Mr Big wanting to know where his missing gang member was, no doubt," Dillon said, stating the obvious.

"Exactly," Reggie said, nodding his agreement.

"I don't suppose the gang have gotten sloppy by calling anyone else?" Tyler asked.

Reggie grinned. "It's funny you should ask that because 777 has been in touch with two other numbers over the past three days. I've submitted subs and call data applications for both, and I'm currently awaiting the results."

"So, in summary," Tyler said, "the gang purchased four pre-pay burners, which became active on Sunday, the day before the breakout. Gifford and Errol had one each, we know that because we've recovered the phones on them. We believe that the mysterious doctor, who's obviously the mastermind behind the breakout, has the 777 number, and by default, Angela Marley has the 321 number. The 777 number has also called two other – as yet – unidentified numbers. Anything else, Reggie?"

"Yep, a couple of other things. Firstly, I've managed to obtain the SIM information for all four numbers. Long story short, the SIM cards they're using run in consecutive order, suggesting they were all purchased at the same time from the same store. The service provider checked their distribution records to see if they could identify the store they were purchased from and, get this…" Reggie licked his lips and then performed a drum roll on Jack's desk "…I've got the address in Barking where the phones were purchased from"

"That's great work, Reg," Tyler said. "I want someone over there first thing in the morning to check for CCTV and get a copy of any payment details."

"I've already put all the info into Mr Q's MIR," Parker said proudly, "and I'm told a HP action will be coming out to do exactly that."

A HP – High Priority – action was one that had to be resulted, or at least significantly updated, within twenty four hours of allocation.

"And what was the other thing?" Dillon asked.

"The 777 and 321 numbers are both still active, so I've had the TIU periodically reviewing their calls and movements over the last twenty four hours. It looks like they bedded down together last night and woke up this morning at the same location. I last spoke to the SPOC at five o'clock, and at that time neither phone had moved all day"

Parker pulled out his final map to illustrate the point. "The cell they're pinging on covers this area here…" He pointed to a large circle he had drawn on the map. "It's a fairly big area north of Barking Road so I'll need the services of an analyst to narrow it down further, but it's looking very promising that they're still together."

"They could have dumped the phones at that location and buggered off without them," Dillon pointed out.

"They could have," Reg allowed, "but I don't think that's the case because of the calls that 777 made during the day to the two unidentified numbers I told you about."

"Is there any way you can narrow it down?" Tyler asked, indicating the circle Parker had drawn. "This is far too big an area to search."

Reggie shook his head. "That's a bit too technical, even for me, which is why we need to get an analyst on board, ASAP."

"Explain why you can't do it," Dillon said.

"Generally speaking, cells are split into three sectors, and each sector has its own antenna. The antennas are erected at 120-degree intervals to ensure the cell gets the best all-round coverage. Each 120-degree arc is called an azimuth. Analysts have access to specialist software that enables them to narrow down a signal to a specific azimuth, whereas I can only tell you which cell the signal went through."

Dillon's brow creased into a deep furrow. "So, at best, we can only reduce the search area to a third, not down to a street or a house?"

Reggie nodded. "That's right."

"And you can't work out which azimuth thingy the phone is located within without an analyst?"

"When I make an application for cell site data, I get sent the CELL ID, its location and postcode, which is how I can say which cell covers the area the phone is pinging in and show you the overall radius of its reach. The data also contains the grid reference and the azimuths, but to be able to extract the relevant information and convert it into a chronological report or an evidential package, you need to have analytical training and access to the specialist mapping software. I don't have either."

Dillon scratched his head. "I see," he said, but from the blank look on his face, it was clear that he didn't.

Jack tried to remember the telephone input he'd received during his SIO course the previous year. As he understood it, at its most basic level a mobile telephone was simply a receiver that worked by using radio waves to communicate with individual masts. The masts then interacted with the host network.

In busy urban areas like Plaistow and Barking, a lone cell might service an area with a one-kilometre radius, and at any given time a mobile phone might be able to detect and measure the signal from as many as six cells.

The instructors had explained that phone analysis, which was still in its infancy in many ways, was a complicated science. Due to their nature, radio signals tend to propagate in an irregular manner, influenced by things like building clusters and topography, which is why the nearest mast isn't necessarily the one with the strongest signal.

"I'll speak to Mr Holland first thing in the morning and badger him into providing us with an analyst as a matter of urgency."

After Reg had departed, Dillon turned to Tyler. "I didn't understand any of that," he admitted.

"Don't worry," Tyler said, grinning. "You can't help being thick."

"I'm not thick," Dillon replied indignantly, and then his face broke into a wry smile, "just technologically challenged!"

Tyler's leaned back in his chair, interlocked his fingers and rested his hands against the back of his head. "Dill, first thing in the morning, can you check with Reggie to confirm that the 777 and 321 numbers bedded down together again within coverage of the same cell. If they did, and I'm fairly confident they will have, I'll need you to get straight onto the TSU to see if we can arrange for them to send out a signal detector van tomorrow night."

The TSU - Technical Support Unit – were based at Lambeth in South London and, as the name suggested, they handled all the Met's technical deployments. A signal detector van was basically a vehicle that performed a similar function to a TV licencing van, except that it searched for phone signals and not unlicensed televisions. Of course, it didn't always work. Sometimes the phone they were hunting was switched off, or it had been left in a room that didn't receive a signal, but the tactic was definitely worth a try.

"When it's arranged, can you immediately give George Holland a heads up and then knock out the relevant paperwork."

"What about if they can't help?" Dillon asked.

Jack shook his head. "That's not an option. Tell them this will go all the way up to the Commissioner if they want to argue the toss."

"Fair enough," Dillon said, making a note in his daybook. "Leave it to me, oh mighty leader."

"I have one more request," Jack said. "I want you to phone the Duty Officer at Plaistow on my behalf and ask the night duty to conduct an early hour's street search of the area Reggie's circled on this map." He held it aloft for Dillon to see. "They'll be looking for a red four door Rover 216 hatchback."

Dillon grimaced. "That's going to make me bloody popular," he complained.

"Can't be helped," Jack said firmly. "Explain that we think it was involved in the murder of a colleague. That should motivate them. As an added incentive, tell them that if any of the cars they put up turns out to be the right one, whoever spotted it gets a crate of beer and a bottle of scotch on me."

Dillon smiled. "That might soften the blow," he said. "What's the index number and are there any distinguishing marks or dents on it?"

"Unfortunately, we don't have an index, and we're not aware of anything that makes it stick out."

Dillon's raised eyebrow was an inverted tick of incredulity. "Seriously? There could be hundreds of cars that fit the description."

"I know," Jack said, "and I want a PNC printout for every car they find, along with details of the exact location where it was parked."

Dillon sucked in air. "Maybe you should make it two crates of beer," he suggested.

Leaving Dillon to make the call, Tyler ventured out into the main office to check in with the Intel Cell. As ever, Dean was hunched over his keyboard, tapping away furiously. Wendy was standing by the printer, having just run off some stuff to submit to the MIR. Both looked absolutely shattered.

Thankfully, Dean had swapped the morose sounds of his preferred classical radio station for the more upbeat tunes of Magic. The velvety smooth saxophone solo from Spandau Ballet's *True* was currently playing and Jack nodded his approval.

"Any updates on this Rodent character that the pilot put up?" he asked them.

Wendy shook her head regretfully. "Afraid not, guv," she said. "I was certain he would be in the system, but he isn't, so whoever he is, he hasn't got any form and he hasn't come to the attention of the locals."

"That's a bit of a bummer," Tyler said. "I was really hoping something would come up regarding him."

"Me too," Wendy confessed. "I feel like I've let you down."

"Don't be daft," Dean said, looking up. "We can only mine the databases for what's in them. If he isn't there, we can't do anything."

"Dean's right," Jack said. "We can only do what we can do."

Dick Jarvis and Paul Evans had driven down to Vicarage Lane, E15 to keep an eye on the squat where Angela resided.

In order not to stand out, they had been forced to park in Byford

Close, which was so far away from the address that it was nigh impossible to recognise any individuals entering or leaving, even using binoculars.

"Well, this is a complete waste of time," Evans moaned. He had the car radio tuned into talkSPORT and was currently listening to a bitter dispute between a couple of Arsenal and Spurs fans who were at loggerheads over who the history books would see as the rightful kings of North London.

"Anyone could go into that place and we would be none the wiser," he pointed out.

"I think Steve just wanted us to get a feel for how much movement there was," Jarvis said, trying to remain positive. "Besides, if we hadn't been sent here, we might've been lumbered with something far worse."

"True," Evans allowed, "but you've got to admit, this is so boring."

"What's boring is that rubbish you're listening to," Jarvis said, pantomiming a yawn.

"You think football's boring?" the Welshman eyed him as if he had suddenly sprouted a second head.

Jarvis shrugged. "Prefer cricket myself."

"At least tell me you like rugby," Evans pleaded after a moment's reflection.

Jarvis turned his nose up. "Not really."

"Bloody heretic, you are," Evans said, shaking his head in dismay. "How can you not like rugby?"

"I don't dislike it," Jarvis explained. "It just doesn't do anything for me."

Evans didn't know what to say. Growing up in the valleys, he didn't think he'd ever met anyone who didn't like rugby before; it wasn't normal. "You're not - you know...", he flapped his wrist effeminately, "... batting for the other side, are you?"

Jarvis rolled his eyes in exasperation. "No," he said with studied patience. "And what's not liking rugby got to do with my sexual persuasion anyway? For your information, Mr Neanderthal, I have a gay friend who loves football and rugby and is bloody good at both, so don't be so closed-minded."

Evans blushed. "Well, I..."

"I like boxing too," Jarvis added as an afterthought.

Just then, a figure appeared at the top of the road, walking straight for the target address.

"Here we go, posh boy," Evans said, nudging his colleague's arm.

Jarvis raised the binoculars to his eyes and twiddled the focus. "This is NOT easy," he complained as the figure moved in and out of sharpness. "Right, we've got an IC3 female, slim, wearing a green Parker with the hood up. Can't make out her face yet."

Evans was writing the time of the sighting and the woman's description down in the log.

The woman stopped outside the street door and banged on it with her fist.

"Whoever she is, she doesn't have a key, so unlikely to be our girl," Jarvis said, sounding disappointed.

The door opened inward and the caller's face was suddenly bathed in bright light. At that exact moment, she pulled down her hood and shook her hair loose. To Jarvis's shock, the woman had a deep scar running down the right side of her face. He gripped the binos tighter, virtually screwing them into his eye sockets in order to get a better view. "Oh my God!" he exclaimed, astonished. "You're not going to believe this, but I think that's Angela Marley."

Evans snatched the binoculars from his hand. "What? Are you sure?" he gasped, trying to adjust the focus. "Gordon Bennett!" he said a moment later, "I think you're right."

Handing the binoculars back to Jarvis, he pulled an A4 sheet of paper from his daybook and stared at the image on it. "It's her," he said with confidence. "We need to phone this in."

CHAPTER TWENTY-TWO

Jack Tyler was back in the CCTV viewing room talking to Darren Blyth about CCTV from the area where the HEMS bird had been forced to put down. He knew it had been collected but he wanted to know if any of it had been viewed yet.

"Afraid not, gov'nor," Blyth said in his deep Mancunian voice. "Bearing in mind the murder only occurred yesterday, Mr Quinlan wanted me to focus on the hospital stuff today so that the interview team could show it to that toe-rag, Mullings."

Jack thought that he sounded overly defensive, "I accept that," he said, trying not to lose his temper, "but someone else could and should have been tasked to start checking the Canning Town footage for the Red Rover's index while you were sorting out the hospital stuff."

"But I'm the CCTV officer," Blyth protested. "That's my job."

Jack knew he could be a hard taskmaster; when a new job broke, he invariably wanted everything done at warp speed. His team was used to the way he worked, and they understood that the first few days of any new case with him at the helm were going to be gruelling, but they didn't mind because Jack Tyler got results, and he tended to get them quickly. Andy Quinlan seemed to have a very different work ethic, and that reflected in the way his team worked.

"Okay, leave it with me," Tyler said brusquely, realising that Blyth wasn't on the same wavelength and was struggling to grasp his need for urgency.

"I'll get you some help, but I want someone to start looking at that footage tonight to see if they can locate the Rover and get me the registration number. We've got the local plod out doing a street sweep for us during the early hours, and it would help them massively if we could at least supply them with the Rover's index."

Blyth didn't look overly happy about this. "But if someone views it too quickly, they might miss something," he protested.

"I think you're the one who's missing something, Darren," Jack pointed out, tetchily. "I'm asking for flash viewing to get the Rover's index, not evidential viewing for court. That can be done later."

"But isn't that just duplicating work? Surely, it's more efficient to take a bit more time and do it properly all in one go, the way we usually do?"

"Darren, you need to consider the bigger picture. If the pilot's information is accurate, we need to find that car within the next couple of days, before they all fuck off to the coast and Winston hops on a boat to the continent. This is a priority –"

Blyth interrupted. "But Mr Quinlan doesn't like it done that way," he said adamantly.

Tyler felt his knuckles whiten as he clenched his fists in frustration.

"When Mr Quinan returns," he said with forced patience, "he can do it any way he pleases but, for now, I'm running the show and it gets done how I say and when I say. Are we clear on that?"

Blyth averted his eyes. "Yes, sir," he said meekly.

As Tyler stood up to leave, Reg Parker came bursting through the doors. "Got some important updates from the TIU for you, boss," he said, breathlessly.

"Run me through them on the way back to my office," Tyler said, and strode out of the room without a backward glance. He needed to get away from Blyth while he could still control the urge to throttle him.

He was aware of Parker rushing along behind, trying to catch him up. "Come on then Reggie, what have you got for me?" he asked.

"Both the 777 and 321 numbers have been on the move during the last three hours," Reg said, waving a sheet of paper in his hand.

Tyler stopped dead in his tracks, allowing Parker to catch up.

"Are they moving together?" he asked.

Reggie shook his head. "No, they've gone in different directions."

"Shit," Tyler said, taking the proffered piece of paper and reading Reggie's hastily scribbled notes. "Do you think they've split up for good, or just popped out for a little while, intending to regroup later?"

Parker shrugged. "No way of telling at the moment," he said.

Tyler considered this. "So, where are they now?" he asked.

Reggie held out his hand and Jack returned the sheet of paper to him.

"Er, according to the latest TIU report the 777 number has been to Mile End and is now near Aldgate, on the outskirts of the City, while the 321 number went over to Barking earlier, but is currently somewhere in the Stratford area."

"Why weren't we told they were on the move earlier?" Jack asked, annoyed that there had been a delay.

"The TIU was doing live monitoring for us, but the signals didn't move all last night or all day today, so they cut us back to three hourly updates. Can't blame them really."

Tyler sighed. "No, I suppose not. Will they revert to live monitoring now that they're on the move?"

"The SPOC's agreed to continue with live monitoring up until eleven p.m. unless a live kidnap case comes in, but after that, he goes off duty. The TIU only has minimum cover on for night duty so they won't be able to resume live monitoring again until seven o'clock tomorrow morning."

Tyler was nonplussed. "Unbelievable, isn't it? The Met is the biggest police force in the UK, capable of assembling and deploying enormous resources to deal with any threat conceivable – unless it happens at night or during the weekend when we're running on minimum strength!"

Parker gave Tyler a 'what can I do' shrug. "I'll speak to whoever's on night duty," he offered. "They might be able to sort something out for us."

"Thanks, Reg," Tyler said, feeling a tad jaded. "Anything else?"

"One other thing," Parker said. "The subscriber checks I requested on the two unknown numbers 777 called have just come back in. The first belongs to a bloke in East Sussex, and the second is an unregistered pre-pay."

Jack grunted. "These people do love their pre-pays, don't they?"

"They do," Reg agreed. "But just to dot the I's and cross the T's, I asked Tom Wilkins to run both numbers through HOLMES. Guess what…?" Reggie stared at Tyler expectantly, waiting for him to ask.

Jack sighed theatrically. "Okay, I'll indulge you. What?"

"The pre-pay number belongs to Errol Heston's next of kin."

Tyler's jaw tightened with anger. "You've got to be shitting me?" he said.

The smile fell from Parker's face. "No, honestly, guv. It definitely matches," he said, confused by Tyler's furious response.

Jack shook his head. "What I mean is, why hadn't the MIR already run these numbers through HOLMES? They've had them all day."

Reg looked uncomfortable. "Er, I don't think they're used to working at quite the speed we do," he said tactfully.

"Right," Tyler said, storming off towards Quinlan's MIR, "I want someone to visit the next of kin tonight to see who made that bloody call to them from the 777 number."

Parker was left standing all alone in the corridor, feeling dejected. "Well done, Reggie," he said, lamely reaching over his shoulder to pat his back. "Great job, Reggie, proud of you for using your initiative." He waved his hands in the air in celebration. "Yaaay Reggie." If no one else was going to praise him, he figured he might as well do it himself.

―――――

Jack Tyler returned to his team's general office ten minutes later, fresh from putting a flea in the ear of Tom Wilkins for not running the two telephone numbers through HOLMES earlier. He'd upset him further by ordering the OM to issue a HP action for someone to visit Sonia Wilcox that evening. Just to make sure there were no misunderstandings, Jack made it very clear that he wanted to be told the moment the result came in.

As soon as he entered the room, Dean Fletcher looked up from his desk and thrust the phone he had been speaking into towards him.

"Guv, I've got young Dick Jarvis on the blower, said he needs to speak to you urgently."

Tyler crossed the room, flopped down on Dean's desk to field the call.

"What is it, Dick?" he asked wearily.

"Guv, we've got a bit of a development here. Both Paul and I are confident that the woman who's just turned up at the squat is our target, Angela Marley. What do you want us to do?"

The news caught Tyler off guard because he really hadn't expected Marley to return to the squat. "Was she alone?"

"Yes."

Jack liked that about Jarvis; he was always succinct, like a living advert for the old training school motto: '*Accuracy; brevity; speed.*'

"Did she arrive by car or on foot?"

"On foot," Jarvis confirmed.

"Okay, here's what I want you to do," Tyler said, thinking fast. "If she leaves, follow her until she's away from the squat and then arrest her. In the meantime, I'm going to get a warrant organised. If either Winston or the bogus doctor turns up, I want to know immediately. Do not engage them without armed back up."

"Okay boss, but we're parked a fair way back and if she comes out and turns the other way, I'm worried she might disappear before we could catch up to her."

Jack considered this. "Alright, hang tight and I'll rustle you up a couple more bodies to come down and cover the road from the other end." He wasn't sure where he was going to find the people to do this, but it was important, so even if it meant dragging officers away from another assignment, he would get it done.

At that moment, Tony Dillon and Carol Keating came in, laughing and joking. Jack signalled for them to go straight into his office. "I'll join you in a minute," he said, covering the mouthpiece with his hand.

Dillon gave him a thumbs up and the pair continued walking. As they reached Jack's office, Dillon did his impression of Sid James's trademark dirty laugh. Carol responded with her imitation of a Hattie Jacques giggle, clutched her chest romantically and cooed, "Ooh Sid."

Closing the door behind them, the pair burst into laughter once more.

"Why does everyone feel the need to do *Carry On* film impressions around her?" Jack asked Dean. To his surprise, the normally taciturn researcher burst out with, "Ooh, Matron," in his best Kenneth Williams voice.

It was a very surreal moment.

Replacing his reading glasses, Dean turned to his computer and began typing as though nothing unusual had happened.

Tyler shook his head in disbelief. "The world's gone mad," he said, standing up.

"Did you know," Dean suddenly pipped up, "Hattie Jacques appeared in fourteen Carry On films, and played a Matron in five of them?"

Jack raised an eyebrow. "You seem very well informed," he said.

"Can't beat a good Carry On film," Dean said emphatically. "I've got all of them on tape at home."

Before Jack could respond to this useless bit of trivia, Susie Sergeant popped her head around the door. "Guv, can I have a word, please?"

"Of course," Tyler said, walking over to join her. "What can I do for you, Susie?"

"Tom Wilkins tells me you want someone to go around to speak to Sonia Wilcox tonight, is that right?"

"It is," Jack said. "Why?" He hoped Wilkins hadn't gone whinging to Susie behind his back, complaining that Tyler was working him too hard.

"Well, the only person I have available is Kevin Murray, and he's not exactly the most tactful person for something like this."

Jack grinned. "Murray's about as tactful as a brick through a window," he agreed, "but if he's all we've got..." he left the sentence unfinished.

Susie seemed genuinely surprised. "Well, if you're sure, I'll get him straight onto it."

"Just to add to your woes," he said as she turned to leave, "Angela Marley has turned up at the squat in Vicarage Lane, and I need you to find me two officers to shoot down to the address to cover it from the other end of the street."

"But everyone else is tied up," Susie protested.

Jack shrugged. "Then find out who's doing the least important task and get them to divert."

Susie nodded reluctantly. "Okay, leave it to me. I'll get straight on it."

Jack felt guilty for burdening her like that, but she was the Case Officer and, unfortunately, organising resources to carry out the SIO's directives was one of the joys that came with the role.

He recalled something that a wizened old DCI had said to him the first time that he'd performed the role of Case Officer, back when he was still a junior DS: *'Remember, Jack, your job is to find me solutions, not put more obstacles in my path.'* They had been wise words indeed, and he often shared them with his own Case Officers when things got tough.

"Dean," he shouted across the office, "before I forget, can you have a word with Reggie. I want you to conduct some urgent research on a man in East Sussex who's mobile has been in contact with the 777 number."

"Leave it to me," Dean said. "I'll get the details from him and get it sorted."

"Cheers mate," Jack said, knowing that Dean would get straight on it. When he returned to his own office, he was delighted to see that Carol had used the time to prepare them all a nice cup of coffee.

"White, with two sugars, if I remember correctly," she said, handing him over a brew.

"Thank you," Tyler said, returning to his desk.

"How did it go at the SPM?" Tyler asked her.

"Exactly as expected," Carol told him flatly. "Cause of death was a single gunshot to the head. The pathologist recovered the slug from inside Morrison's cranium. It was a .22 calibre, and the pathologist thinks he was shot at point black range. Juliet Kennedy agrees; she said the pillowcase they'd found on the bed next to Morrison's corpse appears to have been used as a make-do suppressor. It had been shot through, and there were scorch marks on one side and blood all over the other, which supports the working hypothesis that it had been placed against his head just before the shot was fired."

"Poor bastard," Dillon said, morosely.

"Any update on Andy?" Jack asked. "Did he get home safely."

Carol nodded. "I spoke to Alison a little while ago. It took her ages to get him back home. She had to keep pulling over so he could throw up, poor thing."

Dillon grimaced.

"Let's hope he makes a speedy recovery," Jack said. "In the meantime, I need one of you to sort out getting an out of hours warrant, and the other to speak to the Chief Inspector at IR to see if he'll release a couple of TSG carriers from the Commissioners Reserve for a raid on a squat. If he does, you'll need to prepare a briefing document for when we execute the warrant."

"When you say squat," Dillon said, "should I assume you're talking about the dive where Angela Marley lives?"

"That's the one. Dick Jarvis and Paul Evans have been keeping an eye on it, and they've just phoned in to say that Angela has returned."

"Why not just go in under Section 17 of PACE and arrest her? Then we can search under Section 18 or 32?" Carol suggested. "It would be much quicker and it would save a lot of paperwork."

Jack shook his head. "I've considered doing that, but there are too many risks involved. I'm happy we have a power of entry to arrest under Section 17 because the boys have seen someone fitting her description go in. But if we gain entry and she's not there, we can't make an arrest, and without that, there's no power to search. Also, if she is there, but the house is divided into bedsits, then we only have the power to search the room she's using and any communal areas. I'd rather have a Section 8 PACE warrant in my back pocket, allowing us to search the whole premises."

"I'll sort out the warrant," Dillon offered. "I'll get on the phone to the Duty Clerk and see who's available to deal with the application."

"In that case," Carol said, "I'll phone Information Room at the

Yard and work my charms on the Duty Chief Inspector, then I'll knock out a briefing."

The two Detective Inspectors rose as one to follow out their orders.

"To arms!" Dillon proclaimed with a smile. "I'm off to find myself a friendly Magistrate."

"To the toilet," Carol countered. "That coffee has gone straight through me!"

CHAPTER TWENTY-THREE

Inside the squat, Angela had taken a long shower and changed her clothing. The grimy nurse's uniform had been tossed in the corner. She would come back and burn it as soon as Winston was on his way to Sussex, but for now, it would be fine where it was.

As soon as she finished towelling off her hair, Angela retrieved her burner phone from the bed. She needed to remind Garston that Cribbins was coming around to the flat at some point after nine, and that he needed to be there to pay the embalmer for his services. After making the call, she planned to shoot up with the emergency smack that she kept hidden under her floorboards and then crash out on her nice warm bed while the Golden Brown worked its magic.

She would go back to the flat later this evening, or in the early hours of the morning, depending on how long she slept for. Garston would be furious, but it would be worth it to have a few hours of freedom.

Her face fell as she saw that the battery was dead, and she angrily threw it on the bed, where it bounced on the mattress and then toppled to the floor.

"Shit!"

Angela frantically started searching her messy room for the charger but it was nowhere to be found. "No good bunch of motherfuckers," she cursed, realising that someone must have come in and taken it while she was out. Was nothing safe in this damn house?

Angela stormed out into the hall, shouting and swearing, demanding to know who had 'tiefed' her charger. When her aggressive approach didn't get her anywhere, she changed tack and went around the rooms trying to sweet-talk the other girls into letting her borrow one of theirs.

That didn't work either.

This was terrible news. It meant that she would have to go back to Rodent's flat instead of staying here and getting high. In a foul mood, she marched back to her room, threw a few bits and bobs into a duffle bag, snatched the useless phone from the floor and slammed the door on her way out.

As she reached the bottom of the stairs, two of the other residents turned up with four very noisy, very drunk punters in tow. They were National Front types from the look of them, with buzzcuts and flattened noses. One of the hookers, a loud-mouthed Asian girl who called herself Lola, spotted Angela and invited her to join the party. "Some easy money if you want it," she said, slurring her words, "but it's gonna be wild!"

The thuggish punters looked like they had come here to do some heavy partying, and Angela suspected they would pay well for the privilege of doing so, but she had to get back to the flat in case Cribbins turned up and there was no one there to admit him.

"Can't," Angela said. She couldn't rely on Garston getting back in time to sort Claude out, and if he didn't, they would both take it out on her.

As she walked towards the front door, one of the drunks veered into her path, wrapped his arm around her waist and pulled her to him. He immediately started to gyrate against her, dry fucking her like a dog in heat. He was a real charmer, with a small Swastika tattooed on the right side of his neck, just above his collar line.

"Stay and have some fun," he said, huskily. She could feel his erection pressing against her like a tent pole. As she tried to back away from it, the man laughed, exposing uneven yellow teeth, and squeezed her even more tightly.

"I've taken two Viagras and snorted a tonne of coke," he boasted, "and I'm ready to fuck you girls, one after the other, until I break you all."

His mates all cheered; one patted him on the back, while another passed him a half-empty bottle of Russian vodka.

He released Angela and took a long swig. "Want some..." he asked, turning to offer the bottle, only to find that she had vanished.

Angela made her way through the kitchen and left the squat by the rear entrance, knowing from experience that it would be far quicker to do that than try and get past the four drunken idiots Lola had brought back for an orgy.

A gig like that might pay well, she reflected, but you always had to work really hard for your money, doing whatever the deviants wanted for as long as they wanted. Sometimes the shagging went on all night as the girls were passed around like toys. The last time she'd participated in one of those debauchery-filled marathons, she hadn't been able to walk properly for the best part of a week.

She emerged into Evesham Road and headed down to Portway, keeping the hood of the Parka up to ward off the wind. Walking as fast as she could, her heels clackety-clacked off the pavement like a pair of badly played castanets. As soon as she reached the main drag, Angela headed for the local mini-cab office that the girls all used. With any luck, she would be back at the flat in next to no time.

Steve Bull pulled the car up outside a three-storey Victorian house with an imposing stone façade.

"Is this it?" Dillon asked, squinting into the darkness to try and work out the number.

"I think so," Bull said. He reached into the back, where he retrieved a small torch from his jacket pocket. Unwinding his window, he switched it on and shone the weak beam of light over the street door and ivy-covered wall adjacent to it.

"Yep. This is definitely the place," he said a moment later. Winding his window back up as quickly as he could to close out the arctic wind that battered his face, Bull turned to Dillon. "Do you want me to wait here or come in with you?" he asked.

Dillon grimaced. "You'd better come in with me," he said. "If this old dragon is half as bad as the on-call Clerk said, I'll need all the support I can get."

When the Duty Clerk, a bubbly lady called Stephanie, had called Dillon back after checking the out of hours Magistrate availability, she had sounded apologetic – almost remorseful – when she'd informed him that the only person available in East London was Mrs Hilda Baxter. He'd immediately picked up on her regretful tone and asked if that was a problem.

"*Not for me,*" the Clerk had replied jauntily, "*but she has a reputation for being a mean old troll who enjoys giving the boys in blue a really hard time.*"

That didn't sound good. "Surely she can't be that bad?" Dillon had asked hopefully.

"*Imagine a demon from the bowels of hell, but uglier and meaner.*"

Dillon didn't like the sound of that at all. "Oh dear," he had said, wishing he'd opted to call IR and draft the briefing document instead.

"*Just make sure your paperwork is mistake-free, and don't try to bullshit her,*" the helpful Clerk had advised. "*That woman can spot a fib a mile off.*"

Dillon alighted the car, nervously adjusted his tie and then did up the first two buttons of his Pierre Cardin suit jacket. Satisfied with his appearance, he grabbed the folder containing the warrant and information, and the other little bits he had brought along to support his application, from the back seat. Followed by Bull, he made his way along the path and knocked loudly on the door. "Well," he said, "here goes nothing."

He heard footsteps approaching from inside. "Wait one moment," an authoritative voice barked.

"Doesn't sound like she's terribly pleased to see us," Bull whispered.

Dillon turned and winked at him, full of bravado. "Don't worry, as soon as I turn on the fabled Dillon charm, she'll be putty in my hands."

Bull groaned. "Why did you have to go and tempt fate by saying something stupid like that?"

Before Dillon could respond, a latch turned, a bolt clunked, and then the heavy wooden door slowly swung inwards, spilling light onto the doorstep where Dillon waited with bated breath to catch his first glimpse of the demon that was Hilda Baxter.

"You must be the police officers Stephanie told me about," the diminutive woman in her sixties who answered the door said.

Dillon stared at her in open-mouthed surprise. Mrs Baxter didn't look anything like a demon. The tiny woman was wearing a big, fluffy red dressing gown with little Beatrix Potter animal imprints, a pair of bunny rabbit slippers – complete with floppy ears – and she had her grey hair up in curlers. The eyes, which he had expected to be little black holes that sucked the life force from her victims, were warm and friendly. "Come in out of the cold," she said and ushered them into the hall like a mother hen.

"Go straight through to the kitchen at the back," she said, following on behind.

They traversed a long, tastefully decorated hall with a beautiful tiled floor until they came to an enormous kitchen with wood flooring. A centre island dominated the middle of the room and behind that stood a gigantic Rangemaster oven.

"Let's sit at the dining table," Mrs Baxter said, pointing towards a huge oak table off to their left. "While you sort out your paperwork, I'll put the kettle on." With that, she shuffled off to one of the cupboards and removed three mugs from it. "Coffee or tea?" she asked, glancing back over her shoulder at them.

"Coffee would be great," Dillon replied, feeling a little shell shocked. It dawned on him that the bloody Clerk had been winding him up. Feeling a little silly for having fallen for it, he turned to Bull and whispered, "See, what did I tell you? Putty in my hands."

As soon as coffee was served – she had thrown in an assortment of biscuits and told them to help themselves – they got down to business.

"Will you be taking the oath or making an affirmation?" Mrs Baxter asked.

"The oath, of course," Dillon replied. In his experience, Magistrates always preferred it when people swore on the bible before giving evidence.

Mrs Baxter smiled approvingly. "Good," she said, removing a King James Bible and a laminated card from one of the drawers in the cupboard nearest to them. The card had the oath written on it in big bold letters. Dillon took the bible in his right hand, held it up and recited the oath. He didn't need to refer to the card she offered him; he knew it off by heart, a fact that was not lost on the wily old Magistrate.

After formally introducing himself by name, rank and the unit he was attached to, Dillon explained that he was there to apply for a search warrant under Section 8 of PACE. He provided her with three copies of the warrant, a written Information – an official document outlining the nature of the offences under investigation, the type of warrant being applied for, the grounds for making the application, and the evidence sought – and then gave a detailed overview of the case and Angela's involvement. He was pleased to see Mrs Baxter listened to his every word in rapt silence, appropriately nodding enthusiastically and shaking her head sadly at every juncture.

He explained that he was asking for a single-entry warrant to cover multiple premises, by which he meant that the house that they wanted to search was a squat. As such, it was possible that the transient occupants moved around, sleeping in different rooms on different nights, depending on which one was available for occupancy at the time.

When he was finished, he took a deep breath and helped himself to a slice of shortbread.

"Very well," Mrs Baxter said, "before I make a decision, can you tell me if there are likely to be any children or animals at the premises?"

Dillon shook his head emphatically. "No children or animals. Our intelligence suggests this is a large house in a state of disrepair that has been used as a squat by a number of local prostitutes for the last few months. Some of them, like Angela Marley, live there on pretty much a full-time basis while others doss down for a night or two here and there. The local authority is currently trying to get it closed down as some of the hookers have started bringing punters back for sex parties on an increasingly regular basis, and the squat has effectively turned into a self-ran brothel."

"I'm sure the neighbours love that," she said, raising an eyebrow.

"I'm told there have been one or two agitated complaints," Dillon informed her.

"I bet there have," she replied, shaking her curler-laden head disapprovingly. "Very well, Detective Inspector Dillon, I'm happy to authorise the warrant." A pen magically appeared in her hand and she began to sign the copies. "Please make sure a copy is returned to the court as soon as it's executed. I wish you luck with your investigation and I would be grateful if you could let me know how it all turns out."

"Thank you, ma'am," he said, taking possession of the signed copies one at a time. "And thank you for seeing us at such short notice, and for your hospitality with the coffee and biscuits," he said as she escorted them back along the hall to the street door.

"You're very welcome, Inspector," she said, smiling sweetly. "One last thing," she said as she showed them out.

"Yes, ma'am?"

"I have a hard-earned reputation for being a rather formidable lady in court, so if either of you dares to tell anyone how I was dressed tonight, or that I was nice to you, I will have no alternative but to hunt you both down and kill you."

Dillon's face broke into a huge grin. He liked this woman – a lot. "Don't worry," he assured her. "Your secret is safe with us."

Garston was sitting in the bedroom with Winston when Angela finally arrived back at the flat. She poked her head around the door sheepishly. "Everything okay?" she asked timidly.

"Where have you been?" he demanded, standing up angrily. "You were supposed to come straight back here after going around to see Horace." He looked at his watch and scowled. "That was over three hours ago! What have you been doing since then?"

Angela couldn't meet his eye. "Sorry," she muttered contritely, looking down at the floor. "Needed to go home and get changed."

Garston moved towards her with menace. The slap he had given her the day before had changed the dynamic between them, knocking some of the arrogance out of her. Maybe she needed a little more of the same today? "What did I say to you?" he snapped, spraying her with spittle. "You don't go anywhere near the squat until I give you permission. If I find out that you opened that horrible big gob of yours and blabbed to anyone about where we're holed up..." He raised a hand as if to slap her.

"I didn't say anything to anyone, I swear," Angela cried, cowering in fear.

"Leave the bitch alone," Winston said, speaking for the first time. "She knows I'd gut her like a fish if she dropped me in the shit. Ain't that right, girl?"

Angela nodded, too afraid to even speak, not with Garston looming over her, looking for an excuse to lash out.

There was a knock on the door.

"Who's that?" Garston asked, suddenly looking worried. Rodent had a key, and they weren't expecting visitors. And then he remembered that Cribbins was meant to be popping around, and he let out a sigh of relief.

"Make yourself useful," he said, shoulder barging Angela out of the way. "Clean Claude's wound while I let our guest in."

Angela went over to the bed and began to remove Claude's bandages. "How are you feeling?" she asked him.

He shrugged grumpily. "How would you be feeling with half your insides hanging out?"

Angela wondered why men were prone to such over-exaggeration. She was just about to peel the dressing back when she noticed some tablets in plastic foil on the bedside table, next to a half-drunk glass of water. "He got you some antibiotics, then?" she observed.

Winston grunted. "Just gave me the first couple of pills. Massive things, they are too. Had trouble swallowing the fucking things."

Just then, Garston returned with Cribbins. The latter was carrying a small brown medical bag of the type favoured by doctors making house calls.

"Who the fuck's this motherfucker?" Winston demanded, eyeing the newcomer suspiciously. Garston noticed his right hand had slipped under his pillow, where the gun was no doubt hidden. He raised his hands placatingly. "It's all cool, Claude," he said hurriedly. "This is Horace. He's come to stitch up your wound."

Winston's hand slowly reappeared from beneath the pillow. Thankfully it was empty. "You took your motherfucking time coming," he complained. "Fucking useless wanker."

Ignoring the insult, Horace Cribbins opened his bag and removed a pair of rubber gloves. "You're a lot more vocal than my normal clients," he said conversationally.

Garston and Angela exchanged nervous glances, suddenly allies again. If Winston found out what Cribbins did for a living, and what he had been dismissed for doing in his previous occupation, he was quite likely to shoot all three of them.

"Let's have a look at the wound, shall we?" the white-haired embalmer said, demonstrating the perfect bedside manner. He sat down next to the gangster and gently peeled the dressing back. Winston swore as the sticky gauze came away, but Cribbins took no notice of the outburst.

"Hmmm," he said, examining the wound. "There was obviously widespread infection of the inner lining of the abdomen, which is why the surgeon has made a wider than usual incision. The procedure is called a laparotomy."

"Do I look like I give a flying fuck what it's called?" Winston growled. "Just sew the damn thing up so I can move around again."

"It looks like there has been some bleeding under the skin, which is why there's a firm swelling here," he indicated an area below the scar. "That's called a haematoma," he said with a helpful smile. "It should get better on its own, but if you're concerned you can always consult your GP."

"There was some puss coming out of the wound yesterday," Angela said, "but that seems to have eased off now."

"He might still have an infection, but the antibiotics you're giving him should take care of that. Is this them?" he asked, picking up the tablets and reading the label. His eyes narrowed and he turned to Garston with a questioning look on his face. "But these are –"

"Horace, let's just concentrate on stitching up the wound for now, and we can discuss Claude's medication later," Garston said, grabbing the embalmer's arm and squeezing hard.

"Ouch," Cribbins yelped. "That hurt."

"The boy's right," Winston said impatiently. "Just get your needle and thread out and patch me up."

"Very well, "Cribbins said, still rubbing his arm. He turned to Angela. "What have you been cleaning the wound with?"

"Iodine," she said.

"That won't do," Cribbins told her sternly. "Warm soapy water is what's required. Can you get me some, please?"

Angela bristled. "Why are you asking me to get it?" she demanded. "Is it because I'm a woman?"

"No," Cribbins told her patiently. "I'm asking you because you strike me as being far more capable than him," he indicated Garston with a jut of his chin.

"Oh," Angela said, genuinely surprised. "In that case, I'll get right on it."

Cribbins raised an eyebrow. "According to the news reports, Mr Winston, you've been running around fighting with the police. That wasn't very wise, was it? Didn't your surgeon tell you to avoid any strenuous exercise for the first two to four weeks after the operation?"

Winston looked from Cribbins to Garston. "Is this dude shitting me?" he asked. He couldn't tell if the man was being serious or taking the piss out of him.

"Mr Winston," Cribbins said with a fatherly smile, "In a few minutes I'm going to stitch you up, but the sutures won't be any stronger than the ones you were given in hospital. The point I am trying to make is that if you exert yourself too much there is a very good chance they will tear apart and you will be back to square one."

"So, what? I'm supposed to be bedridden while I recover? That what you're trying to say?"

"You can move around slowly and carefully, ideally with assistance. You cannot roll around on the floor, fighting with policemen. That's what I'm trying to say."

Angela returned with the soapy water and towels. They weren't exactly clean, but they were the best she could come up with.

After washing and drying the wound, Cribbins set about stitching it up. "We don't have anything to give you for the pain, I'm afraid, so you'll just have to grin and bear it."

"Get on with it," Winston snapped. "I'm not a pussy. I can cope with a few stitches without crying like a baby."

"Let's hope you can," Cribbins said. Without another word, he removed the equipment he needed from his medical bag and laid it out in front of him.

He was going to be using swaged – or atraumatic – needles. These basically came prepacked with the required length of thread attached.

Cribbins used a technique known as the 'simple interrupted stitch'. Its name is derived from the fact that the surgical thread is cut – interrupted – after each individual stitch. Cribbins had mastered this over the years, although he had never actually practiced it on anyone who was still alive.

Cribbins had surprisingly nimble fingers and he worked with great dexterity. The sutures were placed in position by mounting the swaged needle onto a pincer-like needle holder. The needle point was then pressed into Winston's flesh on one side of the wound until it emerged again on the other side and the trailing thread was promptly tied with a surgeon's knot. Starting at the bottom, he methodically worked his way upwards, humming contentedly as he worked.

Winston's face quickly contorted with pain, but true to his word, he managed to suffer his way through the procedure in silence.

"Not too much longer now, Mr Winston," Cribbins said cheerfully.

Winston nodded gratefully.

When he had finally finished, Cribbins tidied up and applied a new dressing. "I'll leave you to bandage the patient," he told Angela.

Standing up to take his leave, Cribbins paused for a moment. Then, for no apparent reason, he reached down and touched the tip of Winston's nose with the back of his hand.

Winston swatted it away. "What the fuck you doing?" he snarled, his patience now completely at an end.

"Just checking to see if your nose is moist," Cribbins said, staring pointedly at Angela. There was a mischievous twinkle in his eye, and she had to look away to avoid smiling.

Winston was clearly at a loss. "My nose is what? I thought that's what vets did with animals?"

Horrified, Garston grabbed hold of Cribbins' arm and virtually frog-marched him out of the room. "Shall we discuss your fee outside?" he said, glancing nervously back over his shoulder at Winston, half expecting him to be reaching for the revolver.

CHAPTER TWENTY-FOUR

Wednesday 12th January 2000

The TSG carrier pulled up outside Arbour Square at exactly one minute past midnight. Another carrier was already parked in front of it, along with a marked station van and an IRV. The carrier's crew, six PCs and a PS, all rushed out and hot-footed it into the building.

"If we're late for the briefing, Reevo, it'll be your fault for lumbering us with that useless stop in Commercial Street," PC Ron Stedman complained. He hated the idea of entering a briefing that was already underway and having every set of eyes in the room turn on them scornfully.

"Sorry," PC Patrick Reeve said, "but you have to admit it looked like a good stop when I put it up."

They had just stopped a beat-up car full of scruffily dressed teenagers on their way to the briefing because the occupants were brazenly passing around what PC Reeve thought was a giant spliff, only to find that it was nothing more sinister than an oversized roll up.

"Everything looks like a good stop to you these days," Stedman said, contemptuously. "You need to get your eyes tested. I reckon all that wanking's sending you blind."

Reeve came to an abrupt stop. "What did you say?" he bristled.

Reeve sported a Poncho Villa style moustache that drooped miserably over the sides of his mouth. Whenever he was annoyed, like now, he tended to compress his lips and grate his teeth from side to side, which made his facial hair ripple like something alive was moving around inside.

"It's obviously affecting your ears too," Stedman said sarcastically.

"Get a wiggle on, the pair of you," their leader, Sergeant Bob Beach, shouted from behind.

When they finally reached the conference room, they found the assembled officers standing around chatting, and they were able to slip in without the embarrassment of having a string of people looking at their watches and tutting disapprovingly.

"Talk about cutting it close," PS Martin Brent said, appearing out of nowhere to join them. Brent was the skipper of the other TSG carrier. "Lucky for you, there's been a five minute delay or you would have looked like a right bunch of knob-heads."

"Would've been here much earlier if Seventies Cop hadn't put up a rubbish stop," Beach said. Everyone on the unit called Patrick Reeve Seventies Cop as he had joined the job in 1979 and all his mannerisms belonged to that era.

At that moment, Tyler, Dillon and Carol Keating entered the room. Locked in conversation, they walked over to Susie Sergeant who was trying – and failing – to reproduce an accurate copy of a road layout on the whiteboard. Holding a red board marker in her right hand and a photocopy of a map in the other, she was desperately trying to get the diagram ready in time for the meeting.

As soon as Beach caught sight of Carol Keating, his face split into a wide grin and he rushed over to say hello.

"Oooh Matron," he said, tapping her on the shoulder.

Keating's face blossomed with affection when she realised who had addressed her. "Little Bobby Beach!" she exclaimed, and immediately wrapped her arms around him and gave him a crushing hug. "I haven't seen you in ages," she said when she finally released him.

"You haven't changed one bit," he told her. "If anything, you look more like Hattie Jacques than ever."

"Jack, this is Bobby Beach. He used to be on the crime squad with me when I was a DS over at Edmonton, and he's the bugger who started all this 'Oooh Matron' malarkey off."

Tyler arched an eyebrow. So, this was the culprit. "You've got a lot to answer for," he said ruefully.

Beach belly laughed at that. "I didn't think it would catch on the way it did," he confessed.

"Listen, I hate to be a party pooper but I'm afraid I'm going to have to drag Carol away from you so we can get started."

"No worries, boss," Beach said. He gave her a little wave. "Catch you later, Carol," he said with a wink.

Brent sidled up to him the moment he rejoined his colleagues. "Look at you, fraternising with the head suits," he said, nudging Beach's arm playfully. "And I think you're in there, son – with the Hattie Jacques lookalike I mean, not the DCI."

Tyler's voice boomed out, stopping all conversation in the room. "Right, ladies and gentlemen, can you all be seated as we're ready to start the briefing."

There was confusion and chaos as everyone scrambled to get to their preferred spot, either at the front or the back or in the middle with their mates, before someone else nabbed it. It was like watching a game of musical chairs without the audio. Tyler waited patiently until they had all sorted themselves out and were sitting quietly in the three rows of plastic chairs that had been set out for them.

"Thank you all for coming at such short notice," he began, looking around the room. There were fourteen TSG officers, four uniforms from Newham Borough, and eight detectives from the murder squad.

"For those of you who don't know me, I'm DCI Jack Tyler from AMIP. Tonight's operation is connected to the murder of PC Stanley Morrison, which occurred at the Royal London Hospital on Monday afternoon. He and two colleagues were performing a hospital watch on a drug dealing pimp called Claude Winston, who had been taken to hospital for emergency surgery after collapsing at Forest Gate police station last week with peritonitis. Ironically, Winston was due to be escorted back to Pentonville that afternoon, but before his escorts arrived, a gang of armed suspects burst in and broke him out."

As he spoke, Steve Bull was walking around the room, handing out briefing packs.

"Of the four people involved in the breakout, one was arrested at the scene, while another was fatally shot by SO19 during the escape. That leaves two suspects outstanding. Tonight, we're going after the only female in the gang, an IC3 called Angela Marley. Her photograph is in the briefing pack that DS Bull is currently distributing and I would be grateful if you could all study it carefully."

There was a rustle of paper as virtually everyone started flicking through the document to find the most recent custody image of Marley.

"The information we have is that at approximately eight-fifteen last night, Angela Marley returned to the squat in Vicarage lane, E15 where she has resided for the past few months. The info comes from two officers who are currently conducting surveillance on the venue and is, therefore, reliable. Marley arrived alone, and to the best of our knowledge, she is still inside. The intention is to arrest Marley and search the premises for evidence relating to PC Morrison's murder. The method will be for the TSG to gain rapid entry into these premises, secure them and everyone inside, and then call the enquiry team forward to search the address in slow time. We have a multi-occupancy Section 8 PACE warrant authorising us to do this. The warrant is with DI Dillon, the big gorilla sitting to my immediate left, and you are all very welcome to have a gander at it before we leave."

It had become customary to make the warrant available for officers to inspect during briefings so that they could, hand on heart, say that they'd had sight of it before being deployed, should they ever be cross-examined about this at court.

"Before we started the briefing, DI Dillon and PS Brent from 3 Area TSG sat down and discussed tactics regarding the entry. I don't intend to cover what came out of that here. Suffice to say that PS Brent will conduct a separate briefing for his TSG colleagues before deployment to fine-tune their individual roles and responsibilities."

Jack walked over to a whiteboard and stared at Susie Sergeant's handiwork in bewilderment. The road lines were wonky, the junction names were illegible, and a five-year-old with a crayon could have done a better job at drawing the houses.

He glanced down at her and raised an eyebrow.

"Don't," she warned.

Tyler turned to face his audience, smiling devilishly. "Now I appreciate that some of you may be looking at this –" he tapped the board "—in confusion and wondering if it's a work of surrealist impressionism." A few people chuckled. "Others may have understandably assumed that we left a care in the community patient alone in here, and the drawings on the board are the doodles of a badly disturbed mind."

Several officers, mainly the detectives who knew Susie, were openly laughing now. Even Susie was giggling.

"Neither of those very reasonable suppositions would be correct," Tyler continued. "In fact, this strange tangle of lines is actually just a very badly drawn roadmap."

"I think a care in the community outpatient might have actually done a better job," Tony Dillon suggested, generating more chuckling.

"Anyway, rather than us being reliant on the board, can I invite you all to turn to page four in your briefing pack, where you will see the actual ordinance survey map this is meant to represent."

There were more rustles as pages were turned.

Holding the briefing package map up for comparison against what was drawn on the board spawned quite a few more giggles.

"I think we'd better book DS Sergeant an urgent appointment with the force optician," Steve Bull said in between bouts of laughter.

Susie held up her middle finger and pulled a face at him. "I'll have you know that it's not as easy as it sounds to recreate a perfect street map," she said cattily, but there was no malice in her voice.

The jibes flew in thick and fast after that, but they were all said in good humour.

"Should've waited till you were sober to draw it, sarge…"

"I didn't know you had Parkinson's…"

"So, I'm guessing you didn't get an A level in art…?"

Jack allowed them a moment more of laughter and then waved them all to silence.

"Okay," he said. "As we can just about make out from this amazing illustration, this is the target address." He pointed to a red square with a tilted triangle on the top and an oblong shape in the middle that was supposed to represent the door. "It's located in Vicarage Lane, almost directly opposite Hurry Close. According to intelligence, this squat is actually two houses that have been knocked into one, and it's been awaiting demolition for the best part of a year. I'm told that a TSG unit searched it in late November and helpfully drew the internal layout on the back of the Prem-Search Book 101. Unfortunately, this has been filed on division and we can't access it until the stores at KF open in the morning."

Beach held up a tentative hand. He'd thought the address sounded familiar when he'd heard it, but hadn't realised why until Tyler mentioned that the TSG had recently searched it.

"Excuse me boss, but it was my carrier that spun that address last November. We nicked an Asian prossie called Lola for possession with intent to supply. I don't know the layout of the whole house, as we only searched the prisoner's room and the communal areas, but think I can just about remember what they looked like if you want me to draw it."

Jack considered the offer. "I think it'll be sufficient for you to just describe the layout as best you can to us, although it might be worth doing a rough sketch for your TSG colleagues when you sit down to go through who's doing what during the rapid entry."

"Fair enough," Beach said. He cleared his throat, aware that everyone was staring at him expectantly. "Feel free to correct me if I get anything wrong," he said to his crew, who were sitting in a line beside him.

"So, from memory, all the windows and the street door are boarded up. The door is bolted from inside, so to gain entry you have to be let in by someone who's already there."

"I take it that means the premises is never empty?" Dillon asked.

"That's right boss," Beach confirmed. "This lot are pretty clued in on squatter's rights and they make sure the house is never vacant so it can't be repossessed."

"You wouldn't think a bunch of drug-addicted hookers would be that well organised," Carol said, impressed.

"The street door opens up onto a large hallway," Beach continued. "There are four rooms on the ground floor, two on each side of the hall, and a big kitchen at the rear. The downstairs rooms contain a mix of beds and armchairs, and I get the feeling that this is where the girls bring their punters when they entertain at home. Upstairs, there are seven –"

"Eight," PC Jay Smith corrected him.

"Upstairs, there are eight bedrooms. Some of these are little more than broom cupboards in which random girls can doss down on a scabby mattress for a night or two whenever they want. Others have been taken over by permanent residents, who have turned them into half-decent bedrooms. Lola, the girl we nicked, had a room at the rear of the house overlooking the garden."

"That's very useful," Jack said. "Am I right in saying that the only way in or out is via the front door?"

Beach shook his head. "Actually, no. The garden backs onto a house in Evesham Road, and there are fence panels missing between the two, so egress into Evesham Road is easily achieved by cutting through the back gardens."

Jack's face hardened. "Are you sure?"

"Positive," Beach said. "When we went in, a punter saw us and had it on his toes. He went straight out the back, through the missing panels and out into Evesham Road. PC Smith caught him after he'd made a hundred-yard dash. The bloke cried his eyes out when he was dragged back. Turned out he had only run because he was convinced that we would tell his wife what he'd been up to."

Jack turned to Dillon. "When you're dishing out the postings, can you make sure we've got the back well and truly covered."

Dillon nodded and made a note in his daybook.

Tyler looked around for Steve Bull. "Stevie, can you just nip out and phone Dick Jarvis for me. Give him the update about there being a back way out."

Bull raised his thumb in confirmation and slipped out the door.

"Right, as far as the risk assessment goes, the latest update from the officers watching the address is that, in addition to Angela Marley, there are at least two other working girls and four men, presumably punters, inside. They were very boisterous when they arrived. There may be more people inside, but we have no way of knowing. We know Angela's a heroin addict so there may be exposed needles. There's nothing to suggest that anyone inside will be carrying weapons, but there may be kitchen knives and other sharps around the place that some idiot might be stupid enough to pick up and use against the officers trying to effect entry, especially if they're spaced out on booze or drugs."

Beach said, "Last time we went inside we found a baseball bat hidden behind the door and a kitchen knife concealed under the pillow in Lola's room."

"Thank, you," Tyler said. "Taking into account that Angela Marley is now wanted for murder, I think the unknown risks are high enough that the TSG should make entry in full public order kit, and this has been agreed by PS Brent."

Tyler looked up as the door opened and Bull reappeared. He shot him a questioning look and was rewarded by a nod that confirmed he had spoken to Jarvis.

PC Stedman raised a hand. "Any suggestion that there will be firearms present?" he asked. It was a reasonable question, bearing in mind guns had been used during the escape.

Jack shook his head, emphatically. He needed to quell this idea fast, before they started giving themselves the jitters. "We're confident that only the male suspects were carrying guns and there is absolutely no intelligence to suggest any firearms will be present tonight."

"Thank you," Stedman said, looking relieved.

"Communications," Tyler said, moving swiftly on. "The TSG will use their own back-to-back channel until the premises are secured. If it all goes pear-shaped, switch straight to Kilo Foxtrot's radio link and call for support."

Tyler turned to Susie. "This is DS Susie Sergeant. She might not be all that as an artist, but she is a cracking detective, and she's the Case Officer for this investigation. All paperwork goes through her, and no one goes off duty until released by myself or one of the DIs. Right, I'll hand you over to DI Dillon and DS Sergeant to go over the route we are all going to take to the venue, the way the vehicles will line up for the convoy, and what everyone is going to be doing when they get there. Thank you for your attention, and good luck everybody."

At 1 a.m. a six-vehicle convoy – two TSG carriers, two unmarked AMIP pool cars, one marked Immediate Response Vehicle and a marked station van left Arbour Square for the four-and-a-half-mile journey across East London to the squat in Vicarage Lane.

They travelled on blue lights, with the unmarked cars sandwiched between the carriers and the IRV. Turning left into Commercial Road, they headed for the Limehouse Link Tunnel, their route taking them through some of the City's less salubrious areas. Emerging from the tunnel, they sped along West India Dock Road and Aspen Way, taking the exit for the Royal Docks and City Airport. Cutting onto the A13, they continued to make good progress, ignoring the flashing speed cameras, and took the A1011 exit for Stratford and Canning Town.

They drove along Plaistow New Road until the junction with Densham Road came into sight. At that point, the convoy killed their blue lights and pulled over against the nearside kerb as had been agreed before they set off.

Dillon was travelling in the first pool car with Tyler and Susie Sergeant. While Tyler got out to have a final word with the TSG skippers, Brent and Beach, he used the time to ring George Copeland, who was with Kelly Flowers in the car that Susie had dispatched down to the scene earlier to cover the other end of Vicarage Lane.

"George," he said as soon as the Yorkshireman's bored voice answered, "we're almost with you. Can you and Kelly relocate to outside the house in Evesham Road that backs onto the target address, just in case there are any runners."

"*We can, but I'm no Linford Christie, so you might want to send someone else. Otherwise, I'll probably be lagging way behind Kelly if anyone has it on their toes.*"

Dillon grinned as he imagined the comical sight of the overweight exhibit officer trying – and failing – to climb over garden fences in pursuit of a fleeing suspect. "Don't worry," he said. "I'm sending an IRV around to back you up. They can do all the footwork if it's required."

Copeland sounded relieved. *"In that case, as soon as it joins us, we'll move into position. I'll call you back once we're set up. Make sure the TSG doesn't go in until we say so, just in case we have any problems working out where we need to be."*

He terminated the call and dialled the number he had for Paul Evans. "Taff, Dillon here. We're just around the corner in Densham road. Any sign of movement out the front?"

"*No, quiet as the grave here,*" Evans replied. "*Three white females came out about half an hour ago, and there's been no other activity since.*"

"Are you sure Marley wasn't amongst them?"

"*Absolutely positive.*"

"Silly question, but do you reckon the three who left were hookers?

Evans laughed. "*Well, they were all dressed as you'd expect prostitutes going out to work on a cold winter's night would be: low cut blouses under flimsy jackets, short skirts, fishnet stockings and suspenders, high heels. Poor cows will end up with frostbite in their nether regions if they're not careful.*"

Dillon heard Jarvis chuckle in the background. "*You can laugh, young Dick,*" Evans scolded him playfully, "*but it can't be pleasant having hyperthermia of the muff.*" That only creased Jarvis up more.

"Never mind their frozen fannies," Dillon snapped, attracting a puzzled look from Susie, "how many people do you think there are inside?"

"*At least seven, possibly eight. There's Marley and whoever let her in – that could have been one of the three girls we saw leave or someone else entirely – and there's also the two hookers and four punters who arrived after her. When you rang to say you were setting off from Arbour Square, Dick took a stroll past the address to see if there were any signs of life inside.*"

"And...?"

"*There was loud music playing inside, along with some raucous singing. Dick thought it sounded as though they were having a bit of a party.*"

"Okay mate, I'll let the TSG know. We're going to be working off their back-to-back channel so you'll need to change to that." He gave Evans the frequency and rang off.

"So," Susie quizzed him, "who's got a frozen fanny?"

Dillon grinned. "You'll have to ask Paul Evans, I'm far too shy to discuss such things."

Susie snorted, derisively. "Shameless, yes. But shy? Definitely not."

"It's the new, sensitive me," he told her, and before she could ridicule him, he nipped out to join in the little huddle outside the lead carrier, where Jack was still talking to the TSG skippers.

"Guys, I just spoke to the DC who has eyeball on the address. All quiet in the street outside, but it sounds like a bit of a party going on inside the squat."

"Any idea how many are inside?" Beach asked.

"They reckon at least seven or eight," Dillon said.

"Is that going to be a problem?" Jack asked.

Beach shook his head. "No, I don't think so. Have you had enough time to let the two units you've already got on plot know we're about to effect entry?"

Dillon nodded. "They've been updated, they're now on your channel, and they're in place and waiting for the fun to begin."

"Good," Beach said, slipping his NATO riot helmet over his head. "In that case, let's do it."

With everyone back in their respective vehicles, the convoy moved off, turning right into Densham Road.

Moments later, it snaked left into Vicarage Lane. The road ahead was straight, except for a slight kink about a third of the way along, which gave the impression that two competing teams of builders had started at either end and then bodged the join in the middle.

Hugging the pavement line so that other traffic could overtake, the motorcade crawled towards the junction with Hurry Close. They were now less than one hundred metres from their destination. Fortunately, traffic was almost non-existent, enabling the line of police vehicles to swerve onto the wrong side of the road for the final approach. The vehicles coasted to a silent halt outside an unobtrusive house that stood virtually opposite the junction with Byford Close.

The station van had long since dropped back and was waiting near the junction with Densham Road. It would only come forward if it was needed for prisoner transport.

The two semi-detached houses that comprised the squat, built in the early fifties from the look of them, boasted a fairly large frontage, with a tarmac driveway big enough to accommodate four or five cars, although only one, a beat-up Ford Escort, occupied it at present.

The police drivers had switched their lights off as soon as they turned into Vicarage Lane and, as a precaution, a complete radio silence was in force as they prepared to exit their vehicles.

The Territorial Support Group officers were dressed in full public order attire, including black, flame-retardant overalls, NATO helmets, and short shields. Having carried out similar raids many times before, they alighted quickly and quietly, immediately taking up positions that had been designated to them in the rushed briefing an hour ago.

The AMIP cars pulled up behind them.

Looking around to see if he could spot his colleagues, Jack was pleased that there was no sign of the eyeball car containing Jarvis and Evans. That demonstrated good fieldcraft on their part.

"I hope that IRV has found George," Dillon fretted. "Just in case Angela goes out the back when the TSG make entry."

"It'll be fine," Susie reassured him.

The house, like most others in the street, was in total blackness. Up close, it appeared shabby and neglected in comparison to the properties on either side. The walls were pebbledashed a depressingly dull brown; all the upstairs windows had been boarded with ply; the downstairs windows and street door had been secured with thick timber, although a gaping rectangular hole had been chiselled out of the right side of the door in order for the squatters to install a crude locking system of their own.

The muffled sound of repetitive dance music escaped from inside, and the steady boom, boom, boom of a bass drum punctuated the still night air around them.

"It must be a delight living next to this lot," Tyler remarked, feeling sorry for the neighbours.

The officers stood motionless as they waited for confirmation that the back was covered. They felt exposed, vulnerable; all they could do was hope that no one inside would see them. The boarded-up windows worked in their favour, as did the darkness; things would have been much tougher had the raid been carried out in daylight. Trying to make a discreet approach to a target address wasn't easy when there was a small crowd of onlookers gathering, shifting from foot to foot and asking each other what was going on.

Finally, after what seemed like minutes but was, in reality, only seconds, George's taut voice came over the radio in a tinny whisper. *"Copeland to Dillon, we're finally in place, guv. Sorry we took so long but we've managed to gain access into the gardens directly behind you. For your info, the target address is in total darkness at the rear."*

"Received, George. Stand by," Dillon responded. He turned to see if Tyler was going to give him the green light and was rewarded with an affirmative nod.

Dillon crossed the drive in five purposeful strides and gave the TSG lads a thumbs up. He leaned into PS Beach's ear and spoke quietly. "Time to use the big red key."

Beach grinned, then turned and patted Ron Stedman on the shoulder. "Go, go, go," he whispered urgently.

With that, Stedman removed the red 'Enforcer' battering ram from his shoulder, where it had rested, and hoisted it into a readiness position. Through the gap in the timber, they could see that the original door was a cheap, mass-produced model. There was a sturdy looking Chubb lock, but it was unlikely to offer much resistance to the kinetic force generated by the heavy ram, especially when it was wielded by someone as proficient as Stedman.

WHACK! WHACK!

The door flew open and Stedman stepped aside as a posse of officers surged into the hallway of the house.

"POLICE! POLICE! STAY WHERE YOU ARE!"

The ghastly music sounded even louder now that they had gained entry.

PS Brent and his PCs were first through the door, and they veered left, headed straight for the ground floor room from which the hellish racket was coming. The lights were on inside so at least they could see where they were going.

His ears throbbing, Brent's eyes followed the cable that ran from the sound system sitting on top of an old cupboard against the far wall to the wall socket beneath. Gritting his teeth, he strode across the room and pulled the plug.

The room immediately went silent.

There were two large leather sofas, one on each side of the room, and both were occupied by a couple attempting drunken copulation.

"You can stop all that nonsense immediately, you randy bastards," Brent ordered, his harsh voice sounding incredibly loud in the sudden silence.

The instructions turned out to be superfluous. On seeing the riot trained police officers standing before them, helmet visors down, shields held at the ready and batons raised, both couples sprang apart as though they had just been electrocuted.

Lola screamed, lowered her skirt and covered her breasts with her hands. She didn't show them to anyone who wasn't paying for the privilege.

The man who had been pumping away on top of her sprang to his feet, naked as a newborn.

Brent grimaced at the sight. "Cover that bloody thing up before I arrest you for possessing an offensive weapon," he shouted at the tattooed man, whose manhood was so hard that it had turned purple.

The couple on the other couch was far slower to respond, but the reason for this instantly became obvious when an officer shook the man lying on top of the prostitute and discovered that he was fast asleep. The girl pinned underneath him seemed quite relieved when he was unceremoniously dragged into a sitting position, allowing her to wriggle free.

Now that entry had been gained, the TSG officers scattered in all directions, securing every room in the premises. Shouts reverberated throughout the building as officers banged loudly on locked doors, demanding that they be opened up quickly. The alternative to rapid compliance, they warned, was to have the locks forced open by a pair of size twelve keys.

A naked man with the numbers 18 tattooed into the base of his shaven skull was dragged, screaming and swearing, from the downstairs toilet, where he had been taking a leak.

The numbers signified his membership to Combat 18, a violent neo-Nazi group that had chosen its name in honour of Adolf Hitler. The number 1 represented the first letter of the alphabet: A for Adolf, and the number 8 represented the eighth letter of the alphabet: H for Hitler.

The far-right extremist was taken into a vacant downstairs room and ordered to sit in a chair. Clad in nothing but a stained pair of shreddies, he did as he was told, looking bleary-eyed and confused from all the drugs and alcohol he had consumed during the last few hours.

While Brent and his officers had deployed across the ground floor, Beach had led his crew straight upstairs.

Considering that they didn't know the exact layout of the house, which caused some minor confusion in the first crucial seconds of the raid, he still managed to get his officers into most rooms inside of a minute.

Only three of the eight bedrooms failed to respond.

On Beach's instruction, these were forced open.

One of the rooms was clearly unoccupied, much to the disappointment of the officer who had just booted in the door, but the second contained a slim white male in his middle thirties who was spooning a dark-skinned woman on a tatty double bed that had definitely seen better days. The woman was so completely spaced out that she hardly even noticed the violent entry, but the man was up in an instant. Naked as the day he was born, he grabbed a clear bag of white powder from the bedside table next to him and made a dash for the en-suite loo, clearly intent on flushing the incriminating drugs away.

A Parteiadler tattoo – the German eagle sitting atop a wreath containing a Swastika that had become the emblem of the Nazi party – spanned his entire back, with the wingtips reaching from shoulder to shoulder. Staring at the tattooed man in disgust, PC Stedman sent him flying across the room before he could pull the chain and dispose of the evidence. His colleague, PC Smith, casually strolled over to the bowl and peered in. "Well, well, well, what have we got here?" he enquired aloud.

As the unfortunate skinhead staggered up from the floor, clutching his stomach and complaining about police brutality, he was met by a satisfied smirk that spoiled his entire day.

Fishing the bag of cocaine out of the bowl with a coat hanger, PC Jay Smith raised his visor and said with great pleasure: "You're nicked sunshine."

Downstairs, Dillon had sneaked into the venue on the tail of the last officer. He knew he ought to have waited outside, but he just couldn't help himself. There was no way he was going to miss out on all the action.

"Copeland to Dillon. Guv, we've got someone coming out of a back window, top floor, furthest window on the right." George's voice announced over the radio as the final bedroom door was kicked open.

As Dillon ran up the stairs towards the room in question, he heard an officer shouting for the suspect to stop.

Predictably, the runner ignored the order. Several officers stampeded down the stairs, intent on giving chase through the gardens. They nearly knocked Dillon over in the process.

"Bloody suits! You were meant to wait outside until you were called forward," one of them called over his shoulder.

Dillon ignored the rebuke. "George, tell me you've caught the bastard!" he yelled into the handset. "George!" he said again, annoyed by the lack of response. Cursing profoundly, Dillon followed the small group of officers into the rear garden.

"Have you got the suspect?" Dillon demanded when he caught them up.

"Sorry, boss, whoever it was shot over the fence like a whippet. I didn't have a chance." PC Reeve apologised sheepishly. He was out of breath and covered in mud, where he'd slipped in one of the garden's flowerbeds.

Dillon shook his head in disappointment, then patted the TSG officer on the shoulder.

"Never mind, you did your best," he told the older man.

"I know, Sir. But it wasn't good enough, was it?" PC Reeve said, disappointed.

"*DI Dillon from DC Copeland, receiving, over,*" George transmitted.

"Yeah, go ahead, George," Dillon replied, trying not to sound too pissed off.

"*Sorry about the delay, boss, but we got the fucker, two gardens down.*" Copeland couldn't keep the pleasure from his voice.

"Well done, George," Dillon beamed. "Is it Angela?" He crossed his fingers, hoping the answer would be a resounding 'YES'.

"*Negative, boss. Just some Asian twat who says he ran because he's wanted on a warrant.*"

"Received," Dillon acknowledged glumly. "Do a namecheck to confirm he's wanted, and then take him straight out to the van. I'm going back inside to supervise the search."

He found Tyler and Susie Sergeant waiting for him in the communal hallway. Unlike him, they had played by the rules and waited in the car until called forward.

"What are you like?" Jack said, shaking his head at Dillon's antics.

Dillon blushed. "Sorry, got a bit carried away."

"Have we found Marley?" Susie asked.

Dillon shrugged. "Haven't had a chance to take a look at any of them yet."

PS Brent emerged from the downstairs boudoir sniggering to himself like a naughty schoolboy. "I think I'm going to have to call an ambulance," he informed them casually.

"Has someone been injured?" Jack asked, confused by Brent's obvious lack of concern.

Removing his NATO helmet, the TSG skipper cackled in wicked delight. "Nah, it's one of the blokes in there. He's got such a stiffy that he's literally crying out in pain. Reckons he's had this monster erection for the best part of four hours now and, no matter what he tries, he can't get it to go down."

"That must be hard on him," Dillon said, grinning at his little quip.

"Sounds like a load of cock and bull," Susie joined in.

"Trust me," Brent said, dabbing at an eye, "I don't know about bull, but it certainly is a load of cock!"

Susie gagged at the thought.

Bob Beach jogged down the stairs and walked over to join them. "The top floor's all secure," he reported happily. "We've got one male under arrest for possession with intent to supply, and a black female who's out of her head on drugs."

Hope blossomed on the faces of the three detectives.

Beach saw this and quickly shook his head. "Sorry, it's not the girl you're looking for."

"Of course not," Dillon said. "That would have been too easy and we don't do easy, do we Jack?"

"Not often," Tyler said, ruefully. "So, we've got two detained upstairs, and I heard about the runner out back. How many have you got in there, skip?"

"We've got two men and two women in the living room," Brent told him.

Jack considered this. "Jarvis reckons there should be at least seven or eight people in the house. How many people have we actually rounded up?" he asked the TSG skippers.

"Well, there's the two Bob's crew detained upstairs," Brent said. "The four we found in the lounge, and the runner outside."

"I make that seven,"

"Which is what your man said," Brent pointed out.

Jack shook his head. "The number he gave us included Angela Marley, so unless one of the girls in the room where the party was going on is her, we're one person adrift."

"One of the girls is Asian, the other is black, but she definitely doesn't have a scar on her face, so it's not Marley," Brent said.

"Are you happy every room has been thoroughly checked?" Jack asked, looking from one TSG skipper to the next. "Is there anywhere she could be hiding?"

"We'll check again," Beach said, "but I'm confident that she's not upstairs."

"Likewise, for downstairs," Brent said.

"Get your troops to check again," Tyler instructed, "and while they're doing that, let's have a word with the two hookers in there in case they can shed any light on where Angela bloody Marley is."

Dillon was sceptical. "I don't think the question should be if they can shed any light; I think it should be will they?"

"Well, we might as well try while we're here," Jack said, spreading his arms as if to say 'what else can we do?'

Tyler and Dillon set off towards the lounge, but Susie lingered behind. "I think I'll wait out here if it's all the same to you?" she said. "I ate just before we came out and I think the sight of that poor man's engorged member might make me chunder."

"I wouldn't feel too sorry for him," Brent said. "He's an obnoxious bloke, covered in tattoos of Nazi emblems and ICF slogans."

Dillon paused when he reached the door, and after a moment's contemplation, he turned to address Susie. "Strange," he said, "I wouldn't have thought that being in close proximity to a giant prick would bother you, not after having spent so much time working with Kevin Murray."

CHAPTER TWENTY-FIVE

The LAS had arrived and the paramedic, struggling to keep a straight face, was checking out Charlie Dobson, the skinhead with the hard-on.

As Dillon had predicted, Lola had been totally uncooperative; she had never heard of anyone called Angela Marley and claimed no one of that name resided at the squat. It transpired that the male George Copeland had detained in the rear gardens was her younger brother, who lived there and acted as a house sitter when the girls were out so that the authorities couldn't move in and repossess it.

The other sex worker in the room, a young black girl of Jamaican descent called Anita, had refused to speak to them, but Jack got the feeling she might have been a little less hostile if Lola hadn't been staring daggers at her the whole time. It was obvious that she was the one running the show.

"It seems to me," Jack said, looking at the bag of cocaine on the coffee table beside the sofa that Lola and Dobson had been cavorting on, "that you have a very simple choice to make, Lola." He gestured at the drugs – in addition to the cocaine, there was some cannabis and a small bottle of blue pills. "From here, it seems obvious that you're using these premises as a brothel and supplying customers with a selection of controlled drugs."

"They're not mine! You can't fit me up with those," Lola said defiantly. Her brown eyes simmered with hatred as they flicked from Tyler to Dillon to Dobson.

"They're not mine," Dobson said quickly.

Lola turned on him in an instant. "You dirty lying cun –"

"That's enough," Dillon bellowed, and the force of his outburst shut her up instantly.

"I'll ask you one last time, Lola," Jack said patiently, "where is Angela Marley?"

The sex worker stubbornly folded her arms and said nothing.

"What about you?" Jack said, turning to the other girl.

"Don't say nothing," Lola snapped before Anita could even open her mouth.

Jack shrugged. "Fair enough. Sergeant Brent, would you and your officers be kind enough to arrest everyone in the room for possession with intent to supply. Let's see if any of them are willing to talk back at the station. If not, they can all be charged."

"Be my pleasure," Brent said, nodding for the officers standing quietly in the background to move forward and lay hands on the four prisoners.

"Oh, and let's also arrest little Miss Smarty Pants for running a brothel, shall we?" Jack said jovially.

"Why not," Brent said, grinning enthusiastically.

"That doesn't include me, does it?" The man who had fallen asleep on Anita asked. He was hard-faced and sinewy, wearing a pair of jeans and nothing else.

Jack couldn't help but notice the letters ACAB had been crudely tattooed into the knuckles of his left hand in green ink. It stood for 'ALL COPPERS ARE BASTARDS' and was a homemade prison tattoo if ever he had seen one.

Another equally distasteful tattoo took up most of his left shoulder, only this one looked like a professional job rather than something which had been inked inside a cell. There were two circles, an outer one of claret and an inner one of blue. The outer circle contained the slogan: 'THESE COLOURS DON'T RUN.' The inner circle was home to a pair of crossed iron worker's hammers. The initials ICF were also present, with the I to the left of the hammers, the C above them and the F to their right. Beneath the hammers was the British Rail emblem. The tattoo clearly denoted the wearer's affiliation to the Inter City Firm, a well-organised group of football related hooligans who were mostly associated with West Ham United. They had been particularly active from the 1970s to the early 1990s.

The last bit of visible body art consisted of the letters NF – an abbreviation for National Front – which were tattooed on his right shoulder.

Jack took an instant dislike to him. "Are you in the room or not?" he asked politely.

The thug, who was called Harry Taylor, considered this as if it might be a trick question, and then he stupidly looked around to confirm that he was. "Er, yeah," he eventually said.

Jack smiled sweetly. "There you are, then. You've answered your own question."

Taylor held his hands out in front of him and waited for the arresting officer to apply the quick-cuffs.

Lola wasn't so savvy. "Get your fucking hands off me, you cunt," she screamed, trying to pull free from the female officer who had just taken hold of her wrist. Without batting an eyelid, the officer swiftly applied a rear arm lock that forced Lola to bend over double. A second officer took hold of the hooker's other arm, and they expertly restrained her.

"Slap on the bracelets and get her out of here," Brent said, shaking his head disapprovingly.

Watching on in amusement as the handcuffs were applied, Dillon started singing the words to Eric Clapton's *Layla*, substituting Lola's name in all the relevant sections of the song. This only served to infuriate the prostitute further, but with her hands now securely cuffed behind her back, she could do nothing about it.

Bobby Beach popped his head around the door. "Guv, could I have a word outside?" he asked, indicating for Jack to follow him with a quick jerk of his head.

Tyler glanced across to Dillon, who had thankfully stopped singing, shrugged, and then followed Beach out of the room.

"What is it?" Tyler asked when they were alone out in the hall.

"Couple of things, but first you might want to come up and speak to the girl who was asleep when we kicked her door in. She's a little more with it now, and she's quite chatty, unlike those two minxes in there."

Signalling for Susie Sergeant to tag along, Tyler followed Beach up the stairs into a reasonably sized room on the left side of the building. A black girl in her early twenties was sitting lethargically on the edge of a dishevelled double bed. Jack dreaded to think what the various nasty looking stains splattered over the sheet were.

The girl had a faded and threadbare dressing gown wrapped tightly around her. She had a thin, blotchy face and there were dark bags underneath her eyes. As they entered, she ran a quivering hand through lank hair that was badly in need of a wash.

She was unquestionably an addict.

"This is Prudence," Beach said by way of introduction. "Pru, be a love and tell these detectives what you told me a few minutes earlier."

The girl looked up at the new arrivals with uncertainty. After a beat, her eyes nervously flickered back to Beach and he nodded encouragingly.

"I hear you're interested in Angela," Prudence said hesitantly, and her voice was every bit as listless as Jack had imagined it would be. She sat there worrying at her fingernails as she waited for him to reply.

"That's right," he encouraged. "Is there anything you can tell us that might help us to find her?"

"Is she in trouble?" Pru asked, deflecting his question.

Jack hesitated, wondering how best to respond. If he said yes, the girl might clam up on him. If he said no, he would be lying. He took a deep breath and released it slowly. "Yes, she's in a lot of trouble," he confessed.

The girl nodded once, seemingly satisfied. "Good," she said, her voice laced with bitterness. "It'll serve her right for being such a mean bitch all of the time."

Tyler glanced over at Beach, who winked at him.

"Now tell the officers what you told me," Beach encouraged her gently.

Prudence shifted uncomfortably on the bed. "Angela lives here," she said, her voice a disinterested monotone. "Her room's two doors along. She hasn't been here for a couple of nights but she came back earlier this evening. Bitch was ranting and raving about someone stealing her phone charger; went around all the rooms accusing people of all sorts of shit. Then, when everyone blanked her, she was suddenly all sweetness and light, trying to persuade us to lend her ours."

"Where is she now?" Jack asked.

Prudence shrugged heavily as if the simple movement had all but drained her. "Dunno. I heard her come out of her room about half-eight, so I poked my head out to be nosey. She was going downstairs with a bag over her shoulder. Lola and her friend had just arrived with four punters and she couldn't get by them. I think she must have gone out the back because I didn't see her anymore."

"What about you? Did you go straight back to your room?" Susie asked.

Prudence shook her head. "No. I heard Lola offer Angela some money to join the party. She refused, but I needed the cash so I went downstairs and offered my services. Been up here with a client ever since."

"Have you any idea where she might have gone?" Jack asked.

"Probably gone out to work," the girl replied with a half shrug. She didn't have the energy for anything more substantial. "She used to work in Whitechapel, but then her pimp got banged up. She's working for his nephew now, but I don't know where."

Jacks exchanged a quick glance with Susie. "This new pimp," Jack said casually. "Don't suppose you happen to know his name, do you?"

Prudence nodded very slowly, and for a moment Jack thought that she was actually drifting off to sleep. "It's Deontay," she said falteringly. "Deontay Garston."

"Thank you," Jack said, placing a hand on her shoulder. "You've been very helpful."

Prudence smiled up at him, but he could tell that it was just muscle memory, and there was no happiness in the act.

Beach motioned for Tyler to follow him with his eyes. They stepped outside the room and Beach leaned in, lowering his voice. "She also told me that the skinheads they've been entertaining make a living by supplying illegal firearms and that the one who was with her drunkenly boasted about selling the guns that had been used to shoot the copper during the hospital breakout."

"Fucking hell!" Jack exclaimed. "Will she make a statement to that effect?"

Beach spread his arms in exaggerated perplexity. "I haven't got a clue," he admitted, "but she didn't seem opposed to the idea when I floated it by her. I think, with the right help and encouragement, young Prudence might jump at the chance to get off the game and turn her life around."

"Okay," Jack said, thinking aloud. "Let's make sure the skinheads don't get a whiff about us knowing what they do for a living. Susie, shoot back downstairs and discreetly let Dill know what we've got. I want all the prisoners taken back in different vehicles. I don't give a toss if that ruffles feathers or causes delays. You'll have to ring around to sort out suitable cell space for them all, but I want them going somewhere with different cell blocks so they can't talk to each other while they're banged up. I want them kept incommunicado while prem-searches are organised for their homes and any other premises we can attribute to them."

Susie blanched. "You don't want much then?" she said, sarcastically.

Tyler raised an eyebrow. "You think I'm asking a lot? I haven't even started yet."

It was Susie's turn to raise her eyebrows. "I'd better get on with it then," she said.

"Anything else?" Tyler asked Beach after she had gone.

The TSG skipper beckoned him with a crooked finger. "One last thing," he said walking into the room Prudence had identified as Angela's. He pointed to a pile of clothing on the floor in one corner. It contained the unmistakable uniform of a Royal London Hospital nurse.

"Wow!" Tyler said, grinning like a Cheshire Cat. "You really are the man who never stops giving."

Beach laughed heartily. "I aim to please," he said.

———

It was 7 a.m.

Jack sat at his desk, sleeves rolled up, tie off, writing up his decision log. He had been at work for twenty three hours on the trot now, and he was fit to drop. He ran a hand through his mop of unruly brown hair and then vigorously dry washed his face, enjoying the feel of a day's stubble brushing against his palms.

Yesterday, he had been so desperate to be involved, so missing all the excitement that came with leading a fast-moving murder enquiry, that he would have given virtually anything to be the SIO. Now that he was, and he was experiencing that familiar 'death warmed up' feeling, he wasn't so sure that getting his wish had been such a good thing.

Gerry Rafferty's *Baker Street* was playing quietly on the radio, and he stopped writing to listen to it while he drank his latest cup of coffee.

The TSG had been absolutely brilliant. Although they were due off duty at 2 a.m., they had volunteered to make all the arrests, transport the prisoners back to the various stations CCC had allotted – two of the skinheads had gone to Forest Gate, while the other two had gone to Barking – and book them in. Lola, her brother, and Anita had been taken to Plaistow, where the local CID had kindly offered to deal with them.

By the time the prisoners had gone through the custody procedure and been placed in a cell, it had been three-thirty a.m. They were all put straight into an eight hour sleep period, meaning that they couldn't be disturbed for an interview during that time. Solicitors were arranged by phone, with instructions to be at the relevant station, ready to begin consulting with their clients, at 11.30 a.m. that morning.

Prudence had been asked to pack up her belongings, and she had been taken to a nearby station to be key witness interviewed on tape. Jack had half expected the FME to proclaim her unfit for this, but Dr Mackintosh had declared that she was good to go, so Susie had cracked on and taken a very powerful statement from her. After this, she had been booked into a local motel they sometimes used, with a view to being properly relocated in the morning. Jack planned to put her in touch with a lady called Sarah Pritchard, who ran The Sutton Mission in Whitechapel, a charity that was dedicated to helping people like

Prudence and ran programmes to help prostitutes and people with drug and alcohol dependencies to get their life back together and move on.

The good news, as far as the local authority was concerned, was that the squat was now empty. Dillon had contacted the emergency out of hours number and explained that, if they wanted to reclaim the premises, they had until the search and record photography was completed to send someone along to secure it. A boarding up team had arrived just as the officers were getting ready to release the scene, and the council had finally taken possession of the condemned building.

Jack suspected that the neighbours would be overjoyed when they awoke and found out that the brothel had been closed down.

Jack checked his watch. He would give it another half-hour before calling George Holland.

To his surprise, there was a knock on his office door. "Come in" he called, wearily.

Reggie Parker entered the room. "Morning, guv. Heard things got a bit hectic after I went home last night?"

Tyler grunted. "You could say that," he said, breaking into a yawn. "What can I do for you Reg?"

"Got the latest on the 777 and 321 phones," Parker said, waving a sheet of paper in the air.

Tyler groaned and then reached for a pen. "Have a seat."

"So," Reggie began, checking his notes after he'd made himself comfortable, "after going walkabouts during the evening, 777 returned to the same cell it bedded down at the night before, but 321 dropped off the grid at about eight o'clock last night, either because it was deliberately switched off or because the battery died. The good news is that both phones are active again this morning, and they are together. It means Angela and mysterious doctor –"

"His name's Deontay Garston," Jack interrupted.

"What?" Reggie looked confused. "How do we know his name all of a sudden?"

Jack allowed himself a brief smile. He was too tired for anything more. "One of the girls at the house we raided last night told us."

"Cool," Reggie said, looking suitably impressed. "Does Deano know yet?"

Jack nodded. He'd told Dean the moment he'd walked through the door some twenty minutes ago.

"Anything else, Reggie? Only I've got a lot to do before the eight o'clock team meeting."

Parker shook his head and stood up. "That's it from me," he said. And then a thought occurred to him. "Guv, have you been home since the last time I saw you?"

Tyler smiled wanly. "Nope. You know me, Reggie. When a new job breaks, this becomes my home."

"Thought that might be the case," Reggie said, "Because you look like shit."

Jack couldn't help but smile. "Yeah, I know. I'm gonna finish up this entry, phone the DCS and then grab a shower to freshen myself up."

Reggie shook his head in despair. "You're gonna burn yourself out, you know, carrying on like this."

Jack shrugged. "It's only for a day or so, then I'll have a day off and sleep to my heart's content."

On his way out of Jack's office, Reggie passed Dillon coming the other way. Despite only having had four hours of sleep on his office floor, he looked fresh and ready for another day of manic action.

"Morning guv," Parker said.

"And a fine morning it is too," Dillon beamed, closing Jack's door behind him.

Jack cringed. *Oh God*, he thought, *Dillon's in one of his 'the morning's the best time of the day' moods...* "Dill," he warned, "be gentle with me. I'm feeling fragile."

Dillon looked confused and then angry. "I thought you were gonna grab some shut-eye when we got back? Please don't tell me you've been sitting here for the last four hours, writing that stupid log up?"

"It won't write itself, will it?" Tyler said, irritably. "And I'm not going to have the time to play catch up today, not when we've got so much going on."

"Jack," Dillon said, softly, "go and have a shower and a bit of breakfast, then we can divide the workload and get through it together."

"I need to finish –"

Dillon's tone became firm. "You look knackered, Jack. You clearly need a break. Don't argue with me, just go and take a shower and have some breakfast."

Tyler opened his mouth to protest, realised that Dillon was right, and tossed his pen onto his desk. "Fine," he said. "I'll be back in time for the meeting." With that, he stood up, snatched his jacket from the back of his chair, and walked out.

The team meeting started promptly at 8 a.m. in Andy Quinlan's main office. Jack was feeling much better, having showered and shaved. He had also grabbed a bacon sandwich from the local café, where Dillon had dragged him for breakfast.

He'd phoned Holland from the café to update him on where they were, and he'd requested additional resources to help out with all the searches, which Holland had reluctantly promised he would try to provide, not that he had many to spare with the Commissioner pressuring him to plough everything he had into tracking down Craig Masters.

Tyler started off by giving them a rundown on what had happened overnight and outlined the massive amount of work they would have to get through before the end of the day.

"DI Keating's preparing the briefing document for all the prem-searches," Jack said. "Mr Holland has promised to provide us with enough additional officers to enable us to hit each address simultaneously, and we will keep the skinheads incommunicado until we have control of all the addresses."

A Superintendent's authority was required to hold a detainee incommunicado, and the authorising officer had to have reasonable grounds for believing that informing anyone of their arrest could lead to interference with evidence related to an indictable offence, cause physical harm to other people, alert other persons suspected of being involved in the offence but not yet arrested, or hinder the recovery of evidence.

"Have we got any actual evidence, yet?" Charlie White, a bow-legged Scotsman with a badly broken nose and a thick Glaswegian accent asked.

Jack nodded. "Prudence Hardy provided a very compelling statement outlining the admissions that her neo-Nazi client made to her."

"What exactly did he tell her?" DS Wilkins asked.

"Basically," Susie Sergeant said, "he bragged that their night out was being financed by the money they had made from selling the two darkies – his words, not Prudence's – the guns that had killed the policeman during the hospital escape. He also boasted that they had plenty more guns to sell, and said if she knew any gangster boys who were in need of a shooter, she should send them his way and there would be a drink in it for her."

"Do we have anything to corroborate what she said?" Wilkins asked.

"Afraid not, Tom," Jack said.

"Wi'out anything to corroborate her accusation, those nasty wee buggers will all go 'no comment' and we willnae have enough to charge them," Charlie White predicted.

Jack thought that he sounded a bit like Frazer from Dad's Army, and he half expected the gloomy DS's prophecy to end with the sitcom character's catchphrase, 'We're doomed!'

"I know," Jack said, "which is why it's all going to come down to if we find anything incriminating at any of the addresses that we've linked them to. On that subject, Deano, how did you get on with your research?"

"Well," Dean said, lowering his reading glasses to focus on his fellow detectives. "I've got home addresses for all four, but those are family addresses, so I'm not expecting us to find much there. However, as luck would have it, I stumbled across a CRIMINT entry dated three days ago, and there was something about it that made me want to dig a little further. Glad I did because, as a result, I found out that Dobson is renting a lockup behind a little parade of shops near Rathbone Market in Canning Town."

Jack leaned forward in his seat, intrigued. "How exactly did you stumble across this information, if you don't mind me asking?"

"Well, I had no luck looking for addresses that were linked to our suspects so I thought I'd try different search parameters. I ran one looking for any recent incidents involving skinheads and property. There were only four hits, so I worked my way through them and this one was the last on my list."

"So, what's the information, Dean?" Steve Bull asked.

"A few days ago, the owner of all the lockups complained to his local Beat Bobby about a skinhead who's renting a unit from him. The bloke's causing him problems by not complying with the terms of the rental agreement. He wanted the PC to go around and have a quiet word with the yobbo, but the PC wasn't interested. He said it was a civil matter and told him to go to his local Citizen's Advice Centre or speak to a solicitor. I'm surprised the PC even bothered to put the CRIMINT on, to be honest."

"That's it?" Steve asked, sounding surprised.

"That's all that's on the CRIMINT," Dean confirmed, "but I wanted to know more. On a whim, I rang the informant, a bloke called Aaron Stein, and he told me he was renting the unit to Charlie Dobson. The terms of the rental are that it can only be used for storage or parking, not as a workshop, and he's been getting it in the neck from all the shopkeepers because Dobson's got machinery set up in there, and he's coming and going at all times of the day and night, often bringing what appear to be dodgy looking customers with him. Not only that, but there have been strange banging noises coming from the lockup during the night – like someone setting off fireworks."

"Or someone test-firing guns?" Jack suggested.

"Exactly," Dean said. "Anyway, When Mr Stein popped around to the lockup to have a word with Dobson the other day, he was promptly seen off by some of Dobson's skinhead mates."

"That's a great bit of work," Jack said, "and it sounds quite promising." He turned to George Copeland. "George, can you check the property page of Dobson's custody record, see what keys he's got on him?"

"Stand by," Copeland said, hurriedly sorting through the pile of forms on his lap. "Here we go," he said, reading from the printout. "Five keys in total, two Yale, two Chubb, and a chunky padlock key."

"Fingers crossed, one of those will fit the lockup," Jack said. "Fingers, toes and everything else crossed, the lockup will contain something we can use against him."

"Mr Stein told me that, as long as Dobson isn't being taken along, he's happy to meet the searching officers and point out the lockup. They just need to phone him ten minutes before they get there," Dean said.

"Okay," Tyler said. "Susie, now that we know all the addresses we want to search, can you liaise with the PACE inspector at the relevant stations and get all the Section 18 searches authorised?"

"I'll get straight on it after the meeting," she promised.

"Kevin, how did you get on with Sonia Wilcox, Errol's fiancée?" Jack asked.

"Miserable cow was totally unhelpful," Murray told him sulkily. "Blamed us for lover boy getting himself shot, silly tart."

"I'm sure you were very tactful in your reply," Jack said, very much doubting that was the case.

"I literally bled sympathy," Murray assured him. "Although, at one stage, I did feel obliged to point out that if her fella hadn't just murdered a policeman, hijacked a car, and then pulled a gun on the officers who stopped him, he might still be alive. I assure you I said this very politely, but it still seemed to cause offence." Murray appeared genuinely surprised by this. "I guess there's just no pleasing some people," he said with a dismissive shrug.

"Did she say anything about the calls between her mobile and the 777 number?" Jack asked. "Or did the situation deteriorate too quickly for that?"

"She had the gall to tell me she hadn't received any calls from that number and that she didn't know anyone called Claude Winston. She even offered up her phone so I could scroll through the address book and the incoming and outgoing call logs. Of course, the sly old hag had already deleted her call history by then."

"Well, the call data says otherwise," Reg Parker said. "Pity you didn't seize her phone, then we could have tried to recover the erased data."

Murray reached behind him and produced a clear evidence bag containing a Nokia handset. "Ta-da!" he said triumphantly.

"I bet that went down well," Reg said, grinning.

"Well, to be honest, I think she had pretty much decided that she didn't like me by that stage," Murray admitted, grinning to himself.

"Okay," Jack said. "I think it might be worth us getting a statement from Sonia at some point. If she commits the lies that she told Kevin to paper, we may want to consider bringing charges of perverting the course of justice against her when the dust settles."

Murray didn't look too keen on the idea. "I'll happily try," he said, "but I don't think she'll be willing to speak to me again." He had only just about got out of the house without being assaulted the last time.

"I don't think the boss was planning to send you, Kevin," Susie explained.

Murray looked relieved.

"Indeed not," Jack confirmed, inwardly shuddering at the thought. "I have no doubt that Sonia Wilcox knows exactly who's using the 777 phone and now, thanks to young Prudence, we do too. She told us that since we banged Claude Winston up last November, Angela's been working his for nephew, Deontay Garston. We believe he's the bogus doctor, which also makes him the man with the 777 phone. Wendy, how you getting on with your research on Garston?"

Wendy Blake cleared her throat. Although she was a well-liked and respected member of the team, she suffered from stage fright and always got nervous when she had to speak during office meetings.

"I started work on him first thing this morning sir," she said quietly.

"Speak up," Murray griped. "Some of us don't have super hearing."

Wendy blushed. "Sorry," she said, making an effort to project her voice. "There's surprisingly little in the system about him. PNC-wise, there's some petty form as a juvenile, just TDA, possession of cannabis, that kind of thing. Nothing for violence or weapons. There's hardly anything about him on CRIMINT either, which does seem at odds with him taking over Winston's drug and pimp business."

"Do we have a current address for him?" Dillon asked.

"Sort of," Wendy replied. "He was stopped in a BMW a few weeks ago in Barking. I did a check on the car he was driving. It's registered to him at an address in Bow several years ago, but there's no way of knowing if that address is current."

"Is he shown on the voter's register as living there?" Susie asked.

Wendy shook her head. "No, there's an Asian family shown on voter's."

"Okay," Jack said. "Let's get a drive-by done at the address to see if the car's there. Without more to link him to it, we're going to really struggle to get a warrant at this stage. Wendy, can you get the car circulated on the PNC. If seen, it's to be stopped. If either Garston or Angela are in it, they are to be arrested. Put a firearms marker on the PNC that the car is not to be approached without Trojan assistance. I don't want some local lid getting killed trying to make a name for themselves by nicking the bloke who shot PC Morrison."

"I'll get straight on it."

A horrible thought occurred to Jack. "Dean, can I confirm that Winston, Garston, and Marley are actually circulated as wanted on the PNC?" he asked.

Dean's scowl translated to: 'Oh puh-lease!' and the stern-faced researcher raised an admonishing eyebrow as it if say, 'Do I really even have to answer that question?'

Jack took the hint. "I'll take that as a yes," he said, grinning. "While we're dealing with Intel matters, are either of you any further forward identifying this Rodent character?" he asked.

"Sorry boss," Wendy said. "I can't find anything on him."

Jack grunted his disappointment.

Darren Blyth raised a hand. "Sorry if it's jumping the gun," he said, "but after our chat last night –"

You mean after the bollocking I gave you, Jack thought.

"– I started going through some of the footage from the cameras surrounding the wasteland where the HEMS bird went down. I've managed to find what I believe is the red Rover fleeing the area, and I think I've actually got the car's index."

Jack had mixed views about this revelation. On the one hand, he was very pleased that Darren had responded to his criticism positively, and he was delighted that the man had found what could be a very important lead. On the other hand, he was angry that Blyth had waited until this morning's meeting to tell him, instead of letting him know right away, which is what his own officers would have done. He could only put it down to the difference between the ways that he and Andy ran their respective teams and conditioned their staff to think.

Andy was a plodder; he was happy to move forward slowly and methodically, dealing with one strand of an investigation at a time, knowing that he would get the right result in the end. In contrast, Jack was totally driven; he wanted everything done yesterday, and he expected his people to aggressively chase all lines of enquiry from the second the job broke right up to the moment that the suspect was charged. Considering that the two men were such polar opposites, not just in their working methods but in their appearances and backgrounds, it sometimes surprised Tyler that they got on so well.

"Well done, Darren," Jack said. "Can you play the clip for us now?"

Blyth seemed caught out by that request. He obviously hadn't prepared anything, which a CCTV officer on Jack's team would have done without having to be asked, knowing that it would be expected of them.

"Er, no, not yet," Blyth replied uneasily. "I've printed off some stills though," he said, handing them over.

That was something, Jack thought, gratefully accepting them. It was impossible to make out any of the car's occupants, but the registration number was just about readable. He passed the stills to Carol Keating, who was sitting next to him. "Pass them around when you've had a gander so that everyone gets to see them," Jack told her.

"I got Dean to do a quick check on the PNC before the meeting started, and it came back as having no reports on it and no current keeper since May 1997," Blyth informed him.

"Dean, I need you to run the car's index through CRIMINT to see if we can work out who's been using it since then," Tyler instructed. "And can you also circulate it on the PNC – same conditions as the BMW."

"Leave it to me," Dean said, jotting down notes.

Tyler turned to Wilkins, the Office Manager. "Tom, I need a High Priority action issued for the last known keeper to be contacted urgently. It's a long shot, I know. It's probably passed through half-a-dozen different keepers since he got rid of it, and it was probably sold for cash with no records kept, but we have to try."

Wilkin nodded. "I'll get it issued as soon as the meeting's over," he promised.

"Anything else before we wrap up?" Tyler asked, looking around the room.

"I've got the results of the overnight street sweep," Tom Wilkins said, waving several sheets of A4 paper in the air. Today, he wore a yellow and blue polka dot bow tie over a pale blue shirt. "The Duty Officer emailed them to me at the end of his shift. Unfortunately, they didn't manage to complete the sweep because they had to rush off and deal with a fatal accident on the Barking Road, but he's promised to send his troops back out to finish it off tonight. Basically, it's just Star Lane and half a dozen streets branching off of it that need checking."

"Can you have a quick look to see if the car Darren has found is on your list?" Jack asked him.

Wilkins shook his head. "I've already looked, boss, and it's not."

"When did you do that?" Jack asked, frowning suspiciously. He hadn't seen Wilkins referring to a list during the meeting.

"Before we started," the OM informed him. "Darren came to see me earlier."

Jack felt a bubble of anger forming in his chest. Blyth had found time to inform the Office Manager about the red Rover's index before the meeting, but he hadn't thought to tell the SIO. He took a deep breath. Now wasn't the time to have another dig at Blyth.

"Right," Jack said, looking around the room and making eye contact with as many people as he could. "I know you're all tired, and I appreciate that the last thing you want is another full-on day with me cracking the whip like a slave driver, but I'm pushing you like this for a very good reason. Claude Winston is an evil man and a danger to the public. He shot two of your colleagues last November, and he killed another one on Monday afternoon. If we don't catch him in the next couple of days, there's a very good chance he'll quietly slip out of the country and evade justice. We're making great progress, but the clock is against us, so let's grit our teeth and keep up the pressure for just a little while longer. I'm going to hand you over to DI Keating and DI Dillon to go through operational roles and responsibilities for the day. Keep me updated on your progress. I wish you all good hunting." With the pep talk delivered, Jack gathered up his things and rushed down to see Mr Holland in order to sort out the additional resources he was going to need.

CHAPTER TWENTY-SIX

Claude Winston was feeling much better today. Now that the wound had been stitched back together, he was moving with a little more freedom. This morning, he had gone to the toilet independently for the first time since they had arrived, which had pleased him greatly. The antibiotics he'd started taking the previous evening were also having a positive effect, and his fever seemed to have more or less vanished overnight.

His mood had obviously improved too, because he hadn't shouted at Angela or threatened her with violence once while she was changing his bandage and cleaning the wound, and to her great surprise, he'd even grunted out a sullen thank you to her as she'd left the room.

"Oi, Deontay," Winston shouted, summoning his nephew into the bedroom.

"What is it, Claude?" Garston asked, poking his head around the door. He had been halfway through his breakfast when called.

"I've been thinking about that white-haired doctor you brought me yesterday." Winston was sitting up in bed, drinking coffee, and his brows were drawn together in thoughtful consideration.

Garston stiffened. "What about him?" he asked, cautiously.

"I think he was taking the piss when he touched my nose. Do you think the cheeky cunt was implying that I'm some kind of animal?"

"No, of course not," Garston said quickly. "He was probably just checking to see if you were dehydrated."

Winston scowled at him suspiciously. "How the fuck can he tell that by putting his grubby hand on my nose?" he demanded.

Garston's burner phone started to ring. Thankful for the interruption, he checked the number and saw that it was the Sussex fisherman. "I need to take this," he said, slipping out of the room.

Alone in the hall, he pressed the green button and raised the phone to his ear. "Hello...?"

"It's me, Kenny Meade," a jarring male voice with a slightly rural twang announced. *"There's been a slight change in plans. Can you bring the cargo down tonight?"*

"Tonight?" Garston replied, confused. "I thought you didn't want him there until tomorrow night so you could go across in the early hours of Friday morning."

Meade was short with him. *"Like I said, the plan's changed and you need to bring the cargo down tonight."* His tone became surly. *"I would've thought you'd be pleased to be a day ahead of schedule."*

"I am," Garston said defensively, "but it might be too early to move him."

Meade tutted irritably. *"Listen, I've been asked to run another cargo over as well as yours, and this new job pays a hell of a lot more than the chicken feed you're giving me. I'm not sure if it's arriving tonight or tomorrow, but I need to be ready to set sail as soon as it gets here, so I need you to get your man down to the cottage by ten o'clock tonight just in case."*

"What you're asking is going to be difficult," Garston complained. "I'm going to have to rush around like a lunatic to make it happen, and for what? You might not even end up sailing tonight."

Meade grunted ill naturedly. *"Don't make a plank out of a splinter, son,"* he complained. *"Just do what you need to do to get your man down here tonight. If all goes well, he'll wake up tomorrow morning in La Belle bloody France. Worst case scenario is he gets to spend a lovely day by the sea at no extra cost to himself and we go on Friday as originally planned."*

"I don't like the sound of this," Garston said aggressively. They had an accord and it wasn't right that Meade had just upped and changed the conditions of their deal just because someone else had come along and offered him more money to go a day earlier.

"*I can't help that,*" Meade said bluntly. "*Be here for ten p.m. tonight. If you're not, and my other cargo is, you'll have to wait until next week for it to be safe for me to make another night time crossing.*" With that, the cantankerous fisherman hung up, leaving Garston staring at the handset in silent fury.

He paced the hall, wondering what to do. Had there been a viable alternative, he would have told the pirate to shove his mainsail right up his inbred arse, but people smugglers were hard to find at short notice and he needed to get Winston out of the UK as quickly as possible.

He daren't mention this to Winston, or his uncle would probably shoot the fisherman as soon as he saw him. Realistically, there was no real choice but to comply with the instructions he'd been given. If Meade sailed tonight, without Claude Winston on board, he would be stuck with his uncle for another week, and he doubted his sanity would be able to withstand that.

Garston stormed into the lounge, where Rodent was curled up in his sleeping bag in the centre of the room, snoring away contentedly. Feeling the need to vent his frustration, Garston kicked him viciously in the side. "Get up," he snapped.

Rodent cried out in pain. When he sat up, his eyes were full of fear and confusion. "What's the matter?" he whimpered, looking around in a panic. "Are we being raided?"

"No," Garston said irritably. "I need you to get up and run some urgent errands for me, and then I need you to go and get your mate's van like you said you could."

Rodent unzipped the bag and gingerly rose to his feet, still favouring his side. "But I'm not supposed to be getting that until tomorrow," he mewled.

To Garston's disgust, the small-time drug peddler was still clad in the same clothes he'd worn when he had picked them up from the hijacked helicopter, and the ripe smell of his body odour came flooding out of the sleeping bag with him.

"Yeah, well, there's been a change of plan and we need to drive him down to the coast tonight, so you need to have a word with your mate and borrow his van this evening instead. Tell him I'll make it well worth his while."

"But he uses it for work during the week," Rodent snivelled. "What if he can't let us have it tonight?"

Garston stepped forward and slapped him around the top of the head, making him flinch. "Tell him if he doesn't, I'll put a fucking bullet through his head. I'm sure that'll convince him to make his poxy van available."

Motioning for Rodent to follow him, Garston went through to the cramped kitchen. His half-eaten poached egg on toast had gone cold, and he pushed it aside as he sat at the small Formica table.

"You stink," Garston told him bluntly, his voice dripping with contempt. "Don't you ever change your clothes?"

"Normally I change them every day," Rodent told him, and his young face flushed with shame.

"So why haven't you changed them since we've arrived?" Garston taunted him.

Rodent stared down at the floor. "Because," he said meekly, "every time I try to go into my bedroom to get anything, Mr Winston shoves a gun in my face and shouts at me to get out."

Garston's face softened. "You should have told me," he said.

The kid shrugged. "I'm not a grass."

Garston nodded. "Good for you," he said, "but even if you can't change your clothes, you could still shower and spray on some deodorant."

"I'm sorry," Rodent said, feeling browbeaten.

A notepad and pen were lying on the kitchen worktop. Garston ripped a page out of the notebook and began to scribble frantically. When he'd finished, he reached into his pocket and pulled out a large wad of cash. "I need you to get some more medical supplies, some men's clothes in the sizes I've written down, and some food for Claude to take with him. Also, pop into a phone shop and buy yourself a cheap burner phone and fifty quid's worth of credit. Tell them you want a pre-paid unregistered phone. Whatever you do, don't give them your details. Got it?"

Rodent nodded uncertainly. "Pre-paid unregistered. Don't give them my details," he recited.

Garston thrust the shopping list and cash into Rodent's hand and shoved him towards the door. "That's right. Now, I want you back here by two o'clock at the latest, so you'd best get a move on."

"But I haven't had any breakfast yet," the boy protested. He looked close to tears.

Garston rolled his eyes, peeled off another tenner and threw it at him. "Stop off at a bloody café, and while you're out, buy yourself some deodorant with the change."

―――

The morning had sped by in a sustained flurry of frantic activity. The meeting with George Holland had gone better than expected. Although it wasn't their core business, he was all in favour of trying to recover the skinhead's gun stash, and he had been able to recruit an entire unit of TSG – four carriers, each containing a PS and six PCs – to help out with the searches, plus a half-dozen detectives to assist with the interviews.

The local CID had kindly offered to deal with the back-garden runner, who was wanted on a fail to appear warrant, which left AMIP with six prisoners to be interviewed: four men and two women.

Having been put straight into a mandatory sleep period upon arrival, they hadn't been roused until eleven. Of course, they then had to be given sufficient time to shower, eat some food, and then consult with their solicitors before they could be questioned. As a result, although it was now getting on for one o'clock, most of the interviews were only just beginning.

The searches had taken far longer to organise than Jack had hoped. One of the hardest challenges had been tracking down the PACE Inspector to authorise them. It turned out that he had gone into a meeting and switched his radio off for the duration.

By the time that Carol had completed the briefing and risk assessment documents, all the staff being deployed on the searches had arrived at Arbour Square. They had been hurriedly divided into search teams and whisked off for a quick briefing. Then there was a mad scramble as officers ran around the building trying to round up enough vehicles to ensure everyone had transport, and Jack had been annoyed that none of the officers participating in the searches had thought of doing this before they were ready to set off.

The net result of all the fluffing around was that the premises searches didn't begin that much earlier than the interviews.

Steve Bull was leading the search of the lockup behind the parade of shops near Rathbone Market. With no occupants to worry about, it was the smallest of the search teams. In addition to Bull, there were only three other detectives, Kelly Flowers, Paul Evans, and Kevin Murray, who was to be their advanced exhibits officer.

Upon their arrival, they were met by Aaron Stein, a short, fat man in a creased suit, with a wrinkly bald head and bulbous nose.

It transpired that the lockup was actually an end garage in a block of ten units situated behind the shops. They had brought along the five keys that had been in Charlie Dobson's possession when he'd been arrested and were pleased to see that the chunky key was a perfect fit for the padlock attached to the side of the lockup The first of the two Yale keys didn't want to know when it was inserted into the lock in the handle protruding from the door's centre, but the second one turned smoothly and they were able to raise the door upwards and gain entry.

"Well, well, well," Bull said as he looked inside. "What do we have here?"

Although it was dark inside, Bull immediately made out the large Nazi flag that was hanging in the centre of the left-hand wall. It pictured the swastika in a white circle on a background of red. Directly beneath this was heavy-duty safe that Bull suspected was probably either bolted into the wall or, more likely, the concrete floor.

A penny to a pound, he thought to himself, *if we're going to find anything incriminating, it will be locked in there.*

Aaron Stein started to walk towards the opening, clearly intent on having a nose around inside, until Murray placed a restraining hand across his chest.

"Where do you think you're going then?" he demanded.

The bald man seemed startled by the question.

"Why I'm going inside to see what that hooligan has done to my property," he said as if it should have been obvious.

Murray shook his head. "No, mate, you're not."

"But I own it," the man protested.

"You might own it," Murray said, patronisingly, "but right now it's a potential crime scene and only authorised personnel are allowed inside, and you ain't authorised."

Stein opened his mouth to object, but Murray raised a warning finger to shush him. "It's not up for debate, so be a good chap and go and wait in your car."

Out of the corner of his eye, Steve Bull saw the lockup owner pivot angrily and storm off towards his vehicle. He walked over to Murray, who was slipping into a Tyvek oversuit. "Not been upsetting people again, have you, Kev?"

"As if I'd do that," Murray said, working the fingers of his right hand into a latex glove one by one. Maybe it was just Steve's imagination, but he could have sworn that Murray deliberately left his middle finger extended far longer than all the others.

"Come on you bunch of losers," Murray said when he had finished. "You need to suit up if you want to come into my crime scene." With that, he reached into the back of his car and threw them each a set of barrier clothing.

When they were finally ready, Steve led the way over to the entrance and they all had their first proper look inside. The interior was ten foot wide by sixteen foot deep. A single fluorescent tube hung from the ceiling. Murray hit the light switch, which was located just to the left of the door, and the bulb flickered on and then stabilised, bathing the interior in a sickly yellow glow.

Apart from the hefty wall safe, there was no other furniture along the left hand wall. The right hand wall was occupied by an eight foot long heavy-duty workbench, and just beyond that stood a rusted, three drawer filing cabinet that was covered in dents.

What really caught the eye – apart from the huge Nazi flag – was the way that the back wall was set up. It was covered from floor to ceiling with thick sheets of metal, and these were all peppered with small dents and impact craters.

Murray let out a low whistle. "This place looks like a homemade firing range to me."

Evans nodded his agreement "I reckon we've found ourselves a little armoury in here."

"Look at the wall safe," Flowers said. "Unless Dobson's given you the combo, we're going to have to call out a locksmith to crack that little beauty."

A thick yard broom was leaning against the wall in the far left corner of the lockup, and there was a metal bucket on the floor beside it. "I wonder," Bull said, ambling over. He broke into a large grin when he peered inside. "Guess what's inside here?" he said to the others, beckoning them to come and have a look.

Murray hazarded a guess. "Spent cartridges?"

"Yep," Bull said happily. "Lots of them."

Murray sauntered over to join him, his plastic overshoes scraping along the floor with each lazy step. Kneeling down, he inserted the tip of his biro into one of the cartridges and raised it for a closer inspection. Although he was wearing two pairs of latex gloves, he didn't want to risk smearing any latent prints that might be on the brass cases. He held it up to the light and tilted it from side to side, seeing if he could spot anything of interest with the naked eye.

"Kevin, you better get on the blower mate, we're definitely going to need the services of a safecracker," Bull said with a grin.

The final errand Rodent had to run before heading back to the flat was to stop off at the chemist in Barking Road and pick up some more dressings and bandages. He'd already purchased the thick winter clothing that Garston had sent him out for and some groceries for Winston to take with him to France.

None of the local shops had stocked any coats big enough to

accommodate the gangster's gargantuan frame, and the staff in the shoe shops he'd tried had all looked at him as though he were mad when he'd asked if they stocked anything in size fourteen. In the end, fed up with getting nowhere, he had found a phone box, called Garston and asked him where Winston normally purchased his clothing from. Inevitably, he'd received an ear-bashing for not having had the brains to do that before leaving the flat.

With Garston's earlier comments about his lack of personal hygiene still bothering him, Rodent had grabbed himself a can of Lynx antiperspirant when he'd stopped off at Tesco to pick up Winston's food supplies. As soon as he'd returned to the Rover, he'd sprayed himself all over so that he wouldn't reek of sweat if he was lucky enough to be served by Jenna Marsh.

Just thinking about her made his pulse race. He knew a girl like that could never fall for someone like him, but even being around her made him feel better about himself.

To his delight, Jenna was standing behind the counter on her own, serving an elderly woman. His heart missed a beat when he saw her. Ducking behind one of the display racks so that she couldn't see him, he had a quick sniff of his armpits. Thankfully, all he could smell was the pleasant musky scent of the aerosol he'd doused himself in a few minutes earlier.

It suddenly occurred to him that he hadn't even washed his face or cleaned his teeth before leaving the flat that morning. He self-consciously cupped his hands to his mouth, exhaled into them a couple of times and then sniffed to see if his breath smelled. Then he quickly ran his fingers through his straw-like hair to smooth it down.

He passed the woman on his way to the front of the shop, politely moving aside to let her pass him in the narrow aisle.

"Hello again," he said as he reached the counter. He could feel a goofy smile spreading across his face, but there was nothing he could do about it.

Jenna didn't smile back, but she looked relieved to see him. "I was hoping you would come in," she said.

"Well, here I am," he said, spreading his arms wide and giving her a twirl.

Jenna's face remained serious. "I need to ask you something, but I don't want you to be annoyed," she told him when he was facing her again.

The smile fell from his face as he realised it was going to be one of *those* conversations. In his experience, an opening statement like that was usually the precursor to a telling off or a lecture.

"What's wrong?" he asked, wondering what he could possibly have done to offend her.

"I watched the news on TV last night," Jenna began, watching him carefully for a reaction. "And I was really concerned when I saw the segment about the man who murdered that police officer at the Royal London Hospital on Monday afternoon and then escaped from custody."

Rodent didn't like where this was going. "And what's that got to do with me?" he asked, guardedly.

He could see that she didn't like the standoffish tone of his voice, but he couldn't help that. This wasn't a conversation he was prepared to have.

Jenna didn't take the hint. "While I was watching the telly," she continued doggedly, "I remembered you telling me about your friend's stitches popping open after his operation, and him not being able to go back to the hospital because the police were looking for him."

Rodney affected a perplexed expression. "So...?"

"So," she said, and there was an edge to her voice now, he noticed, "it seemed to me that it was too much of a coincidence for the two things not to be linked."

"Don't be silly," Rodney said dismissively, but even he could hear the tension that had crept into his voice.

"Rodney," Jenna said gently, "I promise I'm not having a go at you; I just don't want to see you getting in trouble."

"Why would I be in trouble?" he scoffed. "Even if I was helping Mr Winston, it's not like I was involved in the murder or in breaking him out of hospital, is it?"

"Rodney, the police won't see it that way," she said in exasperation. "You'll get done for assisting an offender or something even worse, and you'll end up going to jail."

"Look, don't worry about me," he told her, but he could tell from the look on her face that she was indeed worried. After glancing around to make sure they were still alone, Rodent leaned in close to whisper in her ear. "We're driving him down to the coast tonight and some fisherman bloke's gonna smuggle him over to France in a boat." As soon as the words left his mouth, he realised it had been a mistake to tell her that. She looked horrified.

"Tell me something, Rodney," she asked, her big eyes full of confusion, "is someone forcing you to help him against your will"

Rodent didn't know how to respond. If he told her that he was being coerced, she would think he was pathetic; if he admitted that he was being well paid for his services, she would assume he was just as bad as Winston. Either way, she would lose any respect that she had for him.

"It doesn't matter why I'm helping," he told her. "Anyway, after tonight, Mr Winston will be out of my hair for good and then I can get back to normal."

"Rodney, please don't help him to escape," Jenna implored him. "It's wrong. Men like that are evil, and they ought to be locked up in jail, not left free to roam the streets hurting people."

"For fuck sake, I've got no choice!" Rodent shouted, and immediately regretted raising his voice to her. "I – I'm so, so sorry," he said, feeling truly awful. "I didn't mean to snap at you like that."

Jenna shook her head, "It doesn't matter," she said, but he knew it did; the disappointment in her eyes told him so.

When Jenna next spoke, her voice had taken on the hardness of steel. "If you're so sorry, prove it by calling the police and telling them where he is."

Rodent shook his head sadly, knowing that his refusal would bring about an abrupt end to their brief friendship. "I wish I could, but I can't."

"Yes, you can," she said fiercely, and he was taken aback by the raw anger in her voice. "Because if you help him to escape, then you're no better than he is and you're not half the man that I'd hoped you were."

The words hurt him more than Garston's kick to the ribs had

earlier. "I told you, I can't do that," Rodent said, almost choking on his shame.

"Well I can," Jenna said, bluntly.

Tears were running down the side of her face. "I'll give you till six o'clock tonight to do the right thing," she told him. "That's when I finish work. If I haven't heard from you by then, I swear I'll call the police myself."

Rodent didn't know what to say, so he didn't say anything. Spinning on his heel, he stormed out of the shop without a backward glance.

"Please Rodney," Jenna called after him. "I'm begging you, don't go down with this man. He's evil, and he deserves to rot in jail for the rest of his life. Do the right thing – call the cops."

CHAPTER TWENTY-SEVEN

The locksmith had finally arrived. His name was Leonard Rhymes and he was a short, tubby man with a greying comb-over and a very noticeable lisp.

Lenny, as he preferred to be called, didn't seem too impressed when Murray insisted that he don a full set of barrier clothing before being allowed to examine the safe, complaining that the paper oversuits severely restricted his range of movement.

Murray rolled his eyes theatrically. "I just want you to unlock the bloody thing, Lenny, not Moondance across the top of it like Whacko Jacko."

Lenny struggled into an extra-large Tyvek suit and then had to fold the arms and the legs up because they were way too long. He complained constantly throughout the process. "These things are ridiculous. Look how far I've got to roll the bloody legs up," he moaned.

Murray was having none of it. "It's your own fault for being such a short arse," he said. "They're not made for midgets like you."

"I'm not a bleedin' midget," Lenny objected.

"Course you are," Murray insisted. "You're short and fat, and you look like one of the Teletubbies."

"This is not helping my self-esteem," Lenny told him.

"Shut up, Tinky Winky."

When he was finally kitted out, Murray led him over to the safe, where he knelt down awkwardly to examine it.

Earlier in the day, Juliet Kennedy had arranged for a local SOCO and a photographer to attend the scene, and while they had been waiting for the locksmith to arrive, they had cracked on with their respective tasks; the SOCO had fingerprinted the safe's exterior, the filing cabinet, some of the tools and anything else that might yield prints, like the light switch. He had also taken a multitude of swabs for DNA and GSR testing.

Ned, the SO3 photographer from Lambeth, had completed as much record photography as he could. Both men had then gone off to a nearby café in order to warm up over a cup of coffee, and Murray had promised to call them back as soon as the safe had been opened.

Murray gave the poor man a whole minute to examine the safe before his impatience got the better of him. "How long is this going to take, Lenny?" he demanded, testily.

"This is a good bit of kit," the locksmith said, looking up at the detectives. "It's a Chubbsafes Executive model. These babies have a door thickness of sixty six millimetres and a body thickness of fifty millimetres, and they're tested to International Standard UL73 Class 350 and NT Fire 017-60." He said all this as though it should mean something to them, and was disappointed to receive blank looks in return.

"I'm sure that's all very interesting," Murray said, sounding bored out of his head, "but the only thing I care about is, can you open the bloody thing or not?"

Lenny snorted as though he'd never heard anything so ridiculous in all his life. "Course I can. I'll have you know there aren't too many locks that I can't open after all these years in the business," he announced with great pride.

"Well get a move on then," Murray said, irritably snapping his fingers at the locksmith. "We haven't got all day."

"Give me a chance," Lenny shot back. "I've only bleedin' just got here."

Leaving them to it, Bull wandered back to the warmth of the pool car where Kelly was topping and tailing the paperwork for the search. So far, all they had seized was the bucket of spent cartridge cases and an innocuous-looking thick green book that had been buried at the bottom of the filing cabinet underneath a load of far-right extremist literature.

The book was in a clear plastic evidence bag waiting for Kelly to seal it up. Slipping on a new pair of nytril gloves, he carefully removed it and folded it open at the page containing the latest entries.

"What are you doing?" Kelly asked. "I'm just about to index that and seal it up."

"I need to take a quick look first," Bull said. "Just in case there's anything in it that the boss needs to know about in fast time."

"Okay, but hurry up," she told him. "I don't like having loose exhibits inside the car.

Despite his many other faults, Charlie Dobson's bookkeeping was immaculate. The book was neatly divided into bought and sold ledgers. In the first, every single outlay the skinhead had made over the past year was meticulously itemised. However, it was the sold ledger that grabbed Bull's attention. The last entry was dated Thursday 6th January at nine p.m. It read: *Two Brocock ME38s at £300 each plus a free box of .22. Paid in cash by D.G. Tested prior to sale by client.*

Steve felt his heart rate increase. If this meant what he thought it did, it was pure gold. "Kelly, take a look. What do you think this means?"

Kelly leaned over, read the entry and raised an eyebrow. "DG could stand for Deontay Garston, I suppose," she speculated.

"I reckon it does, and if Garston test fired the two guns in that lockup the spent cartridges ought to be in amongst all the others that were swept into the bucket we've seized."

"Makes sense," Kelly agreed.

Steve let out a low whistle. "If there are spent cartridge cases in that bucket from the gun Winston used to kill PC Morrison, we'll be able to match the hammer marks on them to the murder weapon once we've recovered it."

"Let's not get ahead of ourselves," Kelly cautioned him. "We've got to recover it first."

Steve nodded. "True, but I'm confident we will, and then the FSS can test fire the weapon and compare the striations on that slug against the ones on the bullet that was removed from PC Morrison's brain during the post mortem."

Striation marks are caused by a bullet passing through a gun's barrel during discharge, and they are totally unique to that weapon. The same was true of the mark a firing pin left in the back of a cartridge case when the trigger was pulled.

One of the things the Forensic Science Service at Lambeth in South London would do as part of the ballistic investigation was run the striation and firing pin data they retrieved through the National Ballistics Intelligence Service - or NABIS for short – to see if there were any matches against weapons that had been involved in previous shootings. Steve was convinced that the gun used on PC Morrison was a new weapon, but some of the other cartridge cases might have come from firearms that had, by now, been in circulation for a while.

"I'll tell you something else," Steve said as the cogs in his brain worked overtime. "If Dobson, his mates or Garston have handled the cartridges in that bucket, we're going to get fingerprints and or DNA from them."

"Assuming they weren't wearing gloves," Kelly pointed out.

Steve shook his head emphatically. "They won't have worn gloves here. This is their safe place, and they won't ever have expected us to find it."

Hardly able to contain his excitement, Steve was just reaching for his phone to let Tyler know when he caught sight of Murray waving at him out of the corner of his eye.

He nudged Kelly's arm. "Looks like lisping Lenny has opened the safe," he told her. "Coming for a look?"

"Wouldn't miss it," Kelly said, grinning like she was on her way to a party, "but why do you call him that?"

Steve grinned mischievously. "Trust me, as soon as he speaks it'll become self-explanatory."

Jumping out of the car, they pulled their coats tight against their bodies to keep out the wind, lowered their heads, and set off towards the comparative shelter of the lockup.

"What have we got?" Bull asked excitedly, looking from Murray to the locksmith.

"Have a look for yourself," Murray said, standing aside.

Bull knelt down next to the locksmith and peered inside.

There were two shelves, both of which were crammed full of stuff.

"Use this," Lenny offered, handing over a pencil torch.

"Thanks," Bull said, accepting it gratefully. The top shelf housed what appeared to be two bulky objects wrapped in leather shammies. Next to these were several unopened boxes of .22 ammunition. On the lower shelf, several bigger boxes sat on top of each other, and when he read the packaging, he saw that each one contained a Brocock ME38.

"My bet," Murray said, "is that the bottom shelf contains the legally purchased stock that's waiting to be converted into guns that will fire real ammunition. The replicas that've already been adapted and are ready to be sold are safely tucked away up on the top shelf, along with the ammo."

Bull nodded. That made perfect sense. "We need to get this lot photographed before we remove any of it," he said.

"Well, duh," Murray responded. "I've already rung the photog and told him and the SOCO to hotfoot it back here with some takeaway coffees for us."

"That'll be lovely," Leonard said appreciatively. "I'm freezing my bollocks off in this cold, and I could murder a hot drink."

"I didn't tell them to bring you anything," Murray said. "You can sod off and get your own in a few minutes."

Lenny looked crestfallen.

When Tyler hung up after receiving the update from Steve Bull, he turned to Dillon and smiled like the cat who had just got the cream.

"It looks like they've found two firearms down at the lockup and several boxes of .22 ammunition," he announced.

"That's great news," Dillon said, smiling back at him.

"It gets better," Jack told him. "Charlie Dobson maintained a very detailed ledger outlining all the transactions he made. The last entry in the book is him selling two Brococks to a client whose initials are DG –."

"That'll be Deontay Garston," Dillon interrupted.

"– who test fired the guns at the lockup last Thursday."

"I'd better let Susie know," Dillon said. "She's going to have to incorporate that into her advanced disclosure."

Jack said nothing. He was too busy trying to work out how long it would take to get any useable results back from the lab. It would take the officers down at the scene a little time to package everything and get it back to the office, say another hour or two, and then Murray would have to type out the lab forms and get them approved by the CSM. That would easily take up another hour. Once all that was done, someone would have to blue light any exhibits they wanted testing up to the lab for forensic examination.

Under the Police and Criminal Evidence Act 1984, the police were allowed to detain a prisoner without charge for up to twenty four hours following arrest. Should the investigation require additional time, as this one was undoubtedly going to, a Superintendent not directly involved with the case could authorise an additional twelve hours detention.

Would that be sufficient time for the lab to do all the work necessary to produce the evidence that he would need to charge Dobson and his cronies? If not, Tyler would have to make an application at Magistrates court under S. 44(1) PACE for a warrant of further detention.

Tyler needed to prioritise the work he asked the FSS to undertake. Clearly, he wanted the hammer markings of all the cartridges to be run through NABIS, but that would take days to complete and would have to be done at a much later stage.

Likewise, he wanted all the casings fingerprinted and DNA swabbed. If they found either Garston or Dobson's dabs on any of those it would be evidential dynamite. Again, the process was slow and laborious, especially as Bull had told him there were in excess of forty cartridges to get through. This would also have to be done in slow time.

The various entries in the green book would need to be examined by a handwriting expert and compared against samples provided by Dobson. Of course, the skinhead could always refuse to cooperate, but that would hurt him at court as an inference could then be drawn by the prosecution. Getting handwriting comparisons carried out was always a mega slow process, and was generally not even worth considering until post charge.

So, what did that leave?

He wanted the converted weapons fingerprinted and swabbed. The print results could potentially be back by the end of the day, and the DNA swabs within thirty six hours.

The sheets in the ledger would need to be checked for Dobson's fingerprints, but he would need to liaise with Juliet Kennedy to see if this could realistically be achieved within the time that they had remaining on the custody clock before pushing for that.

Since its discovery by Siegfried Ruhemann in 1954, Ninhydrin treatment was the preferred method for obtaining latent fingerprints from paper or other porous surfaces. Basically, Ninhydrin is a chemical powder that is soluble in ethanol or acetone. The process works by dipping the item to be tested in a tray containing a Ninhydrin mix and then allowing it to dry off at room temperature.

The fingerprint development occurred slowly over the next twenty four to forty eight hours. Jack knew the process could theoretically be speeded up by putting treated items in an oven for twenty minutes, but he didn't know if there were any risks associated with doing that, or if the lab would be willing to deviate from their normal practices.

He reached for his phone. Juliet would set him straight on that, one way or another. Before he could enter the digits for her mobile, his landline rang. It was Steve Bull and he seemed very excited about something.

"Boss, you're not going to believe this," he said breathlessly, "but we've just found a hidden motion activated CCTV camera clipped to the wall. We followed the wiring and found a hard drive hidden behind the filing cabinet. There's a little monitor attached to it. Although the quality isn't great, I think we've got footage of Garston and Errol Heston test firing the guns with Charlie Dobson last Thursday."

DC Colin Franklin had been given the unenviable task of leading the interview with Charlie Dobson. The athletic-looking officer was in his mid-twenties and had recently become a father for the first time. He had also completed the Tier Three interviewing course the previous year, making him an ideal candidate to conduct an interview that promised to be as challenging as this one. His obvious skills as an interviewer were one of the reasons that Susie Sergeant had picked him; his skin colour was the other.

Franklin was of Jamaican descent, and with Dobson's Aryan white supremacist links and National Front allegiances, she figured that being questioned by an ebony-skinned officer would, at some point in the proceedings, provoke a response from Dobson that would expose him as the reprehensible creature he undoubtedly was.

Susie had discussed her plan at length with Colin first, making sure that he understood her rationale and was comfortable performing the role. After all, she reasoned, they had achieved some big successes by having strong women officers interview wife-beaters and rapists, so why not have a black man interview a white supremacist?

As a precaution, Susie had partnered him with the taciturn Colin Stone. While the square-jawed detective with the broad shoulders might not say a lot, there was a certain physicality about him that was hard to ignore, and just having him in the room was usually enough to dissuade most criminals from even thinking about kicking off.

Predictably, Dobson had gone 'no comment' to every question that had been put to him during the afternoon, but when the tapes had been switched off, he had tried to goad Franklin by making random monkey noises. Once, he had asked Franklin what his favourite chocolate bar was. "I'm guessing you like Bounty Bars," he taunted. "You know the ones, white on the inside but black on the outside, a bit like darkies who became police officers."

Franklin had completely ignored the baiting and, in the end, Dobson had grown tired of it and shut up.

At least Dobson's solicitor, Martha Fischer, had had the decency to look embarrassed at her client's disgraceful behaviour and, at one point, when they had stopped for a quick toilet break, she had sidled up to Colin outside the interview room and whispered, "If it's any consolation, I don't think he likes my kind any more than he does yours."

Colin had glanced sideways, confused. "Your kind?"

Fischer was in her thirties, slim, with a permanently serious face and a severe haircut. She had been looking down at the glasses she was polishing when she'd made the comment, but when she looked up at him and smiled conspiratorially, there was a wicked glint of humour in her brown eyes. "I'm Jewish and I'm gay. I think if he knew that, he would probably refuse to let me represent him."

Colin laughed. "How funny."

"More ironic than funny," she said, and then allowed herself a self-deprecating laugh. "Stupid isn't it? I know he hates people like me, and yet I still do my utmost to protect and advance his rights, just the same as I would if I were here representing Mother Teresa." She shrugged as if to say, 'I must be raving mad.'

Colin nodded, solemnly. "I know exactly what you mean," he told her. "I took an oath to perform the duties of my office fairly and impartially, without favour or rancour. Believe it or not, if he's innocent, I'll do my best to prove it even though I know he would happily put a bullet in my head if he got the chance."

"Nice speech," she said, giving him a wry smile. "Do you stand in front of the mirror and practice it every night?"

Franklin grinned. "Corny, I know, but I meant it."

Fischer looked around to see if her client had reappeared yet. He had, and he was glaring at her like she was a traitor consorting with the enemy. "I hope you're gonna wash your hands after being near him," Dobson shouted across the custody office to her.

With a weary sigh, Fischer turned to Franklin. "Between you and me, I'm really hoping that you're going to throw the book at this vile man." With that, she put her game face back on, turned and smiled at her client. "Just seeing how much longer the police intend to keep wasting your valuable time," she told him.

Dobson seemed to like that, and he laughed all the way back to the interview room.

After he had gone through the introductions and caution, Franklin made a point of smiling at Dobson, who scowled back at him through beady, hate-filled eyes.

"Okay, Charlie, in our previous interviews we've covered the drugs that were found on the table beside where you and Lola were cavorting."

"No comment."

"We've also gone through the witness statement that describes your associate, Peter Roach, openly boasting about how the four of you financed last night's binge of drink, drugs, and hookers by selling firearms to criminals."

"No comment, boy." A derogatory emphasis was placed on the last word.

Colin's eyes narrowed at the slur, but he didn't bite. "And we've gone over the fact that Roach also boasted that the four of you are arms dealers and that you're regularly selling guns to anyone who has the money to pay for them."

Dobson crossed his arms and fidgeted in his chair. He had clearly had enough of being interviewed. "No comment. No comment, no-fucking-comment. When will you get it through your thick black head that I'm going to say no comment to every stupid question you ask me?"

His solicitor gave him a warning look, which was accompanied by an almost imperceptible shake of her head.

"I take it from the fact that you're covered in neo-Nazi type tattoos and the way you constantly refer to me by inflammatory names like 'boy', that you don't particularly like black people. Is that true?"

Franklin could see that Dobson really wanted to say something in response to this, to spout some grandiose white supremacist rhetoric, no doubt, but his solicitor had warned him to stick to 'no comment', which is precisely what he did.

"Oh, come on," Franklin encouraged him. "Show me that you have the courage of your convictions? At least tell me why you think you're so much better than me. Or, when push comes to shove, are you just a cowardly wimp without your friends to back you up?" His tone had started off as blasé, but it had hardened with every word, finally becoming accusatory.

He and Susie had discussed their tactics in light of the new information they had received, and she had decided that it was time to go up a gear and transition from passive to aggressive questioning. That was fine by Franklin.

"I don't need anyone to back me up," Dobson said defiantly. "And, for your information, the Nazis have scientifically proved that the Herrenmenschen – that's white people – are on a higher evolutionary scale than the Untermensch – that's the lesser races like Jews, Negros and gypsies." he turned his nose up as he said the last three words as though merely mentioning the so-called lesser racial groups had left a nasty taste in his Aryan mouth. "It's why Hitler wanted to eradicate them," Dobson said, looking at Franklin with the superior sneer of a true zealot. "Old Adolf had the right idea if you ask me, because white folk are at the top of the racial hierarchy, and if we don't do something to stop it, your lot will try and pollute us through interbreeding."

That seemed a little ironic to Franklin, considering Dobson had been arrested while shagging an Asian prostitute, but he seemed to have conveniently overlooked that.

Franklin literally didn't know whether to laugh at the man sitting opposite him for his amateurish attempts to combine historical facts with outlandish propaganda in order to add verisimilitude to the cause of white supremacy, or lean across the table and slap the arrogant smirk from his ugly face. His eyes flickered to Martha Fischer, who had gone pale and looked like she wanted to throw up. From the severity of her reaction, he suspected that members of her family had ended up in the concentration camps during the Second World War.

"So, if I understand you correctly, you're saying that black men are inferior to white men," Franklin said, struggling to keep his voice even.

"Obviously," Dobson replied as though it were a given.

"Do you have any black friends or associates?" Franklin enquired, keeping his voice level, even though his temper was beginning to boil.

Dobson shook his head and laughed at the ridiculousness of the question. "Don't be fucking stupid," he snorted, "I would cross the road to avoid one."

"So, you've never sold a gun to a black man?" Franklin asked.

The smile evaporated from Dobson's face. "I've never sold a gun to anyone," he said.

"What about to Deontay Garston?"

"Never heard of him."

Franklin slid an old custody image photograph of Garston onto the table. "For the sake of the tape, I'm showing Charlie Dobson a photo of Garston, which is exhibit number CF/1. Do you recognise this man?"

Dobson shook his head.

"Please answer the question," Franklin said politely, "this is an audio recording, not video."

"No, I don't recognise him, but you all look the same to me anyway," he said with a nasty grin. "All smell the same, too," he added for good measure.

Gritting his teeth, Franklin placed another still on the table. "Again, for the benefit of the tape, I am showing Charlie Dobson a photo of Errol Heston, which is exhibit CF/2. Do you recognise him?"

Dobson sighed impatiently. "I've told you, you all look –"

Colin brought his palm down hard against the desk, making both Dobson and his solicitor jump. "Answer the question, do you recognise him?"

"No," Dobson said.

"What would you say if I told you I could prove you sold both of these men two Brocock ME38 Magnums on Thursday 6th January?"

"I'd say prove it."

"What would you say if I told you they used one of these guns to murder a police officer in cold blood at the Royal London Hospital on Monday 11th January?"

Dobson lazily shrugged his lack of concern. "I'd say pigs are no better than coons so who gives a fuck?"

Franklin slid another sheet of paper onto the table. "Take a look at this," he told Dobson. "For the tape, this is exhibit CF/3, and it's a photocopy from a ledger we seized during the search of a lockup you rent from a nice Jewish man called Aaron Stein. Do you know him?"

"No comment," Dobson said, but his face had drained of colour.

"Well, he knows you. Apparently, you're only supposed to use the lockup for parking and storage, but you've turned it into a workshop for your gun selling business, haven't you?"

"No comment." Dobson was starting to look a little hot under the collar, Franklin noticed with satisfaction.

"And when he came around to see you a little while ago, because the residents in the flats above the shops had been complaining about the loud bangs coming from inside your lockup some evenings, you and your skinhead mates gave him a hard time. Isn't that right?"

Dobson swallowed hard. He wasn't looking so smug now. "No comment," he said, casting a worried glance at his solicitor.

"Well, my colleagues searched that lockup today and, amongst other things, they found a ledger. The photocopy I've just shown you relates to the last entry. Would you care to read it aloud for us?"

"No comment."

"I take it you can read?" Franklin asked innocently. He was starting to enjoy this. "I mean, what with you being one of the Master Race and all."

"No comment."

"Never mind, I'll do it for you," Franklin said, scooping the exhibit up off the table.

Dobson's eyes followed his every movement like a hawk.

"The entry reads: 'Two Brocock ME38s at £300 each plus a free box of .22. Paid in cash by D.G. Tested prior to sale by client.' Is that your handwriting, Dobson?"

"No comment."

"The writing's very neat," Franklin observed. "Should be easy for a handwriting expert to say whether or not it's yours." He produced a sheet of paper and a biro and offered them to Dobson. "Why don't you copy this entry down three times in your normal writing for comparison purposes? That way, if it's not your writing, we will be able to prove it, which will be good for you."

Dobson snatched his hands away and folded them firmly under his armpits. "You can stuff that pen and fucking paper where the sun don't shine," he shouted.

"Are you refusing to cooperate?" Franklin asked.

Dobson turned to his solicitor. "This is a fit-up," he snarled. "They've got someone to forge my writing so they can stripe me up for something I didn't do."

"We don't fit people up," Franklin said, making no effort to hide his irritation. "So, why don't you just tell the truth and stop whinging like a pathetic coward? This is your handwriting, and this entry was made when you sold Deontay Garston two converted Brocock revolvers and gave him fifty rounds of .22 ammo as a sweetener. Isn't that right?"

"Lies, all lies," Dobson shouted. "You're only doing this to me because I'm white and I want Britain to remain white."

"Then why did you sell a gun to a black man who used it to murder another white man?" Franklin demanded.

"I didn't know he was gonna shoot a white man," Dobson screamed in exasperation When he realised the significance of what he'd just said, he looked around, flustered. "I – I mean…What I mean is I didn't know he was going to shoot a white man because I didn't sell him no guns."

Franklin laughed, mockingly. "Is that so?"

"Yes, it fucking well is, you dumb Jigaboo."

Franklin stiffened at the insult, involuntarily clenching his fists.

Surprisingly, it was DC Colin Stone, his number two in the interview, who stood up, his jaw quivering with anger at Dobson's use of the racial slur. "What did you just call my colleague?" he demanded in a voice that was thick with menace. It was the first time he had spoken during the entire interview process, other than to introduce himself at the beginning of each tape.

"You think I'm scared of you?" Dobson said defiantly; his eyes suggested he was.

You really should be, Franklin thought as he indicated for the square-jawed detective to return to his seat. Stone had been a paratrooper before joining the job, and he was a very hard man, unlike Dobson, who merely thought that he was hard.

"Do you even know what that word means?" Franklin asked Dobson in disgust. "It's a Bantu word meaning meek or servile, like a slave. I might be a public servant, but I'm no one's slave," he said fiercely.

"Whatever," Dobson said sullenly, but he couldn't meet Franklin's eye.

Still inwardly simmering, Franklin leaned back and pulled the TV and video combination that was standing on a trolley behind him closer to the interview table. It had already been plugged into a power socket ready for use. Taking his time, and trying to bring his breathing back under control, he removed a VHS tape from the bag by his feet and inserted it into the player.

"My colleagues found your secret CCTV system," he informed Dobson conversationally. "That's good news for us, but not so good for you. Footage from last Thursday evening has been copied onto this tape, which is exhibit RP/1. I'm going to play that for you now. There's no audio, but it clearly shows you and your three Aryan friends entertaining Deontay Garston and Errol Heston. Heston's the one with the bald head. It clearly shows you – you, not your skinhead friends – removing two guns from the safe, demonstrating how they work and then letting the client's test fire them. It also shows them paying you for the merchandise and leaving with the guns. You all have big smiles on your faces, parting company like you're the best of friends. Strange, considering you claim not to know them. Let's watch the clip in silence, and then I'm going to invite you to comment. I must say, I'm really looking forward to what you have to say about this footage," he said with a mocking grin.

It had now dawned on Dobson that he was in deep trouble, and he was shaking with rage at the way the black detective had played him. "You fucking cunt," he hissed, and without warning, he stood up and launched himself over the table at Franklin.

Unfortunately for him, Stone had been prepared for this. In one fluid movement, he leapt out of his chair, grabbed hold of Dobson's head as it hurtled forward and slammed it into the wooden table so hard that it sounded as though a firearm had just been discharged. Without breaking stride, he rammed Dobson's right arm so far up his back that it almost came out of the socket.

Dobson's actions had sent his solicitor sprawling backwards onto the floor and, as she scrambled unsteadily to her feet, glasses askew, she could only watch on in shock as Stone restrained the prisoner and

Franklin pressed the alarm button. Within moments, several uniformed officers came running in to assist.

Handcuffed, his face bleeding profusely, Dobson was unceremoniously dragged back into the custody area.

The sergeant behind the desk lazily raised an enquiring eyebrow as they approached him, but he didn't seem particularly fazed by the sight of the skinhead, bleeding and battered, being frogmarched up to the counter.

"Anything I need to know about," he asked casually, as though this was an everyday sight.

"Prisoner didn't like the way the interview was going," Franklin said. "Decided to take a pop at me. DC Stone was forced to restrain him."

The custody officer shook his head in despair. "When will these people ever learn?" he said to no one in particular. "Alright, put him back in his cell. Looks like he's got a nasty bump on his head so we'd better call the FME." He turned to Martha Fischer. "You're his solicitor, aren't you?"

"Yes, that's right."

"Were you present?"

"I was."

The custody Sergeant let out a long sigh. "In that case, are there any observations you'd like noted in the custody record?" he asked, pen resignedly paused to record her bleating complaint about police brutality.

"Yes," she said, looking across at Dobson, who was now sitting on the bench, dazed. "The officers were very professional, and they acted with great restraint when my client launched an unprovoked attack on them."

The custody Sergeant did a double-take. Not much surprised him, but the solicitor's unexpected endorsement of the detectives' actions had.

CHAPTER TWENTY-EIGHT

Jenna Marsh stopped outside the graffiti-covered phone box in Barking Road. Chewing her lip anxiously, she stared at it as though it might bite her if she tried to enter. It was coming up to six-thirty, a full half an hour beyond the deadline that she'd given Rodney. She felt so conflicted inside that it hurt. Had he done the right thing? Had he called the police and told them where to find Winston?

Somehow, she doubted it.

It was heading towards the end of the rush hour, but traffic was still busy along the Barking Road, and as she stood there, watching the never-ending sea of headlights streaming towards her, she wondered what he had done after storming out of the shop.

Jenna's breath clouded around her, and she rubbed her gloved hands together to generate some much-needed heat. God, it was so cold out here! The weather forecast predicted snow over the coming days, and from the arctic temperature, she could well believe it.

Jenna felt sick. She wondered how Kevin would react if he knew what she was contemplating. He wouldn't be happy about her ratting someone out, especially not the younger brother of his best friend, a timid man-boy who in many ways was still as guileless as a child. Even her parents, who were as law-abiding as they came, would take a dim view of her telling tales out of school. The truth was that she really didn't want to grass Rodney up to the police, but she had warned him she was going to do exactly that unless he contacted her to say that he'd called them himself, which he clearly hadn't.

Jenna took a deep breath and opened the door. It felt as heavy as her heart, and for a long moment, she hesitated, feeling as though she were about to step into a gas chamber and not a telephone kiosk.

The cramped space inside smelled of piss. As the door slowly swung shut behind her, she pulled off her gloves and reached into her coat pocket for the loose change she would need to make the call. Most of the kiosk's glass had been smashed, so it was no warmer inside than it had been out on the street. It wasn't any quieter, either.

She had found the number for the Incident Room in an article from yesterday's *London Echo* and had written it on the palm of her left hand before leaving work. She stared hard at the smeared digits for several seconds before plucking up the nerve to lift the handset and start dialling.

"Oh, Rodney, why did you have to turn out just like your brother," she said, shaking her head sadly.

Jenna almost jumped out of her skin when the telephone was picked up and a disinterested male voice said, "*Incident Room. DS Wilkins speaking. How can I help you?*"

Jenna opened her mouth to speak but no words came out.

"*Hello... is anyone there?*" The voice sounded impatient, unhelpful. Maybe its owner was just really busy and could do without the distraction?

Jenna hung up the phone and pushed open the door to leave, eager to escape into the fresh air, but then she hesitated. If she didn't do this now, she never would. Her stomach was doing little flips, and her head was spinning, but she picked up the phone and redialled.

It was seven o'clock and, in light of the anonymous phone call that had come in half an hour earlier, Jack Tyler was holding an impromptu supervisor's meeting in his office. Dillon, Carol Keating, Steve Bull, Charlie White, and Tom Wilkins were all gathered in a little semi-circle around his desk. It was a bit cramped, but just about doable.

Carol had been the first to arrive, and she had immediately set about organising hot drinks and chocolate Hob-Nobs for everyone. As each of the others had arrived, they had greeted her with the customary, "Oooh Matron," receiving a delighted smile and a little quip in return.

Despite her no-nonsense demeanour, she really was a very sweet woman, Jack decided, and he could see why everyone warmed to her.

"Right," Jack said, after taking a tentative sip of the boiling hot coffee she'd just handed him, "things are moving fast, so I thought we should get together for a quick pow-wow." He was tired and he was crotchety, and he wanted to get through this as quickly as possible.

"Have you got a particular order of business in mind?" Dillon asked, looking irritatingly fresh.

"Well, the main thing we need to do is discuss our plans for tonight, but before we get started on that, I'd like to top and tail where we are with the four skinheads and the two hookers."

Jack turned to face Carol Keating, who had been tasked with reviewing all the evidence against them and liaising with Susie to see what had come out of the interviews. "How close are we to being able to charge them?"

"Well," Carol said, thoughtfully. "I think we're pretty much there. The interviews for all six prisoners have been concluded. The three skinhead lackeys, Roach, Taylor and Higgins all went 'no comment' throughout. No surprise there. Charlie Dobson tried to do the same, but his arrogance occasionally got the better of him, and he ended up blurting out answers when he really would have been better off staying schtum."

"Anything, in particular, that was worthy of note?" Jack asked.

Carol referred to her notes. "He admitted in interview that he didn't like black people, so Colin Franklin asked him why he'd sold Garston and Heston guns that they'd promptly used to murder a fellow white man. His reply was, and I quote: 'I didn't know he was gonna shoot a white man.'"

Dillon's breath escaped in a low whistle. "That'll go down well in court."

"Dobson realised he'd made a bit of a faux pas as soon as he'd opened his mouth," Carol explained, "and he tried to brush over it but, by then, the damage had been done."

"That's why solicitors always tell idiots like him to go 'no comment'," Wilkins said. "Because every time they open their gobs, they drop themselves further into the shit."

"How did the suspects react to seeing the CCTV from the lockup?" Dillon asked. "I would've loved to have been a fly on the wall when that was played."

"It didn't go down very well," Carol admitted with some satisfaction. "They were all shell shocked, to put it mildly. Dobson's reaction was more extreme than any of the others. He completely lost the plot and tried to attack poor Colin Franklin."

Jack looked up from the notes he had been making. "Is Colin okay?" he asked.

"Perfectly," Carol said, smiling sweetly. "DC Stone prevented the attack by ramming Dobson's face into the desk, which split his head open and left him in a crumpled heap. They had to take a lengthy break for the FME to examine Dobson, who refused to go back into interview afterwards."

"I bet he did," Dillon said, grinning widely.

"Please tell me the interview was videoed," Steve Bull said in anticipation of being able to watch the former Para nullify Dobson.

"Afraid not," Carol told him, "but Susie said that Dobson's face was a right mess afterwards."

"Couldnae have happened to a nicer bloke," Charlie White said with a malicious grin.

Jack didn't share their amusement. "I'm not having Dobson dictate to us whether he's interviewed," he announced, irritably. "Tell Susie to carry on, even if it means she has to set up portable equipment outside his cell and conduct the rest of the interview through the open wicket."

"That's exactly what she did do," Carol Keating reassured him. "Dobson sat on the cot in his cell, facing the wall. Refused to speak a single word, but they put all the evidence to him and the interview has been satisfactorily concluded."

"Good," Jack said, somewhat mollified. "So, apart from Dobson's admission, what other evidence have we got?"

"Well, I would say we have plenty," Carol said. "The quality of the footage from the concealed camera in the lockup is very good. Reg Parker burned several copies onto VHS for the interview teams and he assures me that everyone's faces are easily recognisable, so I'm convinced a jury will readily accept that it's Dobson, Higgins, Roach, and Taylor. And just to make our lives slightly easier, the considerate little dears were only wearing T-shirts so a lot of their tattoos were visible. Naturally, we've had every tattoo on their bodies photographed while they've been in custody, so it won't be too hard for the graphics department to put together a body mapping package to illustrate that the defendant's tattoos correlate exactly to those of the people featured in the CCTV."

As she spoke, Jack furiously scribbled notes in his daybook so he could update his Decision Log after the meeting.

"Then there are the witness statements," Carol continued after he'd caught up. "You already know about Prudence, the girl who received the confession evidence from Roach. What you might not be aware of is that Anita, that's the hooker who was found in the downstairs living room with Lola, was very forthcoming in interview."

"I wondered if she might be," Dillon said. "She gave the impression that she would have spoken to us at the scene if Lola hadn't been there. What has she said?"

"She told her interviewers that the skinheads brought all the drugs with them. She admits to being a sex worker and claims that Lola's the house Madame, having been installed by none other than Deontay Garston. She also told the interviewing officers that Dobson and Taylor – he's the man she was shagging when the TSG burst in – had openly boasted about selling the guns that were used in the policeman's murder. She said they seemed really proud to have done so."

"Low life shite-bags," Charlie White mumbled under his breath.

"Susie's instinct is that if we NFA her, Anita can be persuaded to make a statement repeating what she said in interview," Carol said.

Jack considered this. If they charged the girl with an offence, they wouldn't be able to use any of what she'd said in her interview against another defendant, whereas if they took no further action against her, they would then be free to take a detailed witness statement from her. "What charges are we realistically looking at for her anyway?" he asked, struggling to concentrate. Although he'd managed to take a power nap in his office for an hour or so earlier in the day, it had been fitful and uncomfortable, and he was now so tired that he could hardly think straight.

"She was arrested for the collective possession of drugs, along with everyone else, just because she was in the room and no one was putting their hands up to owning them," Carol said. "Nothing worth getting worked up about."

"NFA her then," Tyler said. "She's small fry. I'm happy the drugs will either have been laid on by the skinheads or Lola, and she's far more useful to us as a witness."

Carol made a quick note. "That's my view, too. If you don't mind, I'll pop out and let Susie know straight away, so she can grab a statement from the girl before she changes her mind." Excusing herself, Carol left the room to make the call.

Closing his eyes, Jack pinched the bridge of his nose. He had taken some paracetamol before the meeting but it was doing little to dull the throbbing ache in his head. Maybe he needed to drink some water to rehydrate himself as he'd been living off coffee all day.

"How's the lab getting on with the exhibits you had rushed up there, Stevie?" he asked wearily.

Bull consulted his notes. "I spoke to the FSS just before we sat down, boss," he said. "They've done the presumptive testing on the drugs from the squat. The white powder is definitely cocaine. There is also some herbal cannabis and a small amount of a prescription drug called Viagra."

Dillon chortled. "I think Charlie Dobson's already tested the Viagra out for us. It worked a little too well for his liking, mind you," he said, recalling the man's acute discomfort as he'd waited for the paramedic to come and examine his engorged manhood.

"The lab has also found several prints on the drug's outer packaging," Bull continued. "There are definite matches for Dobson, Higgins, and Lola."

"Good," Jack said, writing this all down.

"As for the firearms we seized from the lockup safe, they've found fingerprints matching Dobson and Roach on the two converted guns. Under UV light, they can make out some latent prints on one of the boxes of ammo and on at least two of the three unopened Brocock boxes, but it'll require Ninhydrin treatment to bring them out. You know the score as well as I do," he said, shrugging his shoulders resignedly, "it'll take a day or two before we see any results. I did broach the subject of them fast-tracking the process by using an oven, but they were unhappy about doing that in case it compromised the quality of the evidence."

"Fair enough," Jack grunted. He hadn't expected anything else, but it had been worth trying. "I suppose they said the same about the ledger?"

Bull nodded. "Yep, afraid so."

Carol returned. "Have I missed anything important?" she asked.

Jack shook his head. "Steve was just telling us where the lab was in regard to the priority submissions that we sent up earlier."

"Oh, is that all?" Carol asked, waving her hand dismissively as if it were old news. "I already know about all that stuff."

"In that case, we'll carry on," Jack said.

"Carry on Matron, you mean," Dillon said, and did another rendition of his Sid James laugh.

"Oooh Sid," Carol responded, and everyone except Tyler laughed.

Jack stroked his stubbled chin thoughtfully as he flicked through his notes, finding the sensation strangely soothing. "It seems to me," he said, when they had quietened down, "that we have enough evidence to charge the four skinheads with possessing two firearms and a quantity of .22 calibre ammunition without a licence. We can also charge Dobson, Higgins, and Lola with possession of controlled drugs with intent to supply. I take it she didn't say anything when interviewed?"

Carol shook her head. "Not a dicky bird, and Susie said she's a nasty piece of work."

Tyler arched an antagonistic eyebrow. "Is that right? In that case, on the strength of the statements from the two working girls, I'm minded to add on an additional charge of running a brothel for Lola as well as the drugs," Jack said. "Does anyone disagree?"

No one did.

"Okay then," Jack said, tossing his pen onto his desk and leaning back in his chair, "Tell Susie to start the necessary paperwork for the prisoners to be charged with the offences we've discussed. Obviously, I'll expect them to be remanded in custody."

"Obviously," Carol echoed.

"Carol, can I ask a favour of you?"

"Of course," she said, with an indulgent smile.

"Before Susie informs the skinhead's solicitors that they're going to be charged, can you speak directly to someone senior at the CPS and see how they would feel about us also charging Dobson and his three buddies with offences relating to the manufacture and distribution of firearms and ammunition without a licence. Ultimately, these bastards are arms dealers so let's see if we can sheet them for that as well. I did plan to do this myself, but I don't think I'm going to have the time."

"I'm way ahead of you," Carol informed him. "I took the liberty of contacting the CPS earlier to discuss the possibility of going down that route. The lawyer seemed very receptive but he wanted to wait until the lab had confirmed that they were real guns before making a decision."

Jack was suitably impressed. "Excellent. In that case, can you get back onto him and seek a formal charging decision as quickly as possible."

"Do you want me to do it now or wait until we finish here?"

"I think it can wait ten minutes more while we thrash out the plans for this evening," Tyler said. "And can you inform Susie that she can keep three people to do the charging and put the case file together, but I want everyone else back here ASAP. We're going to need every available person for tonight."

"I'll let her know before I call the CPS back," Carol promised.

"Thank you," Jack said, making a mental note to phone Holland as soon as the meeting concluded. Charging the bastards who'd sold the guns to PC Morrison's killers might not bring their dead colleague back, but it would hopefully offer some degree of comfort to his grieving family, and by taking two weapons and a load of ammunition out of circulation, they might have prevented other innocent families from having to go through the same torturous experience at some point in the future.

Smothering a yawn, Tyler wearily turned to Wilkins. "Tom, can you talk everyone through the call you received earlier, please."

Wilkins cleared his throat. "Yes, the call came in at six-thirty-three. We've traced the number to a phone box in Barking Road. It's not covered by CCTV, which is a pity. The caller was a youngish sounding female with a London accent. She refused to give her details, but she provided some very important information."

"Which is…?" Tyler prompted impatiently.

Wilkins shifted uncomfortably in his seat, unsettled by Tyler's relentless intensity. "She used to go to the same primary school as a boy called Rodney Dawlish," he said hurriedly. "Apparently, their brothers were best buds. She hasn't seen him for years, but yesterday, out of the blue, he strolled into the chemist where she works and asked for a load of bandages, dressings, steri strips and pain killers. When she got home, she saw the news and wondered if Rodney's visit could be linked to Winston's escape. Today, when he came back into the shop to purchase some more supplies, she confronted him and he reluctantly admitted that he was helping Winston. What's particularly worrying is that he told her they were planning to drive him to the coast during the early hours. She doesn't know where Rodney lives, only that it's somewhere in the vicinity of Star Lane."

"Wasn't Star Lane one of the few roads that got missed when the night duty had to abandon the street search to rush off and deal with a fatal RTA?" Charlie White asked.

"It was," Dillon said, "and although our illustrious leader –" he nodded towards Tyler "– was desperate for us to send staff down there this morning to finish it off, we had well and truly run out of people by that stage."

"Anyway," Wilkins continued, "Rodney's nickname is Rodent, as in the name that the HEMS pilot overheard."

"Thank you, Tom," Jack said. He took a deep breath and studied the faces of his subordinates one by one. "I think it's fair to say that almost all of the pieces of the puzzle are now in place. On Monday afternoon, all we knew for sure was that Winston had escaped from the RLH with the aid of two unknown suspects in a hijacked helicopter. After it put down in wasteland near Canning Town the trail went cold. Since then, through sheer hard work and tenacity, we've worked out that someone called Rodent picked them up in a red Rover 216. We've identified Winston's helpers as Deontay Garston and Angela Marley, and we've worked out they're using mobile telephones that end with the respective numbers 777 and 321. Thanks to the TIU, we know that these numbers have been predominantly pinged by the cell covering Star Lane, going to sleep there every night and waking up there every morning. Finally, we've received information that Rodent is Rodney Dawlish and he lives in the vicinity of Star Lane. When you add all this information up, it's not unreasonable to conclude that Winston, Garston, and Marley are staying with Rodent at his place in or near Star Lane. Unfortunately, we don't know the actual address. What we do know is that at some point overnight, the gang are planning to drive Winston down to the coast where, presumably, he'll hop onto a boat and be smuggled across the channel. Without wishing to be overly dramatic, I think that the manhunt for Winston and his odious little crew is likely to reach its zenith tonight, and I'm really worried that if we don't have him in custody by the morning, it'll be because he's slipped the net and made it to France."

Steve Bull frowned. "Surely, if the TIU is still live monitoring their phones, it'll be simple enough for us to follow them?"

Jack pulled a face like someone had just passed wind. "We'll be able to follow their general direction, Steve, yes. But we'll be playing catch up every step of the way, and we'll only know the rough area the handsets are in, not their specific location. If Rodney drives somewhere remote and Winston jumps straight in a boat when they get there, we won't be able to get to them in time to stop him. And consider this: what happens if they split up or turn their phones off or go into an area without reception?"

"I hadn't considered any of that," Bull admitted, sounding depressed.

"I have," Jack said. "I've been thinking about little else since Tom came in and told me that the girl had called the MIR."

"So, what do we do?" Dillon asked. "Knowing you as I do, I'm confident that you have something in mind."

"There are two questions we have to address," Jack told him. "Firstly, what's our plan of attack to arrest them all tonight, before they leave Rodent's address? Secondly, what's our back up plan if we miss them and they set off for the coast?"

"Oh, is that all?" Carol asked, managing to sound underwhelmed. "And here was me thinking this was going to be hard."

Even Tyler had to laugh at that.

"Perhaps it'll be easier if I tell you my initial thoughts and we can build on that," Jack offered.

"Och, I can hardly wait," Charlie White said with a wry grin.

"I've had Reg check in with the TIU to make sure that they're going to continue to live monitor the 777 and 321 numbers for us," Tyler said. "They've been appraised of the situation and they've promised to continue the live monitoring throughout the night as long as we pay the overtime bill."

Dillon rolled his eyes. "It always comes down to money," he said, scathingly.

"Right now, both phones are still in the same cell where they've been for the majority the past two days," Jack continued.

"The cell that covers Star Lane?" Steve asked.

"That's right," Jack confirmed. "The chances are that they won't dare move Winston until the early hours when the roads are at their quietest. With that in mind, DI Dillon's arranged for the Technical Support Unit to deploy a signal detector van before midnight to see if it can narrow down the location of the two phones to a specific address. Dill, what's the score with that?"

"Sorry – a what?" Wilkins asked, looking confused. He wasn't the only one. Carol and Charlie White appeared equally bewildered.

"It's a van equipped with directional tuning equipment that can search for individual IMEIs and isolate where phone signals are coming from," Dillon explained. "Unfortunately, they can't deploy until after eleven p.m., but that might work in our favour as telephone traffic will be considerably lighter by then."

"I would have been much happier if we could have got them out on the streets for ten o'clock," Jack said, "but that's clearly not to be so we'll have to settle for what we've got. I'm planning to send out a couple of pool cars with people in scruffs to start cruising the area from nine-thirty onwards. There's no point doing it any earlier as the Rover might not be there. If either car spots the Rover, we'll try and plot up around it and wait for the suspects to approach the car. As soon as they get inside, we can move in and arrest the bastards."

"Surely that's too dangerous," Wilkins protested. "As far as we know, they still have one of the firearms that they bought from the skinheads so only armed officers should approach them."

Jack treated him to a mirthless smile. "I'm well aware of that," he said patiently. "That's why Mr Dillon has spoken to SO19 and arranged for a team of SFOs to be on standby."

"Oh," Wilkins said, blushing.

"With luck, the TSU will be able to identify the house that the suspects are holed up in before they set off for the coast, and then we can all sit back and enjoy the show as SO19 move in and arrest them," Jack said. "However, if Winston and his cronies move off before the TSU has located their hidey-hole, it won't matter too much if we've already got their car under our control because we can just call the SFOs forward to carry out a hard stop."

"Winston won't come quietly," Dillon warned them. "Trust me, he will go out in a blaze of glory rather than surrender."

"Let's just hope it doesn't come to that," Bull said.

Dillon shook his head, grimly. "I'm telling you now, when he's challenged, he's going to open fire and it's going to be a blood bath."

The room went eerily quiet as the implications of his words set in, and Wilkins and Keating looked at him and then each other with growing unease.

"What happens if they manage to get Winston out of London before we locate them?" Bull asked.

"Then we're in the shit," Jack said, glumly. "I can only think of one other tactic we might be able to employ, but I don't want to discuss that until I've firmed up its viability."

"That's very cryptic of you," Steve said drily, "and not very confidence-inspiring if you don't mind me saying so?"

"I don't mind at all," Jack said, blithely, "seeing as you're the person I'm going to be entrusting to make it happen."

"Me?" Bull swallowed hard and a look of dread swept over his features. "In that case," he said timidly, "I recommend that we all start hoping and praying that plan A comes off without a hitch."

There was nothing that Jack could say to that, so he started issuing orders, which seemed to galvanise the others into action. "Steve, can you go and get Dean and Reg for me. I need to discuss something with the three of you. Then I'll need you to knock up a couple of Directed Surveillance requests in case we need them for later. I'll phone Mr Holland and warn him that they're coming his way. Dill, can you get the SFO team and TSU crew here as soon as possible so that we can get them fully briefed. Carol, can you speak to Susie and then get back onto the CPS. Tom, can you start ringing around and spreading the word that I want every available officer in the main office for a briefing at nine o'clock sharp. Make it clear I will not be a happy bunny if there are any stragglers. Right, we've got a lot to do and not a lot of time to do it in, so let's crack on and make a start."

CHAPTER TWENTY-NINE

Melissa Smails was on the final leg of her five-kilometre run. Despite the blistering cold, she was sweating profusely inside her tracksuit as she puffed a trail of breath out like an old-fashioned locomotive.

With Dave suddenly coming down with man-flu, the trip to his parents in Cornwall had fallen through at the last minute. It had been a relief in a way; after Monday's awful drama on the ward, she was quite content to spend a few days at home with her big bearded Teddy Bear, vegging out on the sofa and watching old films on TV.

On a positive note, the heating was working again. The landlord had finally sent someone around to sort the boiler out this morning, which meant that she would be able to enjoy a nice hot shower when she got back and then lounge around in her jimjams for the rest of the evening without worrying about frostbite setting in.

Mel turned the corner into her road and jogged along the perimeter of the park. She checked her watch and saw it was coming up to a quarter to nine. Easing into warm down mode, she took it nice and slow over the last couple of hundred yards.

When she came to a stop outside the communal entrance of the house that contained her flat, Mel placed her hands on her knees and lowered her head, sucking in air hungrily. Keeping her diaphragm extended, she breathed in deeply and concentrated on lowering her pulse rate. As Mel began to stretch off her hamstrings, she became aware of a red car pulling up beside her.

"Evening," the scrawny looking white male who lived in the ground floor flat called cheerfully as he slammed the driver's door shut. "You must be mad going running in this weather." He gave her a wonky smile that exposed prominent front teeth.

"Rubbish," she said, grinning back. "You don't even notice the cold once you get going."

Mel followed the boy – she didn't even know his name – up the steps. As he keyed them through the communal front door, Mel immediately became aware of raised voices coming from inside his flat.

He glanced nervously over his shoulder at her. "Sorry about the racket," he said, seeming genuinely embarrassed. "I've had some friends staying with me for a couple of days, and I think they're starting to go a bit stir crazy."

"Don't worry about it," Mel said, dismissively. Thankfully, living on the top floor, she couldn't hear what went on down here, but she felt a twinge of sympathy for the man who was sandwiched in the middle flat.

"I'm Mel, by the way," she said, figuring that she ought to introduce herself as they did live in the same house. "I live in the top flat."

"Rodney," he said. "I live in the bottom flat."

Mel laughed, thinking he was making a joke, but then she realised he was being serious, and the penny dropped that he was a bit simple.

"Nice to meet you," she said.

The voices inside were becoming more heated, with a deep-voiced man shouting aggressively at a woman. "Is everything alright in there?" Mel asked, concerned. Some of the language was quite strong, and the woman had started crying.

"Sorry," Rodney said, slipping the key into his door and opening it inwards. "I'll ask them to keep it down."

Mel was still standing on the stairs as he slipped into the flat, and from her elevated position, she was afforded a brief glimpse inside. What she saw nearly caused her legs to buckle, and she had to grab hold of the bannister to steady herself.

A gigantic black man with shoulder-length dreadlocks had been looming over a woman who was cowering on the floor. One hand was raised above his head, as though he was about to strike her, the other was clutching his stomach protectively. Layers of thick white bandages were wrapped around his shirtless torso.

Mel had instantly recognised the brutish face. She had seen it a number of times during the past week or so, while its owner had been a patient in one of the private rooms outside her ward at the Royal London Hospital. It belonged to Claude Winston, the cop killer.

———

"Please! Mr Winston," Rodent pleaded as soon as he'd closed the door. "You need to keep the noise down. The lady in the top flat was just asking if something was wrong and I'm worried that she might call the police." He turned to Garston for support, but none was forthcoming.

Winston bounded across the room and tore open the door into the hall. There was no sign of anyone so he slammed the door shut and stormed back into the lounge. "If she does, I'll hold you personally responsible," he snarled.

Garston checked his watch. Rodent was late – again. He had been nearly an hour late coming back from his errands this morning, and when he'd finally turned up, the stupid boy had forgotten the medical supplies and had had to be sent back out for them.

"Claude, put your sweater on," Garston said. "Rodent's right, we can't take chances." They hadn't planned to leave for another couple of hours, but there was no point in waiting any longer, especially not with Winston being in such a volatile mood. He had just threatened to beat Angela to a pulp simply because she'd forgotten to put sugar in his coffee.

All of their planning and hard work – all of the money he had forked out – would be for nothing if they ended up getting arrested because a nosey neighbour had called in a suspected domestic disturbance.

"Since when have you been the one giving the orders, nephew?" Winston demanded, turning on him in an instant.

"Since you put me in charge," Garston said, keeping his voice level even though his temper was in danger of bubbling over. "Rodent, get Claude's things. They're in a rucksack on the bed. Angela, help him put his top on, and be careful not to disturb his bandages."

Garston watched as Rodent scuttled off to load up the car and Angela fussed over Winston. His uncle seemed to have calmed down now and he was talking to her as if nothing had happened. The man was clearly psychotic, and he had to be treated with kid gloves, especially as he still had the Brocock revolver and access to forty rounds of ammunition.

Five minutes later, they were climbing into the red Rover, with Claude and Angela cramped in the back and Rodent and Garston sitting in the front. With a careful glance over his shoulder to make sure that nothing was coming, Rodent indicated and pulled out, pushing and pulling the steering wheel through his hands the way he had read you were supposed to do in the Highway Code. When he finally got around to taking his test, he thought he would make a very good driver.

Mel locked and bolted the door to her flat the moment she got inside. Standing with her back pressed against it, her head spun as she tried to bring her spiralling thoughts back under control. How the hell could Claude Winston be in the same house as her? It seemed inconceivable. What had the toothy boy said to her out in the street? *'I've had some friends staying with me for a couple of days, and I think they're starting to go a bit stir crazy...'*

She did a quick calculation. If they had been here a couple of days, it meant that the most wanted people in London had been hiding out in the ground floor flat, right under her bloody nose, since Monday afternoon, and to have done that, they would have had to have come here straight after decamping from the hijacked helicopter.

"Shit!"

This was just insane; thinking about it blew her mind.

She clamped her hand to her mouth, wondering what to do. Obviously, she needed to call the police, but was it wise to do that from inside the flat? Maybe it would be better – safer – to grab Dave and get away from this place first. She could just as easily ring the fuzz from the call box on the other side of the park.

The sound of the street door slamming down below interrupted her thoughts.

Had someone come in or left?

She placed her ear against the back of the door and listened carefully, but all she heard was silence. Running into the lounge, which overlooked the street, Mel cautiously peeled back the curtain and checked outside. The boy who had introduced himself as Rodney was placing a duffle bag into the boot of his red hatchback. As she watched, he stood up and started back towards the house, but then he suddenly stopped and looked straight up in her direction.

Her breath catching in her throat, Mel immediately dropped the curtain and flung herself against the wall. The lights in the lounge were off, but the TV was playing and it was possible the flickering picture had caught his eye.

Less than six feet away, Dave was fast asleep on the couch, oblivious to the dilemma that she now found herself in.

Mel ran back to the door and listened again, half afraid that Rodney had seen her and was about to come charging up the stairs, demanding to know why she had been spying on him. What would she say if he asked? Her mind had gone completely blank, and for the life of her, she couldn't think of anything that wouldn't sound suspicious.

Thankfully, no one came up the stairs, and after a minute of indecision, she decided to take another look outside, in case Rodney had gone back into the street without her noticing.

As she stepped away from the door, she heard movement down below. There were muffled voices too, three of them. Mel listened until the street door slammed and it went quiet again, and then she sprinted back into the lounge, turning the TV off as she flitted past it. Breathing heavily, she peeked out of the window for a second time.

"Mel...?" a groggy voice called out from behind.

"Shhh!" she hissed without looking around.

"What's going on?" Dave asked, full of cold.

She heard him lumbering to his feet.

"Stay there," she whispered, but he ignored her.

Typical.

Dave yelped as he stubbed a toe on the leg of the coffee table. "Why is it so dark?" he said angrily.

When he started fumbling around awkwardly, Mel realised that he was groping for the light switch.

"Leave the lights off," she growled.

"But I can't see a bloody thing," he complained, sounding all bunged up.

"David, do NOT turn on that light," she ordered in the scary voice that she reserved for when he'd given her the raging hump.

Dave froze on the spot. With a low moan that signalled his surrender, he stumbled across the room – stubbing his toe on the coffee table leg once again.

"What the hell's going on?" he demanded, leaning down to rub his foot.

"You know the gangster who murdered the policeman at work and then hijacked the HEMS helicopter?"

Dave nodded. "Yeah."

"Well, I've just found out that the bastard's been staying in the ground floor flat since he escaped, and him and three of his dodgy mates have just left the building."

"You're shitting me?" Dave said, incredulously.

"No, David. I'm not." It was too dark for him to see the withering look she fired in his direction but there was no mistaking the irritation in her voice.

"Show me," he said, excited. In his usual clumsy fashion, he pulled the curtains wide open and thrust his big hairy face up against the window.

"My God," Mel blurted out, pulling him away from the window. "Do you want to get us both killed?"

"Easy princess," Dave soothed, holding up his big hands to calm her. "It's okay, they've already driven off."

Mel cursed, pushed him aside and pushed opened the window, letting cold air into the cosy room. She leaned as far out as she could, cursing under her breath.

"What are you doing?" Dave asked, mystified by her actions.

When Mel closed the window, she turned on him with a face like thunder. "I didn't even get the index thanks to your bloody interference."

By the time the two unmarked murder squad cars arrived at Mel's flat, the suspects had long since gone. The 999 call had come out as they were travelling from Arbour Square to Star Lane to start searching for the Rover. Local uniforms were already on scene, and the surrounding area had been flooded by units hunting for Winston and his associates.

"Do you want me to boot the downstairs flat's door in, skipper?" the driver of the RT car asked Charlie White.

The Scotsman shook his head. "No, but thanks for the offer."

Leaving an officer to guard the door, he trotted up to Mel's flat to take a statement from her. She was sitting on the sofa next to a red-nosed bear of a man who had a box of tissues on his lap and was coughing and spluttering like he was about to die.

"Got a wee cold then, have you?" he asked, keeping as far away as possible.

Dave nodded, looking sorry for himself. "Flu," he said miserably.

"Can I get you a cup of coffee?" Mel asked, standing up.

"Aye, that'd be lovely," White said. "Perhaps we could go into the kitchen and leave your hubby and his germs in peace," he suggested.

Mel led him into the flat's cramped kitchen and switched the kettle on. "I can only do instant, I'm afraid," she told him, pulling three mugs from a cupboard above her head.

"That'll be fine," he said with a warm smile. "I gather you met my boss, Mr Dillon, at the hospital on Monday. Sounds like you went through a bit of an ordeal, what with walking in on the killers and all."

Mel shuddered at the memory of being chased along the corridor by the fearful bald-headed man. "It was a little harrowing," she admitted.

When someone from the murder squad had rung on Tuesday morning to inform her that Heston had died from his injuries, she had experienced a frisson of guilty pleasure; at least he would never be able to terrorise anyone else the way he had her.

"Forgive me for asking," White said, "but are you one hundred percent sure the man you saw was Claude Winston?"

"I'm one million percent sure," she replied. "Not only did I have to put up with his histrionics at the hospital for a whole week, I saw him standing above two of your colleagues with a bloody great big gun in his hand just two days ago, and I will never – ever – forget the cold-blooded way he looked at me when I entered the room, or the way he told that bald-headed bastard to get me. He was issuing a death sentence, and you don't easily forget the face or the voice of the man who does that to you."

"No," Charlie said, "I don't suppose you do. Look, I know you've already gone through this with the local officers, but can you tell me anything about the people he was with?"

Mel considered this as she spooned coffee into the three mugs. "My downstairs neighbour's called Rodney. He's a skinny white lad with pronounced front teeth and overgrown sideburns. He can't be more than twenty, I would say, and I get the impression that he's a bit simple if you know what I mean. He drives a red hatchback but I couldn't tell you which model. I'm not very good with cars. There was a black woman on the floor when I looked into the room." Mel closed her eyes and replayed the scene in her head. "I think..." she said as she scrunched her face up in concentration "...I'm almost certain she had a long scar down the right side of her face like she had been bottled in a fight."

"That's really helpful," Charlie White encouraged. "Anything else?"

Mel shrugged. "There was another black man in the room with them, but I only got a fleeting glimpse of him and he was standing with his back to me. He was slim, I think."

"Did you get the impression they were just popping out for a little while or did it seem more like they were going for good?"

"I'm not sure, but when I looked out the window, Rodney was loading a big bag into the boot. I don't know if that helps?"

"It might do," Charlie said. "One last thing: I dinnae suppose you got the registration number, did you?"

The fugitives had almost certainly driven off in the Rover 216 that had been used to spirit Winston away from the wasteland in Canning Town – in which case they already had the index number – but it would have been nice to have conformation, just in case the Rover had been swapped for a different red car. Stranger things had happened, after all.

"I would have," Mel said ruefully, "if my oafish partner hadn't woken up and got in the bloody way."

Charlie White's mobile started to ring. It was Tyler. "Excuse me," he said, stepping out into the hall to take the call.

"Charlie, Jack Tyler here. What's the score?"

White looked over his shoulder to make sure that Mel was out of earshot. "You willnae believe it, boss, but the informant's the ward sister from the RLH who walked in on Winston just after he'd shot Morrison," Charlie told him quietly. "She reckons her downstairs neighbour, Rodney, drove Winston, Garston, and Angela off in his wee red car about five minutes before the lids got here. She doesnae know which direction they were heading in, but she saw Rodney load a big bag into the boot, so it looks like they've set off for the coast ahead of schedule."

Tyler swore profoundly. *"What could have made them do that?"*

Charlie was struck by how worried the boss sounded. He was usually as cool as ice in situations like this. "I havenae got a clue," he said.

When Tyler next spoke, there was great urgency in his voice. *"If they're heading for Sussex the most likely route from there would be to take the A13 up to the M25. Leave it with me, I'll have Kent and Sussex informed that it might be heading their way."*

A wise move, Charlie thought; although ANPR cameras had been installed at various points along the M25, it was a big road to police, and unless there were units close enough to respond to any activations all the hard work of getting it onto the system would have been for nothing.

"Have we gained access to the downstairs flat?" Tyler asked, changing tack.

"Afraid not boss," Charlie said. "It's locked and secure. I've got a lid standing guard outside, but we're gonna need a search warrant to enter."

Jack grunted. "*I suspected as much. Don't worry, mate. Mr Dillon's got the number for a friendly out of hours Magistrate. I'll get him straight on it.*"

"I'll crack on with taking a statement from the informant then, and await word from you about the warrant."

Jack reluctantly dismissed the team for the night at eleven o'clock. There hadn't been any further sightings of Rodney's car since Mel had seen it drive off, and despite the TIU live monitoring, there hadn't been any activity on either the 777 or 321 numbers. As he watched his team grab their things and wearily trudge out of the office, Jack prayed that Winston wouldn't be gloating at them from the other side of the English Channel come tomorrow morning.

Charlie White's team was the last to leave the building. They had just returned from searching Rodent's flat, which had been small, dirty and smelly. They had found some blood smeared bandages in a bin that had, no doubt, come from Winston. These had been seized for DNA comparisons. A local SOCO had attended to take fingerprints, of which there had been an abundance. At least putting Winston and the others inside the flat should prove easy enough with the forensic finds, and it would all be used as evidence against Rodney Dawlish in due course.

The TIU had agreed to continue the live monitoring overnight, and Reg Parker had volunteered to sleep in the office on a little camp bed that was kept for such occasions in case any activity was detected. Dean had also offered to remain behind, to perform any fast time searches that might be required, but Jack had decided against this, explaining that Dean would be of more use to him if he were fresh and ready for action in the morning.

Dillon had stood down the TSU signal detector van and the SO19 SFO team. Without a location for the suspects, or at least an idea of the general area they were in, both were redundant.

Kelly was going to spend the night at Jack's, and Dillon had offered to drop them off and pick them up again in the morning to save tying up two pool cars. As they settled in for the journey home, Jack seemed unusually morose.

"Cheer up mate, it might never happen," Dillon said.

Jack's face said that it already had.

"I really thought we'd get them tonight," he said miserably. He was silent for a few moments as he stewed the situation over in his mind. "Do you think that girl who rang in deliberately sold us duff info to buy them time?" Tyler asked, referring to Jenna Marsh's phone call.

Dillon shook his head. "No, I think she was genuine," he said.

When he spoke, Jack sounded deflated. "Me too, so why did they leave so early? I just don't understand it."

"Me neither," Dillon admitted, "but it is what it is and we just have to play the hand we've been dealt."

"Even if Winston does get away," Kelly said, reaching forward from the back seat to squeeze Tyler's right shoulder consolingly, "we've still got enough evidence to charge Garston and Marley with a joint enterprise murder, and this Rodney boy with assisting an offender."

"Kelly, darling, that really doesn't feel like much of a consolation at this moment in time, if I'm honest," Jack said, placing his left hand over her right.

"I know," she soothed, "but wherever Winston eventually ends up, we can always apply for an extradition warrant, so I'm sure we'll get him before the court eventually."

Jack twisted around and smiled. "That's one of the many things I like about you, you're ever the optimist."

Dillon tried to lighten the mood by talking about football. "I can get us tickets if you fancy a trip to Highbury this weekend," he said enthusiastically. The Gunners were due to play Sunderland. "Maybe you could bring young Kelly here along and broaden her horizons."

Kelly grimaced. "You must be kidding, Tony. I'd rather watch paint dry."

"Let's take a quick drive past Star Lane on the way home," Tyler said on a whim.

"What?" Dillon and Kelly blurted out in perfect unison.

"I said, let's –"

"I bloody well heard what you said," Dillon interrupted him. "But why would you want to do that? It's getting on for twenty past eleven now, and we've got to be back in for an eight o'clock meeting, which means you'll want to be at the office by seven-thirty, which means I've got to get up at stupid o'clock to collect you, and you're going to be in a shit awful mood, and –"

"Dill," Jack said firmly. "The quicker you get us there, the quicker we get home."

Dillon looked at Kelly in the rear-view mirror. "Don't just sit there," he pleaded, "tell him it's a ridiculous idea."

"Don't drag me into this," she said quickly. Like everyone else on the team, she knew that when these two started arguing like an old married couple, as they were prone to do from time to time, the best thing to do was stay out of it.

"Fine," Dillon snapped, swinging the wheel around to set them on a new course, "but I don't know what you're hoping to achieve, other than making us all feel even more tired and cranky than we already do."

Jack said nothing. He didn't have a clue what he was hoping to achieve by taking a detour to Star Lane either, but he felt compelled to do so. Quite often, Tyler liked to spend a few minutes alone at a scene, just soaking up the atmosphere. It didn't always work, but sometimes it gave him a sense of what had happened and a feeling for the killer. It was almost as if he was subliminally tuning into his quarry's mind, or perhaps it was more akin to a hunter getting a scent. Maybe, he admitted to himself, that was why he was being drawn to the flat now, because of some weird primal urge. He knew that if he tried to explain that to Dillon, the big man would say it was all poppycock, and that he was just a tired man grasping at straws. Maybe he was right?

They drove in silence, which was a sure sign that Dillon was sulking; he was never that quiet for that long. As they came off the A13 at the Barking flyover, they caught a red light. Dillon pulled up the handbrake with a huff and turned to address Jack for the first time in ages. "This is such a waste of time," he said belligerently. "If he was on a promise tonight," he said, glancing over his shoulder at Kelly, "I really hope that you'll tell him that ship has well and truly sailed."

"Dill!" Jack exclaimed, but Kelly just laughed.

A battered red car pulled up next to them, screeching to a halt in typical boy racer style. A dreadful racket was coming from its sound system and, almost immediately, the Astra's chassis began to pulse in time to the bass.

"For fuck sake!" Dillon said, glaring angrily at the hatchback. He couldn't see inside due to a combination of tinted windows and condensation, but he figured there had to be at least four people in it.

"Turn that bloody racket down," he yelled, not that there was the slightest chance of them hearing him over the blare of the garage music that was being pumped out.

As soon as the lights started to change, the red car accelerated away with a wheelspin, leaving a frustrated Dillon staring at a plume of exhaust fumes.

"Er, boys," Kelly said, leaning forward with some degree of urgency. "I don't want to alarm you but unless I'm very much mistaken, that was Rodney Dawlish's car."

CHAPTER THIRTY

The Astra wasn't equipped with a Force Main-Set radio, so Tyler had to dial 999 and go through the emergency operator to call for help, which seemed to take an infuriatingly long time. Eventually, he found himself speaking to someone at Information Room, who put the request out over the working channel and got the ball rolling. While Jack provided a commentary that was relayed to the responding units by the very efficient woman he was now talking to, Dillon did his best to keep the red Rover 216 in sight without showing out.

"Can you believe this?" Dillon blurted out as they drove along Barking Road. "I really thought we'd blown our chances of ever finding them again."

Jack couldn't answer; he was too busy providing updates. "Yes, I'm certain it can only be stopped by Trojan units," he was telling the IR operator.

The Rover pulled up outside a little parade of shops and a hooded figure jumped out of the driver's seat and ran into a fast food outlet selling fried chicken.

"That must be Rodent," Dillon said, pulling into a gap a few car lengths back. "How long till the Trojan units get here, Jack?"

"There are two of them running from Limehouse," Jack informed him. "ETA three minutes."

Dillon considered this. "With a bit of luck, they should arrive before Rodent comes out of there with his bucket of chicken."

"I bloody well hope so," Tyler said, although he wasn't sure that carrying out an armed stop with a fast food shop packed full of customers serving as a backdrop was a good idea.

A thought occurred to Tyler. "Kelly, can you ring Reg and get him to check whether there's any activity on either of the phones that the TIU are live monitoring for us."

While Kelly made the call, he gave the operator at IR an update.

"Apparently, the ARVs are just coming into Barking Road from the A13," Tyler told the other two a few seconds later. "We should see their blue lights in a minute or so."

The hooded figure emerged from the chicken shop carrying a large bag of food, which he passed through an open window to the front seat passenger before jogging around to the driver's door and getting back in. Within seconds, the car pulled away, treating them to another wheelspin.

"Here we go again," Dillon said, pulling out behind them at a more sedate pace. Thankfully, traffic was extremely light so it wasn't hard to keep up.

Kelly's phone rang. It was Parker, calling back with the update she had requested. "Reg said the phones are all still quiet," she informed them.

"I've got little blue pinpricks in the distance," Dillon announced after looking in his rear-view mirror.

Jack and Kelly glanced over their shoulders in concert.

The blue lights gained on them rapidly, and it became apparent that there were three police vehicles, not two. That was fine by Tyler; as far as he was concerned, with a man like Winston, it was a case of the more the merrier.

The operator told Jack that the lead Trojan car now had the target in its sights, and instructed him to stop following as soon as the marked units got behind the bandit vehicle. "Of course," Jack said, intending to do no such thing.

Seconds later, three liveried Vauxhall Omegas whizzed by, leaving the Astra rocking in their wake. They took up station behind the

Rover and the lead car flashed it to pull over. The Rover duly indicated left and started to drift towards the nearside kerb.

Brake lights came on as it slowed down.

"Well, I didn't expect that," Dillon said, almost sounding disappointed.

"Nor me," Jack admitted.

The lead Omega followed it into the kerb, while the second and third cars held back, hugging the crown of the road. By now, the Rover had slowed to a sedentary crawl, although it still hadn't quite come to a halt.

The second Omega started to accelerate past it, intending to cut in front and force it to stop. This turned out to be a big mistake as the Rover suddenly swerved directly into its path, causing the startled driver to pull onto the wrong side of the road and brake hard to avoid a collision. Luckily, nothing was coming the other way.

"Shit!" Jack said, tensing up. "Did he just try and ram the gunship?"

"It certainly looked like it," Dillon said, wondering what was going to happen next.

What happened next was that the Rover took off like a rocket, spewing clouds of black fumes from its gurgling exhaust. In an instant, the three ARVs were back in formation and, sirens blaring, they set off in pursuit. Slipping the lumpy gearstick into second, Dillon floored the diesel in an effort to keep up.

Leaving them way behind, the bandit car hurtled along Barking Road, recklessly weaving in and out of traffic with the three Trojan units right on its tail.

"Don't lose them," Jack shouted above the roar of the engine.

"I'm doing my best," Dillon promised, stamping his right foot to the floor.

Up ahead, the traffic lights controlling a busy four-way intersection turned red against the Rover.

"I don't think he's going to stop," Tyler said, cringing as a stream of traffic started to cross in front of it.

At the last possible second, the Rover's brake lights came on and car slewed sideways, with smoke billowing from its wheels. Miraculously, the driver somehow managed to straighten it up by coming off the brakes and steering into the skid.

With its horn blaring, the Rover tore through the junction at suicidal speed.

The three pursuit cars slowed down and negotiated the junction more carefully, which allowed Dillon to catch them up and follow through in their slipstream.

"I think this boy knows how to drive," Dillon said as they cleared the junction.

Two drunks who had just staggered out of *The Abbey* public house watched on in amazement as the Rover's driver turned right into New Barnes Street like a seasoned rally driver. One of the inebriated onlookers actually started clapping.

The Rover then made a handbrake turn to the left, cutting into a narrow winding street called Esk Road that ran parallel with Barking Road.

"He obviously knows the area," Kelly said, as she was flung around in the back.

Esk Road was littered with savage speed humps, each one sending the Rover airborne as it was lunched over it. The bouncy landings were so out of control that it was a miracle it didn't wipe out any of the vehicles parked on either side of the road.

With the three Trojan vehicles still in pursuit, but proceeding more cautiously over the speed bumps, the bandit soon started to open up a gap on them. Turning left at the end of Esk Road, the Rover went straight through a pair of 'NO ENTRY' signs, and powered along Cumberland Road, going the wrong way along the one-way street.

Thankfully, nothing was coming the other way, because there wouldn't have been enough room for it to squeeze past an oncoming vehicle. Moments later, the Rover reached Barking Road, where it turned right, getting back on its original route.

Jack glanced sideways at Dillon. Their old pool car didn't have blue lights or an audible warning system, and it was as about as manoeuvrable as a mobility scooter. If Dillon crashed, a garage Sergeant would throw the book at him for his unauthorised participation in a high-speed pursuit. "This is getting a bit hairy. If you want to drop out, I'll completely understand."

"Be quiet and let me concentrate," Dillon snapped. "There's no way I'm pulling out now."

"I bet that's what you say to all the girls," Jack said, treating his friend to a devilish grin.

Kelly leaned forward and slapped him.

They quickly built up speed again as the Rover raced along Barking Road, and before they knew it, they were bearing down on another major intersection, with Prince Regent Lane on the right and Greengate Street on the left.

Jack saw that the traffic lights were red against them yet again. Up ahead, a marked police van was sitting in the middle of the junction with its blue lights flashing. In addition, several RT cars could be seen waiting in the mouth of Greengate Street, roof bars strobing bright blue in the dark.

"Looks like there's a reception committee waiting for young Rodent," Dillon said, happily.

The police vehicles had been positioned in such a way as to discourage the Rover from turning off the main road. They obviously wanted it to continue straight ahead, which probably meant that a Traffic unit had deployed a Stinger further along Barking Road to burst its tyres.

Unfortunately, Rodent had other ideas.

Ignoring the 'KEEP LEFT' bollard in the middle of the road, he swerved onto the wrong side of the road, jerking up his handbrake and skidding the car into Prince Regent Lane.

"He likes his handbrake turns," Jack observed.

"He certainly does," Dillon said, drily. "That car's gonna fall apart by the end of the chase."

"Well, he won't be needing it where he's going," Jack said. "So, I suppose he might as well have a bit of fun running it into the ground tonight."

In addition to the three Trojan ARVs, there were now three marked RT cars, or pursuit cars as they were called these days, behind the fleeing Rover. Dillon hadn't been impressed when they'd zoomed past him, forcing him down to seventh vehicle in the pursuit's pecking order.

The chase hurtled along PR Lane, passing Newham Sixth Form College on the right, the entrance to Newham General Hospital on their left, and then Plaistow fire station on the right. "I think they're heading for Newham Way," Kelly shouted from the back seat.

Tyler didn't like the sound of that. If the Rover got onto a dual carriageway, it would really be able to start motoring.

"If we start going much above seventy, I don't think this heap will be able to keep up," Dillon warned them.

As Kelly had predicted, the Rover turned left onto Newham Way and the driver immediately floored the gas pedal, taking the chase up to ninety miles per hour.

Kelly looked out of the window and tilted her head upwards. "I think we've got India 99 above us," she told them.

Jack's mobile started to ring. Without taking his eyes from the road, he pulled it from his jacket and answered.

"*Boss, it's Reggie, the TIU has just reported activity on two of the phones you asked them to monitor.*"

Tyler pulled a pen from his pocket and opened his daybook to a blank page. It was all he could do to keep it steady on his lap. "Go ahead with the details," he said.

"*The 777 number has been onto the 989 mobile that's registered to the bloke in Rye, East Sussex. It was a two minute call. I've got the cell site coordinates for both phones but it'll take me a few minutes to work out where they are.*"

"Let me hazard a guess and say that the 777 number is currently traveling along Newham Way at warp factor five," Tyler said, closing his daybook. It was a good job he hadn't actually needed to make any notes. With the way the car was flying into bends, he would have had trouble writing anything clearly.

Reggie paused. "*What makes you think that?*" he asked.

"Oh, just a hunch," Tyler said. "Call me back when you've checked."

Annoyingly, another couple of RT cars breezed past them and bolted themselves onto the ever-growing convoy. "There must be eight or nine cars behind that Rover now, not including us," Dillon complained, gripping the steering wheel tightly to cope with the vibration.

Jack shrugged. It was always like this when a chase occurred during night duty. Even though the Met SOP stipulated that no more than two pursuit cars could participate in a chase unless specifically authorised by the Yard, it always ended up with many more units tagging on.

The Rover came off the A13 onto the slip road for the A406, cutting over the cross hatchings at the last moment and dangerously swerving in and out of the cars that were slowing down on the approach to the roundabout.

"Where's this fucker taking us now?" Jack wondered aloud. It had been exciting at first, but now the chase was starting to wear very thin.

"I dunno," Dillon said, tensely, "but if he carries on like this, he's going to kill someone."

"As long as it's only himself and the other occupants of his car, I really don't give a toss," Tyler said, although he did. He badly wanted to see Winston stand trial.

They were now heading northbound along the North Circular Road with the Rover still weaving dangerously in and out of lanes, trying to throw his pursuers off. There seemed to be no planning or thought behind the route he was taking, and the longer this went on, the more erratic his driving was becoming.

At some point, the Chief Inspector at IR was going to have to make a decision about bringing the pursuit to a forced stop, and Jack wondered if trained TPAC units were already converging on the Rover to do just that.

Tactical pursuit and containment — or TPAC — is the term used by UK law enforcement to describe the range of special measures available for managing and terminating vehicle pursuits.

One of the most commonly used tactics was the deployment of a hollow spiked tyre deflation device — a HoSTyDS — such as a Stinger. Jack suspected they had already tried — and failed — to execute this tactic back in Barking Road, when Rodent had frustrated them by turning into Prince Regent Lane.

Boxing would be the next option. That involved several police vehicles positioning themselves around the vehicle being pursued, bringing it to a slow and gradual stop by boxing it in on all sides. From what he'd seen of the boy's driving so far, Jack didn't think Rodent was going to allow the TPAC officers to get away with this, and even if he was, Winston would be taking pot-shots at them out of the window from the moment they came into range.

Tactical contact was likely to be more successful. This involved a TPAC police car carefully hitting the back end of the target vehicle with the intention of causing it to spin around and lose traction. As such, it was very similar to another slightly more aggressive tactic called the PIT manoeuvre.

The PIT manoeuvre involved the pursuit vehicle pulling alongside the bandit in such a way that its bonnet aligned with the fleeing vehicle's trunk. The pursuer then initiated contact with the target's side by steering sharply into it. If timed correctly, this caused the bandit's rear tyres to lose traction and sent the car into a 180 degree spin.

Whatever option they went for, they needed to do something – and fast.

Jack let out a frustrated grunt. "I wish we'd thought to bring the Ford Escort. We could have listened to the chase commentary on the Main-Set if we had." Apart from the Omega, it was the only car on the team that had one.

"If I'd known you planned to drag us off to Star Lane and get us involved in a high-speed chase, I would have bloody well booked it out," Dillon said acerbically. "But not being a mind reader, I didn't, so stop moaning, sit back, and enjoy the ride."

"The first three exits we're going to come to will be the ones for Barking, Redbridge, and then the M11," Kelly called from the back, putting her local knowledge to good use.

"It doesn't look like he's going to take the first one," Jack said.

No sooner had the words left his mouth when the bandit suddenly veered from lane three, where it had been sitting, across the other two lanes and onto the slip road that led down to the large roundabout at the start of Barking Road.

"What were you saying?" Dillon smirked, risking a quick sideways glance.

There were two lanes on the slip road, and each had a stationary vehicle waiting in it for the traffic lights to change to green.

At the end of the slip road, instead of joining the roundabout and going clockwise around it, Rodent initiated another handbrake turn and drove anti-clockwise, trying to force a path through oncoming traffic.

Unfortunately for him, the lumbering goods vehicle coming the other way was bigger, heavier and driven by someone who had no intention of giving way. With a screech of brakes, the Rover swerved to the left, narrowly avoiding a head-on collision that would have, in all probability, proved fatal.

With a bone-jarring crash, it careered straight into a thick concrete pylon, hitting it so hard that the bonnet crumpled inwards like a concertina. There was a horrendous bang, followed by thick clouds of acrid smoke. Nobody inside the car moved.

Firearms officers spilled out of the three Trojan vehicles, instantly surrounding the Rover and shouting out a string of commands at the dazed occupants as they bought their weapons to bear. One by one, the four stunned passengers were unceremoniously dragged from the car and placed face down on the floor, where plasticuffs were applied and they were secured.

One of the officers ran over to the Rover and used an extinguisher to put out the fire that had started in the engine.

When everything was finally under control, Tyler, Dillon and Kelly Flowers were allowed to come forward.

Three men and a woman lay cuffed on the floor. The driver, recognisable from his hoodie, had blood streaming down the side of his face where his head had smashed into the windscreen.

"Stupid fucker wasn't even wearing a seatbelt," the skipper in charge of the ARVs commented with a grin. "So, are these the bastards who killed PC Morrison?" he asked, staring down at the human dross on the floor.

Jack borrowed the AFO's torch and shone it over their faces. He had no idea what Rodent looked like, but he would easily be able to identify the other three without a problem.

With a frustrated sigh, Jack turned off the torch and returned it to the ARV skipper. "Slight problem," he said unhappily. "The three suspects from the hospital are black. All four of these are white."

Just then his mobile rang. It was Reggie calling him back. "*Boss, I've worked out the cell coordinates of the 777 phone and the 989 number it called. They're not in Newham Way, they're both in Sussex.*"

CHAPTER THIRTY-ONE

Thursday 13th January 2000.

The eight o'clock meeting was delayed by half an hour so that all the overnight updates could be collated. Most of the detectives were clad in scruffs – jeans and jumpers – today, in accordance with the instructions that had been given to them by Reg Parker when he had started ringing around the team at six-thirty that morning.

Looking like death warmed up, Tyler sat with his back to the tea urn, with Dillon flanking him on one side and Holland on the other. Carol Keating, looking more like Hattie Jacques than ever, and Susie Sergeant, looking tired and drained, sat quietly next to Dillon.

By the time they had got back to Jack's place, it had been getting on for one a.m., and he and Kelly had collapsed into bed, too tired to even speak.

Dillon had taken the spare room to save himself from having to do any additional driving. Of course, Dillon being Dillon, he'd woken up looking as rested and refreshed as if he'd enjoyed nine hours of uninterrupted slumber instead of five hours of fitful sleep.

"How do you do it?" Jack had asked when they'd sat down together for coffee before setting off. "Even Kelly looks tired and she's wearing makeup."

"It's because I'm pure of mind and soul," he'd explained piously, "so I drop off into a deep sleep the moment my head touches the pillow. You, on the other hand, are obviously troubled by the sins of your wicked past and they keep you awake at night."

Kelly had laughed, but Jack had just sat there and stared at him, feeling too exhausted to even attempt a pithy retort.

"Okay," Jack said, calling the meeting to order. "Apologies for the delay, but we've got a lot to get through, so let's crack on."

He began by telling the assembled officers how they had stumbled across Rodent's car on their way home, and then described the lengthy chase that had ensued. "So, it turns out that Rodney Dawlish, aka Rodent, drove to his friend's house after leaving the flat in Star Lane. He then borrowed his mate's work van to drive Winston down to the coast and promised to bring it back in a day or so, leaving his own car behind so the guy had a set of wheels for the weekend."

"And why did his mate fail to stop?" Wendy Blake asked. "It seems a bit silly to me."

"Ah, I managed to speak to Norman Crouch – that's the bloke who lent them the van – before he was carted off to Newham General with an assortment of lumps and bumps and a suspected concussion. He told me that the man who was with Rodent gave him two hundred quid and a big bag of cocaine in return for borrowing his van until Saturday at the latest. To celebrate, Crouch invited some friends over to have a few beers and join him in getting stoned. After a while, he developed a bad case of the munchies and decided to grab a takeaway. Crouch failed to stop because he knew he'd get nicked for driving whilst under the influence of drink and drugs, and because he wasn't insured to drive Rodent's car."

"What a wanker," Dean observed, drily.

Dillon nodded approvingly. "Couldn't have put it better myself, Deano."

"He was also worried that he'd get done for possession with intent to supply as there was a decent sized bag of cocaine in the car with him," Jack pointed out. "He didn't trust the lads he'd left back at his place not to steal it, so he took it with him for safekeeping."

Wendy turned her nose up in disgust. "What lovely friends he's got."

Dean nudged her elbow. "Like I said, the bloke's a wanker."

"Anyway," Jack continued, "the long and the short of it is that I've got the van details and registration number, and Dean has already circulated it on the PNC. The red Rover, which is now considerably shorter than a Mini, has been taken to Charlton car pound for a proper examination, but there's no urgency to do that. While we were fannying around chasing the Rover, it turns out that Rodent had driven Winston and the others to Sussex in his mate's van. Reggie's been looking at the data we received from the TIU to try and narrow down their current location. Reggie, over to you."

Parker stood up and circulated amongst the detectives, handing out an A4 Intel bundle he and Dean had put together before the others had arrived.

"Okay," he said, returning to his seat at the front. "Pages one to three are bios for Winston, Garston, and Marley. They contain custody imaging photographs, a detailed physical description and a synopsis of their offending histories. Page four is a photocopy of a photograph of Rodney Dawlish standing next to his mum – she's the one on the left. This was found in his flat. Mel Smails, the ward sister who lives in the flat above him, has confirmed it's an accurate current likeness of Dawlish."

"You know, I still can't get over the serendipity of her living there," Dillon said, only to be met with a sea of blank stares. "It's a happy coincidence, you bunch of ignoramuses," he explained with a disappointed sigh. He turned to Tyler. "We really must try and recruit some more intellectuals on this team."

"Yeah, right," Reg said. "Anyway, moving on, page five is a photo of a white Ford Transit van of the type being used by Dawlish. The registration is there too, for those of you who can actually read." His eyes shot sideways towards Dillon as he said this, but if the big man noticed the jibe he didn't respond. "The van has the legend, 'Patterson's

Plumbing' written along the side. That's who Crouch works for, by the way. Apparently, he was going to phone in and pretend to be sick today."

"At least he won't have to pretend anymore," Tyler informed them with an impish grin. "He had a lump on his forehead the size of a golf ball, and he needed fifteen stitches to sew up the wound in his scalp."

Dean raised a hand. "Just out of interest, did he blow over when they breath-tested him?"

"He wasn't fit enough to provide a sample, so they took blood," Tyler said. "He'll get a four-week bail date in relation to that, but I don't think there's any doubt he was well over the limit."

"Can you all turn to page six in the bundle you've been given," Reggie said. He waited patiently while everyone did this.

Page six was actually an A3 sheet of paper folded in half.

"This is a map of a place called Peasmarsh, a remote area in East Sussex near the Kent border," he said. "As you can see, the mast that's currently serving the 777 number is marked A and has the grid reference underneath." He tapped the copy he held in his hand at the relevant point, which resembled a small Eiffel Tower.

"The circle surrounding this is the cell radius," he explained, "and you will see it has been divided into three slightly differently shaded areas, which are marked AA, AB, and AC. These are the cell's azimuths. Turn to page seven now, please."

There was a loud rustling of papers as another A3 sheet was unfolded.

"This is a blow-up of the relevant azimuth, AC. The 777 mobile is currently at an address within this area. This is both bad and good news for us. Bad because it's a bloody huge area, but good because according to the ordnance survey maps, there aren't that many properties within it. I've marked out the three most likely locations, which are two little hamlets and a cluster of farm properties dotted along a long and winding country lane called Mackerel Hill, as M_1, M_2, and M_3."

"That place sounds a little fishy to me," Murray said, and then sniggered.

Dillon shot him a warning look, and Murray quickly averted his eyes.

"Sussex had their force helicopter fly over the area for us this morning and they found two very remote clearings that we didn't know about from the map. These also contained a scattering of cottages, and they can only be reached from unnamed roads that are basically dirt tracks," Reg said, ignoring the interruption. "These are marked as C1 and C2. Guv?"

"Thanks, Reggie," Tyler said. "Okay, so in case you're wondering why I had Reggie phone you all up at the crack of dawn and tell you to come in dressed in scruffs, and to bring an overnight bag with you, it's because we're going to check out all of these potential addresses today to see if we can identify which one our suspects are holed up in. To assist, we've scrambled together a host of specialist support personnel, who Mr Dillon will brief you about shortly. The more eagle eyed amongst you will have noticed that Steve Bull, Dick Jarvis and Paul Evans are conspicuous by their absence. That's because I shipped them off to East Sussex late last night to start watching a bloke called Kenneth Meade, a low-level criminal who runs a small fishing boat out of Rye Harbour, a couple of miles down the road from Peasmarsh. Sussex Constabulary and Her Majesties' Customs and Revenue both have files on him, and they suspect him of being involved in small-time smuggling, although they've never been able to prove anything. His mobile is the one that Garston has been in contact with over the last few days via the 777 number. Is that right, Reggie?"

"Yeah, that's right, guv. At the moment, it's in the cell that covers his home address, and the only time it moved during the last day or so was to go to the cell covering the harbour where his boat is moored."

Jack took a deep breath. "So, here's the plan," he told them. "We know they've moved to a location near the coast. We know they're in contact with a suspected smuggler, and we know their plan is to ship Winston over to France. In a minute, Susie's going to put you all into teams. You will be deployed to recce the addresses we've already mentioned. You will be assisted by a TSU signal detector van. Once we get a positive contact, a team of SFOs will be called in to make entry and – hopefully – detain our suspects. In the meantime,

Steve'll keep the fisherman's address under observation. If he moves, Steve and his team will go with him. If they get a sighting of our suspects, the SFOs will be called in to make the arrest. The Coastguard has been put on notice in case Meade's boat departs before we're in a position to move in. If that happens, there will be an interdiction at sea. So, fingers crossed, we've got all the bases covered." Tyler laughed, but there was no mirth in it. "Sounds easy in theory, I know, but putting all this into practice is going to be pretty tricky."

He paused to let the words sink in, taking the time to let his eyes wander around the room and engage as many of his staff as he could. "It stands to reason that if Winston's moved from London to the coast his departure to France is imminent, and as Meade has a boat moored at Rye Harbour my money is on him leaving from there. Make no mistake, this is going to be a gruelling couple of days for us. I wish it were otherwise, but if we're going to catch this bastard, I think we're going to have to go through a little pain. I hope that you all agree with me when I say it'll be worth it to prevent a nasty, lowlife scumbag like Claude Winston from getting away."

He was relieved to see they were all nodding determinedly if not enthusiastically. Satisfied that they were suitably motivated, he handed over to his friend. "Dill, can you give an overview of the back up that's been arranged."

"I just want to start by saying a quick thank you to Reggie and Dean for all their hard work getting everything ready for this morning," Dillon began. "While we were all fast asleep in bed last night, Reg was stuck here in the office liaising with the TIU over the live monitoring of the 777 and 321 numbers, and also for Meade's phone. What does that end with, please, Reg?"

"It ends in 989," Parker said. "It's on page eight of the briefing pack everyone was given, along with a Sussex police custody image of Meade, his address and vehicle details, and a snapshot of his form."

"Thank you, I'll read that in a minute," Dillon promised. "In addition to lumbering Reg with all the live monitoring, we also called Dean in at the crack of dawn to help Reg cobble together the intel packs and start liaising with the County Mounties."

"I don't think we're allowed to call our colleagues in the rural Constabularies that anymore," Holland said with a wry smile.

"What about carrot crunchers? Can I call them that?"

"No."

"In that case," acknowledged with a humble bow of his huge head, "what I meant to say was Dean came in mega early to liaise with our splendid colleagues in Sussex Constabulary to let them know we've got an operation running that's likely to stray onto their patch."

"Very helpful they were, too," Dean said.

"After a little encouragement from Mr Holland, the TSU reluctantly agreed to let us take a signal detection van on a jolly to East Sussex for the day," Dillon continued. "We've also got a team of SFOs coming down with us. The PS in charge is called Tim Newman. I've worked with him before and he's a good lad. While the detector does the rounds, Tim's team will be on standby at the local nick in readiness for a rapid deployment. If we do identify an address, I'll hotfoot it straight over to the local Magistrate's court to get a warrant for the entry."

"Do we have a surveillance team available, boss?" DC Stone asked. "Just in case they leave the venue before the SFOs get there." It was a decent question.

Dillon shook his head. "No, we don't. There just isn't sufficient capacity for C11 to write a team off without a clear pick-up point. And don't forget, bearing in mind that the target is armed, it would have to be an Alpha team." An Alpha team was a surveillance unit with a firearms capacity, and there were very few of those.

"That's why Susie has tried to put at least one P9 surveillance trained officer in each car," Jack explained. "If we can follow them safely, without showing out, that's what we do. If we can't, we drop back and hope that they will be heading to the boat that Steve, Dick, and Paul will have visual control of."

Holland cleared his throat, and every eye in the room turned on him. "We all have to accept that this is going to be a fast-moving and very fluid situation where ongoing dynamic risk assessments will have to be continuously made and reviewed. My priority is the safety of my staff and the public, so I'm telling you now, in no uncertain terms, that you do not take chances and you do not put yourselves, your colleagues or Joe Public in the firing line. Better that Winston gets away and we nab him another time than anyone gets hurt. Is that clear?"

As one, every officer in the room chorused, "Yes, sir." Holland had that kind of effect on people.

"Good," he said, seemingly satisfied. He turned to Jack. "I'm going to remain here at Arbour Square all day, and I expect to be updated immediately if anything of substance occurs. I'll be popping in and out of the office regularly, but come and find me if anything happens or if – God forbid – the shit hits the fan."

Tyler nodded. "As soon as I know anything worth knowing, you'll know it too," he promised.

Rodney Dawlish stumbled into the cottage's cramped downstairs toilet, freezing cold and still half asleep. He had hardly slept at all, tormented as he was by the painful memories of yesterday's distressing encounter with the lovely Jenna. It had ended so horribly, with him storming out of the shop and her screaming after him, and he desperately wished that he knew her telephone number so he could call her and apologise, although he very much doubted that she would want to speak to him ever again after the disgraceful way he'd behaved.

Unable to find the light switch in the dark, and shivering with cold, he shuffled forward on the dirty lino floor and unzipped his fly. Rodney's bladder was close to bursting, and he sighed with relief as he started to pee. He was so busy trying to avoid splashing the toilet seat that he didn't notice the large wall-mounted cistern protruding from the wall above the bowl, and he banged his head straight into it. Cursing as a hot trail of urine soaked his bare foot, he rubbed his head and concentrated on not making any more mess.

Garston was sitting in the kitchen clutching a steaming hot cup of coffee to his chest when he entered, a few minutes later. "Morning," Rodney said, only to be ignored. He wandered over to the kettle and switched it on.

"Nice here, isn't it?" he said after looking through the window into the darkness beyond. In the daylight, he suspected the views out of the window would be beautiful.

Garston just grunted dismissively. He looked like he still had the raging hump. After putting himself out to get everything organised in time to bring Winston down to the cottage the night before, Garston had received a call from the stroppy fisherman saying the trip was off and they would have to wait until the following evening. Rodney didn't know the exact details, only that the other cargo hadn't turned up yet.

With Winston and Garston both in foul moods, Rodney felt like he was treading on eggshells. "So, do you need me to stay on any longer?" he asked. "Otherwise, I'll take Norman's van back and return in my own car to collect you later on." He crossed his fingers behind his back, praying that Garston would release him.

Garston snorted. "Yeah, go back to London," he said without even looking at Rodney. "Nothing you can do here, and you'll only get in my way if you stay."

"Should I take Angela with me?" Rodney asked. He knew she was as keen as he was to escape the horrid atmosphere.

Garston shook his head. "No, leave the whore behind. I need her to nursemaid Claude."

"Okay. Well, in that case, I'll be off," Rodney said backing out of the door. He was starving hungry but he would rather stop off at a café and get some breakfast than eat here. Rodney pulled out the shiny new pay as you go mobile that he'd purchased the day before. "I just want to make sure I've got your number, he said, pressing the green button. A couple of seconds later, Garston's phone started to ring.

"Do you want to call me back to make sure you've got my number?" Rodney asked, killing the call.

"No need," Garston said curtly. "It came up on my caller ID when you just rang me."

"Oh, I see," Rodney said, not really sure that he did. The man in the shop had set the phone up for him and explained how it all worked, but most of what he'd said had gone in one ear and out the other.

"I'll see you bit later, "Rodent said, waving goodbye.

Garston didn't bother to respond. He just sat there staring into his mug.

Rodent didn't mind; he was used to being ignored, and anyway, it was better than being insulted or finding himself the butt of someone's cruel joke, which is what usually happened when people bothered to reply.

CHAPTER THIRTY-TWO

For centuries, the remoteness and isolation of Romney Marsh, with its flat, barren landscapes and numerous waterways had made the area a smuggler's paradise. Largely inaccessible because of its geography and topography, this bleak and desolate land had been the last bastion of malaria in the United Kingdom, and the disease, known locally as marsh fever, hadn't truly been eradicated until the early part of the twentieth century.

Smugglers on the Marshes were known as 'Owlers', a term rumoured to have been derived from the owl-like noises they used to communicate with each other during the hours of darkness. Kenny Meade liked the expression, and he considered himself to be a modern-day Owler.

At fifty-six, he had worked on small fishing boats for most of his adult life, and he reckoned he knew the coastal seas as well as any man alive.

He also knew the layout of the land and its history like the back of his hand. Dungeness with its shingle beaches, seven lighthouses and two nuclear power stations; Dymchurch with its five mile long stretch of sandy beach, and its famous landmarks like *The Ship* public house, where Russell Thorndike wrote his Dr Syn stories about smuggling and law-breaking on the Marshes, and Martello Tower number twenty-four, built between 1805 and 1815 to defend against the threatened French invasion that never came.

Then there was the nature reserve and all the surrounding countryside and its abundance of flora and wildlife. This place was in his blood and he couldn't imagine ever living anywhere else, although that wasn't what he said when the wind was blowing a gale and the sky was full of bruise covered clouds that boded the imminent arrival of a storm.

Meade had hoped to sail his cargo over to France the previous night, but the second passenger hadn't arrived in time so they had missed the tides. That had meant he'd had to fork out another night's rent for the cottage where the black gangster was staying, and shell out for separate accommodation for the newcomer as well, all of which was biting into his profits.

Meade looked in the mirror and ran a hand through his thick grey mane. He badly needed a shave, but he couldn't be bothered, so he decided to wait until the weekend, even though his wife of thirty years had complained over breakfast that he was starting to look like Captain Birdseye with his white whiskers and stupid sailing cap. He liked his cap, so he had bitten his tongue, refusing to give the old cow the satisfaction of seeing that she had got under his skin.

As he studied his rheumy eyed reflection, he thought he bore more of a resemblance to Quint, the character played by Robert Shaw in the 1975 hit movie, *Jaws* than the crusty old bloke who advertised fish fingers.

"Captain fucking Birdseye, my arse," he said, angrily slipping his battered cap onto his head and adjusting it so that it sat at a suitably jaunty angle.

Walking through to the kitchen, his knees and hips aching from the arthritis that was beginning to plague him as it had his father at his age, he scooped up his mobile phone from the dining table and dialled the number for Garston.

"It's me, Kenny Meade," he said as soon as Garston picked up. "Everything's good for tonight. Keep yer phone on and await my call. I'll be sending a car to pick you up and I'll let you know the moment it sets off."

As soon as he hung up, he called his second passenger and repeated the message. That was another unnecessary expense, arranging transport for two people instead of one. He decided to borrow a van and pick them both up himself in order to save on costs.

Rodent was on his way back to London. Despite stopping off for a lovely fry up in a little roadside café on the A28, he had made very good time. His route had taken him along the A21, onto the M25 and then onto the A2, and he was now chugging along in the noisy diesel van towards the Blackwall Tunnel Southern Approach. With luck, he would be back on his own manor by half-eleven.

He was in turmoil over what to do about Jenna. Perhaps, if he drove straight to her chemist shop and threw himself at her mercy, she would take pity and forgive him for yesterday's wretched behaviour.

He had been stressed at the time and she had flustered him, and he had responded badly, which he very much regretted. He was hoping that now Winston was out of the way life would quickly return to normal, and they could repair their damaged friendship and put this silly misunderstanding behind them.

He had been so worried about getting back to the Big Smoke and putting things right that he'd hardly slept a wink, and at one point, about halfway through the night, he had woken up gasping for air, the weight of his emotions crushing him like a huge stone slab.

Perhaps he should stop off at Tesco and buy her some flowers and a box of chocolates? He'd heard that girls liked that sort of thing.

He suddenly became aware of sirens coming up on him from behind. When he looked in the mirror, there were two big police cars sitting right on his tail, and the lead one seemed to be trying to get him to pull over.

Rodent's stomach turned to ice.

What could they possibly want with him?

He hadn't been speeding and he was wearing his seatbelt.

Rodent took a deep breath and tried to work out what to do next, but his brain seemed to freeze, the way it always did when he needed to think fast.

Was there anything in the van that could get him into trouble with the police? No, Winston and the others were all back at the cottage, and they had taken all their belongings with them. He began to breathe a little easier.

Maybe he had committed a minor traffic violation that he was unaware of?

That wouldn't be a problem if he held a full licence and had insurance. Unfortunately, he didn't have either. Of course, he could always pretend to be Norman – he'd found his mate's driving licence in the glovebox yesterday when he'd been looking for the Sat Nav – but that would just mean dropping one of the only friends he had in the shit, and that just didn't seem like the right thing to do, not after Crouch had loaned them his works van.

Without realising, Rodent had been steadily gaining speed, and when he glanced down at the speedometer a few seconds later, he was surprised to see that he was now doing eighty five miles per hour instead of the steady fifty he'd been doing when he'd first spotted the police cars. His heart rate started to climb; they would think he was making off from them.

A third police car joined the others, but instead of dropping in line behind them, it accelerated past Rodent's van and pulled directly in front of it. Then the rear police car pulled out and accelerated until it drew level with him. Looking down, he found himself looking into the flint-like eyes of the car's front-seat passenger. As soon as the police cars finished hemming him in, the lead car's brake lights came on and he was forced to apply his own brakes to avoid running into the back of it.

What was going on? Were they trying to make him crash?

As he began to lose speed, it dawned on him that there was no other traffic on the road. Looking in his wing mirrors, he saw two marked police vehicles way back in the distance had stopped all northbound traffic.

Would they go to all the bother of doing that just for a traffic violation?

The three police units surrounding his van were aggressively shepherding it onto the hard shoulder and forcing it to stop. As soon as it came to a halt, policemen with assault rifles were jumping out of the cars and pointing their big fuck-off guns at him.

"ARMED POLICE! SHOW ME YOUR HANDS!" they screamed, snapping at his heels like a bunch of rabid dogs.

Frozen with fear, Rodent found his hands had become glued to the steering wheel. He couldn't move, not even to turn his head away from them.

They seemed to take this as open defiance, and he felt the tension outside the van crank up a notch.

Rodent wondered if these were the same armed officers who had stopped Errol. If so, were they going to shoot him, too?

Rodent swallowed hard; he didn't want to die.

"D-d-don't shoot," he pleaded as tears prickled his eyes. The words came out as little more than a croak.

"SHOW ME YOUR HANDS!"

"Please, I'm unarmed. Don't hurt me," Rodent whimpered, feeling his bladder loosen.

"SHOW ME YOUR FUCKING HANDS – NOW!"

Shaking with fear, Rodent finally managed to prise his hands away from the wheel and place them in the air.

One of the firearms officers immediately rushed forward and yanked open the driver's door, while another thrust a gun muzzle straight into Rodent's face. A third officer grabbed hold of his wrists and he was manhandled out of the van and brought down onto the floor, where his face was rammed into the cold, hard concrete. A knee was placed in his back so hard that it took his breath away and his arms were thrust behind him, making him cry out in pain. He heard a sound like fabric tearing as the plasticuffs were applied and pulled tight.

"Prisoner secure," someone shouted.

All Rodent could think about as he lay on the floor crying, a gun pointed at the back of his head, was that he wasn't going to be able to go and see Jenna and tell her how sorry he was.

Dillon thrust his head into Jack's office without knocking. "Just had IR on the phone. The white van Dawlish used to take Winston to the coast activated an ANPR on its way towards the Blackwall Tunnel a little while ago. It's just been stopped by SO19 and Dawlish is in custody."

"And the others?" Jack asked, holding his breath in anticipation.

Dillon shook his head. "Sorry mate, it's just Dawlish. He's being taken to KO and the van's being lifted to Charlton."

"Okay, thanks for letting me know," Jack said. He picked up his landline and dialled Steve Bull's number from memory. "Stevie? Jack Tyler here. Listen, Rodney Dawlish's just been nicked driving the van he borrowed back to London."

"*Great news,*" Bull said, sounding dog tired. "*Was he alone?*"

"Afraid so. What's the score at your end?"

Jack waited while Steve let out an expansive yawn. "Keeping you awake, are we?" he asked with a smile in his voice.

"*Sorry boss, haven't had much sleep. You'd think I'd be used to it by now, after all these months working with you.*"

"Think of the paycheck you're going to get," Jack said brightly.

"*Yeah,*" Bull said wearily, "*but you've got to be alive to spend it.*"

Jack laughed. He could picture Bull slouched in the car, hair sticking up, clothing dishevelled. "You know you love it," he said. "So, what's the latest with our people smuggler?"

"*Meade's still in his little house,*" Bull half said, half yawned. "*He hasn't been out all night. We've booked a couple of rooms in a little Bed and Breakfast nearby and we're doing three hour stints watching the premises. The other two have a car so if there's any movement they can be here within five minutes.*"

"Okay, Jack said. "Did you know there was a call from Meade to Garston earlier this morning?"

"*I did,*" Steve confirmed. "*Between them, Reg and Dean have been giving us regular updates. How are the rest of the team getting on?*"

"They've all arrived down your neck of the woods, and they've had a little scout around to get a feel for the place. Now, we're waiting for the signal detector van to deploy to see if we can narrow down where Winston's staying."

"I hope they can find him," Bull said, *"but even if they don't, I'm quietly confident that Meade is going to lead us to right to him when the time comes."*

"Let's hope you're right," Jack said, feeling that they were running out of time. The officers he had spoken to at Customs and the Coastguard service had said that most attempts to smuggle people into the country occurred at night, and these were nearly always illegal immigrants, but they didn't have too much data about people being smuggled out.

After he'd hung up, Tyler went out into the main office to see how Reg, Dean, and Wendy were getting on with the phones and research. There had been no further activity on any of the phones, which worried him greatly, and the research was progressing slowly. With most of the team deployed to East Sussex, he didn't have many people left at his disposal.

"A penny for your thoughts," Kelly said, joining him as he walked out into the corridor. She looked tired, like everyone else on the team, but when she smiled at him her face seemed to light up from within, sweeping all the weariness away in an instant.

Jack glanced around to make sure they couldn't be overheard. "My God, even when you're exhausted you're beautiful," he whispered.

Kelly blushed. "I bet you say that to all your DCs," she replied coyly.

"I'm sorry we haven't been able to spend much time together recently," he said, subtly brushing his hand against hers. "Maybe, when we've got this one wrapped up, we can make up for that?"

"I'd like that," she said with a demure smile.

When they reached the entrance to Andy Quinlan's MIR, Jack stopped. "Well, this is my exit," he said jerking his thumb towards the door.

She smiled and gave him a little wave. "Catch you later?"

"Definitely," he said, feeling better for having spent a few precious moments alone with her.

Inside the MIR, he found Susie Sergeant and Tom Wilkins hunched over a HOLMES terminal, going through statements. "What are you two up to?" he asked.

"Just getting the relevant witness statements printed off for Dawlish's interviews," Tom Wilkins said.

"Susie, who have you got in mind to deal with him?" Jack asked.

She shrugged. "To be honest guv, I was thinking of doing it myself as we've hardly got anyone available, what with most of our combined teams down in Sussex."

Jack considered this. "Okay," he said. "But I want someone to high-tail it over to Plaistow right now to see if he's willing to tell us where Winston is holed up before a solicitor gets his hooks into him and tells him to go 'no comment.' Plus, the first thing he's gonna want to do when he gets there is make a phone call, and we can't allow that, so someone needs to ring the custody officer and explain we're going to be making a request for him to be held incommunicado as there are three suspects still adrift who might evade capture if word of his arrest gets out."

"Leave that to me," Susie said, reaching for a phone. "I'll make the call and then shoot over there to see if he's willing to tell me what we need to know."

"Thank you," Jack said, turning to go. "I'll speak to Mr Holland now and get his authority for an urgent interview without legal representation," he promised.

Urgent interviews of a suspect at a police station without legal representation were permissible under Code C Para 6.6 or Code H Para 6.7. of PACE. They required the authority of an officer of Superintendent rank or above but, unusually, the authorising officer didn't necessarily have to be independent of the investigation. The authorising officer did, however, have to have reasonable grounds for believing that delay might lead to interference with, or harm to, evidence connected with an offence or lead to interference or physical harm to other people.

Garston sat in the cosy lounge watching the ancient TV and drinking yet another cup of coffee. The day was dragging, and he desperately wished that nightfall would hurry up and come so that he could finally be free of his troublesome uncle and move on with his life.

He glanced down at his expensive wristwatch for the umpteenth time and was annoyed to see that it was only one-thirty, just seven minutes later than when he'd last looked.

Garston picked up his mobile to ring Rodent and remind him to tidy up the flat and get rid of anything they had left behind. There hadn't been time before they left, and he recalled there were some of Claude's blood-stained bandages to be disposed of.

To his intense irritation, his device didn't have a signal. "Useless piece of shit," he grumbled, tossing it onto the sofa next to him.

Winston had skulked off back to bed straight after breakfast, which suited Garston, but so had Angela, which didn't, and he decided that it was about time the lazy cow got out of her festering pit and prepared lunch for them.

He stood up lazily and slipped his phone in his back pocket lest he forgot where he'd left it. As he headed into the hall, intent on calling Angela down, he noticed a dark coloured van drive very slowly past the front of the cottage.

His suspicion aroused, Garston slinked over to the window and gingerly pulled the net curtain aside to get a better view. The van contained two unshaven white men in builder's overalls. They looked bored, like they really didn't want to be there.

He knew exactly how they felt.

He relaxed, confident that they were just a couple of tradesmen searching for an address where they were due to carry out some work. After giving the cottage the once over, they moved on towards the next place fifty yards further along the road.

Panic over, Garston let the curtain slide back into place and strode out into the hallway. "Angela," he called up the stairs. When there was no reply, he cursed under his breath and started to climb the steep narrow staircase.

He found her, fast asleep in the smaller of the two bedrooms, the one that he'd used overnight while she and Rodent were forced to make do with the sofa and an armchair in the lounge. He tried nudging her arm, but she was dead to the world, so he grabbed hold of her elbow and shook it repeatedly until her eyes fluttered open.

"Get up, you lazy good for nothing bitch," he scolded. "It's lunchtime. We need food and Claude needs his bandage checked."

Angela sat up groggily and wiped the drool from her mouth, staring up at him from glazed over eyes. She was starting to cluck, he realised with contempt. As much as it went against the grain, he would have to give her something if he wanted her to remain functional.

"Go into the bathroom and wash your repulsive face," he said disdainfully. "When you come downstairs, I'll give you something to make you feel better, but I expect you to earn it, so don't keep me waiting."

He turned to go but then a thought struck him and he held out his hand impatiently. "Give me your phone," he demanded, snapping his fingers to hurry her up. "I need to see if yours has a signal because mine doesn't."

Angela sluggishly reached behind her and retrieved it from the bedside table. She handed it over without a word.

Garston pursed his lips in anger as he studied the screen. He pressed the power button on the side but nothing happened. As he'd feared, she had allowed the battery to run down again.

Garston let out a sigh of frustration. "You stupid bitch, the battery's dead. How many times have I told you to make sure you keep it charged in case I need to call you?"

"I'm sorry," she said lamely.

He threw the handset at her and stormed out of the room. "Plug it in to charge and then get your scrawny arse downstairs," he shouted over his shoulder.

Going into the kitchen at the rear of the property, Garston realised that he hadn't inspected the power bar on his own phone for a while so he pulled it out to check. Thankfully, the battery was almost full and, to his delight, he now had a signal. The cottage was in a dip, and it suddenly occurred to him that it might not be possible to get a signal unless you were at the rear of the property. Sitting on a wooden chair to await Angela's arrival, he scrolled down his saved numbers until he found Rodent's and pressed the green button.

In the custody office at Plaistow police station, a phone started to ring. "No phones allowed in here," the custody officer shouted, looking up from a record she was updating. It was just after two p.m., and although she had only just come on duty and completed the handover with her early turn counterpart, it was already turning into one of *those* days.

"Sorry," Susie Sergeant said, holding up a transparent property bag, "It's my prisoner's mobile. The boss didn't want me to turn it off in case there were any incoming calls from the people we're looking for."

The custody sergeant frowned disapprovingly, looking down on Susie from her raised dais like a schoolmistress addressing a pupil who had submitted shoddy homework. "That may be, but if I let you get away with it, then I have to do the same for everyone else."

"Fair enough," Susie said, scooping up her stuff. "I'm all finished now anyway, so I'll be out of your hair in a jiffy."

She had just returned from placing a disheartened Rodney Dawlish in a cell. The urgent interview she had conducted with him hadn't gone well. Unable to even meet her eye, Dawlish had sat down opposite her, a broken man. When the questioning began, Dawlish had refused, point blank, to tell her where Winston was hiding out. Acting as though it was a virtue to be proud of, he declared that, whatever faults he might have, being a grass wasn't one of them.

As she closed the heavy cell door, leaving Rodent to fester in solitude inside the hollow concrete cube, he surprised her by politely apologising for not being more helpful during the interview. For a moment, she had thought that he was taking the piss, but then she had realised that he was being genuine.

Taking the still ringing phone with her, Susie punched the four-digit code into the keypad next to the security door and departed the custody area. She went straight up to the second-floor canteen, taking the lift because she was too tired to use the stairs, purchased a strong cup of tea and a cereal bar, and sat down at the nearest Formica table. The lunchtime trade had died off and, apart from her and a jaded looking middle-aged woman in canteen staff attire, the room was completely empty.

Susie was absolutely shattered. Although she had heard that working a new job with Tyler was akin to being put through a particularly punishing endurance test, she hadn't quite realised how close to the mark the observation had been. The man was like a tsunami, pushing on relentless, sweeping everything in his path aside.

That said, they had made incredible progress since he'd taken over the enquiry, and as much as she liked Andy Quinlan, she very much doubted they would have come this far this quickly under his leadership. Quinlan was, without doubt, a very experienced and formidable SIO, but he was slow and ponderous in comparison, better suited to protracted enquiries that required lots of meticulous digging and probing to unearth the truth. He certainly didn't possess the brick through a window mindset that Tyler approached manhunts with.

Susie had recently sat the Inspector's exam. If she passed, she was hoping to stay on the new Homicide Command, which was going to be called SO1. She knew she wouldn't be able to remain on her own team, but she wondered if there might be a place on Tyler's team when they moved over to Hertford House in a month's time. She suspected she'd be in for a very steep, but very rewarding, learning curve if she went to work for him on a full-time basis.

After taking a very much needed sip of her tea, Susie examined the caller ID on Dawlish's phone to see who had called him. Her heart jumped when she saw that it was the 777 number. Taking another quick swig to whet her whistle, she hurriedly reached into her shoulder bag for her mobile. Tyler would want to know about this immediately.

CHAPTER THIRTY-THREE

"Boss, I've just had the TSU on the line," Reg said excitedly as he barged into Tyler's office, only to see that Tyler was already speaking on the telephone.

Jack held up a finger and mouthed 'one moment,' before indicating for Parker to take a seat.

"Okay, Susie, thanks for the update. You might as well get back here, and we'll sort out someone to do the slow time interviews on Dawlish in due course."

Hanging up, he turned to Parker, his expression thoughtful. "That was Susie, over at KO. Dawlish was about as helpful as a dose of syphilis during interview, but a few minutes ago his mobile received a call from the 777 number. Did we even know Dawlish had a mobile?"

"No, we didn't," Reg said, "but I suspect it ties into what I've come to speak to you about."

"Which is...?"

"As I was saying, I've just had the TSU on the phone with an update. Firstly, the signal detector van has pretty much covered all the properties we've identified within the area, and so far, it hasn't picked anything up."

Tyler scowled at him. "But we know they're in that neck of the woods from the cell site data, so how can they have suddenly disappeared?"

"It could mean a number of things," Reggie said quickly, "from the 777 and 321 phones no longer being there to them just being switched off, or it could simply be down to them being in a part of the building where there's no signal when the sweep was done. Apparently, in some of the sites they surveyed, the signal strength was much weaker than others, constantly dropping in and out of coverage. They haven't been able to pick up the 321 phone since they arrived, but they were getting a weak reading from the 777 phone. It seemed to be coming from one of two small hamlets set in close proximity to each other. Unfortunately, by the time the van got near enough to be able to distinguish which one it was, the signal just disappeared. Anyway, the crew have broken for a quick lunch and toilet stop, and then they're going to repeat the circuit."

"What about the TIU? Any updates from them?" Jack asked, annoyed that the detector operators were being distracted by their stomachs when the clock was ticking down and they needed to make the most of every second remaining.

Reg nodded and placed a sheet of paper on Tyler's desk for him to peruse. "There was a call from Meade's phone, the one ending in 989, to Garston's 777 number at 10.20 a.m. It was short, lasting only a couple of minutes. The 989 number made another call straight afterwards, equally brief, and I'm awaiting the subscriber results for the number it rang."

"Let me know as soon as it comes in," Jack instructed him.

"I will," Reggie promised. "Also, as you can see from this printout, Garston received a call from an, as yet, unidentified number early this morning. He didn't answer it at the time, but a little while ago he tried to ring it back. It's not a number that's cropped up before, and it ends..." he quickly checked his notes "...in 200. I'll knock out a subs application for it in a minute."

"By all means do," Tyler said, "but I'm confident that the number's going to belong to a phone Susie's bringing back from Plaistow right now. It was in Dawlish's possession when he was arrested, and it suddenly started ringing a few minutes ago, with Garston's 777 number showing up on the Caller ID. That's what she was telling me about when you came in."

Parker nodded thoughtfully. "That makes sense. I'll still get the subscriber check carried out anyway, for the sake of thoroughness, and when Susie arrives back at the office, I'll have a little look through the phone's recent call history to see who else it's been in contact with."

As soon as Reggie departed, Tyler picked up his phone and called Dillon. The big lug had gone down to Sussex to lead the team from the front line. Jack wasn't happy about the crew of the signal detector van taking a lunch break, and he wondered if Dillon was aware of this. His view was that it would be far more productive if they grabbed some sandwiches and ate them on the go, and he wanted Dillon to convey his displeasure to them in no uncertain terms

---

By eight o'clock the sun had long since bid them farewell for the day. Not only was it dark and cold, but in Sussex it had started to rain. Although the day had started out full of promise and excitement, the detector van's failure to locate the suspects had quickly dented morale.

There was only so much that could be achieved by driving around the area in the forlorn hope of spotting the fugitives themselves, so Dillon had radioed the five cars that Tyler had deployed to East Sussex and told them to RVP in the car park of *The Bell* public house in nearby Iden. He had decided against choosing anywhere closer to Rye in case Meade saw them and got spooked.

"This place is in the arse end of nowhere," Charlie White complained as they waited for the others to arrive. "It's very pretty but I wouldnae wanna live around here."

"To be fair, I don't suppose they'd want you," Dillon said. "With a face like that, you'd probably scare all the kids."

"I cannae help my nose being a funny shape," White objected.

"I know, but having a hooter that sits at a right angle to the rest of your mush doesn't do you any favours, does it? No offence, Whitey, but you make Quasimodo look like Sean Connery."

"Aye, well, at least I don't resemble a poor man's Arnold Schwarzenegger," the Scotsman fired back.

Dillon laughed. "No, mate, you don't. You just look like an ugly man with a bent nose and bowed legs."

"My legs are no' bowed. They're —"

Dillon's phone rang, killing the banter. The caller ID said: Number withheld, so it was obviously Job-related. "Dillon speaking," he said.

"*Dill, it's Jack. How's it going at your end?*"

Dillon barked out a mirthless laugh. "It's not," he said. "I've just about had a belly full of Rye and its surrounds."

"*Look, I know they've already been at it all day, but I want the detector van to do one more circuit for us before they go. Who knows, maybe this time around they'll be lucky? In the meantime, we've had a think about this, and come up with a cunning plan.*"

Dillon responded with all the enthusiasm of a man waiting to have a tooth extracted. "Oh good, I can hardly wait to hear the details."

Tyler ignored the sarcasm. "*We know from the signal detector van's earlier findings that there are two little hamlets where the 777 phone is most likely to be holed up. I want you to send a couple of units to each one and deploy people on foot to cover the addresses visually. When your troops are in place, Reg is going to send a text from Dawlish's phone to Garston's, saying he dropped something outside the cottage and asking Garston to go out and have a look for him. With luck, we'll see which house he comes out of.*"

"Good plan," Dillon said, "but aren't you forgetting something?"

"*What?*"

"If Garston's got enough of a signal to receive the message, the detector van will be able to identify the address without your text message. If he hasn't got any signal, then he won't even receive your message and he won't come out to play for us."

"*Believe it or not, we have considered that,*" Jack said, sounding irked. "*But Reg has spoken to the SPOC at the TIU, who's spoken to the service provider, and the consensus of opinion is that the problem might just be patchy reception. They think the detector van's having difficulty locking down the phone's location because the coverage is sporadic and it keeps dropping off the grid when the van's in the area. If they're right, and I'm hoping they are, then a*" text message might take a little while to get through, but Garston will get it eventually. When it does, we might be able to identify the house they're in."

"As long as Garston goes out to check and doesn't just ignore it," Dillon pointed out.

Tyler sounded very tired, but there was resolve in his voice. "*Dill, we blew out last night because Winston left London before the detector van was able to deploy. We've had no luck all day because the signal is lousy down there. We're running out of options, and if this doesn't work, we're reduced to relying on Winston meeting Meade at his boat later tonight. What alternative do I have but to try this out?*"

Dillon sighed in resignation. "Okay, we'll give it a go, but it's just started to rain down here, and it's as cold as fuck, so the troops won't be happy."

"*I'm not happy either,*" Jack said, "*but we're not paid to be happy, we're paid to catch villains. Feel free to tell them I said that, and give me a call when everyone's in place.*" With that, he hung up.

Apart from the control car, which contained Dillon and Charlie White, each of the other four cars had three people in them. That gave Dillon twelve officers to cover fourteen houses. It wasn't ideal, but it was doable. Once everyone had been briefed, those that needed to pop into the public house to use the toilet did so, and then they all set off for Mackerel Hill, some four miles away.

Charlie White had suggested holding the briefing inside the pub over a 'wee dram', which had been well received by everyone apart from Dillon, who had pointed out that as they were on duty it would be a contravention of the licencing regs. "Not the best suggestion you've ever come up with," he'd told Charlie once they were alone.

The small convoy turned right out of the pub into Church Lane, heading west until they reached Coldharbour Lane. They then turned onto the A268 and followed it all the way to Mackerel Hill, arriving some seven minutes later.

The two hamlets were relatively close together, and before long everyone was in place. They were using encrypted Cougar radios to communicate, but there had only been enough to issue one per vehicle. One by one, the four cars radioed in to say they were on plot and about to deploy their crews on foot. Thankfully, the rain had eased off to nothing more than an annoying drizzle, but the wind had picked up and it wasn't going to be fun, having to stand in the open for God knew how long.

It had been decided that the drivers should retain the Cougars, and everyone else would have to communicate with the control car by mobile phone. Of course, as soon as they were in a position to have eyeball on the relevant addresses, they realised that the same poor signal issue that had affected Garston's phone also applied to them, and there were going to be long periods in which some of them had no signal at all.

Dillon phoned the office to let Tyler know they were all in position and as ready as they would ever be.

"We're on plot so get Reggie to send his text," he said, "and let's hope, for the sake of the poor buggers stuck out there in the cold, that it reaches Garson sooner rather than later."

"*Okay,*" Jack said, "*tell the troops that he's sending it right now.*"

Garston was sitting in the kitchen, finishing off the last of the stodgy food that Angela had prepared them for their evening meal. She was a rubbish cook but it was better than nothing. Wiping his mouth along the back of his hand, Garston glanced over at the sink, where the whore was standing with her back to him, washing up the pots she had used to prepare the tasteless gruel he had just finished consuming. He had grown to like her less and less during the past few days, and he couldn't wait to get back to London and be rid of her.

It was getting on for eight-forty-five, and he was growing restless. He had expected to receive an update from Meade by now, and he was wondering how much longer to give it before putting in a call.

As he stared at his phone, sitting on the table in front of him, the screen lit up and there was a soft 'ping' signifying an incoming message. Hoping it was from the fisherman, he picked his phone up and read it.

A frown marred his forehead.

'Think I dropped my flat key outside the front door when I left this morning. Can you check for me? Rodent.'

Garston tossed the phone back on the table. Rodent was a pathetic waste of space. He had only taken the simpleton on as a favour to his brother, who was currently locked up for running drugs. The boy was a retard who would probably forget his balls if they weren't in a bag. Garston couldn't be bothered to go outside and start foraging around in the dark, where it was cold and wet. He would have a look later, when they left – if he remembered.

The phone rang, making him jump. If it was Rodent calling to confirm he'd received the text he would not be impressed.

"What?" he demanded, answering without bothering to check the Caller ID.

"*Someone's in a bad mood,*" Meade taunted. "*What's-a-matter? Wrong time of the month?*" The fisherman cackled at his own joke.

"I'm assuming that you have something worthwhile to say and haven't called just to annoy me?" Garston snapped.

"*Keep yer knickers on,*" Meade told him, the outbreak of humour over. "*A car's coming to pick you up at eleven o'clock sharp. Be ready.*"

Garston's eyes narrowed. "What type of car? And who will be driving it?" he demanded.

"*A car with four wheels and an engine,*" Meade replied, sarcastically. "*You don't need to know the driver's details. He'll knock on yer door when he arrives. Don't keep him waiting.*"

"That's not good enough –" Garston objected, but Meade had already hung up.

"Motherfucker," he cursed, throwing the phone down onto the wooden table.

Angela looked over her shoulder, alarmed by his raised voice.

"What you looking at?" he shouted, seeing an outlet for his anger.

"Nothing," she said, quickly looking away.

An agonisingly slow hour had passed since Reggie had sent the text message. That equated to sixty minutes or 3,600 seconds, and Jack Tyler felt as though he had been staring at the clock on the office wall for every painful one of them.

Depressingly, there hadn't been any response from Garston.

"Do you want me to try again?" Reggie offered, but his face told Jack that he didn't think there was any point in doing so.

They were sitting in the main office with Dean and Wendy. The Carpenters were singing their 1975 hit, *Please Mr Postman*, in the background.

Jack shook his head. "No, but thanks for offering."

He retired to his office and flopped down behind his desk, head thumping. Even taking into account the poor signal issues, Jack had would have expected Garston to have replied by now.

Was it possible that the text they had so carefully drafted had made him suspicious?

Could Garston have worked out that it wasn't from Rodent?

They had thought long and hard about how best to phrase the wording so that the text wouldn't look odd, but perhaps they had inadvertently got something wrong?

Maybe Dawlish would have signed off as Rodney, not Rodent?

Maybe, he hadn't stayed with Winston and Garston overnight as they had surmised?

Tyler let out a frustrated sigh and reached into his top drawer for some paracetamol. He wondered if it was worth trying to speak to Rodent again, to see if he would be more reasonable this time around? He dismissed the notion almost immediately. The chances were that Dawlish had never been to the address he'd taken them to before and would have no idea how to get back there.

As he washed down the two pills he'd just popped into his mouth with a swig of water, a thought occurred to Tyler, stopping him in his tracks. A tremor of excitement rippled through him. *Could it be as simple as that?* he asked himself.

Springing to his feet, he rushed out of his office, straight along the corridor, and into Andy Quinlan's main office, where he found Susie

Sergeant and Carol Keating locked in conversation. "A quick word," he said as he slumped down in a chair next to them.

They stared at him with puzzled faces.

"I don't suppose there were any pieces of paper amongst Dawlish's possessions, were there? Something with an address scribbled on it?"

Susie shook her head. "Sorry, boss, I went through everything he had with a fine-tooth comb. There was nothing like that."

Jack's shoulders slumped with disappointment. "Never mind," he told her. "It suddenly occurred to me that, as Dawlish hadn't been to the address before, he would have written it down in case he got lost and needed to ask for directions." He stood up to leave, but then sat down again as another idea sprang into his head.

"What about the van?" he asked. "Has that been searched?" If Dawlish didn't have it with him, perhaps there was something with the address written on it in the van.

"Not by us," Susie said. "SO19 arranged for it to be lifted to Charlton for us to search properly at our leisure."

"We need someone to scoot over there now and check out that van," Jack said, eyes brimming with excitement.

"I've already sent Kevin Murray over there with the local SOCO," Susie told him. "I'll give him a ring right now, and he can have a gander while we wait." Excusing herself from Carol, Susie popped off to retrieve her mobile and make the call.

"Getting a little tense, isn't it?" Carol observed when she had gone.

"A little too tense, if you ask me," Jack said with a wry smile. "I can feel it in my water Carol, if we don't get him tonight, he's going to get away."

Carol placed a motherly hand on his arm and gave it a gentle squeeze. "You're doing everything humanly possible, don't make yourself ill over this." Her eyes were full of concern.

"Yes, Matron," Jack said, finally succumbing to addressing her by her nickname.

Carol beamed at him. "Trust me," she said, "Matron knows best."

Susie reappeared, her mobile glued to her ear. "Kevin's checking the van's cabin out now," she informed them. "Yes, Kevin, I appreciate it's a plumber's van and it's full of notes and receipts and the like," she said testily into the phone, "but this is crucial so don't leave anything unchecked...Yes, I appreciate it could take you ages..." She raised her eyebrows in exasperation. Murray had that effect on people. "Yes, I am familiar with the expression 'a needle in a haystack'. Are you familiar with that good old Irish saying, 'Get on with it and stop your whinging or you'll feel my toe up your arse.'?"

"I must say, I'm not familiar with that particular expression either," Carol said with a smile.

Susie covered the speaker with her hand. "Made it up myself," she grinned. "I was going to say, 'Is minic a gheibhean beal oscailt diog dunta!' which in Gaelic means 'An open mouth often catches a closed fist,' but I thought that might be a bit too complicated for him, so I kept it simple."

Carol laughed. "I'll have to try and remember that one," she said.

I kept it simple...

A lightbulb came on inside Tyler's head. "Susie," he said, standing up and placing a hand on her arm to get her attention. "Ask Kevin if the van has a Sat Nav fitted. Maybe the address isn't written down on paper after all. Maybe it's been inputted straight into a navigation device." That would be the simplest thing to do, after all.

Susie relayed the message, and they all waited on tenterhooks while Murray checked.

"Come on, come on," Tyler muttered under his breath.

"He's found one," Susie said a moment later. "He's just powering it up and he's going to check it for recent addresses."

It seemed to take forever, and the three of them sat in strained silence until Murray finally came back on the line.

"What's that?" Susie said, plugging a finger into her ear. "You're sure?" A big smile broke out over her face as she turned to look for a pen. "We've got the address," she said excitedly.

CHAPTER THIRTY-FOUR

"Boss, you do know you're doing just over a hundred, don't you," Susie said as she glanced nervously at the speedometer.

"I know," Jack said, pressing his foot down even harder, "but I can't seem to squeeze anything more out of this heap."

"What a pity," Susie said, lacking any sincerity. Without taking her eyes from the road, which was flying by at an alarming rate, she checked her seatbelt to make sure that it was working properly. Not that it was likely to make much difference to her chances of survival if they crashed at this speed.

"Don't worry," he reassured her, "I've done the fast car course so I know what I'm doing." The fast car course was given to officers who worked on specialist squads and were required to drive high powered, unmarked cars on blues and twos. It was one down from the pursuit course in terms of skill level.

"I can tell," Susie said, fearfully.

They were on their way to Sussex. As SIO, Jack knew that he really ought to have remained at the office to maintain overall strategic control of the operation and leave Dillon free to implement tactics out in the field for him. The trouble was, Jack liked being hands on whenever he could, especially when the stakes were as high as they were in this particular case.

Leaving Carol Keating to run things in his absence, he had grabbed hold of the log book and keys for the last remaining car in the building, an aging Vauxhall Astra covered in dinks and dents, and dragged Susie off with him in a mad dash down to the Sussex coast.

Dean had sent a CAD message to IR asking them to notify Kent and Sussex Constabularies that an unmarked MPS car was about to enter their territory on an emergency run and to request that their Traffic patrols give it free passage and not try to stop it if they came across it.

The van's Sat Nav had yielded the address that Winston was holed up in, and to everyone's surprise and annoyance, it hadn't been in either of the two hamlets that AMIP officers had been staking out since the fake text had been sent. In fact, it had been located in a tiny settlement consisting of half a dozen properties about a third of a mile further along the road.

Dillon had passed the information onto PS Newman, the SFO team leader, who had immediately dispatched an officer to carry out a recce while Dillon rushed off to obtain an out of hours search warrant.

Jack knew it was going to be ridiculously tight, but he wanted to be there when the armed entry was made; he wanted – needed – to see Winston dragged away in handcuffs.

They were making good progress and had already crossed the Queen Elizabeth Bridge at Dartford. Jack didn't have a Sat Nav of his own, and he was having to rely on the map reading skills of his co-pilot. Luckily, Susie seemed to be a very competent map reader, unlike Tony Dillon, who usually got them lost at least once whenever he was charged with getting them anywhere.

"Okay, we're going to stay on the M25 till we reach the Sevenoaks by-pass, at which point we take the A21 and stay on that until we get to the A268, "Susie said after checking the map again.

Jack's phone rang.

"Get that for me, would you," he said, removing the handset from his inside jacket pocket and handing the mobile to her, all without taking his eyes from the road.

"DCI Tyler's phone," Susie said, balancing the Geographia on her lap and tracing their route along the page with her left index finger while holding the phone to her ear with her other hand. She listened for a few seconds, said, "Wait one," and turned to face Tyler. "It's Tony Dillon," she informed him. "He's got the warrant and is just leaving the Magistrate's house to return to the target address and meet up with PS Newman and his team. He reckons they'll be ready to effect entry in around thirty minutes."

Jack considered this. "Tell them our ETA is about forty minutes. I would prefer they await my arrival unless operational safety makes it necessary to make entry before then, in which case they should just crack on."

Susie relayed the information and there was a brief pause while she listened to Dillon's response.

"Tony says he's happy to wait, but he wants you to be aware that they don't have visual control of the cottage because the area around it is far too exposed to park a car up in."

Jack wasn't impressed. "Can't he just put someone out on foot, get them to hide behind a tree or something?"

Susie dutifully passed this suggestion on and then listened to Dillon's reply. "Apparently, the SFO who scoped out the property said it's too risky to deploy a footie," she reported back. "Tony says there's no cover whatsoever, and they would stick out a mile unless they were wearing a ghillie suit." A ghillie Suit was a type of specialist camouflage clothing, typically worn by military snipers, designed to help its wearer blend into the background.

Susie made a few 'uh-huh' noises as Dillon provided further information, and when he stopped speaking she turned to Tyler. "Tony says someone did a drive-by about twenty minutes ago, at which time there were lights on in the downstairs living room but no sign of movement."

Jack grunted his disappointment and shrugged. "It is what it is, I guess. Tell Dill to do whatever he thinks is best."

Susie passed the message on and said goodbye. As she put the phone down, a Kent traffic car materialised behind them, its blue lights flashing.

"For fuck sake," Tyler fumed, "why can't these poxy County Mounties just do as they've been told and keep out of our way?" He knew he would have to pull over; otherwise, the idiots might put it up over the radio as a fail to stop, but he would give them the bollocking of their lives for slowing him down.

At that point, the Traffic car pulled into the middle lane, accelerated until it was level, and the female operator mouthed the words, 'follow us,' and gave them a friendly smile. With that, the car slipped in front of them and took up station as their very own escort.

"Oh," Jack said sheepishly. He hadn't expected that.

"Shame on you," Susie said with a wry smile, "bad mouthing those poor County Mounties when all they wanted to do was help us out. Tut-tut-tut!"

Kenny Meade reversed out of his gravel drive, sending stones spraying everywhere. No doubt, his wife would give him an ear full for doing so when he got back home, but he was in too much of a rush to care.

He drove his old Land Rover along the narrow winding lanes at reckless speeds, figuring that he would see the headlights of an approaching vehicle in plenty of time to stop. Unlit, some of these narrow roads were barely more than tracks. There were some nasty bends in them, too, and, over the years, he had seen many an unsuspecting motorist misjudge them and end up in the hedge. Luckily, only locals tended to use this route during the hours of darkness. Meade wasn't remotely worried about having an accident; he had lived around here all his life and he knew these roads and all their danger spots like the back of his calloused hand.

Not long after setting off, he had noticed headlights a little way behind him. It was unusual to see another vehicle on the back roads at this time of night and he had thought it strange, but they had long since disappeared, so it couldn't have been anything to worry about. Dismissing the thought, he concentrated on negotiating the last sharp bend and then he was at the A259. He signalled left, pulled out when there was a gap, and set off towards the cottage to pick up the first of his passengers.

Dick Jarvis unbuckled his seatbelt and opened the driver's door with a shaking hand. He got out gingerly, placing his weight on legs that felt like jelly. He didn't think he was injured, but he was badly shocked by the crash. He had been driving too fast, he knew that, but the smuggler had been going like a bat out of hell and he had been in danger of losing him. He hadn't even had time to put it up over the radio.

The impossibly tight bend had appeared out of nowhere and, as Jarvis had stamped on the brakes and desperately tried to steer the Astra around it, the vehicle had locked up and skidded straight into a great big bush. There had been no warning chevrons or anything to alert him to its presence, and he was furious with himself for having misread the road so badly. Now Meade had got away and it was all his fault.

He walked around to the front of the car and shone his torch on the bonnet, expecting to see it mangled. He was pleasantly surprised to see that it appeared intact. Maybe he would be able to reverse out and get after Meade? First, though, he needed to let Steve Bull know what had happened.

Jarvis pulled out his mobile, but he was in a dip and the signal was rubbish. Cursing, he ran back to the car and searched for the Cougar radio, conscious that with every passing second, Meade was getting further away. The radio had slid under the passenger seat and become wedged, and he had to open the back door and wriggle his arm underneath to reach it. Finally, panting from his exertions, Jarvis had it.

"Jarvis to Bull, urgent message, over."

"*Go ahead,*" Bull responded almost immediately.

"Steve, Meade's on the move. He's in his green Land Rover," Jarvis reeled off the registration number from memory. "I'm sorry mate, but I've lost him in the back roads. He was heading towards the A259, so presumably, he's on his way into Rye. Can you and Paul get to the boat ASAP?"

"*How the hell did you lose him?*" Bull demanded, sounding very angry.

"I stacked the car on a tight bend," Jarvis confessed, feeling incredibly stupid. He cringed in anticipation of the scathing comments that were sure to follow.

"*Are you injured?*" Bull asked, surprising Jarvis. He had expected to be shouted at.

"No, just a little shaken," he admitted.

"*What about the car – is it drivable or do you need a garage skipper to report the POLACC?*"

A POLACC was police speak for a police accident.

"No, miraculously, I can't see any damage at all to the car. I just slid off the road onto the verge and ended up stopping with the bonnet buried in a bush. There might be a few superficial scratches, but this car is so old and battered anyway that it'll never notice."

"*Okay,*" Bull said slowly, and Jarvis could hear the cogs turning as his sergeant thought things through. That was one of the things he really liked about Steve Bull. He was so mellow, and always calm under pressure, unlike Charlie White, whose default setting tended to be one of ranting and raving in such an unintelligible Glaswegian accent that no one could understand a word he said. Invariably, he had to repeat everything again when he had calmed down.

"*Right,*" Bull was saying, and Jarvis could tell that he was walking quickly as he spoke from the change in his breathing pattern, "*me and Paul are hot-footing it over to Meade's boat now. I'll let the boss know what's happened. See if you can get the car out of the bush. If you can, meet us at Rye Harbour.*"

"Will do, "Jarvis said, sounding relieved that Bull hadn't apportioned blame on him for losing the target.

"*And Dick?*"

"Yes, Steve?"

"*Drive carefully.*"

CHAPTER THIRTY-FIVE

At precisely 11:07 p.m. the SFOs set off towards the property. Dressed all in black like Ninjas, they were carrying an assortment of carbines, ballistic shields, and a red battering ram.

Tyler and Susie had arrived just as they were getting kitted up to move in, and they now waited with Dillon and the rest of the team a safe distance back from the property where there was no danger of them collecting a stray round if the situation deteriorated into a firefight.

PC Jim Collier, the officer who had conducted the initial recce, had gone back for a final check just before the team deployed, and he had reported back that, as before, the cottage was in complete darkness apart from the living room.

Ideally, armed dig outs like this were carried out at about four o'clock in the morning, when the human body was at its lowest ebb and everyone inside the premises was likely to be fast asleep and, therefore, at their most vulnerable to being caught off-guard. Of course, there were always exceptions to the rule, when speed was of the essence, and everyone agreed that this was one such occasion.

The SFO team leader was a former paratrooper called Tim Newman. In his mid-thirties, Newman stood five foot ten inches tall, had cropped blonde hair, hard grey eyes, and the wiry build of a marathon runner. His every movement was controlled, economical, and he had a well-deserved reputation for being a strong leader who remained focused under pressure and calm under fire.

Like all SFOs, Newman and the men and women under his command were volunteers who had been approved for specialist training following a rigorous assessment procedure. They had then undergone an extremely intensive training programme that lasted nineteen gruelling weeks.

Newman had led many operations like the one he was about to embark on, and to him, this was just another day at the office.

There were no street lights, and as Newman led his team in single file along the country lane that led to the property, he moved slowly, constantly assessing and reassessing the terrain in front of him.

Each member of the team was equipped with a standard-issue Glock 17 SLP as a sidearm. In addition, most carried a Heckler and Koch G36C carbine.

They were all dressed in black, fire-retardant Nomex overalls, boots, and gloves, and wore MICH/ACH (a tongue-twisting acronym that stands for Modular Integrated Communications Helmet / Advanced Ballistic Combat Helmet) Kevlar helmets over Nomex balaclavas. Their ear defenders were linked to the secure radio system they were using, and the bulging black goggles that gave them such a sinister appearance provided all-important eye protection. To give them the best possible protection against incoming fire, they all wore ballistic resistant Kevlar body armour.

In addition to carrying a heavy metal battering ram called an 'Enforcer,' one of Newman's team was also in possession of a Hatton Gun, a short-stock shotgun that fired 'solid rounds' and was used to blow out tyres on vehicles or blast locks off doors.

During the preceding briefing, they had been reminded of their responsibilities in regard to the use of force and the justification required. The ACPO manual of guidance on the police use of firearms was the SFO's Bible, and it gave step-by-step instructions on how to 'identify, locate, contain and neutralise' any threat posed. It stipulated that firearms officers must identify themselves and warn their target that they intended to shoot, and then give the suspect sufficient time for the warnings to be observed.

Dillon had read from the firearms briefing prompt card when he'd addressed them over the use of force prior to their deployment. "According to ACPO," he'd told them solemnly, "the ultimate responsibility for firing a weapon rests with the individual officer, who is answerable to the law in the courts." They had taken the ominous warning in their stride, having heard it a thousand times before.

When Newman reached the side of the cottage, he paused and listened. When he was satisfied that it was safe to do so, he ducked down and crabbed past the living room window, keeping his head below the level of the sill. One by one, all the others in the team followed suit. As he reached the front door, he held up a clenched fist, indicating for those behind to stop. Newman waved the officer with the Enforcer and the two officers carrying the heavy ballistic shields forward. A small section of the team had peeled off and made their way around to the rear of the premises, quietly slipping over the garden fence and taking up a covering position in case anyone tried to flee out of the back. When he received word from them that they were in place, he indicated for the frontal assault team to take their positions.

When Newman was satisfied that everyone was good to go, he held up his right hand and then raised three fingers, one after the other, giving the team a three-second countdown to entry.

As soon as he reached three, he pointed at the door, giving the signal for the breach to occur.

The Enforcer-wielding officer stepped forward and drove the battering ram into the wooden door with tremendous force. It was old and offered little resistance. As the door flew inwards, he stepped aside to make way for the two officers with ballistic shields who raised and interlocked them. Using them as cover, the team advanced into the hallway. There were shouts of "ARMED POLICE, ARMED POLICE, SHOW ME YOUR HANDS."

The hall was completely empty, and apart from the noise coming from the television in the living room, the premises were silent. The hallway was narrow. There was a steep flight of stairs against the right-hand wall leading up into the darkness. The living room door, to their immediate left, was ajar. Beyond this, there was another door, presumably leading into the kitchen.

The mantra of "ARMED POLICE, ARMED POLICE. SHOW ME YOUR HANDS," was being repeated non-stop from behind the raised shields.

On Newman's instruction, the first officer carrying a ballistic shield moved forward and took up station in the doorway of the living room, accompanied by another officer who was aiming his carbine over the top, ready to engage any armed suspects who appeared. The second shield-carrying officer quickly moved past them, going all the way to the end of the hallway and stopping by the kitchen door, he was also supported by an officer pointing a GS36 carbine over his shoulder. Two more officers stopped at the bannister and aimed their weapons up the stairs, ready to return fire on anyone who might start shooting at them from above.

One by one, the team moved into the downstairs rooms and, after checking them out, gave the 'all clear'. Thankfully, someone switched the TV off, bringing blessed silence and making it easier for them to communicate with each other.

With the ground floor now secured, the firearms team advanced to the first floor, where there were three doors, presumably leading into two bedrooms and a bathroom. Using the ballistic shields, these rooms were cleared in the same efficient fashion as the ground floor ones had been.

Lastly, the loft hatch was pulled down, and a very brave officer offered to pop his gun, and then his Kevlar helmeted head, over the top to check if it was empty.

To everyone's relief, it was.

As soon as the cottage was fully under SO19's control, and Newman was satisfied that it was empty, Jack and his team were allowed in.

"I'm getting sick of this," Tyler growled as he walked into the living room and looked around. "Every time we think we've caught a lucky break, it either turns out to be a false lead or the bird has flown the nest minutes before we've arrived."

"Are we sure that this is definitely the right location?" Tim Newman asked, his weapon cradled across his chest and his beetroot red face covered in sweat from having been ensconced in the Nomex balaclava for the last fifteen minutes.

"We are," Jack said. "This address was in the van's Sat Nav."

George Copeland walked over carrying a wastebasket he had found in the bathroom. "Full of blood-stained bandages," he said, holding it up for them to see. "Pound to a penny they belong to Winston."

"So, where have the slippery fuckers disappeared to this time?" Dillon asked, scratching his head.

Tyler sighed despondently. "God knows," he said. "All we can do now is wait for Meade to move, and pray that when Steve follows him to his boat, Winston is there waiting for him."

Jack and Susie were following Dillon and Charlie White back to their previous RVP at *The Bell* public house in Iden when his phone rang, shattering the heavy silence that had prevailed throughout the short journey. They had swapped drivers, so he was able to answer it himself. It was Reg Parker, and he sounded excited. *"Boss, Reggie here. There are developments you need to know about."*

"What have you got?" Tyler asked, feeling pensive. He hoped it was going to be good news for a change; he could really do with some.

"Garston has recently sent a text to Dawlish's phone. It reads: 'No sign of your flat key. Taking Claude to the boat now. Should be setting sail just after midnight so come to Harbour and collect me ASAP. Text back to confirm you are coming. G.' The TIU has just pinged his phone and they confirm it's moving towards Rye Harbour."

"That makes sense," Jack said. "We've not long finished at the cottage. Although it was empty when SO19 went in, there were signs of recent occupation."

"Is there anything more I can do at this end?" Reg asked.

Tyler considered this. "Actually, Reg, there is. On my desk, you'll find a contact telephone number for the Coastguard. Can you speak to Carol Keating and get her to ring them regarding Meade's intended sailing time? I think his boat's called *The Edna May* but check with Dean. He's got all the details of the vessel on his desk. I need Carol to ask the Coastguard if there's any chance of them readying a boat to intercept *The Edna May*, just in case we don't get there in time to prevent her from sailing? Tell her to make sure that whoever she speaks to is made fully aware that Winston's armed and extremely dangerous, and that we can provide SFOs if they want."

"*Do they even do that sort of thing – board vessels, I mean?*" Reggie asked.

"I don't know, "Jack admitted. "But if they don't, they're bound to know how to scramble a naval vessel, or at least notify the French authorities that the boat's heading their way."

"*Good point*," Reg said excitedly. "*Maybe it can be tracked on radar and intercepted at sea.*"

"Maybe," Jack said. "Get Carol onto this straight away for me. In the meantime, we're almost at the RVP at Iden. As soon as we get there, I'll brief the team and get them redeployed to Rye." As he spoke, his phone beeped, letting him know there was another incoming call.

"Reg, I think Steve's ringing me. It might mean the Meade's on the move, so I'll have to go." He quickly killed the call and then tried to answer the incoming one, but only succeeded in cutting Bull off.

"Bollocks," he cursed, redialling Steve's number. "Sorry, Steve, I accidentally pressed the wrong button," he said as soon as they were connected. "What have you got?"

Tyler listened to Bull's latest update in silence.

"Is Dick okay?" he asked when Bull had finished speaking.

Susie glanced sideways at that.

"*He's fine*," Bull reassured him. "*I've told him to head for Rye and meet us there. Me and Paul are just leaving our B&B and heading down to the harbour to plot up on Meade's boat. From what Dick said, the fisherman should be there very shortly.*"

"Let me know as soon as you've got eyeball on the boat. I want to know the minute there's any sighting of Winston, Garston or Meade."

"*You got it, boss*," Bull promised and hung up.

"What happened to Dick?" Susie asked.

Before he could explain, his mobile started ringing again. Tyler frowned. Why was Reg calling him back so soon? He pressed the green button and raised the phone to his ear.

"What's up?"

"*Boss, Garston has started ringing Dawlish's phone. Three calls so far, one after the other.*" In the background a ringtone became audible. "*Make that four,*" Reg said. "*What do you want me to do?*"

"Don't do anything," Jack said. "If we turn it off, he might get suspicious. This way, he'll probably think Dawlish has just left it in another room or something."

Reg grunted. "*Bloody thing is driving me mad,*" he said. "*Oh, and according to the TIU the 777 phone is now in the vicinity of Rye Harbour, so they might already be on Meade's boat.*"

Jack swore. Had they boarded the boat before Steve and Paul had arrived at the Harbour? That would be bloody typical, the way this job was going. If they went down below without being spotted, how could he ever be certain they were on it?

"Keep monitoring and let me know if the phone moves or there are any calls." He hung up and redialled Bull's number.

"Steve, Reg thinks Winston might already be aboard *The Edna May*. Do you have it in sight yet?"

"*We've just arrived,*" Steve told him. "*No sign of any activity on the boat and Meade's Land Rover is nowhere to be seen.*"

"Terrific," Jack said, despondently. Surely, if they were on the boat, there ought to be lights showing and movement on board, maybe even signs of the engines warming up? And where was the bloody Land Rover?

He couldn't put his finger on it but things just weren't adding up.

Rye Harbour was located one and a half miles downstream of the main town, and about three quarters of a mile inland from where the River Rother joined the English Channel. It was a fully functional commercial harbour that was home to a large fishing and commercial fleet.

Within minutes of setting off from the last hamlet, the two passengers had arrived at the harbour and boarded the vessel that would take them to France.

Meade loved this boat. It was a 1978 Lochin 33 with a ten metre long fibreglass hull, equipped with a Raymarine Hybrid Touch Chart and Radar Plotter, a VHF DSC radio and an Autopilot. Powered by an Iveco 280 hp turbo-diesel engine, it wasn't exactly the fastest vessel afloat, but then, for what he had planned tonight, it didn't need to be.

There were berths for five people down below, with a separate head compartment and a hanging locker. There was also a stove and a hob in case anyone wanted coffee or soup, and Meade dropped the supplies off in there while the passengers made themselves comfortable.

The wheelhouse was relatively spacious, and it afforded good all-round visibility from the helm. As Meade stood in it, looking down into the River Rother that would take them out into the English Channel in a few minutes time, he felt more at home than he ever did on land.

The Lochin 33 was a practical, sturdy vessel, capable of crossing the channel equally well in smooth or rough seas. Mainly used as a fishing charter, this particular boat was licenced to carry up to twelve passengers, so his two travellers tonight would have plenty of space to stretch out and make themselves comfortable in.

Meade's son-in-law, a shaven-headed thug with the broken nose of a street brawler called Peter Gregory, had been waiting for them on the boat when they arrived, and while Meade entertained his guests, Gregory lugged their bags aboard and started the engines.

"Everything's going according to schedule," Meade told the two passengers, "and we should be ready to set off in a few minutes."

The black man grunted at him. He was already starting to look queasy.

"You alright, mate?" Kenny Meade asked.

Winston shook his head. "I don't travel well," he said.

Meade sneered. The swell of the sea had never affected him. "Here," he said, pulling a box of Dramamine from a cupboard and tossing them to Winston. "Take a couple of those and you'll be right as rain."

The second passenger was a stocky white man in his late thirties with a tanned complexion, teeth so white that they could only have been veneers, perfectly manicured hands and the sort of fancy layered haircut that TV celebrities often sported. Then again, bearing in mind that he had starred in one of the most popular new soaps on the box until he'd made the mistake of murdering his girlfriend on New Year's Day, that was hardly surprising.

"Do you need anything for the crossing?" Meade asked Craig Masters.

The surly actor shook his head. "I just want to get going," he said, his voice low and tense. It sounded like a line from a script, Meade thought.

"Me too," Winston echoed, looking greener than ever.

"Won't be long now," Meade said, studying a chart. As he took a swig of the rum-laced coffee his son-in-law had just handed him, he made a mental note to ask the tosspot actor for his autograph before he got off the boat; his wife liked that stupid show, and if he bought her the star's signature it might make her go a little easier on him for churning the gravel up when he'd left home earlier.

Access to the English Channel from the River Rother was very straightforward, but navigation was limited by a bar that fronted the entrance and dried to a metre at low tide. There was ample room to clear it at high tide, though, which was due at eleven fifty three. The harbour entrance was forty two metres wide and marked by a red-painted tripod beacon located thirty-metres seaward of the West Groyne.

In strong offshore winds like the ones they were going to experience tonight, the seas in Rye Bay could get very rough, which meant they were in for a lumpy journey when they cleared the harbour. With that in mind, Meade opened a locker and checked that he had sufficient sick bags. He didn't want the black bastard spewing his guts up all over the floor if he got caught short and couldn't make it to the toilet in time.

Both passengers had been told that they could only bring one holdall each, and he was pleased to see they had adhered to the rule. What they hadn't been told was that in the event of Meade not being able to sail directly into the sleepy little fishing harbour that he used for his clandestine visits, he would have to send them ashore in the Zodiac Rib that was secured to the deck, and that would make for a very rocky ride indeed.

Garston and Angela were standing on one of the many jetties that protruded from the quay, waiting for the boat to set sail. It was a quarter to twelve, and Meade had been adamant that he was going to cast off before midnight.

Garston wouldn't be able to relax until he saw it leave with his own eyes.

Angela seemed to have shrunken into herself. "I'm freezing," she bleated through chattering teeth. Junkies didn't do well in the cold. "Can't we go now?"

There was no protection from the elements where they stood, and the wind coming in from the sea was relentless. "No," Garston snapped. He pulled his collar up and tucked his chin into it, gritting his teeth against the biting cold. He'd found a woollen cap in the cottage and it was now rammed over his head, providing some protection for his ears.

Thoroughly miserable, Angela started hopping from foot to foot. "I'm really busting for a pee," she whined.

Garston shrugged indifferently. "Should have gone before we left then, shouldn't you."

"I did," Angela whined pathetically, "but this cold is going straight through me and it's affecting my bladder."

Pulling off a glove, he reached into his pocket and withdrew a ten pound note. "Go and find a toilet," he said, "and then see if there's anywhere open where you can grab us some coffee. While you do that, I'll try ringing that imbecile, Rodent, again."

Angela didn't need to be told twice. She snatched the money from his hand and set off back towards the town without a backward glance. Watching as her hunched up figure was battered by the wind, he wondered how Claude had managed to put up with her for so long without putting a bullet in her feeble brain.

Not long after he'd boarded the passengers, Meade had asked them if they were tooled up. Naturally, both men had said no, but the fisherman clearly wasn't the trusting type. He had explained that it was his policy to search all of his clients before taking them on trips like this, just to make sure that no one tried any funny business out at sea.

"Just so you know, if you've got any guns or knives on you and you don't hand them over now, I'll refuse to take you if anything's found when you're searched," he'd warned them sternly.

As he spoke, Gregory had appeared from the locker below, ominously brandishing a pump-action shotgun.

"Not gonna be any arguments, are there, now?" Meade had enquired sweetly.

Winston's face twisted into a malevolent sneer at the implied threat, and Garston had immediately feared the worst. Thankfully, Winston seemed to have realised that he needed Meade far more than the fisherman needed him and so he had grudgingly surrendered the revolver to Garston for safekeeping.

The actor had seemed genuinely shocked when the firearm appeared.

No real call for guns if you're only going up against women, Garston had thought, loathingly. It was ironic; he would have happily killed for a lifestyle like the one the soft centred actor had thrown away, whereas Masters had killed to lose it.

Looking onto the boat from the jetty, Garston dialled Rodent's number and listened to the dialling tone. "Come on, come on... pick up the damn phone."

After the eighth ring, he gave up and pocketed the mobile. If he didn't get hold of Rodent soon, he would be forced to find an alternative means of getting back to London, and at this time of night, it might not be that easy.

If Rodent let him down, as was now looking more and more likely, the first thing Garston planned do when he arrived back in London was pay a visit to his slummy Star Lane flat and kick the living daylights out of him.

CHAPTER THIRTY-SIX

Steve Bull was becoming increasingly anxious. *The Edna May* was moored next to several similar boats on a pontoon quite close to the Harbour Master's office, but it was in complete darkness and there was no sign of life on board. Paul Evans had gone for a walk around when they had first arrived, and he had reported back that the area was deserted. Furthermore, there was no sign of the green Land Rover Meade habitually drove anywhere in the vicinity. Evans had braved the cold to take another look around a few minutes ago, and he was now on his way back to the car.

"Something's not right," Evans said as he slid into the passenger seat after completing his latest prowl around the harbour. He blew into his hands and rubbed them together vigorously. "If there was anyone on board that boat, I would have seen them, but it's as dead as a bloody graveyard out there."

Steve chewed his lip as he thought about this. Tyler had called him a couple of minutes earlier to say that the team were on their way and would be arriving shortly, along with the covert van containing the SFOs. He was beginning to wonder if it might be better to redirect them to another part of the harbour. But what was the point of that? Meade's boat was here. Surely, this was where he was going to bring the fugitives?

A thought struck him, and he reached for his phone. Dialling the number for the office, he waited impatiently for the phone to be picked up.

Dean Fletcher's dulcet tone answered after the fifth ring. "*Intel Cell.*"

"Deano, it's Steve Bull. Can you do me a favour and check to see if Meade has access to any other boats, only we're plotted up on his vessel and there's no one here."

"*Wait one...*" Dean said, and Bull could hear him rummaging through papers. Just as Bull was beginning to worry that Dean had been distracted by something else and forgotten all about him, the lead researcher came back on the line. "*I can't find anything that specifically links him to another boat,*" Dean said, "*but when I looked at his known associates, I did see that his son-in-law, a horrible piece of work with a history of weapons and violence, also owns a boat that's moored at Rye. It's called The Eclipse, and it's a Lochin 33, whatever one of those is.*"

"Does it say where in the harbour he berths it?" Steve asked, his voice brimming with urgency.

"*Afraid not,*" Dean said. "*Do you want me to try ringing the number for the Harbour master to see if they can help?*"

"Please mate, and tell them it's extremely urgent. I don't think Meade's planning to smuggle Winston out in his boat, and this *Eclipse* is looking like a good alternative."

As soon as he'd finished the call, Steve rang Tyler with the news. "If I'm right, and Meade's gonna use *The Eclipse* to take them across the channel, it could be moored anywhere in the port," he said gloomily.

"*What are the most likely locations?*" Tyler demanded, sounding agitated.

Bull's voice took on a note of panic. "Well, there's Strand Quay in the town itself, and there are numerous private moorings around the harbour, including some along Rock Channel. I think we need to starburst the team and start checking out as many places as we can."

"*I wish you'd flagged this up earlier,*" Tyler said, angrily. "*If our information is right, they're going to sail before midnight.*"

"I'm sorry, boss," Bull said, sounding crestfallen, but Tyler had already gone.

After a frantic call to Dillon, in which he'd instructed him to radio the team and task them with scouring the town and its environs for signs of Meade and his Land Rover, Tyler instructed Susie to pull over at her earliest convenience so that he could have a better look at the map. Almost immediately, she found a public car park opposite the Rye Heritage Centre and pulled in.

It wasn't easy going, but he started to divide the land around the harbour into grids, noting the location of all the car parks and any roads abutting water. Feeling a bit more organised, he began ringing each of the five cars and allocating them with defined search areas to concentrate on. Hopefully, this approach would add some order to the process and avoid some places being swamped and others being overlooked altogether.

He made it clear that he didn't just want them driving around aimlessly. They were to deploy on foot, as many of the boats were berthed below the line of sight from the road, and the only way to make sure that nothing was missed was to take a stroll along the edge of the river.

They sat in the car park for several minutes, twiddling their thumbs and waiting for updates. The only vehicle to pass them was the Astra containing Dillon and Charlie White, which crawled past as it checked out the cars parked along the main A259 to make sure that the elusive Land Rover wasn't hidden in amongst them.

Tyler fidgeted in his seat restlessly. All he could do now was wait, but patience wasn't one of his greatest strengths. He anxiously checked his watch. It was eight minutes before midnight. "I've got a really bad feeling about this," he told Susie.

Pulling out his phone, Jack called Dillon. "Dill, can you put it over the radio that they're to check out any boat with its lights on or engine running."

"*I've already given that instruction,*" Dillon told him.

Jack cleared his throat noisily. "There must be something more we can do?"

"*Jack, we've got Meade's boat staked out. We've got five units searching the harbour area for The Eclipse, and we're checking out all the car parks and roads for the Land Rover. The TIU has confirmed Garston and Meade's phones are in the vicinity of Rye Harbour. What more can we do? Even Tim Newman's team is unofficially having a drive around for us to see if they can spot anything."*

Dillon was right, but it didn't make him feel any better.

Hanging up, he started drumming his fingers impatiently against his knee.

Susie glanced sideways at him and raised an eyebrow. "That's awfully annoying," she said.

His fingers stopped mid drum. "Sorry," he said, sighing dejectedly.

Susie gave him a sympathetic smile. "Why don't we go for a little drive around," she suggested. "It's got to be better than just sitting here."

"Good idea," Jack said, pulling his seatbelt on.

They turned left out of the car park and drove the short distance up to the roundabout with Wish Street. There was a nice-looking café on their right, and a fish and chip shop directly ahead. Closed now, Jack imagined they both did a thriving business during the summer when the town was full of tourists. Taking the first left, Susie drove them across the River Brede and then continued along the A259.

Rye was like a ghost town, but that was hardly surprising; it was approaching midnight on a cold winter's night and a storm was brewing. Anyone with a modicum of sense was at home, safely tucked up in a nice warm bed.

Susie followed the road around to the left, running parallel with the river until they came to Harbour Road. She turned left into this. "I think we've got the SFOs following us," she said after glancing in her rear view mirror.

Jack checked over his shoulder. Sure enough, the dark blue van containing the SFO team was sitting on their tail. Susie pressed the button to make her hazard lights blink a couple of times and the driver gave them an almost imperceptible flash of his headlights in acknowledgement.

They passed a large stretch of grassland in which boats of all shapes and sizes had been mounted on dry dock stands. A sign read, 'Brede River Moorings'.

Jack noticed a small car parking area next to the boats.

"Slow down," he ordered. "Let's make sure Meade's Land Rover isn't concealed amongst this lot."

Susie obliged, but it soon became evident it wasn't there. "Let's move on," she said, and started to accelerate.

"Hang on," Tyler said, placing a hand on her arm. There was a large crane situated just beyond the car park, from where it towered above the quay. If he wasn't much mistaken, he could see the silhouette of a vehicle parked behind it, almost completely hidden from view.

"Let me just quickly go and check out whatever's behind the crane," he said, unclipping his seat belt and opening his door.

"Wait, take this," Susie shouted after him. When Tyler returned to the car, she handed him a Maglite four-cell torch that was about twenty four inches long and made of metal.

"I didn't think we were allowed to use these big long torches anymore," he said with a wry grin.

An edict had been issued by the Yard that officers were only permitted to carry two-cell torches, which were half the size of the hefty beast he now held, whilst on duty. This had come about following several incidents in which officers wielding the four-cell Maglites had used them to defend themselves when situations suddenly turned nasty. Those on the receiving end had complained that the torches had inflicted far worse injuries than police issue batons would have done if used in their place. Of course, many rank and file officers had seen that as a glowing recommendation for the product, and the attempted ban had merely led to a noticeable increase in sales.

"Oh, really?" Susie said, her face a picture of innocence, "I guess I must have missed that memo."

Shining the light in front of him, Jack carefully made his way through the darkness towards the big blue crane.

Up close, it seemed massive.

As he reached the other side, he saw that it wasn't a Land Rover he'd glimpsed from the road, rather it was an old mini-bus, and it was owned by a local church judging from the livery on the side. As he turned to go back to the car, the wind eased off and he thought he heard faint voices coming from the quay. Could it be a couple of his detectives, following his instructions and checking out the boats that were moored there?

Jack decided to find out.

He set off in the direction that the mysterious sounds had come from, moving away from the road and working his way closer to the river. The wind had picked up again and all he could hear now was its fierce howling.

A few seconds later, having negotiated his way through some very thick foliage, he emerged onto a concrete path that ran along the side of the quay. He gingerly walked to the edge and glanced over, looking down into the murky water. To his left, a variety of boats were moored in close proximity to each other along the side of the river. A few were stern in, but most were tied with their bows facing the quay.

One boat immediately grabbed his attention. It was a thirty footer and, not only were the lights on in the wheelhouse, its diesel engines were running loud and smooth.

The voices he had heard had presumably originated from the two men who were huddled together on the wooden jetty that protruded from the quay.

He couldn't make out much about them in the near stygian conditions, except that one was shorter than the other and seemed to be in charge. From the way he moved and the stoop of his back, Jack would have put him at sixty, give or take a few years. He wore a fisherman's cap at an odd angle. The other man, who was taller and far bulkier, had a shaven head and carried what looked like a Pick Axe handle in his right hand.

As he watched, they were joined by a tall, slim male who wore a thick coat and a woollen hat. Jack couldn't be sure, but he thought the first two men were white and the newcomer was black.

His heartbeat started to climb.

Had he just stumbled upon the crew of *The Eclipse*?

He was too far away to be able to read the boat's name, and there was no way he could get any closer without the risk of showing out. If these were the people smugglers, they would be deeply suspicious of anyone moving about at this time of night, especially a stranger. In tight-knit communities like this, everyone knew everyone else.

Jack was about to retreat, intending to circle around them and try to make his way back from the other side, when the man in the cap lit a cigarette. For an instant, his face was bathed in light, as was the face of the third man. That was long enough for Tyler to recognise them from the stills he had seen of Kenny Meade and Deontay Garston.

A slow grin spread across his face. "Gotcha," he said.

For a moment, Tyler stood there, watching the tip of Meade's cigarette dance around in the cold night air like a demented firefly, and then he turned to go.

Maybe this debacle was salvageable after all.

The SFO team hurriedly formed up outside their van. Dressed in their Ninja costumes, and toting enough firepower to start a small war, they checked and rechecked their weapons as they waited for the word to move forward to be given.

The briefing had been rushed. PC Collier had just returned from carrying out a covert recce of the quay, scuttling forward on his stomach like a crab until he could get no closer and then using night vision binoculars to get a clear view inside the boat. He had confirmed that the vessel Jack had spotted was *The Eclipse* and that it was being made ready to sail.

Apart from the three men up on the jetty, he had seen that there were only two people in the wheelhouse, a gigantic black man with dreadlocks and a stocky white guy. Tyler had asked if there had been a woman present, feeling certain that Angela Marley must be there somewhere, but the SO19 officer was adamant that he hadn't seen one.

The most significant observation to come out of the recce was that the shaven-headed guy was lugging around a pump-action shotgun, not a Pick Axe handle. This obviously raised the threat level substantially. They already knew that Winston had a handgun, but going up against a pump gun raised the ante even higher.

Newman had liaised with his Sussex counterparts to request that specialist ballistic injury trained paramedics be dispatched to the scene. He had also requested the attendance of local units to assist with road closures, not that there seemed to be any traffic on the highway at the moment.

It had reached a point in the proceedings where Tyler felt they couldn't hold off any longer and the SFO's needed to move in now, before the boat could set sail.

A soon as Tyler finished giving Newman his final instructions, he rushed back to the Astra and flopped down in the passenger seat. Closing the door to keep out the cold, he opened the Geographia at the page for Rye Harbour and spread it across his knees. Yanking his mobile out of his pocket, he hurriedly dialled Dillon's number. "Dill, where are you and Whitey now?" he asked the moment his friend answered.

"*Er,*" Dillon said, "*Not sure. Where are we now?*" he casually asked his driver.

Jack rolled his eyes. "Seriously! You're telling me you don't know where you are? What would you do if Winston jumped out in front of you right now with a gun?"

"*We'd run the fucker over, wouldn't we Charlie?*"

"*Aye, guv,*" White confirmed jovially. "*I'd quite happily squash that pile of human shite.*"

Anger crept into Tyler's voice. "Dill, stop clowning around and tell me where the fuck you are."

Dillon became serious. "*We're just driving past the spot where we saw you parked up earlier, opposite the Heritage Centre.*"

"Which direction are you heading in?" Tyler asked, running his finger down the page to pinpoint their current location on the map.

"*We're driving in the same direction as the last time you saw us,*" Dillon said. "*Why?*"

"Listen carefully, we've found the boat. It's moored along Harbour Road. SO19 will be going in imminently, but I need you two fuckwits to get your arses over to Rock Channel Quay urgently. It's not far from where you are so I'll talk you in."

Dillon was all business now, his earlier frivolity forgotten. "*Okay, I'm listening.*"

"Any second now, you'll come to a junction on your right called St. Margaret's Terrace. Turn into that. After about fifty yards, it leads into Rock Channel Quay. I want you to follow the road around to the left. About seventy five yards or so after the bend, you'll see a big blue crane on the opposite shore. Beneath it, there's a line of about thirty boats all moored against the quay. The Eclipse is one of those. She's the fifteenth one along if you take the first boat as being the one nearest the crane."

"*Okay,*" Dillon said, "*we're just turning into St. Margaret's Terrace now.*"

Jack remained on the line until his colleagues had the crane and the line of boats he'd described in their sights.

"*We're here, and we can see one boat with its lights on. I take it that's our target?*"

"Yeah, that's the one," Jack confirmed.

"*What do you want us to do?*" Dillon asked.

"The SFOs are about to move in. I want you to make sure the opposite bank is covered in case anyone jumps in the water and tries to swim across. Thinking about it, you'd better call up another car to back you up, just in case they all go overboard."

Dillon was dismissive of this. "*I can't really see anyone choosing to get wet,*" he said. "*Trust me when I say it's no fun.*" Dillon had wound up taking an unexpected dip in the Thames the previous November, during the hunt for the New Ripper.

"Yeah, well, better to be safe than sorry," Jack told him. "Listen, Newman's calling me so I've gotta go. The fireworks should be starting any minute now."

"*Wish them luck from me,*" Dillon said wistfully.

"A section, on me," Tim Newman whispered into his throat mike as he advanced towards the boat, weapon raised. Moving in single file, with the practiced ease of a well-drilled unit, they set off from the car park and padded stealthily towards the blue crane and the moorings that lay beyond.

He had divided his team into two elements, with him leading the frontal assault and his second in command, PC Louise Richmond, bringing the other half in from a side angle to create a pincer movement that would give both detachments clear lines of fire when they engaged the suspects.

"*B section, on me,*" he heard her say through his earpiece

PC Collier had been sent back to act as their scout and to guide the two sections into their target. He had just radioed in to say that all three men had just gone up onto the deck of the boat, leaving the jetty and abutting quay temporarily empty.

Knowing they probably wouldn't get a better chance to close the distance without being seen, Newman had given the order to move in.

They covered the ground quickly, moving past the row of parked cars, and then the crane, and finally the old church mini-van. Crouching down, they then negotiated a stretch of open grassland and stopped by the thick bushes that led out onto the quay.

"A section now at the halfway point," Newman announced. "Can we have an update on the target please, eyeball?"

"*The quay's still clear,*" Collier calmly informed him. "*We have four males on the boat deck and one inside the wheelhouse.*"

"That's all received. Status report, please, Louise?"

"*B section is at the quayside, awaiting instructions,*" she replied almost immediately.

Although she didn't have the benefit of his previous military experience, Newman had found Louise Richmond to be a remarkably cool customer; she was acutely aware of her working environment, tactically astute and virtually unflappable, even when things went pear-shaped.

Newman took a deep breath and exhaled slowly, taking a moment to centre himself. "Very well," he said. "Standby for engagement."

The Eclipse was moored with its stern facing the quay and its bow looking out into the river. To board it, they would have to traverse one of the seven narrow jetties that jutted out from the quay into the river, but doing that would make them visible to anyone on the boat who happened to glance ashore during their approach.

Newman knew they would only have a very short window in which to act, and if they didn't do so decisively, taking control during those first crucial moments of the attack, there was a good chance that the safety of his officers would be compromised.

As he was about to give the command to engage, Jim Collier came over the radio, his voice suddenly full of urgency. *"Standby, standby! All units from eyeball, the group on the deck have split up and two of them are now walking towards the jetty..."*

"Shit!" Newman cursed under his breath, wondering if they had just lost the element of surprise.

"The tall, slim IC3 and the stocky shaven-headed IC1 with the pump-action shotgun are now walking along the jetty towards the quay..."

"Is the IC1 still carrying the shotgun?" Newman demanded.

"Yes, yes," Collier confirmed. *"It's cradled in his right arm."*

"Lou, as soon as they reach the quay, B section is to engage them. If possible, give them a moment to clear the jetty so that we don't get caught in the crossfire. A section will move straight onto the boat to secure the other males. Is that clear?"

"All clear," Louise confirmed, her voice taut. *"B section to engage the two on the jetty once they reach the quayside. A section will take care of the subjects on the boat."*

"Standby," Collier said. *"Both men now onto the quay. The one with the shotgun has taken up station and is now holding the shotgun in both hands. The IC3 is turning left, left, left and walking straight towards B section."*

That changed things. Newman had anticipated that they would either both stay or both leave, not split up. His mind ran through the options at lightning speed.

"B section from Newman," he said breathlessly, "I'm changing the plan. You are to remain where you are. The IC3 is walking directly towards you and should reach your position in approx. thirty seconds. You are free to engage immediately upon establishing visual contact. I repeat, you are to engage upon visual contact. A section will move in and control the IC1 with the shotgun and the boat immediately upon receiving your contact signal. Please acknowledge my order."

"B section is now to engage the IC3 male walking towards us immediately upon establishing visual contact, and A section will nullify the IC1 and storm the boat. Message received and understood."

As Deontay Garston rounded the bend in the concrete path leading away from the quay, head bowed against the brutal wind and hands tucked into his jacket pockets, he suddenly found himself being confronted by a group of sinister shadows pointing Heckler & Koch GS36 assault rifles at him.

"STOP! ARMED POLICE! SHOW ME YOUR HANDS!" several officers shouted at once as they fanned out to cover him.

Garston froze on the spot, conscious of the ME38's handle against his right hand in his pocket. A week ago, he wouldn't have hesitated to draw the weapon and turn the situation into a Mexican stand-off, convinced that the soft British police wouldn't open fire on him unless he started shooting at them first. Now, though, after what had happened with Errol – a man who didn't even like guns – he wasn't so sure.

"Take your hands out of your pockets nice and slow," a woman was saying to him in a voice that brokered no argument.

"It's all cool," Garston said, removing his left hand from his pocket and making a point of doing so extremely slowly so as not to give them an excuse. For the time being, though, he left the right hand where it was.

From back in the direction of where the boat was moored, there were suddenly more shouts of "ARMED POLICE! DROP THE WEAPON. DROP THE WEAPON NOW!" followed by the deep boom of a shotgun and the harsher cracks of carbines being fired.

Taking full advantage of the distraction, Garston spun on his heels and darted into the thick foliage that bordered the path, ignoring the sharp thorns that scratched his face and snagged at his clothes as he fought his way through it.

"What the fuck....?" one of the officers cursed.

"STOP! GET DOWN ON THE FLOOR!" Louise Richmond shouted, furious that he had given them the slip. She doubted that Newman would have allowed himself to be hoodwinked like that, the man was a war machine.

Garston ignored their shouts, confident that they wouldn't dare shoot him in the back. That would be hard to explain, even with no witnesses. A moment later, he exploded out of the other side of the thicket into open grassland. Without breaking stride, he set off towards the road, hoping he'd be able to flag down a passing vehicle and hijack it.

With her weapon clasped tightly against her chest, Richmond had immediately set off in pursuit of Garston, flanked by two colleagues. As the trio attempted to force their way through the thick undergrowth, they were hindered by their equipment, which snagged continuously. In the end, they withdrew and ran along the outside until they found a patch that wasn't as dense. The detour cost them precious seconds.

As they broke through on the other side, they could hear their quarry running up ahead. It sounded like he had opened up a healthy lead, not that they could see him in the total blackness of the night.

"STOP!" Richmond shouted, only to be ignored.

"Bastard!" one of her colleagues shouted as he tripped on a protruding root and tumbled to the floor.

As she ran, the darkness gradually started to become a little less dense, and before long Richmond was able to make out the shape of the crane towering above them. What concerned her the most wasn't the fact that Garston had got away, it was that he was running straight towards the car park where the two unarmed detectives were waiting.

Suddenly, from beyond the crane, two shots rang out in quick succession and then someone screamed.

CHAPTER THIRTY-SEVEN

As soon as Louise radioed through that she had a visual on the black man, Newman led his section forward to confront the meathead standing by the jetty that led down to *The Eclipse*.

Pump-action shotguns are particularly nasty weapons to go up against. Unlike a double-barrelled shotgun, which only holds two rounds, pump guns usually contain anything from five to seven, and they can be fired as rapidly as the holder can rack a new round into the breech. The two most common gauges are twelve-gauge and twenty-gauge. The significance of this, in layman's terms, is that the smaller the gauge, the larger the round, and the more damage it can cause.

There are three different types of ammunition: birdshot, buckshot and solid rounds, sometimes referred to as slugs. These were basically bullets designed for a shotgun, like the Hatton rounds used by SFOs to take out door locks or tyres.

Birdshot is the smallest type of shotgun pellet, mainly used by hunters to shoot birds and small animals like rabbits or squirrels. Buckshot uses much fewer, but far larger, metal pellets. When fired, buckshot pellets disperse outward in exactly the same way that birdshot does, the only difference being that buckshot causes considerably more damage.

As they broke from cover, the man on the jetty caught sight of them and, after a moment's hesitation, he started to raise the shotgun in a threatening manner.

"ARMED POLICE! DROP THE WEAPON. DROP THE WEAPON NOW!"

Ignoring the frenzied police shouts, the bald-headed man placed the stock into his right shoulder, dropping his weight in readiness to absorb the recoil from the shotgun when it was fired.

"Fuck you," Newman heard him respond.

"ARMED POLICE! DROP THE WEAPON. DROP THE WEAPON NOW!" the shouting continued from the SFOs as they took up their firing positions.

Stepping forward, Newman slid the selector of his GS36 from safety to fire. "DROP THE WEAPON!" he shouted, taking aim at the target's centre mass.

There was a loud boom as the shaven-headed man squeezed the trigger, and the man to Newman's right staggered back and fell to the ground. The shooter immediately racked another round into the chamber and fired again, thankfully missing this time around.

With no time to check on his fallen comrade, Newman focused all his efforts on nullifying the gunman, who was already racking the shotgun in preparation for firing a third time.

Newman returned fire. Two rounds, one after the other. He heard other carbines open fire as his colleagues did likewise. The bald man staggered back, dropped the shotgun and fell to his knees, before keeling over sideways and lying still. Newman and two others immediately rushed forward with their weapons unerringly trained on the unmoving figure of the gunman. One of his officers cautiously stepped forward and kicked the shotgun aside, and then shouted, "Clear."

There was movement on the boat. Leaving one officer to perform emergency first aid on the suspect, Newman and the remainder of his section ran along the jetty towards the boat, fully expecting to come under fire again at any second.

The two men who had been inside the wheelhouse had run out onto the deck. One of them, the white male, appeared to be holding a carving knife, but there was no sign of any firearms. When he saw the officers coming at him with carbines, he tossed the knife over the side.

"ARMED POLICE! STAND STILL AND SHOW ME YOUR HANDS!" Newman shouted; a call echoed by his companions.

For a moment, neither man moved, and then, as though the spell had suddenly been broken, both men turned around and bolted towards the bow, vanishing from sight almost immediately.

"Fuck sake," Newman growled, breaking into a run.

As they boarded *The Eclipse*, weapons held at the ready, his team fanned out around him and began slowly advancing towards the wheelhouse.

"Did anyone see where they went?" Newman asked.

No one had.

With Newman in the middle, the three men continued to move forward, ready to open fire in an instant if they had to.

"In the water," the man to Newman's left suddenly shouted, rushing towards the prow. Sure enough, both of the men who had been on the boat were now swimming across the River Brede towards the far bank.

Newman keyed the throat mic. "Newman to Tyler, come in." He had left the detective one of their hand-held radios to monitor proceedings. If he could get word to him that there were swimmers in the water, there was a good chance that Tyler would be able to get units over to the other side to start searching for them. "Newman to Tyler, urgent message, please come in."

Nothing.

"Newman to Richards. Status report, over."

"*Chasing suspect... heading back towards the van...*" she replied breathlessly.

"Oh, for fuck sake," Newman cursed, turning and running back towards the shore.

"You two, stay here and clear the boat," he hollered over his shoulder. He was fairly confident that it was empty, but it still needed to be thoroughly checked out.

As he sprinted along the jetty and back to the quay, he saw his colleague standing over the fallen suspect. The fact that he wasn't working on him could only mean that the man was already dead. The officer shook his head as Newman ran past, seemingly confirming this.

The SFO Newman had seen go down at the beginning of the deployment was now back on his feet, looking winded but otherwise okay. There was a close-cropped cluster of impact holes in the centre of his vest, but its integrity hadn't been breached.

"Are you okay?" Newman called as he ran towards him.

The constable had pulled off his goggles and balaclava and was grimacing. "Fine," he said. "My vest took the brunt, but it still hurts like a bastard."

"Good man," Newman said slapping him on the shoulder as he ran by.

As he ran, he keyed the throat mic again. "Newman to Tyler, please come in," he said, getting no response. He charged through the coarse thicket of bushes and emerged onto the grassland that led back down to the road. Almost immediately, he heard two shots in rapid succession coming from the direction of the road. They had been fired by a small calibre handgun, not a GS36, of that he was certain.

The gunshots were followed by the sound of a woman screaming.

Dillon stood by the quayside wishing that he had a pair of night vision binoculars handy. He could see the lit wheelhouse of the fishing boat moored on the other side of the river, and he could just about make out the shapes of people moving around inside, but he couldn't see clearly enough to work out who was who, which was annoying. Surely, one of them had to be Winston, but which?

He glanced at his watch. "They should be going in any minute now, Whitey," he called to Charlie White, who was still sitting inside the Astra with the heating cranked up to full. "Why don't you come over and join us for a front-row seat?"

White responded with a disinterested shrug. "I can see fine from in here, where it's nice and warm," he replied.

Dillon shook his large head at White to demonstrate his disappointment. He had assumed that being a Scotsman, Charlie would have been used to the cold. He'd obviously gone soft since moving down south, Dillon decided.

Having been released from their observations on *The Edna May*, Steve Bull and Paul Evans had driven over to join Dillon and White in Rock Channel Quay. Unlike Charlie White, they were braving the cold in order to get a better view of the SO19 interdiction.

"After everything we've been through during this job, it feels a bit odd, us not being there for the takedown," Dillon confided to Steve Bull. He kicked a stone across the quay in frustration, sending it tumbling over the edge and down into the water.

Bull regarded him as though he were deranged. "Speak for yourself," he said. "Personally, I'm quite happy over here, out of harm's way."

"Me too," Evans admitted, stamping his feet to keep warm. "I don't mind the occasional bout of fisticuffs, but these bastards are toting shooters."

Dillon couldn't believe his ears. "You're wimps, the pair of you."

Suddenly, the silence was punctuated by the staccato sound of shouting. There was an awful lot of it, but it wasn't coming from the direction of the boat, which was a tad confusing.

"Where's that racket coming from?" Dillon demanded, scanning the opposite shoreline for the source of the disturbance. It wasn't easy with the wind distorting every sound. "It seems to be coming from way over there," he told the others, pointing to an area about a hundred yards to the left of *The Eclipse*.

"I think I just heard someone scream armed police," Bull said, straining his ears.

Almost immediately, there was another outburst of yelling, this time from directly opposite them, where the boat was moored.

Was it a continuation of the first incident, Dillon wondered, or something altogether separate?

"It must be SO19 moving in," Evans suggested.

Shots suddenly broke out, and all three men instinctively ducked behind Bull's car, fearful of being caught by a stray round. Within a few seconds, it was all over, and several SFOs were running along the narrow jetty towards the boat, their combat boots clanking on the wooden slats.

"It's impressive to watch, isn't it?" Evans said, his voice full of admiration.

"I suppose," Bull allowed, although he was hardly brimming with enthusiasm.

As they looked on, two figures appeared at the boat's prow, one towering above the other.

Dillon tensed. "I think that's Winston," he said, involuntarily clenching his fists.

"Who's the other bloke?" Evans asked.

Dillon shrugged. He didn't know and didn't care. "Probably just one of the crew," he said, dismissively.

Amazingly, the smaller of the two men scrabbled over the side. After a moment of hanging there with his legs dangling, he let go and dropped down into the water.

"He must be raving mad," Bull said, shuddering at the unpleasant thought of being immersed in the freezing river on a night like this. He'd once dealt with a case where a man suffered a fatal heart attack after jumping into an ice bath at a Turkish sauna. Death had resulted from a myocardial infarction, which had been brought on by vasoconstriction; a condition where the heart has to work much harder to pump the same volume of blood throughout the body.

"Perhaps his ticker will pack up on him and he'll drown," Dillon said, hopefully. "That would save the taxpayers the cost of a trial."

But the unidentified man in the river didn't die on them; he kicked off from the keel and started swimming away from the boat, being dragged steadily sideways by the strength of the current. As they watched, the second man lumbered over the side, albeit with far less dexterity, and dropped like a stone into the water. He splashed and spluttered, appearing to be experiencing some difficulty staying afloat, but then he stabilised himself and started doggy paddling towards the opposite bank.

Dillon glanced sideways at Bull and Evans, his eyes burning with mean determination. "You two, grab Whitey and go after the first one," he said through gritted teeth. "The second one's Winston, and he's all mine."

Unlike the clueless TV star, who was trying to swim straight across to the opposite shoreline, Winston was content to drift with the current and let it take him as far away from *The Eclipse* as possible.

He wasn't good in the water and he wasn't particularly buoyant, and his clumsy attempt at a doggy paddle was probably better described as slow drowning than swimming. Nonetheless, he knew his best chance of escape lay in getting as far downstream as he could before making for land, so he flapped his arms and kicked his legs awkwardly, swallowing huge mouthfuls of dirty water every few strokes, and kept repeating his mantra of, "better to die than to be caught."

As Meade's boat receded from view, Winston could feel his energy fading fast, sapped as much by the weight of his waterlogged clothing as by the bitter cold of the water. Thankfully, his stitches appeared to be holding firm and, with each sluggish stroke, he was slowly dragging himself across the Brede and getting closer to his objective on the opposite river bank.

When he was about halfway across, his painfully slow progress hampered by cramping legs and searing lungs, he paused to tread water and catch his breath. Suddenly, his head went under and he felt himself sinking fast. As the dark water closed around him, dragging him down, Winston was overcome by a deep sense of dread. His mouth opened in an involuntary scream but, instead of the air he so desperately craved, polluted river water flooded into his nostrils and gushed down the back of his throat. His body jerked in shock as the foul liquid cascaded into his lungs, causing acute spasms of pain that seemed to spread through every fibre of his being.

Was this it?

Was this the end?

With what felt like a superhuman effort, he thrashed his tired legs and weary arms wildly until he finally forced himself back to the surface. Hungrily gulping down air as every cell in his body screamed for oxygen, Winston tried to suppress the mindless panic that was threatening to take control.

Winston knew that if he didn't get out of the water soon, he would go under again, and the next time he might not be so lucky. Spurred on by fear and adrenaline, he set off with renewed determination towards a half-dozen boats that were moored against what was now the nearest section of Rock Channel Quay. Maybe, he would be able to hide out on one of those until the heat died down?

After what seemed like forever, he reached the keel of the first boat and dragged himself along its length until he came to a wooden ladder that led up to the quay. Struggling for breath, he pulled himself upwards, each step draining him more than he would ever have imagined possible. When he reached ground level, he hoisted himself onto the concrete quayside and flopped down onto his hands and knees. With his head spinning and his limbs trembling, and with water pooling on the floor all around him, he gratefully sucked in air and swore to himself that he would never go swimming again.

Craig Masters was a strong swimmer. At school, he had completed all his swimming badges with ease, and he still regularly went to the pool as part of the rigid exercise regime he carried out to keep himself looking good in his role as Steve Michaels on *Docklands*.

Even as he swam across a freezing river in the middle of a cold winter's night, with the police hot on his trail and his freedom at stake, all he could think about was the lavish lifestyle that had so cruelly been snatched away from him just as his star was finally beginning to rise.

Only the week before Katie's death, his agent had been in contact to say that he was being considered for a big role in an upcoming action film that would bring him to the attention of the big Hollywood studios.

As he carved his way through the water with an effortless front crawl, one thought repeated itself over and over in his mind: How had everything gone so wrong for him so quickly?

He reached the opposite bank and began climbing one of the

wooden ladders that led up to the quay above. He was confident that none of the gun-carrying police officers would have been inclined to jump in and come after him.

A few short days ago, Masters had felt like he had the world at his feet; that it was just sitting there ripe for the taking. Now, the best he could possibly hope for was getting out of the country and setting himself up somewhere that didn't have an extradition treaty with the UK.

But even if he managed to avoid going to prison, his glittering career was over, and he was far more devastated by that than he was over the death of his stunning, trophy girlfriend.

Poor Katie. No one would ever believe him, but he hadn't even meant to hurt her, let alone kill her.

Theirs was a tumultuous relationship, but he had loved her in his own selfish way, and, ironically, it had been his foolish desire to please her that had ultimately led to his undoing.

They had been out partying until the early hours of New Year's Day, and by the time they returned to the luxury flat that they shared, they had both been as drunk as skunks and stoned out of their heads. Instead of calling it a night, they had opened another bottle of bubbly and then snorted a few more lines of cocaine. When they finally retired to the bedroom, Kathie had still been wired, and she had insisted on trying something new – something ultra-kinky.

The strangling had been her idea. She had read somewhere that autoerotic asphyxiation greatly heightened sexual pleasure, and she wanted to find out for herself if this was true. He hadn't been nearly as keen as her, but she had promised to let him do her up the arse if he went along with her warped little fantasy, and she didn't often agree to that, so he had played along.

In many ways, Katie was a wonderful girl, but she was also a wild child who was always looking to push boundaries. Well, she had pushed them a little too far this time, and now they were both paying the price for her licentious behaviour.

Maybe he'd got a little too carried away as he'd squeezed her neck, but in his defence, being throttled had really seemed to be turning Katie on – that is, until it had turned her off, permanently.

It was only after he'd shot his load that he realised Katie had stopped breathing, at which point he began frantically shouting at her and shaking her by the shoulders. When that didn't work, he'd tried slapping her face like they do in the films. Her pretty face seemed frozen in pain and shock, and her bulging blue eyes seemed to be staring up at him accusingly, giving him a bad case of the heebie-jeebies.

Throwing on some clothes, he had run out into the hallway, tearfully shouting for help.

When no one responded, he rushed back inside, hunted around the flat until he found his mobile, and then he'd called for an ambulance. He had stupidly told the 999 operator that he had strangled his girlfriend but hadn't explained that it had been consensual, done as part of an S&M sex game they were playing. The operator had calmly tried to talk him through performing emergency life support, but he was all over the place, his mind fogged by alcohol, drugs, and shock.

Masters had left the front door ajar when he'd returned, and a few moments later his next-door neighbour, whose slumber had been interrupted by his screaming, came barging in to complain about the noise.

The elderly man had stopped in his tracks, stared aghast at Katie's naked body sprawled on the bed, and stammered, "Oh my God! You've murdered her."

It was that comment that had caused Masters to go on the run. Up until that point, he'd had every intention of staying with her and explaining to the ambulance crew that Katie's death had all been a tragic accident. Suddenly, though, it became crystal clear that no one would believe him. With Katie dead, there was no one else who could verify his account, and without a witness to provide corroboration, it looked really, really bad.

Throwing some clothing into a holdall, he had grabbed his Rolex, his car keys, all the cash he had in the flat, and his passport, and then he had fled the scene.

With water streaming off him, and his expensive shoes squelching, Masters ran past some luxury riverside apartments, through a car park and out onto the service road that ran through Rock Channel Quay.

He was acutely aware that it would only be a matter of minutes before the police turned up to search for him.

Masters spotted a building that, according to the sign outside, was used by the Sea Cadet Corps. He did a quick loop of the perimeter, checking for open windows or fan lights. If he could find a way to get inside, it would make an ideal spot to hole up in until the morning, at which point he could reassess his options.

The sound of fast-falling footsteps echoing off the concrete floor came as a complete shock. Ducking into the shadows, he spotted three white men in scruffy clothing running along the quay towards him. The two on the outside were holding torches, and the man sandwiched between them seemed to be their leader.

"He came ashore along here," the man in the middle yelled, indicating for the others to fan out.

They were looking for him, he realised with a sinking heart. The question was, were they cops or private security? Their torch beams crisscrossed each other as they scythed through the darkness, drawing ever nearer. Hardly daring to breathe, Masters stood motionless with his back pressed into the wall.

His pursuers were rapidly closing in on him and Masters calculated that he only had, at best, a few seconds before one of the torch beams lit him up and gave his location away.

Head spinning and heart thumping, Masters took a deep breath and bolted away from the building line, cutting across an almost empty car park that backed onto what he assumed was a small industrial estate. There were a half dozen warehouse type buildings to his immediate left, and another complex of similar interlinked buildings lay just beyond those. Directly in front of him, two rows of heavy goods vehicles had been parked up overnight.

Masters hesitated, trying to decide which way to go for the best. The sound of approaching footsteps forced him to make a quick decision and, on a whim, he ran to his left.

"Oi, You, stop there," a harsh voice shouted as a beam of light immediately illuminated his fleeing form. He had an ear for accents, and he was pretty confident his challenger was Welsh.

"POLICE! STOP!" the leader of the three men hollered after him, but Masters ignored this and kept running for all he was worth.

As he slipped down the side of the nearest warehouse, he could hear the policeman in charge breathlessly talking into a radio, calling for back up. Somehow, he managed to double back towards the service road, leaving the cops searching the area he had just vacated, but as he stepped away from the building line and into the exit road, a security light came on.

"Where's that light coming from?" one of his pursuers exclaimed.

"Over there," another responded, and he heard them break into a collective run.

"Shit," Masters cursed, making a dash for it and praying that he could get across the service road and back under cover before they reached his current location.

Suddenly, a car was powering along the service road towards him, engine roaring as the driver thrashed it in a low gear. The headlights were on main beam, and they were almost blinding him. He tried to shield his eyes as he ran and, as a result, he cannoned straight into the side of an industrial bin that lay in his blind spot and went flying over the top of it.

Covering ground rapidly, the car did a snazzy handbrake turn and skidded to a halt about fifteen feet away from him, whipping up a large cloud of dust that spiralled outwards making him cough. The driver's doors opened and a skeletal thin white man with a goatee emerged from inside.

"POLICE! STAY WHERE YOU ARE," he shouted determinedly, at the same time raising a small cylindrical object in his right hand.

Masters could hardly believe his luck. He almost laughed at the pathetic excuse for a cop who was trying to apprehend him. Spitting on the floor contemptuously, Masters broke into a run and charged straight at him, intending to swat the skinny cop aside and steal his car.

Seemingly undeterred, the plain-clothed officer raised his left arm, palm facing out. He rolled his neck and took aim with the object in his right hand. "STAND STILL, ARSEHOLE," the cop yelled.

Masters didn't like being called names, and he decided to give the dweeb a good hard slap for his insolence. Uttering a battle roar that took him back to his schoolboy rugger days, he bore down on the smaller man at a frightening speed.

The gap between them closed to twelve feet, then ten, then eight, then...

"AAARRGGHH!" Masters cried out as a jet of CS spray hit him square in the face. The pain was excruciating and he clawed at his eyes to wipe the noxious substance off.

"You've just been sprayed with a shitload of CS incapacitant," the copper was casually saying, "and I hope it hurts like a fucking bitch."

As Masters dropped to his knees, unable to open his eyes and struggling to breathe, the three men who had chased him from the Sea Cadets' building reappeared.

"You lot couldn't catch a cold," Kevin Murray said, shaking his head contemptuously. He was leaning on the Astra's roof, watching dispassionately as Masters writhed about in agony.

"What's up with him?" Evans asked.

Murray held up the cannister in his hand. "I wouldn't go too close just yet," he informed them, "only I've just given chummy a liberal dose of CS."

"I can see," Steve Bull said, giving Masters a very wide berth in case the wind started spreading the gas cloud. "You heard me put up the chase over the radio, then?" he asked, joining Murray by the car.

"Good job for you I did," Murray replied. He looked down at the little cannister in his hand. "Always wanted to get a chance to try this stuff out. Turns out it works pretty well."

Bull raised the radio to his lips and announced that they had one in custody, just in case any other units were breaking their necks trying to reach them.

"Well," Murray said, "it was lucky for you I was nearby or this one might've got away."

"We had it under control," Bull said, defensively.

Murray sneered. "Course you did, Stevie boy."

Evans took a circuitous route to join them, leaving young Jarvis to worry about providing aftercare. "Any word from Mr Dillon yet on the other scumbag who jumped overboard?"

"No," Bull said unhappily, "and I can't begin to tell you how much it worries me that Winston's still on the loose."

"Where was he last seen?" Murray asked, getting back into the car.

Steve pointed back towards the river's edge. "Over there, on the other side of the car park."

"Well then," Murray announced casually. "I suppose I'd better go and find the dopey knuckle-dragging twat and save him, too."

CHAPTER THIRTY-EIGHT

The quay on this section of the river bank was home to a myriad of boats that came in all shapes and sizes; some were fishing charters; others were pleasure cruisers. Winston was unable to force entry to the first three that he tried, but on his fourth attempt, he got lucky and found an unlocked door. Thankfully, with no streetlamps or moonlight to illuminate his skulduggery, he'd been able weave his way through the shadows unseen.

The boat was a very well maintained fifty four foot long steel gaff-rigged cutter, and from its pristine condition, Winston assumed that it was its owner's pride and joy.

Dripping water everywhere, Winston poked his head through the wooden door, waited several moments to see if anyone challenged him, and then cautiously descended the deep companionway steps that led down into the unlit pilothouse. Once at the bottom, he paused again, listening like a furtive animal for any sounds of movement coming from further inside.

There was a large, bespoke skylight above the boat's saloon, constructed from stainless steel, wood, and glass, but the sky was so black above them that the ambient light coming in through it hardly made any difference to the darkness inside.

His right hand brushed against something cold and metallic, and when he glanced down, he saw it was a big red fire extinguisher attached to the bow wall by two thick brackets.

The recesses on either side of the companionway steps each contained double berths. The mattresses were currently unmade, but a stack of neatly folded bedding and two puffy pillows sat in the centre of each cot so that it could quickly be made ready for use whenever it was required.

Winston agitatedly fumbled around the walls until he found a light switch. When he flicked it on, the saloon's interior was bathed in a warm glow. His eyes darted around the boat's interior, taking everything in. There was a well-equipped galley running along the port side to his left, and he instantly clocked the two rows of carving knives that protruded from the wooden rack next to a four ring hob.

On the starboard side of the cutter, a full-size chart table was full of dials and instruments he didn't understand. Beyond this was a lavish wrap around seating area, big enough to comfortably accommodate six, with varnished oak shelving containing an assortment of books and nautically themed ornaments above it. A circular table was bolted to the floor directly in front of the plush seats.

Unimpressed by the obvious opulence, Winston rushed straight through the saloon, snatching the largest of the knives from the rack as he went. His first priority was to establish whether there was anyone aboard who might raise the alarm, and with that in mind, he began a frenetic search.

Pulling open a door that led off the main living area, he came upon a toilet and shower room – Meade had told him it was called 'the heads' on a boat. Beyond that, another door led through to a cabin at the front of the vessel that contained the master sleeping area.

A vanity sink in an ornate marble surround was mounted in a cubby hole just to the left of the door. On the right, there was a good-sized storage locker Ahead of him a double cot hugged the boat's contours, tapering gently inwards the nearer it got to the prow. As in the living area, the walls were mainly covered in oak panelling, giving the place an expensive and very classy feel.

Winston noticed there was an access hatch right above the bed.

Secured with steel clasps, it presumably led up onto the deck and provided an escape route for the occupants in an emergency.

To his relief, not only was the boat completely empty, but it bore no signs of recent occupation, and he got the distinct impression that it had been put into a state of hibernation for the duration of the winter. The owners hadn't secured it properly when they'd left it, but that was the trouble with having so much money; it made you sloppy and complacent.

Returning to the saloon, he pulled all the curtains so that no one could see in, and then he set about checking the galley cupboards for provisions. Unfortunately, as he'd expected, there were no supplies on board, apart from a tin of instant coffee and some sugar. He poured some water into the electric kettle, plugged it in and turned it on, hoping a hot drink would warm him up. He was so cold that his teeth were chattering.

As soon as he'd caught his breath, Winston returned to the heads and started pulling off his wet clothing, dropping each item on the shower floor. He would wring them all out and then hang them up to drip-dry wherever he could find a space.

The bandage around his torso was also waterlogged. Removing it carefully, he was both pleased and relieved to see that the stitches had held. Old Horace had done a good job with the repair, he grudgingly conceded.

After a quick rummage in one of the cupboards, he emerged carrying two thick towels and a huge bathrobe. The white towelling robe only just about fit him, but it would have to do. Standing on the first towel to keep his feet warm, he sat on the toilet and began vigorously drying his hair with the second.

Winston decided that the safest thing he could do at the moment was to remain exactly where he was and wait until the heat died down. He wondered what had happened to Garston, Meade and his son-in-law, the wannabe tough guy with the shotgun. With any luck, he'd offed a couple of pigs before they'd taken him down with their return fire.

Winston wasn't sure what to do next. He had plenty of contacts back in the Big Smoke, but none of them were people smugglers. As a last resort, he could always approach that no good weasel, Flogger. The man was an unprincipled cut-throat, but he seemed to have his gnarly fingers in all sorts of pies and he had certainly helped his nephew out by sourcing the medical attire and name tags. Maybe he could put him in touch with someone who could help.

As the kettle boiled, he heard the yelp of approaching sirens. There were lots of them, and they seemed to be converging on the quay from several different directions.

Killing the lights, he pulled back the pilot house curtain and peered out onto the road at the end of the jetty. Almost immediately, several marked police cars came hurtling into view, travelling in convoy along the road that bordered Rock Channel Quay.

―――――

Dillon was furious with himself for having lost sight of Winston as he'd floundered his way across the river towards Rock Channel Quay. The gangster had been making for a cluster of boats that were moored quite a way downstream, and although Dillon had run like the clappers to try and head him off before he reached land, by the time he'd arrived, the fugitive seemed to have disappeared into thin air.

Half hoping that he'd got into difficulty and gone under, Dillon spent the next few minutes frantically sprinting up and down the quay searching for Winston.

Feeling utterly deflated, he rang Bull to organise some back up. Annoyingly, there was no reply, so he tried calling Jack instead. When that didn't work, he tried Susie, but even she wasn't picking up.

He stared at the phone in disbelief. "What the hell are they all playing at?"

Relief flooded through him when a column of Sussex units raced along the quay on blues and twos before pulling into a big car park that adjoined a row of warehouses.

As he ran towards them to enlist their help, Dillon spotted Jarvis and Evans standing beside a bedraggled looking man in handcuffs. From his sodden state, it was clear that this was the first of the two men who had jumped overboard.

Some of the Sussex uniforms stared at him warily as he bore down on them. As their hands instinctively gravitated towards their batons, he hurriedly produced his warrant card and shouted out that he was a Met officer, which seemed to alleviate their fears.

"What happened to Winston?" Evans shouted.

"He's gone to ground," Dillon replied, gathering everyone around him to explain what had happened.

"We need to search this side of the river as a matter of urgency," he said, breathlessly. "We're looking for an IC3 male in his thirties. He's a big ugly fucker with dreadlocks, so you can't miss him. I'm pretty sure he's gone to ground by that long line of boats over there, so as long as we can contain the area, we should be able to flush him out."

After directing them to start the search at the point where Winston was believed to have come ashore, he asked one of the PCs to get on the Force radio and request the attendance of a dog unit. He also asked for Sussex police's helicopter to do a fly over using Infra-Red. If Winston had gone to ground, it would be virtually impossible to spot him in the dark with the naked eye, but his heat signature would radiate him like a beacon to the helicopter. The officer nodded enthusiastically. Happy to do anything he could to assist catching a cop killer, he ran back to his car to radio Sussex police's control room.

Dillon returned to the point where he thought Winston was most likely to have come ashore. Looking over the river's edge, he shone his torch down into the murky water and walked along the quay until he reached a wooden ladder that led down to the waterline. The battery was on its last legs, and the weak beam of light flickered constantly.

"Don't you dare pack up on me now," Dillon warned it.

He shone the light over the concrete beneath his feet, hoping to find a big pool of water from where the soaking wet fugitive had recently ascended from the river below.

The ground was bone dry.

Dillon grunted his disappointment.

The moorings in this section of the river here had steel-piled walls with timber fendering, and access ladders were located at every fifteen metres. Dillon jogged to the next one along, and this time his efforts were rewarded by a large puddle on the concrete next to the ladder.

"Bingo," he said, triumphantly. As he scythed his torch backwards and forwards over the cracked concrete path, he spotted a trail of wet splodges moving away from the waterline. With a little twinge of excitement, Dillon followed its erratic path like a bloodhound that had just caught a scent.

The trail quickly went cold, but it had been heading straight for a group of expensive looking cruisers that were moored about 150 yards further along the quay.

Dillon rushed over to the first boat, climbing aboard via a narrow wooden jetty. He tried the door and windows, but they were securely locked and there was no sign of any attempt to force entry.

He repeated the process with the second and third vessels, but they were equally secure.

The fourth boat was a fifty-plus foot cutter. Dillon climbed onto the deck and tried the door to the wheelhouse, but like the others, it was locked. He couldn't see inside because the curtains were drawn. There was a very impressive skylight beyond the wheelhouse, and he made his way over to this, cupped his hands against the glass and peered inside. He could just about make out a plush living area and a long galley down below, but he couldn't see any obvious signs of habitation.

Seconds later, he was back on the quay, cold and disappointed.

"Excuse me," a timid voice behind him whispered, and it sounded so eerie that he almost jumped out of his skin.

Dillon instinctively spun around, his fists raised in readiness, only to find a slim, elderly man clad in a dressing gown and furry slippers. White hair blowing in the wind, the pensioner was gripping a polished wooden cane in his arthritic hands, ready to let swing if Dillon tried any funny business with him.

Dillon lowered his shovel sized hands and forced a smile onto his face. "Can I help you?" he asked, trying his hardest to be polite.

The distinguished-looking old codger hesitated, and then took a tentative step forward. He shrugged the bony shoulders of his age withered frame. "I – I might ask you the same thing," he stammered. "What do you think you're doing, skulking around in the middle of the night, trying to break into people's boats? Just so you know, I've called the police, so whatever mischief you and your friend are up to, you won't get away with it." As he spoke, he nervously flexed his fingers around the cane's grip, and Dillon saw the veins under his parched skin wriggle like sluggish worms.

Dillon let out a low growl of frustration. Reaching into his back pocket, he pulled out his warrant card and flashed it at the cane-wielding man. "I *am* the police," he said, tersely. "and I'm looking for a dangerous suspect, so I suggest you retire to your boat and let me get on with it."

He started to turn away but then paused. "Hang on a minute grand-dad," he said, glaring at the windswept pensioner, "what exactly do you mean: 'me and my friend?'"

The man huffed indignantly. "The big black man who tried to get into my boat a few minutes before you did. Don't pretend you don't know who I'm talking about."

Dillon's eyes narrowed. "I don't suppose you saw where he went after he left your boat, did you?" he asked impatiently.

The man nodded. "He went aboard *The Golden Sunrise*," he said, nodding towards the boat that Dillon had just vacated.

"Are you sure?" Dillon asked, glancing back at the vessel over his shoulder.

The white-haired man stiffened. "I'm old, not senile," he said, huffily.

"And is he still in there?" Dillon asked.

The old man shrugged. "I don't know that he even went inside," he said, becoming crotchety as his confidence grew, "just that he tried the door. The lights came on a few seconds afterwards, so there must be someone aboard, which probably scared him away."

Dillon grunted. "There aren't any lights on now," he said.

The old man tutted at the stupidity of the statement. "Well, of course not," he said, labouring the last word. "No doubt, they went straight back to bed after seeing the fiend off."

Dillon jerked his thumb at the cutter. "Do you know the people who own that boat?"

"It won't be them," the man said with complete certainty. "They're off skiing in Canada for two weeks. They must have rented it out or asked someone to boat sit for them."

Dillon decided to go back and find out.

"Thank you for your time," he told the elderly man, who was, by now shivering from the cold. "I'll go and have a word with them."

Dillon made his way back to the cutter and knocked on the wheelhouse door loud enough to rattle the glass. "Police. Can you open up." He gave it a few seconds, but when there was no sign of movement inside, he knocked even louder. "Open the door. This is the police and I need to speak to you."

His mobile rang. It was Steve Bull. *"Boss, the dog unit has arrived. Where do you want the handler to deploy his land shark?"*

"Send him over to me," Dillon said. "I'm by a boat called *The Golden Sunrise*. Can't miss it, it's a fifty foot cutter."

Inside *The Golden Sunrise*, Winston had hurriedly dressed in his still wet clothes and then concealed himself in one of the double berths that came off the wheelhouse. He lay with his back pressed against the hull, hardly daring to breathe in case he gave his location away.

His insides twisted with hatred. Dillon had been a constant thorn in his side since they'd first crossed paths last year, and he was determined to take care of him once and for all before making a run for it.

The carving knife's plastic handle felt very comforting in his hand, and he had no doubt that it would feel equally good to ram twelve inches of cold hard steel into the interfering detective's gut.

Sliding across the bed until he reached the end, he crawled across the wheelhouse floor and took up a position behind the door. Heart beating like crazy, he gently undid the lock.

Come on, pig, come in and let me skewer you.

Nothing happened.

Winston visualised sticking the knife in Dillon's stomach and twisting it backwards and forwards as he stared into the pig's dying eyes. "Come on, come on..." he hissed. "Open the fucking door and let me kill you."

Still nothing.

Growing impatient, Winston reached out and gently twisted the door handle, cringing as the mechanism clicked. Nervously licking his lips, he pulled it inward, allowing the door to open an inch. Surely, the dumb pig would see this and get curious?

———

Dillon had remained on the cutter's deck because, despite being more exposed to the elements up there, its elevated position gave him a slightly better view of the search now being carried out along the quay than he'd get from the jetty.

To their credit, the local officers were systematically working their way along the moorings from the start of the quay towards his current location, while other officers had been given fixed points at strategic locations to ensure that all the possible exit routes were covered.

As he awaited the dog handler's arrival, he casually glanced back at the cutter's door, wondering if he should try and wake up the occupants one last time.

He almost didn't notice that anything had changed at first, and when he did, he wondered if his eyes were playing tricks on him.

"What the...?" Dillon shone the torch onto the door, confirming that it was definitely ajar. His face morphed into a mask of suspicion. It had definitely been locked before. He knew that for sure because he had tried the handle several times, pulling it so hard that it had almost snapped off. Something was wrong here; how could it have possibly sprung open on its own?

"Hello," Dillon called out, walking cautiously towards the door. "Is anyone inside?"

As before, there was no response.

He pushed it open and shone his torch inside, but the beam was so weak by now that it barely illuminated the companionway steps that led down into the saloon. Almost immediately, the light flickered and then went out.

"Great," he said, violently shaking the torch. When that didn't work, he tried slapping it but it was obviously dead. He shoved the torch into his coat pocket, wishing that he'd had the foresight to put new batteries in before leaving the office.

Dillon cautiously poked his head into the blackness within. "HELLO. IT'S THE POLICE," he bellowed. He was about to step inside and feel for a light switch when a shapeless form detached itself from the blackness around it. Ragged breathing accompanied the movement, and Dillon had been doing the job long enough to recognise the sound of a desperate man preparing to make a dash for it when he heard it. Feeling the hairs on the nape of his neck stand up, he retreated into the centre of the deck, running his eyes over it for something that could be used as a makeshift weapon.

"It's over, Winston, so you might as well come out," he yelled, knowing he was wasting his breath but feeling compelled to at least try and reason with the man. He wished the dog handler would hurry up; in his experience, even psychotics like Winston tended to think twice about having a go when a salivating German Shepherd was snapping at them.

"Don't be a mug," Dillon told him. "It won't end well for you if you kick-off, so why don't you just do the sensible thing for once and come quietly?"

As the first bitingly cold drops of rain started to fall, blown inland from the English Channel, Dillon raised his eyes to the heavens. At that precise moment, a huge figure exploded out of the wheelhouse door in a feral howl of rage and charged at Dillon, its right hand held above its head.

Dillon's eyes widened as he caught sight of the fearsome blade protruding from the gangster's hand, and he instinctively took a hurried step backwards to put some distance between them.

There was no time for conscious thought, only instinctive reaction as Dillon somehow managed to duck under the incoming blow and swivel out of harm's way.

Winston's forward momentum carried him straight past the detective, who shoved him hard in the back, propelling him into the ship's wheel at the bow of the boat.

Snagging his arm on one of the protruding spokes, Winston

screamed in anger as he wrenched it free and spun to face the detective.

The rain was getting heavier by the second.

"Drop the knife," Dillon yelled, crouching to meet the next attack.

"Ain't gonna happen, pig," Winston snarled, his eyes blazing with madness.

Aware that there wasn't a lot of room for manoeuvre on the deck, Dillon backed away until he bumped into the wheelhouse door. He knew he could probably slip inside before Winston reached him, but it had never been Dillon's style to retreat. Besides, if he did that, Winston would just kick it open and follow him in, at which point he would find himself trapped in a confined space and completely at the gangster's mercy.

Grinning insanely, Winston made a show of twirling the knife in his hand as he advanced, enjoying the look of fear that flitted across the detective's face. Suddenly, he lunged wildly at Dillon, unleashing a vicious horizontal backhand slash that was intended to separate his head from his shoulders.

Dillon instinctively threw himself sideways, smashing into the wheelhouse doorframe with his left shoulder as the steel blade missed his throat by millimetres.

Winston took a step backwards and then came straight back in, this time trying to stab Dillon through the abdomen. Sucking his stomach in, Dillon pivoted sideways like a matador, but not in time to avoid the incoming blow altogether. The wickedly sharp blade effortlessly sliced through his coat and jumper, and he felt a burning flash of pain as it made contact with his flesh.

The rain was coming down in great force now, making the deck slippery underfoot. As Winston circled him, getting ready to attack again, Dillon swiped his hand across his face, desperately trying to wipe the water away from his eyes

There was a flash of lightning out at sea, and for a moment the hulking form of the gangster was illuminated. "I'm gonna skewer you, pig," he taunted, "and then I'm going to cut off your ugly fat head and mount it on the ship's wheel for all to see."

"Bring it on," Dillon growled through gritted teeth. He could already feel the hot trickle of blood running down his skin but the battle rage was on him now and he didn't care.

This time, Winston came at him with a fierce backhand slash, and Dillon sprung backwards moving just out of range. Winston advanced relentlessly, slashing inwards this time, but instead of retreating, as he had for both previous attacks, Dillon stepped straight inside the swinging arm and grabbed hold of it, pulling it tight against his body. The gangster reacted by trying to yank his arm free, and as he did, Dillon drove his right elbow back into his opponent's face with jarring force. There was a deeply satisfying crunch, and Winston yelped in pain.

Stunned by the blow, Winston's arm went slack, and Dillon took advantage of this to smash his opponent's knife hand against the boat's safety railing. Once, twice, three times, he struck bone against metal, but the gangster stubbornly refused to let go.

Suddenly, Winston reached over Dillon's head with his left hand and dug his fingers into the detective's eye sockets, yanking backwards with all his might.

Flexing his enormous neck muscles, Dillon shook his head left and right, like a dog drying itself, but he couldn't break free of the other man's grip. Before long, Dillon's head had been pulled against his adversary's shoulder, leaving his neck dangerously exposed.

With Dillon now totally off balance, Winston found himself in the ascendancy, and he lost no time in trying to drive the knife upwards into his adversary's throat, laughing maniacally as it closed in on its target inch by inch.

As the blade drew nearer, Dillon grew increasingly desperate. In a last-ditch effort to break free, he stamped the heel of his foot into Winston's instep. The gangster screamed, and his grip slackened for long enough for Dillon to take a sideways step and drive his fist downwards until it smashed into Winston's groin. The fugitive howled in pain and doubled over, dropping the knife.

Dillon spun around and drove his fist into the other man's jaw, sending Winston staggering backwards into the wheelhouse door. As he rebounded, Dillon stepped forward and grabbed him by the lapels. Using the powerful muscles of his neck to catapult him forward, Dillon drove his large forehead into the centre of Winston's face, causing the gangster's nose to explode in a cloud of red mist.

Winston collapsed in a crumpled heap against the side of the boat, but then he spotted the knife laying a few feet away from his hand and made a dive for it.

Dillon's eyes widened in horror as the gangster's fingers curled around the handle.

"No fucking way," he yelled, rushing forward to kick the big man's head as though he were taking a penalty kick during a football game.

Winston's head jarred forward so violently that, for a millisecond, Dillon was worried that he might have overdone it and broken the gangster's neck.

Dillon's foot was throbbing wildly as he cautiously approached the unmoving form and knelt down to check that he was still alive. Finding a strong pulse in Winston's neck, Dillon breathed a huge sigh of relief and flopped down beside him, ignoring the freezing rain that immediately soaked through his trousers and the pulsating agony in his right foot.

It was finally over. They had recaptured Claude Winston. The satisfaction was indescribable, or at least it was until he thought about the dead constable and his family, at which point the victory seemed somewhat hollow.

As he was catching his breath, Dillon heard footsteps moving along the jetty towards the boat. Seconds later, a middle-aged PC with thick, rain-smeared glasses clambered aboard, holding his flat cap onto his head to stop it from blowing it away in the wind. Rain splashed off of his shoulders and ran down his Gore-Tex jacket in tiny rivulets. "I'm looking for DI Dillon," the officer announced, ineffectually wiping at his thick lenses with a gloved finger.

"You've found him," Dillon panted.

"I'm PC Goodman," the officer told him, watching on in confusion as wearily Dillon stood up and pulled open his coat. Then, raising his jumper, he started examining his exposed torso, eventually letting out a huge sigh of relief.

"Are you okay?" Goodman asked, clearly alarmed at the sight of the blood that had run down one side of the detective's body from his ribs to his jeans.

"I'm fine," Dillon told him, covering up. "It's just a superficial cut."

Goodman's eyes narrowed as he finally spotted the motionless form sprawled across the deck. "Don't tell me I've missed out on all the fun?" he said, sounding bitterly disappointed. "I've never arrested a murderer before, and I was hoping that me and Rex would be the ones to find him."

As he spoke, a furry creature with beady eyes and very sharp teeth bounded over the side of *The Golden Sunrise*. Tail wagging, the German Shepherd went straight over to Winston's prostrate form, sniffed him intently, and then raised a leg and urinated over him.

"Rex!" PC Goodman chastised the dog. "Sorry about that," the dog handler said, looking extremely embarrassed as he reined the dog in. "Rex has developed this really bad habit of doing that to suspects of late."

Dillon grinned and patted the dog's shaggy head. "That's alright," he said. "He can take a shit on him too, for all I care."

CHAPTER THIRTY-NINE

Garston wasn't used to strenuous exercise, and his lungs were fit to burst as he ran a race in which the prize was his freedom. Praying that he wouldn't twist an ankle on the uneven terrain, he blindly sprinted across the grassland, feeling his legs growing heavier with every step.

A wave of relief washed over him when he spotted the massive blue crane and realised that he was almost back at the road. Behind him, his pursuers were still noisily fighting their way through the shrubbery. His face was crisscrossed with deep scratches where numerous sharp thorns had cut into his flesh, but it had been worth the pain to gain the minute or so lead that he had given himself.

As Garston reached the old church van that he and the others had been driven here in, he glanced over his shoulder and saw a thin beam of light burst through the foliage separating the quay from the open grassland that he had just cleared. Almost immediately, it began weaving its way towards him, bouncing up and down in a steady rhythm.

As he emerged into the car park, his breath exploding from him in great gasps, he spotted a vehicle parked on the gravel by the edge of the road.

The car had its sidelights on, and he could just about make out the shape of a man and woman sitting in the front. He assumed they were a couple of young lovebirds who had stopped off there to enjoy a little canoodling.

As he ran towards them, he clumsily pulled the Brocock from his coat pocket, hoping they weren't locked in the throes of passion, because he didn't have time for them to fuck about pulling their clothes back on.

He skidded to a halt and snatched open the driver's door, making the blonde woman sitting behind the wheel jump with fright. Beyond her, the well-built man in the crumpled suit who was sitting in in the passenger seat with a large map unfolded across his lap seemed equally startled. A handheld radio was balanced on the armrest between them, Garston noticed, realising that they were cops, not lovers.

"What the fuck...?" the woman spluttered as Garston thrust the business end of the gun into her face. Her accent was Irish, he noted.

"Get out of the car," he screamed, grabbing hold of her hair.

"Let her go," the man shouted bullishly, opening his door to get out.

To dissuade him from doing anything silly, Garston swivelled the gun on him, levelling it straight at his chest. "Not you," he said fiercely. "You stay exactly where you are until I tell you to move."

Shaking with rage, the male cop froze, one hand on the door handle, the other down by his left leg.

Keeping the gun pointed at him, Garston glanced nervously over his shoulder, looking back in the direction he'd come from.

The torchlight he'd spotted earlier was already much closer, and now there were two others flanking it.

His stomach knotted.

The moment Garston averted his eyes, Jack Tyler grabbed hold of Susie's heavy-duty Maglite, which was in the passenger footwell by his left leg, pushed open the door, and rolled out of the car.

Garston reacted by pinning Susie to her seat and taking aim at Tyler's fleeing figure. He fired twice, shattering the nearside front and rear passenger windows in quick succession, and sending a shower of glass raining down on Jack as he scuttled along the side of the car towards the boot on all fours.

The explosions were incredibly loud, filling the car's interior with the acrid stench of smoke and cordite.

Almost deafened by the noise of the gun being discharged right next to her face, Susie screamed and tried to grab it from Garston's hand.

As Tyler reached the rear of the Astra, shaking tiny shards of glass from his hair, he was aware of manhandling a battling Susie away from the car. Peeking over the top of the boot, he saw the enraged fugitive shove her roughly to the ground.

The sight made his blood boil, but there was nothing he could do about it.

To her immense credit, Susie grunted in pain, spat out a mouthful of dust, and immediately tried to scrabble to her feet.

"Stay there," Garston snarled, pointing the gun at her face, "or I swear I will shoot you."

Tyler's head whirled in confusion. What was Garston doing down here in the car park when he was supposed to be up on the quay by the boat?

Since the earlier outbreak of gunfire, both he and Susie had been trying to establish radio contact with the SFOs to get a situation report, but the handset Newman had left them was only picking up static. Either it was broke or it hadn't been tuned to the correct frequency. They had tried ringing Dillon and Bull, and then White and Evans, in the hope that they would be able to see what was going on from their position on the opposite side of the river, but none of them had answered their phones. It hadn't boded well, and the detectives had been so engrossed in their efforts to re-establish contact with their colleagues that they hadn't noticed Garston's approach.

The fact that he was running around down here in the car park, and not under arrest up at the boat, could only mean that something had gone dreadfully wrong during the armed deployment, but there was no time to dwell on that, not with their lives in danger.

The rain that had been threatening for some time chose this precise moment to start falling, bombarding Tyler with icy drops of water the size of fifty-pence pieces. Almost immediately, there was a flash of lightning out in the channel, and its glow briefly lit up Garston's sinister figure as it loomed over Susie.

Tyler decided to try and jump Garston while his back was still turned, but before he could act, the gunman turned away from Susie and rushed over to the car. He jumped into the driver's seat, but then stopped abruptly, and Tyler could hear him muttering, "No, no, no," under his breath as he fumbled around on the dash, searching for something. The words became increasingly manic, making him sound a little unhinged. A split second later, he sprung out of the car in a state of agitation.

"The keys, where are the fucking keys?"

Susie held up her right hand and wiggled it triumphantly. "Here," she said, and even from a distance, Tyler could see the smile of satisfaction that had crept onto her face. Despite the terrifying ordeal of being dragged from the car at gunpoint, Susie had somehow managed to remove the key from the ignition.

Visibly shaking with anger, Garston thrust his left hand out towards her. "Give them to me," he demanded, and there was a dangerous edge to his voice. To emphasise how serious he was, he thumbed back the gun's hammer to incentivise her.

Susie disobediently shook her head. "Why don't you come and get them?" she dared him, jiggling the keyring tauntingly.

At first, Tyler couldn't work out why she was deliberately antagonising him like this, but then it dawned on him that she was doing it to create a distraction that would allow him to get clear of the car.

Her bravery brought a lump to his throat.

Tyler hated the repellent ugliness of death; he walked amongst it every day, took its smell home on his clothing every night, even had it visit him during his dreams. Now, as Susie's life hung in the balance, he wondered if death had stowed itself away in their car tonight, and was now gloating at him as it waited for Garston to serve up its next victim.

As Garston took a first menacing step towards her, Jack realised that he had to intervene, even if it cost him his own life. He stepped clear of the Astra and raised the heavy torch to use as a club. As he did, something crunched under his foot and Jack stopped dead in his tracks, hardly daring to breathe.

Please don't let him have noticed, he prayed.

Like a predatory animal, Garston's head came up as he heard the sound behind him and, with a vicious snarl, he spun around, bringing the revolver up in one fluid movement.

Jack dived behind the Astra just as a bullet thudded into the side of the trunk inches from his head.

"Jesus!" he breathed as the rear light cluster was blown apart.

Dropping flat onto his stomach, Tyler anxiously peered under the car. To his relief, Garston's feet were still over by the driver's door. Peering around the side of the car, Tyler cringed at the sight of the jagged bullet hole that had been intended for him.

"Give me the keys," a near-hysterical Garston screamed at her. He emphasised the need for urgency by beckoning her towards him with cupped fingers.

"If you want them," she said, slowly standing up, "you go and get them." With that, she tossed the keys as far as she could across the car park floor.

"No!" Garston cried out as his only means of escape tumbled through the night air and disappeared into the darkness.

Knowing he wouldn't get another chance, Tyler burst from cover and sprinted towards Garston, raising his right arm as he ran. He was about eight feet away when he threw the torch, and it cartwheeled through the air in a blur, covering the eight feet between them in the blink of an eye.

As Garston twisted to face him, squeezing the trigger without even taking aim, the four-cell metal torch hit him squarely in the forehead with a loud clunk. The force of the impact knocked him back several paces, arms flailing as he went.

As the wildly fired round whizzed past his head, Tyler lowered his shoulder and slammed it into Garston's midriff. Wrapping his arms around the man's legs as he let out a long battle cry, he lifted him clear off the floor and carried him backwards.

Sailing through the air as Tyler's feet left the ground, they landed heavily with Tyler on top. He immediately seized the fugitive's right wrist in both hands and began smashing the gun into the floor, trying to shake it loose, but Garston was having none of it. As his senses rebooted, he reached up with his left hand and clawed at Tyler's face.

Tyler swatted the hand away and threw a punch at Garston's chin, but the fugitive was bucking and twisting so violently beneath him that Jack couldn't generate enough leverage to deliver the haymaker he'd hoped for, and his punch glanced ineffectually off his opponent's jaw.

As he wound his arm back for another strike, Susie appeared at his side and commenced pulling the gun from Garston's hand. She had to prise it from his fingers, one by one, but eventually, she snatched it from him and tossed it to one side.

Now that he was able to fight without the fear of being shot, Tyler moved decisively. Pinning Garston's head to the floor with the palm of his left hand, he drew back his right fist and smashed it into the side of Garston's ugly face with everything he had. The blow cannoned Garston's head into the hard floor beneath it. To be on the safe side, Tyler followed up with a second punch, and this one connected with considerable force. With a low groan, Garson's eyes fluttered, his body went limp and his arms flopped down beside him.

Tyler spun him over onto his front and then rammed his right arm up behind his back just as Susie produced a pair of quick-cuffs.

"You okay?" he asked her, panting from the struggle. His right hand was throbbing and he flexed it to make sure that no serious damage had been caused.

"Never been better," she told him, blowing a strand of strawberry blonde hair from her face as she knelt down to apply the handcuffs.

Now that the dust had settled, Tyler was finally able to catch his breath and take stock of the situation. The boat, the jetty leading to it, and the quay where the fatal shooting had occurred had all been cordoned off and preserved as a crime scene, as had the Astra that Garston had shot up in the car park off Harbour Road.

Winston, Garston, and Kenny Meade – who had been found hiding inside a locker aboard the boat – were all in custody, and the first man to have gone overboard as SO19 boarded *The Eclipse* had been identified as Craig Masters by a female officer who happened to be a big fan of the show. Holland had been over the moon when Tyler had called him a few minutes ago to inform him that the soap star had been detained.

Meade's son-in-law, the mindless thug with the pump-action shotgun, had been pronounced dead at the scene, and both the CIB and the IPCC had been informed. With the rain having intensified, a tent had been rushed down to cover the body until it was released by the CSM.

Newman didn't seem in the slightest bit fazed by what had happened. It was, he had informed Tyler stoically, all part of the job, and he was confident that the subsequent investigation would conclude this was a clean shoot and therefore a lawful killing.

Tony Dillon and Charlie White had driven across from the industrial estate by Rock Channel Quay to the car park in Harbour Road to collect Tyler and Sergeant as their car would have to remain in situ until it had been photographed and examined by the duty SOCO. By the time they arrived, Tyler and Sergeant looked like a pair of drowned rats.

"So, what's the plan of action?" Dillon asked as soon as Tyler climbed in the back of the car, dripping water all over the seats.

"The plan is to find somewhere quiet where we can dry off and warm ourselves up over a cup of coffee," Tyler said. "Then I suppose we had all better write up our notes."

Dillon had already arranged for the prisoners to be taken back to the Met, where they would be interviewed in the morning. The Astra that Tyler and Sergeant had driven down from London would be removed by a full lift and transported to Charlton car pound in due course.

"Any sign of Angela Marley?" Tyler asked.

Charlie White shook his head. "The wee girl seems to have vanished into thin air," he said. "We've circulated her description and the locals are gonna keep looking for her during the night."

"How did Garston get that great big lump on his head?" Dillon asked. He'd noticed it as he was being placed in the back of a car.

"Bit embarrassing that," Susie Sergeant said glancing sideways at Tyler.

Dillon's interest was piqued. "Do tell," he said eagerly.

"Do you remember the instruction that came out from The Yard a little while ago about officers not carrying torches with more than two batteries while on duty?"

"Aye, what of it?" White asked.

"Well," she said, savouring the moment, "the boss used one of them to brain Garston with." She turned to Tyler and winked mischievously. "Can't wait to see how you're going to justify that in your notes," she said with a wicked grin.

CHAPTER FORTY

Tuesday 18th January 2000

It was a bitterly cold night in Whitechapel, and it had recently started snowing. A light dusting of powder had already settled on the pavement but, so far, it hadn't affected the roads and traffic was still flowing freely. For once, the authorities had been ahead of the game and most of the roads in the borough had already been gritted in readiness for the precipitation that was expected to fall over the coming days.

A slim black woman stood alone on the corner of Quaker Street, outside the used car lot. Her ill-fitting Parka was wrapped around her as she huddled against the wire mesh fencing, trying her best to look alluring to passing motorists.

There was hardly anyone around, and the few pedestrians who did cross her path rushed by without giving her a second look. Feeling invisible, she brushed a thin layer of white powder from her shoulders with a gloved hand and stamped her feet to keep warm.

It was getting on for midnight and, thanks to the inclement weather, business had been almost non-existent for the past two hours.

She knew it was only going to get worse; as it was, she could hardly even feel her fingers or her toes.

Sometimes, when she was clucking, she was able to take happy thoughts from her past and use them to anchor her to the here and now, but when she tried to do that now, to combat the cold, she found herself fighting a losing battle. "F-f-fuck this," she stammered to herself as her teeth chattered uncontrollably. Despite not having earned anywhere near enough money to purchase tomorrow's supply of smack, she decided to call it and night and find somewhere warm to thaw out before she died of hyperthermia.

A dark blue Ford Escort, its windows misted with condensation, pulled up next to her and the driver wound down his window. "Evening," he said, cheerfully.

"You looking for business," she asked, pushing herself away from the wire mesh and pulling down the Parka's hood to reveal a once pretty face that had been marred by a long scar down one side.

The driver was a skinny white male with unkempt hair, a goatee beard, and a lived-in face. "Jump in," he said. "It's too cold to talk out there."

With a reluctant shrug, the prostitute scurried around to the passenger side and whipped open the door. She slid in, slammed it shut, and began rubbing her hands together to get the circulation going. "It's too cold out there," she told him, "so if you want to do some business, it'll have to be done in your car. Is that okay with you?" Without waiting for an answer, she reached out and turned the heating up to full.

The driver smiled obligingly. "Sure," he said, "let's do it right here."

The hooker frowned in confusion. "Here?" she said, turning her nose up at the suggestion. "We can't do it here, it's way too public."

"Nah," Kevin Murray said, his smile vanishing, "here will do just fine."

As he spoke a figure appeared outside the car and tugged open the passenger door. Alarmed, the prostitute spun around to face the newcomer, terrified that he was going to deprive her of her hard-earned takings.

A gloved hand reached in, took a firm hold of her arm, and unceremoniously yanked her out of the car.

"Get off me," she screamed, trying to shake her arm free as the man pinned her to the side of the car.

A warrant card was thrust in front of her face. "Angela Marley," Colin Franklin said in a voice devoid of emotion, "I'm DC Franklin from the Area Major Investigation Pool, and I am arresting you on suspicion of the murder of PC Stanley Morrison, which occurred at the Royal London Hospital on Monday 10th January 2000. You are also being arrested for administering a poisonous substance to PCs Alec O'Brien and Sharon Lassiter, thereby causing GBH, and for assisting an offender who was unlawfully at large." As he cautioned her, he spun her around and applied handcuffs to her scrawny wrists.

"No, no, I didn't kill anyone," Angela blurted out, her eyes darting imploringly from Franklin to Murray, who had alighted the car to assist his colleague. "I admit I drugged the other two, but only because Deontay Garston forced me to, and it was Claude shot the copper on the bed, not me."

"Save it for the interview," Murray said, dispassionately. "Or better still, for the Judge."

Murray donned a pair of latex gloves and patted down the coat for any sharps she might have concealed upon her. There were none, but he did find a cheap mobile phone, which he held up for Franklin to see.

"Whose phone is this?" he asked Marley.

"It's mine," she said, knowing they would think she had nicked it from a punter.

Murray smiled nastily. "I'm sure it is, treacle," he told her. *And I bet the last three digits of its number are 321*, he thought smugly.

He opened the back door, placed a hand on Angela's head, and guided her into the rear passenger seat as Colin Franklin went around and got into the back from the other side.

Despite having seized the town's CCTV for the night they had arrested Winston, the detectives had never worked out how she had made her way back to London on her own. Somehow, though, she had. Their best guess was that she had hitched a ride back the following morning, but they were resigned to the fact that they might never know. In the end, it was largely irrelevant anyway.

With no money to her name, and nowhere to stay now that the squat had been closed down, she had reverted to type and started soliciting in her old haunt at Whitechapel.

As luck would have it, a local vice officer had spotted her loitering outside the Quaker Street car lot the previous evening. Unfortunately, by the time he'd spun his car around to go back and look for her, she had vanished, presumably having gone off with a punter. The officer had notified AMIP immediately, and they had arranged to swamp the area with staff the following evening.

"Look on the bright side," Franklin said as Murray drove them back to Whitechapel, "you'll have somewhere warm to stay during the worst of the winter and, if you want it, you can get help to kick the addiction."

"I'd rather kick you," she replied, staring at him with the dead eyes of an addict.

CHAPTER FORTY-ONE

Nine months later...

Jack Tyler and Tony Dillon were sitting in the Police Room at The Old Bailey, and both were bored out of their brains. The chairs in the dimly lit area were hard and unyielding, and the place had the feel of a doctor's waiting room.

The other team members who had come up to court for the verdict had all grown bored with the waiting and had popped down to the second floor public canteen to grab a drink.

The jury had gone out three days ago and everyone had expected them to come back within a couple of hours, not to stay out for the rest of the week.

Jack glanced wearily at his watch.

15:20.

He blew out his cheeks. "If they don't come back in soon, the Judge will send them home for the day and we'll have to come all the way back up here again tomorrow."

Dillon stifled a yawn. "Why do you think they're taking so long?"

he asked, tossing the morning edition of *The London Echo* he had been reading onto a nearby table.

Jack could only shrug. "I have no idea. Maybe they're struggling to agree on the Joint Enterprise charges," he said.

Dillon grunted. "It has to be that," he agreed. "The evidence against Winston is overwhelming, so the sticking point must relate to one or more of the others."

Jack leaned back against the wall and stretched his legs out, trying to get comfortable. It didn't work. "Maybe we should go down to join the others and grab a coffee. At least it's more comfortable down there."

Dillon stood up and reached for his jacket. "Good idea," he said, "and it's your round if I'm not mistaken."

Tyler pulled a face as he eased himself to his feet. "It's always my round, according to you."

Just then, the heavy wooden door from the corridor opened and Steve Bull popped his head in. He looked excited. "Just spoke to the usher. The jury has reached a verdict and they're coming back in."

Tyler felt a jolt of adrenaline rush through his system. He swallowed hard and took a deep breath, aware that his heart rate was already climbing. Finally, after all these months of waiting, after all the hard work getting the case trial-ready and the countless hours spent dealing with the never-ending disclosure requests from the four separate legal teams representing Winston, Garston, Marley, and Mullings, not to mention all the underhanded shenanigans they had endured during the six week trial, they were approaching the moment of truth.

The trial had turned into a cut-throat, which meant that three of the four defendants had turned on each other in an effort to clear their own names.

It seemed that blood wasn't thicker than water in the case of Winston and Garston, as the former had tried to put all the blame for PC Morrison's death squarely on his nephew's shoulders. His defence had argued that Garston arrived at the hospital in possession of the weapon that had been used to kill the police officer, and that he had subsequently been arrested in possession of that same weapon a number of days later. Their position was that it had never left his custody and that it had been him, rather than Winston who had callously ended the life of the defenceless policeman.

Garston had retaliated by spilling the beans that Claude had taken the gun from him and needlessly killed the officer even though he had been begging his uncle not to.

Angela Marley had stayed neutral throughout, claiming that she hadn't known Garston and Heston had been carrying guns when they had entered the hospital. During her evidence in chief, she claimed that she didn't know who had fired the fatal shot. She was lying, of course, and the prosecution barrister had exposed the impossibility of her assertions during his brutal cross-examination.

Mullings had stuck to his story that he was just acting as a chauffeur and had no idea they intended to break Winston out of lawful custody, and it was Jack's view that if the jury were going to get twitchy about convicting any of the four defendants, it would be Gifford Mullings. Of course, it hadn't helped Mullings' cause that the CCTV the enquiry team had retrieved from the shop where the gang's four burner phones had been purchased clearly showed young Gifford as being the one who had bought them.

As they descended the stairs on their way to Court Number One, they met the others coming out of the canteen.

"This is it," Andy Quinlan said with an impish grin. "I reckon guilty for Winston and Garston but not guilty for Marley or Mullings. What about you?"

Jack shook his head at that. "All four are going down," he said, adamantly.

As they rushed along the corridor, converging on what is arguably the most famous courtroom in the world, Jack spotted PC Morrison's parents sitting with the Family Liaison Officer and PCs Sharon Lassiter and Alec O'Brien. He nodded an acknowledgement to them as they stood up, but there was no time to stop and talk.

The barristers appeared en masse, led by their man, Jonathan Lacroix, QC, Senior Treasury Counsel.

"Here we go," Lacroix said in his clipped Etonian voice. He was wearing his silk gown with a flap collar and long closed sleeves, the standard attire of a QC, and the reason they are said to have 'taken the silk' after being appointed.

The detectives filed into the court along with everyone else and took their seats under the watchful eye of the court usher, an attractive woman in her early fifties with greying blonde hair.

The clerk, a rather stern-faced lady in her late thirties, nodded at Tyler when she caught his eye, and he returned the gesture in a friendly manner.

Jack couldn't see up into the public gallery from where he was sitting directly behind Lacroix and his junior, but from all the noise coming from above, it sounded full to capacity.

Jack took in his surroundings with the same sense of awe that he always experienced whenever he sat inside this bleak but illustrious room, which had been home to some of the most sensational trials ever to have been held.

It was both a monument and a living tribute to the law of the land, and a place where the moral and social changes of recent history had been charted. Traditionally reserved for the most serious and high-profile crimes, it had first opened its doors in 1907. Since then, Number One Court at The Bailey had heard it all, and human drama, unspeakable tragedy, tales of hatred, greed, revenge, and betrayal had quickly become its staple diet.

A large enclosed dock stood in the centre of the court, dominating everything around it. Measuring sixteen feet by fourteen feet, it was a room within a room, solid and impenetrable.

Defendants who were evil, depraved, and sometimes just plain pathetic had gripped its rails over the years, accused of the most heinous crimes imaginable. William Joyce (Lord Haw-Haw), John Christie, Ruth Ellis, Ian Huntley, Dennis Nilsen, Peter Sutcliffe, the Kray Twins, and Dr Crippen, were just a few of the famous – and sometimes infamous – people to have stood trial within its confines.

From their seat in the dock, the four defendants sat facing the trial judge's seat some twenty five feet away, almost on eye level, but not quite. They were, however, raised above everyone else who had participated in the court proceedings.

Winston, dressed in prison attire, looked as sullen and aggressive as ever, while Garston, who had at least made the effort to wear a suit and tie, looked overwhelmed. Angela Marley appeared much healthier than the last time they had seen her. She had put on some weight and her skin pallor had improved. Mullings just looked confused.

To the judge's left and the defendant's right, there were two rows of benches reserved for counsel. They ran perpendicular to the dock, and the custom was for the prosecution to sit nearest to the judge and for the defence to sit nearest the dock to enable them to take instruction from their clients during the trial.

Lacroix and his junior, a bubbly blonde barrister called Heather Quayle, had made themselves comfortable on the green leather seats that were built into the benches and they were busily sorting their papers out in readiness for the court to convene for its final sitting in this case.

Once everyone was seated, the usher slipped out to bring the jury in.

Conversation was muted as the twelve men and woman filed into the court from the nearby jury room, and virtually every person in the room studied them intently, trying to second guess their decision.

The jury consisted of five men and seven women, and they were from a diverse range of ages, colours, and backgrounds. Their foreman, a smartly suited black man in his mid-forties, looked drained as he took his seat at the front, and he made a point of studiously avoiding eye contact with anyone else in the court.

Dillon leaned over and whispered into Jack's ear. "He looks frazzled," he said.

Tyler nodded. "They all do." He guessed that this hadn't been an easy one for them to all agree on, and he was grateful that it hadn't gone to a majority.

Suddenly there were three loud bangs and the door opened to admit the red-robed trial judge. The room went deathly quiet as everyone stood up respectfully.

As he sat down, Tyler glanced at the defendants. Winston glared intimidatingly at the jury foreman, trying to get his attention.

Not doing yourself any favours there, Jack thought, pleased to see that the judge had also noticed.

Garston looked like he might throw up at any second, and he was wringing his hands together nervously and fidgeting in his seat.

Marley just stared down at the floor, resigned to her fate.

Mullings was more interested in picking his nose than what was going on around him. He looked bored.

A number of security officers stood in the dock behind them, and they had been fully briefed on Winston's penchant for extreme violence. They were prepared for him to kick off if things didn't go his way.

"Will the four defendants please stand up," the Clerk said, breaking the silence.

Garston, Marley, and Mullings rose to their feet straight away, but Winston had to be chivvied along by one of the security officers.

The Clerk turned to the jury. "Mr Foreman of the Jury, I am going to read out the charges in relation to each defendant, and in response, I require you to answer guilty or not guilty. Do you understand?"

"Yes," the foreman replied, sounding like he had a frog in his throat. The usher quickly moved forward and gave him a glass of water, which he downed gratefully. "Yes," he said again, his voice sounding much firmer.

The Clerk nodded. "Very well, with regard to the first defendant, Claude Marcel Winston, do you find him guilty or not guilty of the murder of police constable Stanley Morrison?"

There was a drawn-out silence in which the foreman risked a furtive glance at the dock. "Guilty," he said.

The public gallery erupted in applause, which the judge tolerated for several seconds before indicating that was enough.

"Quiet, please," the Clerk barked, and the noise quickly died down. She returned her attention to the foreman of the jury, upon whose brow a film of sweat had broken out. "With regard to the second defendant, Deontay William Garston, do you find him guilty or not guilty of the murder of police constable Stanley Morrison?"

This time the foreman refrained from staring at the occupants of the dock. Instead, he looked straight at the judge and spoke without hesitation. "Guilty."

There was more cheering from above, but this time the judge

didn't let it pass without comment, and the public gallery was told to refrain from making any further noise.

"Here's where it gets interesting," Quinlan whispered.

Tyler glanced sideways at him. "They're all going down," he murmured under his breath.

"We'll see," Quinan said, noncommittally.

"With regard to the third defendant," the Clerk said, "do you find Angela Coreen Marley guilty or not guilty of the murder of police constable Stanley Morrison?"

The foreman seemed to hesitate, and Tyler felt his stomach tighten. Taking another sip of water, the foreman looked over at Marley and then turned to the judge. "Guilty," he said.

"With regard to the fourth defendant," the Clerk said, "do you find Gifford Anthony Mullings guilty or not guilty of the murder of police constable Stanley Morrison?"

The foreman glanced over at Mullings, and something flickered across his eyes. Was it pity, Jack wondered? Maybe the jury hadn't been convinced about the level of his involvement and had decided to give him the benefit of the doubt? He could hardly blame them if they had, and three out of four was still a fantastic result.

"Guilty," the foreman said.

The public gallery applauded.

A wave of relief flooded over Tyler, who looked at Quinlan and winked. "Told you," he said.

———

The customary piss-up started as soon as the press interviews outside The Old Bailey were concluded, and Tyler knew it would probably go on until the pub that they had wandered into at the end of Old Bailey closed.

In accordance with tradition, the first round had been on Quinlan as the SIO. Having briefly stood in for Andy while he'd been off sick, Jack felt obliged to pay for the second round, which he'd jokingly described as a consolation prize for them having to put up with his manic leadership for a few days.

About an hour in, Jonathan Lacroix and his junior arrived, and the barrister insisted on putting his hand in his pocket and buying everyone a drink.

Murray had been the first to accept the offer. "I'll have a double scotch," he'd declared, eyeing up Heather Quayle hungrily.

Steve Bull saw this and leaned into him with a smirk. "She's way out of your league, sunshine!"

Murray was having none of it. "Rubbish. There's nothing posh totty like her enjoy more than a bit of rough."

Bull nearly choked on his beer. "You really have no idea about women, do you Kev?"

Before long, they had effectively taken over one corner of the pub. Nibbles were organised and then the obligatory speeches started. The first was from Quinlan, who thanked everyone for a job well done, and the second was from Lacroix. The QC was full of praise for the magnificent way in which the murder squad officers had carried out the investigation and prepared the case for court.

After toasting their fallen comrade and the victory they had obtained on his behalf, which left a bittersweet taste in their mouths, Lacroix had felt compelled to touch upon the bravery and professionalism of the officers who had been awarded Judges Commendations for their roles in apprehending those responsible at the end of the trial, namely Tyler, Dillon, Susie Sergeant, Nick Bartholomew and Terry Grier.

Bartholomew and Grier had been gobsmacked to receive the Judge's commendations at court and were dead chuffed to have been invited along to join in the celebrations afterwards.

Lacroix also spoke a little about the sentences that each of the defendants had received, saying how pleased he was with the way that the judge had summed things up. He ended by proclaiming that justice been done today and they could all sleep well tonight, knowing they had played a part in making it happen.

"I'm gonna sleep well tonight because I'm pished," Charlie White had slurred, and everyone laughed.

Tyler was invited to speak next, and after thanking everyone for all their hard work he said that he hoped the harsh sentences that had been handed out today would act as a deterrent for others in the future, and that taking Winston out of circulation had undoubtedly saved more lives.

As he supped his beer afterwards, Tyler reflected that the four defendants were going to serve a combined total of ninety-nine-years. Winston had received thirty-five-years for Morrison's murder; Garston had been given twenty-eight, and Marley and Mullings had got off lightly with a mere eighteen apiece. The judge had explained that his starting point had been a tariff of thirty and that he had then taken into account any specific aggravating or mitigating factors that counsel had flagged up to him when he'd invited each of them to address the bench in turn before he'd passed sentence.

There had been a host of other charges on the indictment, including possession of firearms and ammunition with intent to endanger life and administering noxious substances to PCs Lassiter and O'Brien. The jury had also unanimously convicted the three defendants on all of these.

"I spoke to Winston's QC before I came to join you," Lacroix said when he was alone with Tyler, Dillon, and Quinlan. "His view is that Winston should just plead guilty to the two outstanding attempted murders and not waste everyone's time with a lengthy trial that will inevitably end in a conviction. After all, the CCTV evidence alone is sufficient to prove his guilt."

"I could live with that," Tyler said.

The trial for the two counts of attempted murder had been put back until November. There had been discussions at one point about linking all the outstanding matters together and just holding one trial, but that would have been a logistical nightmare. In the end, Winston's counsel had requested separation, with the murder of PC Morrison to take primacy and the two attempted murders to be dealt with afterwards.

Tyler had always suspected there was a hidden agenda behind the request; if Winston had already been convicted of two attempted murders when the judge passed sentence for PC Morrison's murder, Winston would most probably have been looking at a whole life order being imposed. This way, at some stage in the distant future, he might still qualify for parole.

"Of course, he's yet to persuade his belligerent client to agree to this course of action," Lacroix said, smiling ruefully, "but he seemed fairly optimistic that Winston would go along with it."

Jack wasn't so confident. "I hope he does, but I won't believe it until I see it," he said.

With the murder trial out of the way, and Winston likely to plead guilty to the two attempted murders, there were no other loose ends to tie up.

After his interview at Plaistow police station back in January, Rodney Dawlish had been charged with an offence of assisting an offender contrary to the Criminal Law Act 1967. He had pleaded guilty at his first appearance at Crown Court back in March, at which point the case had been adjourned for pre-sentence reports. As he had no previous convictions and the prosecution had conceded that his learning difficulties made him vulnerable to manipulation by unscrupulous people like Garston, the court had decided to treat him with leniency when it reconvened three weeks later. He could easily have been looking at a five years custodial, but he had instead received a two year suspended sentence. He had also been fined, awarded six penalty points and disqualified from driving for six months for having no driving licence and no insurance at the time that he was stopped in Norman Crouch's plumbing van.

Unlike Dawlish, Norman Crouch did have a full licence and a comprehensive insurance policy that covered him to drive any other car with the owner's consent. Of course, that didn't entitle him to drive like a complete twat when he was three times over the legal limit and high on cannabis and cocaine. In addition to being charged with being unfit to drive through drink or drugs, he had also been charged with dangerous driving and failing to stop for police. Crouch had been fined heavily and banned from driving for two years.

At a separate trial, he had been convicted of possession of cocaine with intent to supply, and for that, he had received a two year prison sentence.

By the time of their trial, the evidence accrued against Charlie

Dobson and his three skinhead mates for supplying firearms and ammunition had been damning.

In addition to the CCTV of them selling two Brocock revolvers to Garston and Heston, their fingerprints were all over the two converted weapons discovered in the safe and the equipment being used to convert the blank-firing replicas into real guns. The detailed ledger that Dobson had helpfully maintained had been treated with ninhydrin, and his prints had been found all over it.

Although he had refused to provide a handwriting sample during interview, alternative source material had been found during the search of his home address, in the form of letters he had written to his girlfriend while previously in prison. Subsequent comparisons by a qualified expert concluded that the writing in the ledger matched that in the signed letters and was unequivocally his.

All the spent shell casings recovered from the bucket in the lockup had been fingerprinted, a time-consuming process that ultimately led to all four suspect's fingerprints being identified on numerous shells. Prints for Garston and Heston had also been found on several of them.

The results were then sent to the National Ballistics Intelligence Service and, after scrupulous examination, the hammer and striation marks were linked to weapons that had been used in three separate murders within the Greater London area during the previous year.

Dobson and his gang were all charged with a wider conspiracy to sell firearms and ammunition in addition to the other matter for which they were to stand trial. The case had been heard in July, and Dobson and his cronies had each been sentenced to twenty years imprisonment.

By the time that George Holland turned up, everyone was well on their way to being merry, and he helped matters along by getting in a round of drinks.

"Bloody nice of you to offer," Kevin Murray slurred, wrapping his arm around Holland's shoulder and treating him to a lopsided grin. "I'll have a double scotch, no ice."

"How's the case against Craig Masters going?" Jack asked when Holland had got rid of Murray.

Holland chuckled. "It's been put back so many times that I'm beginning to wonder if it will ever go to trial. The latest date they've given us is in October."

"What seems to be the problem?" Jack asked.

"Availability of expert witnesses, would you believe. The defence want to rely on a particular specialist to support their death by misadventure claims, and this bloke isn't available until then. There's still a lot of behind the scenes discussion going on between the barristers about whether or not the Crown would be willing to accept a plea of manslaughter."

Jack raised an eyebrow. "What's your view on that?"

Holland shrugged. "I wouldn't necessarily be against it, but there would probably be an uproar from the victim's family."

By nine o'clock, most people were starting to flag, and they started disappearing in dribs and drabs. Holland, Quinlan, Lacroix and his junior were amongst the first to say their goodbyes and head for the door.

Tyler flopped down next to Kelly Flowers, who was sitting with Tony Dillon and his girlfriend, Emma Drew. Emma was a very attractive and bubbly girl who worked as a mortuary technician based at Poplar, and they had been seeing each other for about the same amount of time that Jack and Kelly had been dating.

Dillon was a terrible womaniser, and being with the same girl for this length of time was something of a record for him. To be fair, they seemed to have really hit it off, so much so that Tyler was beginning to suspect that there actually might be some longevity in this relationship after all. Then again, he reminded himself, this was Dillon he was talking about, so he would just have to wait and see.

"When are you two going to go public about the fact you're a couple?" Dillon asked with a silly grin on his face.

Flowers started to giggle. They had been seeing each other for the best part of a year now, and she spent more time at his place than she did at her own, and Jack still insisted on keeping their relationship a secret.

The question made Tyler uncomfortable and he looked around to make sure that no one could overhear them. Luckily, everyone else was over by the bar.

"It's not that simple," he said, shrugging awkwardly. "I'd love to go public, but if George found out, he would probably make Kelly switch teams. I do feel bad about keeping the team in the dark, though," he admitted, which caused Dillon and Kelly to crack up.

Jack stared at Emma who shrugged, and from the expression on her face, she was as bewildered as he was. "Have I said something funny?" he asked, wondering what was so hilarious.

"Jack," Dillon said, wiping tears of laughter away from his eyes, "most of the team worked it out ages ago. It's the worst kept secret on the command, and you seem to be the only person who doesn't realise it's common knowledge."

Tyler looked from one laughing face to the other, unable to believe his ears. "Well, who told them?" he demanded, "because I certainly didn't say anything to anyone."

Dillon leaned over and placed a large hand on his shoulder. "You didn't need to, old son. It's the puppy-eyed look on your ugly face every time you see her, and the lovey-dovey tone that creeps into your voice every time you speak to her, that's what gave the game away."

Tyler looked around the room, taking in his remaining colleagues one by one. "They all know?" he said, sounding dismayed.

Dillon nodded.

Jack's face paled. "All of them?"

Dillon nodded some more. "Between you and me, I think even George has figured it out."

Tyler groaned. "He hasn't said anything to me."

Dillon smiled. "I don't think he will unless you bring it up and force him to address the elephant in the room."

Tyler thought about this for a few seconds while the others sat there looking at him in amusement. Eventually, he turned to Kelly. "Does this mean I can finally kiss you in public?" he asked.

She blushed. "I guess so," she said self-consciously.

"Good," Tyler said, leaning across to tenderly plant his lips on hers, "because I've been wanting to do exactly that for a very long time."

FURTHER READING

TURF WAR
The first instalment in the DCI Tyler Thriller series

An out of town contract killer is drafted in to carry out a hit on an Albanian crime boss.

That same evening, in another part of town, four Turkish racketeers are ruthlessly gunned down while extorting protection money from local businessmen.

As the dust settles, it becomes apparent to DCI Jack Tyler that the two investigations are inexorably linked, and that someone is trying to orchestrate a gangland war that will tear the city apart.

But who? And why?

The pressure is on. can Tyler can find a way to stem the killings and restore order to the streets, or will this be the case that destroys his career?

JACK'S BACK
The second instalment in the DCI Tyler Thriller series

It's been over a hundred years since Jack the Ripper terrorised the gas lit streets of Victorian London, but when a night watchman discovers the mutilated corpse of a local prostitute at a building site in Whitechapel, it quickly becomes apparent to DCI Jack Tyler that someone has taken up the Ripper's mantle and is emulating the terrible atrocities that gained his namesake such notoriety.

Be afraid.
This is only the start...
Jack's Back.

Written in the victim's own blood, the chilling message catapults Tyler into a frantic race against time. Can he get inside the mind of a monster and find a way to stop him, or will more women end up on a cold mortuary slab?

With the top brass breathing down his neck and hampered by an interfering reporter, Tyler knows that if he doesn't catch the man the media has dubbed 'The New Ripper' soon his career won't be the only thing that's left in tatters.

Perfect for fans of gritty London Noir, Jack's Back will keep you turning pages until the bloody end.

THE HUNT FOR CHEN
A DCI Tyler Novella only available from Mark's website:
www.markromain.com

Exhausted from having just dealt with a series of gruesome murders in Whitechapel, DCI Jack Tyler and his team of homicide detectives are hoping for a quiet run in to Christmas.

Things are looking promising until the London Fire Brigade are called down to a house fire in East London and discover a charred body that has been wrapped in a carpet and set alight.

Attending the scene, Tyler and his partner, DI Tony Dillon, immediately realise that they are dealing with a brutal murder.

A witness comes forward who saw the victim locked in a heated argument with an Oriental male just before the fire started, but nothing is known about this mysterious man other than he drives a white van and his name might be Chen.

Armed with this frugal information, Tyler launches a murder investigation, and the hunt to find the unknown killer begins.

THE CANDY KILLER

The fourth instalment in the DCI Tyler Thriller series

Love. Obsession. Betrayal. Revenge.

When DCI Jack Tyler is called upon to investigate the murder of a man killed while trying to protect a girl from an aggressive drunk, he thinks the case is going to be fairly straightforward. He should have known better.

Recently released from prison, a convicted rapist is desperate to track down the love of his life and rekindle their relationship, but she has very different ideas, and would rather die than have him come anywhere near her.

When a kidnap plan goes wrong, those involved begin to turn on each other.

As their fates become increasingly entwined, not everyone will survive the fallout.

GLOSSARY OF TERMS USED IN THE JACK TYLER BOOKS

AC – Assistant Commissioner
ACPO – Association of Chief Police Officers
AFO – Authorised Firearms Officer
AIDS – Acquired Immune Deficiency Syndrome
AMIP – Area Major Investigation Pool (Predecessor to the Homicide Command)
ANPR – Automatic Number Plate Recognition
ARV – Armed Response Vehicle
ASU – Air Support Unit
ATC – Air Traffic Control
ATS – Automatic Traffic Signal
Azimuth – The coverage from each mobile phone telephone mast is split into three 120-degree arcs called azimuths
Bandit – the driver of a stolen car or other vehicle failing to stop for police
BIU – Borough Intelligence Unit
BPA – Blood Pattern Analysis
BTP – British Transport Police
BTNA – Blackwall Tunnel Northern Approach
C11 – Criminal Intelligence / surveillance

CAD – Computer Aided Dispatch
CCTV – Closed Circuit Television
CIB – Complaints Investigation Bureau
CID – Criminal Investigation Department
CIPP – Crime Investigation Priority Project
County Mounties – a phrase used by Met officers to describe police officers from the Constabularies
CRIMINT – Criminal Intelligence
CSM – Crime Scene Manager
(The) Craft – the study of magic
CRIS – Crime Reporting Information System
DNA – Deoxyribonucleic Acid
DC – Detective Constable
DS – Detective Sergeant
DI – Detective Inspector
DCI – Detective Chief Inspector
DSU – Detective Superintendent
DCS – Detective Chief Superintendent
DPG – Diplomatic Protection Group
Enforcer – a heavy metal battering ram used to force open doors
ESDA – Electrostatic Detection Apparatus (sometimes called an EDD or Electrostatic Detection Device)
ETA – Expected Time of Arrival
(The) Factory – Police jargon for their base.
FLO – Family Liaison Officer
FME – Force Medical Examiner
Foxtrot Oscar – Police jargon for 'fuck off'
FSS – Forensic Science Service
GP – General Practitioner
GMC – General Medical Council
GSR – Gun Shot Residue
HA – Arbour Square police station
HAT – Homicide Assessment Team
HEMS – Helicopter Emergency Medical Service
HIV – Human Immunodeficiency Virus

HOLMES – Home Office Large Major Enquiry System
HP – High Priority
HR – Human Resources
HT – Whitechapel borough / Whitechapel police station
ICU – Intensive Care Unit
IFR – Instrument Flight Rules are used by pilots when visibility is not good enough to fly by visual flight rules
IO – Investigating Officer
IPCC – Independent Police Complaints Commission
IR – Information Room
IRV – Immediate Response Vehicle
KF – Forest Gate police station
Kiting checks – trying to purchase goods or obtain cash with stolen / fraudulent checks
LAG – Lay Advisory Group
LAS – London Ambulance Service
LFB – London Fire Brigade
LOS – Lost Or Stolen vehicle
MIR – Major Incident Room
MP – Radio call sign for Information Room at NSY
MPH – Miles Per Hour
MICH/ACH – Modular Integrated Communications Helmet / Advanced Ballistic Combat Helmet
MPS – Metropolitan Police Service
MSS – Message Switching System
NABIS – National Ballistics Intelligence Service
NADAC – National ANPR Data Centre
NHS – National Health Service
Nondy – Nondescript vehicle, typically an observation van
NOTAR – No Tail Rotor system technology
NSY – New Scotland Yard
OH – Occupational Health
OM – Office manager
Old Bill – the police
P9 – MPS Level 1/P9 Surveillance Trained

PACE – Police and Criminal Evidence Act 1984
PC – Police Constable
PCMH – Plea and Case Management Hearing
PIP – Post Incident Procedure
PLO – Press Liaison Officer
PM – Post Mortem
PNC – Police National Computer
POLACC – Police Accident
PR – Personal Radio
PTT – Press to Talk
RCJ – Royal Courts of Justice
RCS – Regional Crime Squad
RLH – Royal London Hospital
Rozzers – the police
RTA – Road traffic Accident
RT car – Radio Telephone car, nowadays known as a Pursuit Vehicle
QC – Queen's Counsel (a very senior barrister)
SCG – Serious Crime Group
Scruffs – Dressing down in casual clothes in order for a detective to blend in with his / her surroundings
SFO – Specialist Firearms Officer
SIO – Senior Investigating Officer
Sheep – followers of Christ; the masses
Skipper – Sergeant
SNT – Safer Neighbourhood Team
SO19 – Met Police Firearms Unit
SOCO – Scene Of Crime Officer
SOIT – Sexual Offences Investigative Technique
SPM – Special Post Mortem
Stinger – a hollow spiked tyre deflation device
TDA – Taking and Driving Away
TDC – Trainee Detective Constable
TIE – Trace, Interview, Eliminate
TIU – Telephone Investigation Unit
TPAC – Tactical Pursuit and containment
TSG – Territorial Support Group

TSU – Technical Support Unit
VODS – Vehicle On-line Descriptive Searching
Walkers – officers on foot patrol
Trumpton – the Fire Brigade
VFR – Visual Flight Rules - Regulations under which a pilot operates an aircraft in good visual conditions

AUTHOR'S NOTE

So, there we have it, you've reached the end of the book! I sincerely hope that you've had as much fun reading Unlawfully At Large as I did in writing it. If you have, can I please ask that you to spare a few moments of your valuable time to leave an honest review on Amazon. It doesn't have to be anything fancy, just a line or two saying whether you enjoyed it and would recommend it to others. I really can't stress how helpful this feedback is for authors like me. Apart from influencing a book's visibility, your reviews will help people who haven't read my work yet to decide whether it's right for them.

The books in the DCI Tyler Thriller series have regularly been praised for their gritty realism. That's great to know because I always try to keep my writing firmly grounded in the real world, ensuring that procedural matters are described as accurately as possible. Of course, there are occasions when, to keep the flow of the story going or to maintain the intensity of the drama, I am forced to apply a tiny sprinkle of artistic licence, but I endeavour to keep to keep those to the minimum.

You know, I actually I started writing the first book in the DCI Tyler Thriller series all the way back in 1998. I must have been a bit naïve in those days because I assumed that it would be an absolute doddle to combine my writing with a very demanding job and a hectic family life. When I first started out, I had no doubt that story would be finished within a year. Of course, realistically speaking, there was no way that was ever going to happen; no matter how hard I tried – and I did try – my work had a nasty habit of always getting in the way, so much so that I eventually conceded defeat and decided to shelve the writing project until I retired. That meant that, between penning those first few chapters and completing the story, a whooping twenty years odd had passed. Needless to say, it hasn't taken me anywhere near as long to write any of the subsequent books!

It's safe to say that I've grown quite fond of Tyler, Dillon, and the rest of the team – even Murray – over the years, and I sincerely hope that you will grow to feel the same way about them that I do.

I'll sign off by saying that, if you haven't already done so, why not pop over to my website, www.markromain.com, and grab yourself a free copy of The Hunt For Chen.

Best wishes,

Mark.

ABOUT THE AUTHOR

Mark Romain is a retired Metropolitan Police officer, having joined the Service in the mid-eighties. His career included two homicide postings, and during that time he was fortunate enough to work on a number of very challenging high-profile cases.

Mark lives in Essex with his wife, Clare. They have two grown-up children and one grandchild. Between them, the family has three English Bull Terriers and a very bossy Dachshund called Weenie!

Mark is a lifelong Arsenal fan and an avid skier. He also enjoys going to the theatre, lifting weights and kick-boxing, a sport he got into during his misbegotten youth!

You can find out more about Mark's books or contact him via his website or Facebook page:

www.facebook.com/markromainauthor

www.markromain.com

Printed in Great Britain
by Amazon